"ARE YOU AFRAID OF ME, CHRISTIANA?"

David's voice was barely louder than a whisper. His breath drifted over her temple, carrying his words. Despite the heat, a chill trembled down her neck and back.

"Of course not."

"You act as if you are."

"I am a bit cold is all."

In response, David drew the edges of his own cloak around her. He was closer now. She could feel the muscles of his chest all along her back. She squirmed to let him know that she wanted him to let go.

He did not release her. Instead he turned his head to kiss her neck. The heat of his lips against her skin produced an incredible shock. His arm pulled her tighter as his lips moved up her neck. He nipped lightly along the edge of her ear. Quivering, delicious tremors coursed through her. A hollow tension exploded, shaking her, and she gasped. The sound woke her from the sensual daze. She turned her head away from his mouth.

"Now I am afraid of you."

"That was not fear. . . ."

ALSO BY MADELINE HUNTER

On sale in September 2000

By Possession

On sale in January 2001

By Design

BY
ARRANGEMENT

MADELINE
HUNTER

Bantam Books
New York Toronto London Sydney Auckland

BY ARRANGEMENT
A Bantam Book / June 2000

ISBN 0-553-58222-4

Published simultaneously in the United States and Canada

Bantam Books are published by Bantam Books, a division of Random House, Inc.
Its trademark, consisting of the words "Bantam Books" and the portrayal of a
rooster, is Registered in U.S. Patent and Trademark Office and in other countries.
Marca Registrada. Bantam Books, 1540 Broadway, New York, New York 10036.

PRINTED IN THE UNITED STATES OF AMERICA
OPM   10 9 8 7 6 5 4 3 2 1

FOR PAM,
WHO KNOWS WHY

BY ARRANGEMENT

CHAPTER 1

IF YOUR BROTHER finds out about this, I'll be lucky to walk away with my manhood, let alone my head," Thomas said.

The moon's pale light threw shadows on the walls of the shops that lined the street. Ominous movements to the right and left occasionally caught Christiana's attention, but she didn't fear footpads or nightwalkers tonight. Thomas Holland, one of the Queen's knights, rode alongside her, and the glow from his torch displayed his long sword. Christiana expected no challenges from anyone who might see them in the city out after the curfew.

"He will never know, I promise you. No one will," she reassured him.

Thomas worried with good reason. If her brother Morvan found out that Thomas had helped her sneak out of Westminster after dark, there would be hell to pay. She would take all of the blame on herself if they were discovered, though. After all, she could hardly get into any more trouble than she was in right now.

"This merchant you need to see must be rich, if he doesn't live above his shop," Thomas mused. "Not my business to pry, my lady, but this be a peculiar time to be visiting, and on the sly at that. I trust that it is not a lover I bring you to. The King himself will gut me if it is."

She would have laughed at his suggestion, except that her frantic emotions had left her too sick to enjoy the dreadful joke. "Not a lover, and I come now because it is the only time I can be sure of finding him at home," she said, hoping that he would not ask for more explanation. It had taken all of her guile to slip away for this clandestine visit, and she had none to spare for inventing another lie.

The last day had been one of the worst in her life, and one of the longest. Had it only been last evening that she had met with Queen Philippa and been told of the King's decision to accept a marriage offer for her? Every moment since had been an eternity of hellish panic and outrage.

She was not opposed to marriage. In fact, at eighteen she was past the age when most girls wed. But this offer had not come from Stephen Percy, the knight to whom she had given her heart. Nor had it been made by some other knight or lord, as befitted the daughter of Hugh Fitzwaryn and a girl from a family of ancient nobility.

Nay, King Edward had decided to marry her to David de Abyndon, whom she had never met.

A common merchant.

A common, *old* merchant, according to her guardian, Lady Idonia, who remembered buying silks from Master David the mercer in her youth.

It was the King's way of punishing her. Since her parents' deaths she had been his ward and lived at court with his eldest daughter, Isabele, and his young cousin Joan of Kent. When he had learned about Stephen, he must have flown into a rage to have taken such drastic revenge on her.

Stephen. Handsome, blond Stephen. Her heart ached for him. His secret attentions had brought the sun into her sheltered, lonely life. He was the first man to dare to pay court to her. Morvan had threatened to kill any man who wooed her before a betrothal. Her brother's size and skill at arms had proven a depressingly effective deterrent to a love match, just as her lack of a dowry had precluded one secured by property. Other girls at court had admirers, but not her. Until Stephen.

This marriage would be a harsh retribution for what had occurred on that bed before Idonia had found them together. And not one that she planned to accept. Nor would this old merchant want it when he learned how the King was using him.

She and Thomas followed the blond head of the apprentice whom they had woken from his bed in the mercer's shop. The young man had agreed to guide them to his master's house. He led them up the lane away from the Cheap and then over toward the Guildhall before stopping at a gate and rapping lightly. The heavy door swung back and a huge body filled it.

The gate guard held a torch in one massive hand. He was the tallest person Christiana had ever seen, and thick as a tree. Whitish blond hair flowed down his shoulders.

He spoke in a voice accented with the lilting tones of Sweden. "Andrew, is that you? What the hell are you doing here? The constables catch you out after curfew again . . ."

"These two came to the shop, Sieg. I had to show them the way, didn't I?"

The torch pointed out so that Sieg could scrutinize them. "He be expecting you, but I was told it was two men," he said warily. "*Ja*, well, follow me. I'll put you in the solar and tell him you are here."

Thomas turned to her. "I will go up with you," he whispered. "If anything happens . . ."

"I must do this alone. There is no danger for me here."

Thomas did not like it. "I see a courtyard beyond this gate. I will wait there. Be quick, and yell if you need me."

She followed the mountain called Sieg. Doors gave out on either side of a short passage, and she realized that this was a building with a gate cut into its bottom level. They crossed the courtyard and entered a hall set at right angles to the first. She caught the impression of benches and tables as they filed through, turning finally into yet another wing that faced the first across the courtyard. Here a narrow staircase led to a second level.

Sieg opened a door off the top landing and gestured. "You can wait here. Master David be abed, so it might take a while."

She raised a hand to halt him. "I didn't expect to disturb him. I can come another time."

"I was told to wake him when you came."

That was the second time that this man had suggested that they expected her. "I think that you've made a mistake . . ." she began, but Sieg was already out the door.

The solar was quite large, and a low fire burned in the hearth at one end. The furniture appeared as little more than heavy shadows in the moonlight filtering through a bank of pointed arched windows along the far wall. She strolled over to those windows and fingered the rippled glazing and lead tracery. Glass. Lots of it, and very expensive. This Master David had done well over the years selling his cloths and vanities.

It didn't surprise her. She knew that some of the London merchants were as rich as landed lords and that a few had even become lords through their wealth. The mayor of London was always treated like a peer of the realm at important court functions, and the families that supplied the aldermen had a very high status too. London's merchants, with their royal charter of freedoms, were a proud and influential group of men, jealous of their prerogatives and rights. Edward negotiated and consulted with London much as he did with his barons.

Sieg returned and built up the fire. He took a rush and lit several candles on a table nearby before he left. Christiana stayed near the windows, away from the light in her shadowed corner.

A door set in the wall beside the hearth opened, and a man walked through. He paused, looking around the chamber. His eyes found her shadow near the windows, and he walked forward a few steps.

The light from the hearth illuminated him. She took in the tall, lean frame, the golden brown hair, the planes of a handsome face.

Humiliation swept her. They had come to the wrong place!

"My lady?" The voice was a quiet baritone. A beautiful voice. Its very timbre pulled you in and made you want to listen to what it said even if it spoke nonsense.

She searched for the words to form an apology.

"You have something for me?" he encouraged.

Perhaps she could leave without this man knowing just who had made a fool of herself tonight.

"I am sorry. There has been a mistake," she said. "We seem to have come to the wrong house."

"Whom do you seek?"

"Master David the mercer."

"I am he."

"I think it is a different David. I was told that he is . . . older."

"I am David the mercer, and there is no other. If you have brought something for me . . ."

Christiana wanted to disappear. She would kill Idonia! Her kindly old merchant was a man of no more than thirty years.

He had stopped in mid-sentence, and she saw him realize that she was not whom he expected either. He took another few steps toward her. "Perhaps if you would tell me why you seek me . . ."

Young or old, it made no difference. She was here now and she would tell her story. This man would not like playing the fool for the King no matter what his age.

"My name is Christiana Fitzwaryn."

They stood in a long silence broken only by crackle of the new logs on the fire.

"You had only to send word and I would have come to you. In fact, I was told that the Queen would introduce us at the castle tomorrow," he finally said.

She knew then for sure that there had been no mistake.

"I wanted to speak with you privately."

His head tilted back a bit. "Then come and sit yourself, Lady Christiana, and say what you need to say."

Three good-sized chairs stood near the fire, all with backs and arms. Suppressing an instinct to bolt from the room, she took the middle one. It was too big for her, and even when she perched on the edge, her feet dangled. She felt the same way that she had last night with the Queen, like a child waiting to be chastised. She reached up and pushed down the hood of her cloak.

A movement beside her brought David de Abyndon into the chair on her left. He angled it away so that he faced her. Close here, in the glow of the fire, she could see him clearly.

Her eyes fell on expertly crafted brown high boots, and long, well-shaped legs in brown hose. Her gaze drifted up to a beautiful masculine hand, long-fingered and traced with elegant veins, resting on the front edge of the chair's arm. The red wool pourpoint was completely unadorned by embroidery or jewels, and yet, even in the dancing light of the fire, she could tell that the fabric and workmanship were of the best quality and very expensive. She paused a moment, studying the richly carved chair on which he sat and the birds and vines decorating it.

Finally, there was no place else to look but at his face.

Dark blue eyes the color of lapis lazuli examined her as closely as she did him. They seemed friendly enough eyes, even expressive eyes, but she found it disconcerting that she could not interpret the thoughts and reactions in them. What was reflected there? Amusement? Curiosity? Boredom? They were beautifully set under low arched brows, and the bones around them, indeed all of the bones of his face, looked perfectly formed and regularly fitted, as if some master craftsman of great skill had carefully chosen each one and placed it just so. A straight nose led to a straight wide mouth. Golden brown hair, full and a little shorter than this year's fashion, was parted at the center and feathered carelessly over his temples and down his chiseled cheeks and jaw to his shirt collar.

David de Abyndon, warden of the mercers' company and merchant of London, was a very handsome man. Almost beautiful, but a vague hardness around the eyes and mouth kept that from being so.

A shrewd scrutiny veiled his lapis eyes, and she suddenly felt very self-conscious. It had been impolite of her to examine him so obviously, of course, but he was older and should know better than to do the same.

"Don't you want to remove your cloak? It is warm here," that quiet voice asked.

The idea of removing her cloak unaccountably horrified her. She was sure that she would feel naked without it. In fact, she pulled it a bit closer in response.

His faint smile reappeared. It made him appear amiable, but revealed nothing.

She cleared her throat. "I was told that . . . that you were . . ."

"Older."

"Aye."

"No doubt someone confused me with my dead master and partner, David Constantyn. The business was his before mine."

"No doubt."

The silence stretched. He sat there calmly, watching her. She sensed an inexplicable presence emanating from him. The air around him possessed a tension or intensity that she couldn't define. She began to feel very uncomfortable. Then she remembered that she had come here to talk to him and that he was waiting patiently for her to do so.

"I need to speak with you about something very important."

"I am glad to hear it."

She glanced over, startled. "What?"

"I'm glad to hear that it is something important. I would not like to think that you traveled London's streets at night for something frivolous."

He was subtly either scolding her or teasing her. She couldn't tell which.

"I am not alone. A knight awaits in the courtyard," she said pointedly.

"It was kind of him to indulge you."

Not teasing. Scolding.

That annoyed her enough that she collected her thoughts quickly. She was beginning to think that she didn't like this man much. He made her feel very vulnerable. She sensed something proud and aloof in him too, and that annoyed her even further. She had been expecting an elderly man who would treat her with a certain deference because of their difference in degrees. There was absolutely no deference in this man.

"Master David, I have come to ask you to withdraw your offer of marriage."

He glanced to the fire, then his gaze returned to her. One lean, muscular leg crossed the other, and he settled comfortably back in his chair. An unreadable expression appeared in his eyes, and the faint smile formed again.

"Why would I want to do that, my lady?"

He didn't seem the least bit surprised or angry. Perhaps this meeting would go as planned after all.

"Master David, I am sure that you are the good and honorable man that the King assumes. But this offer was accepted without my consent."

He looked at her impassively. "And?"

"And?" she repeated, a little stunned.

"My lady, that is an excellent reason for you to withdraw, but not me. Express your will to the King or the bishop and it is over. But your consent or lack of it is not my affair."

"It is not so simple. Perhaps amongst you people it is, but I am a ward of the King. He has spoken for me. To defy him on this . . ."

"The church will not marry an unwilling woman, even if a King has made the match. I, on the other hand, have given my consent and cannot withdraw it. There is no reason to, as I have said."

His calm lack of reaction irked her. "Well, then, let me explain my position more clearly and perhaps you will have your reason. I do not give my consent because I am in love with another man."

Absolutely nothing changed in his face or eyes. She might have told him that she was flawed by a wart on her leg.

"No doubt an excellent reason to refuse your consent in your view, Christiana. But again, it is not my affair."

She couldn't believe his bland acceptance of this. Had he no pride? No heart? "You cannot want to marry a woman who loves another," she blurted out.

"I expect it happens all the time. England is full of marriages made under these circumstances. In the long run, it is not such a serious matter."

Oh, dear saints, she thought. A man who believed in practical marriages. Just her luck. But then, he was a merchant.

"It may not be a serious matter amongst you people," she tried explaining, "but marriages based on love have become desired—"

"That is the second time that you have said that, my lady. Do not say it again." His voice was still quiet, his face still impassive, but a note of command echoed nonetheless.

"Said what?"

" 'You people.' You have used the phrase twice now."

"I meant nothing by it."

"You meant everything by it. But we will discuss that another day."

He had flustered and distracted her with this second scolding. She sought the strand of her argument. He found it for her.

"My lady, I am sure a young girl thinks that she needs to marry the man whom she thinks that she loves. But your emotions are a short-term problem. You will get over this. Marriage is a long-term investment. All will work out in the end."

He spoke to her as if she were a child, and as dispassionately as if they discussed a shipment of wool. It had been a mistake to think that she could appeal to his sympathy. He was a tradesman, after all, and to him life was probably just one big ledger sheet of expenses and profits.

Well, maybe he would understand things better if he saw the potential cost to his pride.

"This is not just a short-term infatuation on my part, Master David. I am not some little girl," she said. "I pledged myself to this man."

"You both privately pledged your troth?"

It could be done that way. She could lie. She desperately wanted to, and felt sorely tempted, but such a lie could have dire consequences, and very public ones, and she wasn't that brave. "Not formally," she said, hoping to leave a bit of ambiguity there.

He at least seemed moderately interested now. "Has this man offered for you?"

"His family sent him home from court before he could settle it."

"He is some boy whom his family controls?"

She had to remember with whom she spoke. "A family's will may seem a minor issue for a man such as you, but he is part of a powerful family up north. One does not defy kinship so easily. Still, when he hears of this betrothal, I am sure that he will come back."

"So, Christiana, you are saying that this man said that he wanted to marry you but left without settling for you."

That seemed a rather bald way to put it.

"Aye."

He smiled again. "Ah."

She really resented that "Ah." Her annoyance made her bold. She leaned toward him, feeling her jaw harden with repressed anger. "Master David, let me be blunt. I have given myself to this man."

Finally a reaction besides that impassive indifference. His head went back a fraction and he studied her from beneath lowered lids.

"Then be blunt, my lady. Exactly what do you mean by that?"

She threw up her hands in exasperation. "We made love together. Is that blunt enough for you? We went to bed together. In fact, we were found in bed together. Your offer was only accepted so that the Queen could hush up any scandal and keep my brother from forcing a marriage that my lover's family does not want."

She thought that she saw a flash of anger beneath those lids.

"You were discovered thus and this man left you to face it alone? Your devotion to this paragon of chivalry is impressive."

His assessment of Stephen was like a slap in her face. "How dare such as you criticize—"

"You are doing it again."

"Doing what?" she snapped.

" 'Such as you.' Twice now. Another phrase that you might avoid. For prudence' sake." He paused. "Who is this man?"

"I have sworn not to tell," she said stiffly. "My brother . . . Besides, as you have said, it is none of your affair."

He rose, uncoiling himself with an elegant movement, and went to stand by the hearth. The lines beneath the pourpoint suggested a lean, hard body. He was quite tall.

Not quite as tall as Morvan, but taller than most. She found his presence unsettling. Merchants were supposed to be skinny or portly men in fur hats.

He gazed at the flames. "Are you with child?" he asked.

The notion astounded her. She hadn't thought of that. But perhaps the Queen had. She looked at him vacantly. He turned and saw the expression.

"Do you know the signs?" he asked softly.

She shook her head.

"Have you had your flux since you were last with him?"

She blushed and nodded. In fact, it had come today.

He turned back to the fire.

She wondered what he thought about as he studied those tongues of heat. She stayed silent, letting him weigh however he valued these things, praying that she had succeeded, hoping that he indeed had a merchant's soul and would be repelled by accepting used goods.

Finally she couldn't wait any longer.

"So, you will go to the King and withdraw this offer?" she asked hopefully.

He glanced over his shoulder at her. "I think not."

Her heart sank.

"Young girls make mistakes," he added.

"This was no mistake," she said forcefully. "If you do not withdraw, you will end up looking a fool. He will come for me, if not before the betrothal, then after. When he comes, I will go with him."

He did not look at her, but his quiet, beautiful voice drifted over the space between them. "What makes you think that I will let you?"

"You will not be able to stop me. He is a knight, and skilled at arms . . ."

"There are more effective weapons in this world than

steel, Christiana." He turned. "As I said earlier, you are always free to go to the bishop and declare your lack of consent to this marriage. But I will not withdraw now."

"An honorable man would not expect me to face the King's wrath," she said bitterly.

"An honorable man would not ruin a girl at her request. If I withdraw, it will displease the King, whom I have no wish to anger. At the least I will need a good reason. Should I use the one that you have given me? Should I repudiate you because you are not a virgin? It is the only way."

She dropped her eyes. The panicked desolation of the last day returned to engulf her.

She sensed a movement and then David de Abyndon stood in front of her. A strong, gentle hand lifted her chin until she looked up into his handsome face. It seemed to her that those blue eyes read her soul and her mind and saw right into her. Even Lady Idonia's hawklike inspections had not been so thorough and successful. Nor so oddly mesmerizing.

That intensity that flowed from him surrounded her. She became very aware of his rough fingers on her chin. His thumb stretched and brushed her jaw, and something tingled in her neck.

"If he comes for you before the wedding, I will step aside," he said. "I will not contest an annulment of the betrothal. But I must tell you, girl, that I know men and I do not think that he will come, although you are well worth what it would cost him."

"You do not know *him*."

"Nay, I do not. And I am not so old that I can't be surprised." He smiled down at her. A real smile, she realized. The first one of the evening. A wonderful smile, actually. His hand fell away. Her skin felt warm where he had touched her.

She stood up. "I must go. My escort will grow impatient."

He walked with her to the door. "I will come and see you in a few days."

She felt sick at heart. He was making her go through with the farce of this betrothal, and it would complicate things horribly. She had no desire to play this role any more than necessary.

"Please do not. There is no point."

He turned and looked at her as he opened the door and led her to the steps. "As you wish, Christiana."

She saw Thomas's shadowy form in the courtyard, and flew to him as soon as they exited the hall. She glanced back to the doorway where David stood watching.

Thomas began guiding her to the portal. "Did you accomplish what you needed?"

"Aye," she lied. Thomas did not know about the betrothal. It had not been announced yet, and she had hoped that it never would be. Master David's stubbornness meant that now things were going to become very difficult. She would have to find some other way to stop this betrothal, or at least this marriage.

David watched her cross the courtyard, her nobility obvious in her posture and graceful walk. A very odd stillness began claiming him, and her movements slowed as if time grew sluggish. An eerie internal silence spread until it blocked out all sound. In an isolated world connected to the one in the yard but separate from it by invisible degrees, he began observing her in an abstract way.

He had felt this before several times in his life, and was stunned to find himself having the experience now. All the same, he did nothing to stop the sensation and did not question the importance of what was happening.

He recognized the silence that permeated him as the inaudible sound of Fortune turning her capricious wheel and changing his life in ways that he could only dimly foresee. Unlike most men, he did not fear the unpredictable coincidences that revealed Fortune's willfulness, for he had thus far been one of her favorite children.

Christiana Fitzwaryn of Harclow. The caves of Harclow. There was an elegant balance in this particular coincidence.

The gate closed behind her and time abruptly righted itself. He contemplated the implications of this girl's visit.

He had understood King Edward's desire to hide the payment for the exclusive trading license that he was buying. If word got out about it, other merchants would be jealous. He had himself suggested several other ways to conceal the arrangement, but they involved staggered payments, and the King, desperate for coin to finance his French war, wanted the entire sum now. Edward's solution of giving him a noble wife and disguising the payment as a bride price had created a host of problems, though, not the least of which was the possibility that the girl would not suit him.

His vision turned inward and he saw Christiana's black hair and pale skin and lovely face. Her dark eyes sparkled like black diamonds. She was not especially small, but her elegance gave the impression of delicacy, even frailty. The first sight of her in the fire glow had made his breath catch the way it always did when he came upon an object or view of distinctive beauty.

Her visit had announced unanticipated complications, but it had resolved one question most clearly. Christiana Fitzwaryn would suit him very well indeed.

He had been stunned when the King had chosen the daughter of Hugh Fitzwaryn to be the bride in this scheme, and had pointed out that she was too far above him. Even the huge bride price that everyone would think he was paying did not bridge their difference in degrees.

The King had brushed it aside. *We will put it about that you saw her and wanted her and paid me a fortune to have her.* Well, now he knew the reason for the King's choice of Christiana. A quick marriage for the girl would snuff out any flames of scandal regarding her and her lover.

It was good to know the truth. He did not like playing the pawn in another man's game. Usually he was the one who moved the pieces.

He walked across the courtyard to Sieg.

"It is done then?" the Swede asked as he turned to enter his chamber off the passageway.

"It was not them."

"The hell you say!"

David laughed. "Go to sleep. I doubt that they will come tonight."

"I hope not. There's more visitors here at night than the day, as it is." Sieg paused. "What about Lady Alicia's guard?"

David glanced to the end of the building, and the glow of a candle through a window. "He knows to stay there. I will bring her to him later."

He turned to leave, then stopped. "Sieg, tomorrow I want you to find the name of a man for me. He is a knight, and his family is from the north country. An important family."

"Not much to go on. There be dozens . . ."

"He left Westminster recently. I would guess in the last day or so."

"That makes it easier."

"His name, Sieg. And what you can learn about him."

CHAPTER 2

CHRISTIANA SPENT a desperate night trying to figure out how to save herself. By morning she could find no course of action except writing to Stephen, bribing a royal messenger to carry the letter north, and praying that he received it quickly. But the betrothal was in a week, too soon for Stephen to get that letter and come for her.

The only solution was to speak with the King. She would not refuse the marriage outright, but would let him know that she did not welcome it. Perhaps, at the very least, she could convince him to delay the betrothal.

Steeling her resolve, she left the apartment that she shared with Isabele and Joan under Idonia's watchful eyes, and made her way through the castle to the room where the King met with petitioners. When she arrived, its ante-room had already filled with people. She gave her name to the clerk who sat by the door, and hoped that her place in the household would put her ahead of some of the others.

Some benches lined one wall. An older knight gave up his place, and she settled down. The standing crowd walled her in while she concentrated on planning her request.

As she waited and pondered, the outer door opened and a page entered, followed by her brother Morvan. She saw his dark head disappear into the King's chamber.

The King was going to tell him about the match now. What would her proud brother say? How would he react?

She had her answer very soon. Within minutes the measured rumble of a raised voice leaked through wall that separated the anteroom from the chamber. She knew that it was Edward who had lost his temper, because Morvan's worst anger always manifested itself quietly and coldly.

She had to leave immediately. With the King enraged, there could be no benefit in speaking with him today, and when Morvan left that room, she did not want him to see her sitting here.

She was rising to leave when Morvan hurried out, his black eyes flashing and his handsome face frozen into a mask of fury. He strode to the corridor like a man headed for battle.

She still needed to leave, but she dared not follow him. He might have stopped in the passageways leading here.

She glanced around the anteroom. Another door on a side wall gave out to a private corridor that connected Edward's chambers and rooms. It led to an exterior stairway, and there were rumors that secret guests, diplomats, and sometimes women came to him this way. Without it ever being formally declared off limits, everyone knew that it meant trouble to be found there. Even the Queen did not use that passageway.

She pushed through the crowd. She would slip away and no one would know that she had even come.

Opening the small door a crack, she slid through. The passageway stretched along the exterior wall of the castle lit by good-sized windows set into shallow alcoves. She scurried toward the end opposite the one with the staircase.

The sound of a door opening behind her sent her darting into one of the alcoves. Pressing into the corner, she prayed that whoever had entered the passageway would go in the other direction. She sighed with relief as she heard footsteps walking away.

Then, to her horror, more steps started coming quickly toward her from the direction in which she had been heading. Crushing herself into the alcove's shallow corner, she gritted her teeth and waited for discovery.

A shortish middle-aged man with gray hair and beard, sumptuously dressed like a diplomat, hurried by. He did not notice her, because he fixed all of his attention on the space ahead of him. It seemed that he tried to make his own footsteps fall more softly than normal.

"Pardon. Attendez," she heard him whisper loudly.

The other steps stopped. She heard the men meet.

They began speaking in low tones but their words carried easily to her ears. Both spoke Parisian French, the kind taught to her by the tutors, and not the corrupted dialect used casually by the English courtiers.

"If you are found here, it will go badly for you," the other man said. His voice sounded very low, little more than a whisper, but the words reached her just the same.

"A necessary risk. I needed to know if what I had heard of you was true."

"And what did you hear?"

"That you can help us."

"You have the wrong man."

"I do not think so. I followed you here. You have the access, as I was told."

"If you want what I think you want, you have the wrong man."

"At least hear me out."

"Nay."

The men began walking away. The voices receded.

"It will be worth your while," the first man said.

"There is nothing that you have that I want."

"How do you know if you don't listen?"

"You are a fool to speak to me of this here. I do not deal with fools."

The voices and footsteps continued to grow fainter. Christiana listened until their sound disappeared down the stairway. Lifting her hem, she ran back to her chamber.

She was sitting on her bed in Isabele's anteroom, fretting over whether to approach the King another day, when Morvan came storming into the chamber still furious from his meeting with the King.

He stomped around and ranted with dangerous anger. Rarely had she seen him like this, and keeping him from doing something rash became her primary concern. She felt guilty calming and soothing him, since she knew that everything was her fault and he, of course, did not. Morvan laid all of the blame on the King and the merchant.

"This mercer did not even have the decency to speak with me first," Morvan spat out, his black eyes flashing sparks as he strode around. He was a big man, taller than most, and he filled the space. "He went directly to the King! The presumptions of those damn merchants is ever galling, but this is an outrage."

"Perhaps he didn't know how it is done with us," she

said. She needed him calm and rational. If they thought about this together, they might have some ideas.

"It is the same with every degree, sister. Would this man have gone to his mayor to offer for some skinner's daughter?"

"Well, he did it this way, and the King agreed. We are stuck with that part."

"Aye, Edward agreed." He suddenly stopped his furious stride and stared bleakly into the hearth. "This is a bad sign, Christiana. It means that the King has indeed forgotten."

Her heart went out to him. She walked over and embraced him and forgot her own disappointment and problems. She had been so selfishly concerned with her own pride that she hadn't seen the bigger implications of this marriage.

Fleeting, vague memories of another life filtered into her exhausted mind. Memories of Harclow and happiness. Images of war and death. The echo of gnawing hunger and relentless fear during siege. And finally, clearly and distinctly, she had the picture of Morvan, ten years old but tall already, walking bravely through the castle gate to surrender to the enemy. He had fully expected to be killed. Over the years, she came to believe that God had moved that Scottish lord to spare him so that she herself would not be totally alone.

When they had fled Harclow and gone to young King Edward and told him of Hugh Fitzwaryn's death and the loss of the estate, Edward had blamed himself for not bringing relief fast enough. Their father had been one of his friends and supporters on the Scottish marches, and in front of Morvan and their dying mother Edward had sworn to avenge his friend and return the family lands to them.

That had been eleven years ago. For a long while thereafter, Morvan had assumed that once he earned his spurs the King would fulfill that oath. But he had been a knight for two years now, and it had become clear that Edward planned no aggressive campaigns on the Scottish borders. The army sent there every year was involved in little more than a holding action. All of the King's attention had become focused on France.

And now this. Agreeing to marry her to this merchant was a tacit admission on the King's part that he would never help Morvan reclaim Harclow. The ancient nobility of the Fitzwaryn family would be meaningless in a generation.

No wonder the Percys did not want one of their young men marrying her. But Stephen's love would be stronger than such petty concerns of politics property. And once they were married, she hoped that the Percy family would help Morvan, since he would be tied to their kinship through her.

The chance of that had always increased Stephen's appeal. The redemption of their family honor should not rest entirely on Morvan's shoulders. It was her duty to marry a man who would give her brother a good alliance.

Morvan pulled away. "The King said the betrothal is to be Saturday. I do not understand the haste."

She could hardly confide to her strict older brother that the haste was to make sure that her lover could not interfere. And maybe also to avert Morvan's anger. If he learned what had happened with Stephen, he would undoubtedly demand satisfaction through a duel. King Edward probably wanted to avoid the trouble with the Percy family that such a challenge would create.

Her attempts at soothing him failed. The storm broke in his expression again. He left as furiously as he had entered. "Do not worry, sister. I will deal with this merchant."

✦   ✦   ✦

David stood at the door of his shop watching his two young apprentices, Michael and Roger, carry the muslin-wrapped silks and furs out to the transport wagon. A long, gaily decorated box on wheels, the wagon held seats for the ladies and had windows piercing its sides. Princess Isabele sat at one of the openings.

The arrival of Lady Idonia and Lady Joan and Princess Isabele today had amused him and awed the apprentices. The ladies ostensibly came to choose cloth for the cotehardie and surcoat that Isabele would wear at Christiana's wedding, but the princess was not his patron. The news of the betrothal had just spread at Westminster, and he knew that in reality Christiana's friends had come to inspect him.

They had almost been disappointed, since he hadn't arrived until they were preparing to leave. His business extended far beyond the walls of this shop now, and he left the daily workings of it to Andrew. He smiled at the memory of tiny Lady Idonia throwing her body between Isabele and Sieg when he and the Swede had entered the shop, as if she sought to save the girl from Viking ravishment.

The boys handed their packages in to Lady Idonia. They peered into the wagon one last time as it pulled away surrounded by five mounted guards.

They had a lot to peer at, David thought, glancing at the crowd of onlookers that had formed on the lane when the wagon drew up. A princess and the famous Lady Joan, Fair Maid of Kent, cousin to the King. Members of the royal family rarely visited the tradesmen's shops. It was customary to bring goods to them instead.

Christiana had not come, of course. He wondered what ruse she had used to avoid it. He was sending a gift back to her with Idonia, however, a red cloak lined with black fur which the tailor George who worked upstairs had sewn at his bidding. The one that she had worn to his house four nights ago looked to be several years old and a handspan too short. Being the King's ward clearly did not mean that she lived in luxury.

She would probably feel guilty accepting his gift. In that brief time in his solar, he had learned much about her character and she had impressed him favorably. Her beauty had impressed him even more. The memory of those bright eyes and that pale skin had not been far from his mind since her visit.

She waited for her lover. How long would she wait?

Unlike most men, he liked women and understood them. He certainly understood the pain Christiana felt. After all, he had lived eighteen years near a similar anguish. Was he fated now to spend the rest of his life in its shadow again? Was that to be the price this time of Fortune's favor? This girl seemed stronger and prouder than that.

He had briefly lost awareness of the street, but its movements and colors reclaimed his attention. He pushed away from the doorjamb. As he turned to enter the building he noticed a man walking up the lane from the Cheap, wearing livery that he recognized. He waited for the man to reach him.

"David de Abyndon?" the messenger asked.

"Aye."

A folded piece of parchment was handed over. David read the note. He had expected this letter. In fact, he had been waiting for the meeting it requested for over ten years. Better to finish it quickly. Betrothal and marriage probably had a way of complicating things like this.

He turned to the messenger. "Tell her I cannot see her this week. Next Tuesday afternoon. She should come to my house."

He entered the shop. Michael and Roger were closing

the front shutters, and Andrew came in with cloth from the back room.

"I put the tallies from Lady Idonia and Lady Joan up in the counting room," Andrew said as he settled his burden down.

David clapped a hand on his shoulder. "So. A whole afternoon with the Fair Joan. Your friends will buy you ale for a month to hear your story."

Andrew smiled roguishly. "I was just thinking the same thing. She *is* very fair. As is Lady Christiana Fitzwaryn. I have seen them together in the city. You might have told us about this betrothal. It was very awkward finding out from them."

The boys stopped and listened. Sieg stood by the door.

"It was just decided."

They all waited silently.

"Let us close and go home. I'll explain all there."

Explain what, though? Not the truth. No one would ever learn that, not even Christiana. He would have to come up with a good story fast.

They were almost ready to leave when the sounds of a horse stopping in the lane came through the shutters. Michael ran over and peered out the door. "A King's knight," he said. "The same one who came looking for you this morning, David."

David knew who this would be. "All of you go back to the house. You too, Sieg. I will take care of this."

The door opened and a tall, dark-haired young man entered. He paused in the threshold and looked around. He wore the King's livery and a long sword hung from his knight's belt. Bright black eyes, so like those others but brittle with a colder light, came to rest on David.

The apprentices filed out around the big man, clearly

impressed with his size and bearing. Sieg glanced meaningfully at David. David shook his head and Sieg left too.

"I am Christiana's brother Morvan," the knight said when they were finally alone.

"I know who you are."

"Do you? I thought that perhaps you mistakenly thought that she had no kin."

David waited. He would let this brother make his objections. He would not assume that he knew what they would be, for there was much to object to.

"I thought that we should meet," Sir Morvan said, walking down the passageway. "I wanted to see the man who buys a wife like she is some horse."

David thought about the two hours he had spent this morning with one of the King's clerks drawing up the marriage contract. It had been impossible to keep out the terms of the supposed bride price completely, because only Edward and he knew its real purpose. Still, David had tried, and finally negotiated only a reference to its amount involving a complicated formula based on the price of last year's wool exports. Only someone very interested would ever bother to make the calculations.

Morvan must have been shown the contract for approval and not missed that particular clause.

"The King insisted on the bride price, as in the old days. I would have been happy to pay nothing."

Morvan studied him. "If she were not my sister, I might find that amusing. You go to a lot of trouble to marry a woman whom you do not know."

"It happens all of the time."

"Aye. If the dowry is satisfactory."

"I have no need of a dowry."

"So I am told. Nor are you much in need of a woman to warm your bed, from what I hear. So why do you pay a fortune for my sister?"

David had to admit that it was a damn good question. He realized that he shouldn't underestimate this young man. Morvan had been asking about him, just as David had been asking about Morvan. Perhaps the King's proposed explanation would work. *We will put it about that you saw her and wanted her and paid a fortune to have her.* Not, he suspected, that a man lusting after his sister would appeal much to this young knight.

"I saw her several times and asked about her. The King was receptive to my inquiries."

"So you offered for her just on seeing her?"

"I have these whims sometimes. They almost always work out. As far as the rest, the lack of dowry and the payment, things just developed as they often do in such negotiations." It sounded almost plausible. It had better. He had nothing else to offer.

Morvan considered him. "That would make sense if you were a fool, but I do not think that you are. I think that you are an upstart who seeks to buy status among his people through this marriage, and who sees his children raised above their natural degree through their mother's nobility."

Another plausible explanation. But if Morvan had spoken with the right people, he would know just how wrong it was.

"You are Christiana's brother, and are thus unaware of just how foolish she might make a man who is otherwise not a fool," David said.

A fire flashed in the young man's dark eyes. Nay, he did not like the idea of a man lusting after his sister.

"I will not permit this marriage. I will not see Christiana tied to a common tradesman, no matter what his wealth. She is not a brood mare to be purchased to ennoble a bastard's bloodline. She does not want this either."

David ignored the insults, barely, except to note that Morvan had been checking up on him quite thoroughly. "She and I have already spoken of that. She knows that I will not withdraw. I have no reason to."

"Let me give you a reason, then. Go to the King and say that the lady has a brother who has threatened you with bodily harm unless you withdraw. Explain that you did not anticipate that when you made this offer."

"And what of the King's displeasure with you if I say this?"

"If need be, my sword can serve another man."

"And if I don't do this?"

"The threat is not an idle one."

David studied his resolute expression. An intelligent man, and probably an honest one. "Do you know why your sister does not consent to this marriage?"

"That is obvious, isn't it?"

So Morvan did not know about Sir Stephen. She had claimed that he didn't, but he may have discovered it nonetheless and been planning to force things with Percy.

"Is it?"

"She is the daughter of a baron. This marriage is an insult to her."

David fought down a sudden profound irritation. He had long ago become almost immune to such comments, and to the assumptions of superiority that they revealed. But he had accepted more from this man in the last few minutes than he normally swallowed from anyone. He leaned against the wall and folded his arms and met Morvan's fiery eyes.

"Will you withdraw?"

"I think not."

Morvan looked him up and down. "You wear a dagger. Do you use a sword?"

"Not well."

"Then you had best practice."

"You plan to kill me over this?"

"I cannot stop this betrothal, but I will stop the wedding. A month hence, if you have not left London or annulled the match, we will meet."

Anger seeped into David's head. He almost never lost control anymore, but he was in danger of it now. "Send word of when and where. I will be there."

He knew that Morvan's own cold fury matched his own. But he also saw the surprise that the threat had been met with anger and not fear.

"We will see if you come," Morvan said with a slow smile. "I think that time will show that you are like most of your breed. Rich in gold but without honor."

"And you are like too many knights these days. Rich in pompous arrogance but without land or value," David replied sharply. It was unworthy of him, but he had had enough.

Morvan's eyes flashed dangerously. He pivoted on his heel and walked the twenty paces to the door. "My sister is not for you, merchant. You have a month to undo this."

Something snapped. As Morvan disappeared into the street, David uncoiled himself with a fluid, tense movement. His hand went to his hip, and a long steel dagger flew down the passageway, imbedding itself into the doorjamb directly behind the spot where Morvan Fitzwaryn's neck had just been.

A blond head moved in the open door's twilight, and Sieg bent into the threshold. He glanced at David and then turned and yanked the still-quivering dagger out of its target. He came down the passageway.

"I suppose that it is still early to congratulate you on this marriage."

David took the dagger and sheathed it. The worst of his anger had flown with the knife. "You heard."

"*Ja.*"

"I told you to leave."

"His sword and face told me to stay. I thought that I would have the chance to repay my debt today."

David ignored him and began walking away.

"Do you want us to take care of him? The girl need never know. There be all of these rivers around. A man could fall in."

"Nay."

"The sword is not your weapon."

"It will not come to that."

"You are sure? He looked determined."

"I am sure."

They walked up the lane toward the house. Sieg kept looking over at him. Finally the Swede spoke. "It is an odd time to be getting married."

"Aye." And it was. Any number of carefully cultivated fields were awaiting harvesting in the next few months.

"It could make things harder," Sieg said.

"I've thought of that."

"You could put the wedding off until next winter. November maybe. All should be settled by then."

David shook his head. He realized that he was not inclined to give her lover a whole year to come back. He also already knew that he had no intention of waiting that long to take the beautiful Christiana Fitzwaryn to his bed. "Nay. It will be safer to have her at the house."

"And if there are problems . . ."

"Then the girl is doubly blessed. She gets rid of a husband whom she does not want and becomes a rich widow."

✦ ✦ ✦

A fine cold mist shrouded the Strand as the little party rode up its length. John Constantyn sat straight and proud on his horse, his fur-trimmed and bejeweled velvet robe barely covered by the bright blue cloak thrown back over his shoulders. He glanced at David's own unadorned and austere blue pourpoint.

"Thank God you at least wore that chain," John said, grinning. "They might mistake you for some gentry squire otherwise. Under the circumstances you might have fancied yourself up some, just this once. It is an odd statement that you make with your garments, David."

David would like to claim that he made no statement at all with his clothes, that their plainness merely reflected his taste, but he knew that wasn't entirely true. Refusing to compete in the nobility's game of luxury was, he supposed, a tacit repudiation of the nobleman's assumption of superior worth.

He felt the heavy gold chain on his chest, arching from shoulder to shoulder. He had even worn this with reluctance, and finally put it on only for Christiana's sake. Her friends would know its value. He would not make this day any harder for her than it promised to be already.

"You should have seen your uncle Gilbert's face when I told him what I would be doing today," John said. "By God, it was rich. Right there outside the Guildhall, I asked him if he would attend, aware that he knew nothing of it. I made him worm the details out of me bit by bit, too. At least twenty of the wardens must have overheard." John's hearty laugh echoed down the Strand. " 'Aye, Gilbert,' I said, 'didn't you know? The daughter of the famous Hugh Fitzwaryn. By the king's pleasure, no less. In the royal chapel with the royal family in attendance.' His face looked the color of ash before I was done."

David smiled at the thought of Gilbert's expression when he learned that David would marry a baron's daughter. It was the first time that this betrothal had given him any pleasure.

He hadn't spoken to any of the Abyndons since he was a youth and had fully realized what they had done to his mother. He also refused to trade with them, and never sold them any of the goods that he imported. It was a childish revenge, but the only one open to him right now. Eventually the chance would come to plant that particular field in a more appropriate way.

John smiled more soberly. "Would that my brother could see this."

Aye, David thought. *But it is just as well that he cannot.* He thought a moment about his dead master and partner, the man who had probably saved him from a life in the alleys. A good man, David Constantyn, whose faith in his young apprentice had made them both rich and permitted David to become the man he was today. He had loved his master more than a son does a father.

It was out of respect and love that he had bided his time and waited. Waited for his master's death before planting those fields that waited to be harvested now. *Better that he is not here, for there is much that honest man wouldn't like,* David thought. *But then, he was shrewd, and might not be so surprised. He probably knew what he had in me.*

They rode through the town of Westminster to the castle and buildings that housed the court and the government. David led the way to the royal chapel.

People milled around outside its doors. The King's approach caused no commotion or even much attention. Edward and Philippa led their children and their closest retainers in for the daily mass. David had no trouble locating Christiana in the group, because she wore the red cloak. Her eyes did not seek him out as she silently between Joan and Lady Idonia.

A page had reserved space for David behind the royal family. At the other end of his row stood the rigid form of Morvan Fitzwaryn. In front of him Christiana focused her attention on the priest at the altar, not once turning her head.

The mass was brief and after it the priest came down from the altar and called Christiana and himself forward. Christiana, her cloak still on to ward off the chill in the chapel, went to her brother, then the two of them joined David in front of the priest. He looked over at her and saw a vacant expression in her eyes as she trained her gaze on a spot somewhere in the distance. She looked noble and calm and emotionally void.

Morvan took her hand and placed it in David's. It felt incredibly small and soft. One slight tremble shook her arm, and then they listened to the priest's prayer before pledging their troth. She recited the words like a school lesson, her expressionless chant suggesting that they held no meaning, if indeed she even heard them.

She turned for the betrothal kiss, lifting her face dutifully but keeping her eyes downcast. David felt an odd combination of sympathy and annoyance.

In the law of the church and the realm, she belonged to him now, but she had carefully managed not to see or acknowledge him since her arrival. It had been subtle, and he knew that she had done it for her own sake and to control her own pain. She had not deliberately tried to insult him. He simply didn't matter. He doubted that anyone but Morvan had even noticed.

He suspected that Christiana sought to turn this betrothal into a dream so that she could wake when her lover came and find that it had conveniently never really happened. That he understood this girl did not mean, however, that he felt inclined to indulge her illusions with the dutiful kiss that she now offered and expected.

He did not care that the King and Queen stood nearby, nor that the angry brother watched. This was solely between him and her.

He stepped close to her and laid his hand on her cheek. A small tremor awoke beneath his touch.

The hood of her cloak still rested atop her head, hiding her hair. He could tell that she wore it unbound, a symbol of virginity, as was traditional for the ceremony. With his other hand he pushed the hood away. The thick black locks cascaded down her back, and his hand followed until he embraced her.

"Look at me, Christiana," he commanded quietly.

The black lashes fluttered. The creamy lids rose slowly. Two diamonds flashed startled alertness and fear.

He lowered his head and tasted the soft sweetness of her trembling lips.

CHAPTER 3

CHRISTIANA STUDIED THE chessboard propped on the chest between her and Joan. She shifted a pawn.

Joan quickly took one of her knights. "You are playing badly today," she said.

They sat by a window in Isabele's bedchamber. The princess had gone to visit a friend in another part of Westminster, and Lady Idonia had accompanied her.

Christiana tried to concentrate on the game and not think about her betrothal three days earlier. In particular she worked hard not to reflect on David de Abyndon, but his intense eyes and warm touch kept intruding on her memory in a distressing way. He had handled the ceremony and dinner very kindly, almost sympathetically. With one stunning exception.

"You never told me what it was like getting betrothed," Joan said.

Christiana shrugged. "I don't remember much. I was most unsettled."

Joan tossed her blond curls and her eyes twinkled. "What was the kiss like? It looked like a wonderful kiss."

Christiana stared at the chessmen scattered on the board. She had been working especially hard not to think about that kiss.

What should she say to Joan? What *could* she say? How could she explain that only the most necessary part of her had paid attention to either the mass or the pledge? That she had deliberately dulled her mind so that she would get through the morning without panicking. That she had filled her heart with Stephen and the trust and knowledge of his love, and that the whole scene in the church had only been a restless dream that would quickly fade.

Until there had been that hand on her face in a gesture of intimacy, forcing her awake as surely as a shake during the night. A voice commanding her to look reality in the face. An embrace and a kiss of masterful possession.

What was that kiss like? Confusing. Frightening. Longer than necessary. Long enough to make clear that one of them intended to treat this betrothal seriously.

The sensation of a streak of warmth flowing through her body licked at her memory. She shifted restlessly and forced all of her attention on the chess game.

Aye, she did not want to think or talk about that kiss very much at all. "It was nice enough."

At least that part of this travesty was over. Now she had only to wait for Stephen to come.

"Have you ever been kissed before?" Joan asked.

Christiana wished that she could confide in her friend, but Joan was a notorious gossip. It had, of course, crossed her mind that if Joan did gossip, and Morvan learned about Stephen, then maybe her brother would encourage the Percys to change their mind. She had immediately felt guilty for that unworthy thought. After all, she didn't want

Stephen offering for her at the point of a sword. That wouldn't be necessary anyway.

The memory of Stephen's mouth crushing hers fluttered in her mind. David's kiss hadn't been at all like that, but then they had been standing in a church in front of a king and a priest. Still ... nay, she didn't want to think about that kiss. "I have been kissed before. Frankly, didn't like it. I think that I am one of those women who doesn't."

Joan's expression contained a touch of pity. "He is very handsome," she said after a pause. "If you have to marry a merchant, he may as well be a rich and handsome one."

Christiana knew that Joan echoed the opinion of the whole court. *Poor Christiana. A sweet girl. Too bad about the King giving her to a common merchant, but at least he is rich and handsome.* It reminded her of the encouraging sympathy offered to a maimed knight. *Too bad that you will never walk right again, but at least you are not dead.*

"Lady Elizabeth buys from him, you know," Joan added very casually. "And Lady Agnes and a few others."

Joan always managed to find out such things. In the last week she had probably learned all there was to know in Westminster about David de Abyndon. She would drop tidbits like this here and there as it suited her.

"They prefer to go to his shop, which is quite wonderful. You really should have come with us, Christiana. He brings in silks from Italy and as far away as India. There are tailors there too. The women who use him treat him like a secret and will go nowhere else. Lady Agnes says that Lady Elizabeth's whole white and silver style was his idea. I'm surprised that you never saw him before this happened if Elizabeth is one of his patrons."

Lady Elizabeth, a widow, had been a special friend of Morvan's for a number of months a year ago. She was at least ten years older than him but exquisitely beautiful. Her most notable features were her prematurely white hair and her translucent white skin. Court rumors had predicted a marriage, but then Elizabeth had accepted the offer of an elderly lord and suddenly her friendship with Morvan had cooled.

For two years now, Elizabeth had affected a highly personal style that enhanced her unique beauty. She wore only white and silvery grays. Even her jewels were reset in silver.

"Isabele is convinced that he will make you work for him," Joan giggled. "Idonia has explained that wealthy merchants don't do that, but Isabele sees the women working in the shops and thinks that you will have to as well."

Dear saints, Morvan would kill her to protect the family honor before he swallowed *that*. "It is your move, Joan," she said, deciding that it was time to end the subject.

A page entered a short time later. "My lady, your husband is in the hall and bids you to attend on him," he said to her.

She stared at the boy as if he had spoken gibberish. "Is that the message as he sent it?"

"Aye, my lady."

"I do not much like this message," she said to Joan.

"It sounds common enough to me."

"He is not my husband yet."

"Oh, Christiana, you know that betrothed couples are often referred to as husband and wife. Saturday was the first part of the ceremony, and the wedding is the conclusion. It is half done."

Not for me, she wanted to shout. *And this man knows it.*

She also didn't like, not one bit, being "bidden" to do anything by David de Abyndon. When Morvan put her hand in David's, it was symbolic of handing over authority and responsibility, but under the circumstances of this particular betrothal, that was meaningless too.

She turned to the page. "Tell my betrothed that I regret that I cannot attend on him this morning. I am grateful that he has visited, but I am not well. Tell him that I have a headache and am feeling dizzy."

"I hope that you know what you are doing," Joan said.

More to the point was the importance that David know what she was doing. She had told him that they would not see each other, and if he mistakenly thought that she meant only before the betrothal, then this should clarify it. She had no intention of explaining to Stephen when he came that she had been playing out this farce more than necessary.

A short while later their door flew open and the page reappeared, red faced and winded from running.

"My lady, your hus . . . that man is coming here."

"Coming here!"

"Aye. I handed him over to another page and sent them the long way, but he will be here soon."

She looked desperately at Joan as the page left.

"I thought that you knew what you were doing," Joan said, laughing.

She jumped up. "Help me. Quickly." She ran into the bedchamber's anteroom and threw back the coverlet on her bed. "Tuck me in and close the curtains. Try not to let any of my gown show."

"This isn't going to work." Joan giggled as she poked the coverlet around her neck and sides.

"Tell him that I am resting and send him away."

Joan grinned and pulled the curtains.

Christiana lay absolutely still in the dark shadows of the bed. She could hear Joan walking around, humming a melody. She felt a little ridiculous doing this, but something deep inside her said that she should not see this man again.

Even though her curtains muffled the sounds, she heard the boots walking into the room.

"Master David!" Joan cried brightly.

"Lady Joan. You, at least, appear to be well."

Christiana sighed. This man's quiet, beautiful voice had a talent for putting a lot of meaning into simple words without so much as changing its inflection. It was very clear that he knew that she lied about being ill, but then she had counted on him seeing that. She just hadn't counted on him coming to confront her and thus forcing her to pretend that she hadn't lied.

"Indeed I am very well, David. And you?"

"Well enough, my lady. Although I find myself recently more short of temper than is normal."

"No doubt it is something that you ate."

"No doubt."

Boots paced across the floor. "I am told that Christiana is ill."

"Aye. She is resting, David, and really should not be disturbed."

"What is the malady?"

"It was really quite frightening. When she awoke this morning she was overcome with dizziness. She almost fell. We put her right back to bed, of course, and that seems to help. She could be abed for days, even weeks."

Don't overdo it. Christiana prompted silently.

"It sounds most serious," David said. "Such an illness is not to be taken lightly. Perhaps I should pay the abbey monks to say masses on her behalf."

"We are very worried, but I trust all will be well soon. We will be sure to send word to you when she is better."

"Is this her bed? I will see her before I go."

"I really don't think that will be wise, David," Joan said hurriedly. "The light seems to make it worse."

A clever touch, Christiana thought approvingly.

But not clever enough. "I will be quick."

Even with her eyes closed, Christiana saw the light flood over her as the curtains were pushed back.

She gasped as he took her firmly by the waist, lifted her up, and dropped her on her back.

She lowered her lids as if the light hurt them, and moaned for effect. She hoped that she looked suitably pale and ill.

David gave her hip a gentle whack, gesturing for her to move over. Biting back her indignation, she scooted a little and he sat on the edge of the bed.

"Well, Christiana, I am very concerned. A headache and dizziness. You seem to have a serious illness indeed."

That hardness around his mouth seemed a bit more pronounced. Something in his expression suggested that he was capable of being the exact opposite of the kindly merchant whom she had first expected.

He rubbed her cheek with the backs of his fingers. "No fever. All the same, I think that we should have a physician see you at once."

"I am sure that isn't necessary." She tried to make her voice a little weak but not too much so. "I am feeling better, and I am sure that this will pass."

He ignored her. "I will have to ask around and see which of the ones at court are any good. Some of these physicians immediately want to bleed the patient, and that is so painful. We would like to avoid it if possible, don't you think?"

She had been bled once when she was eleven. She thought that avoiding it was an excellent idea.

"On the other hand, headaches and dizziness are probably caused by the humors that require it."

"I really find that I am feeling much better. The light doesn't bother me at all now."

"The idea of being bled always makes one feel better, my girl, but it doesn't last. However, if you think that you are recovering a little for now, I would really prefer to get you dressed and take you to see a Saracen physician whom I know in Southwark. He is an expert in ladies' illnesses, and treats all of the whores in the Stews. He is very skilled."

"A Saracen! A whores' physician!" She completely forgot to make her voice weak at all.

"Aye. Trained in Alexandria. Saracen physicians are much better than Christians. We are barbarians in comparison."

"I assure you that going to Southwark is not needed, David. Truly, I am feeling enormously better. Quite myself, in fact. I am confident that I am completely cured."

He smiled slowly. "Are you? That is good news. However, you must be sure to let me know if these spells return. I will be sure to get you to a physician immediately. I am responsible for you now, and would not have your health neglected."

She glared at him. This "husband" who had "bid her attend on him" was reminding her of his rights and warning her not to play this game again. She could think of nicer ways to have made the point without threatening to have her arm cut open.

He rose. Apparently his oblique scolding was finished, and Christiana felt confident that he would leave. She glanced at Joan triumphantly.

David looked down at her. "The day is fair. Perhaps all that you need is some fresh air to clear your head."

"I'm not at all sure . . ."

His gaze lit on the closest ambry. "Are your things in here? We will get you dressed and I will take you out for a while."

She narrowed her eyes at David's handsome face. One farce after another. She couldn't claim to be too dizzy to go out but also too well to see a physician. He had cleverly, elegantly manipulated her ruse against her.

"I am already dressed," she announced, throwing back the coverlet and sitting up, admitting defeat.

"So you are," he said quietly, coming toward her with a vague smile on his face and her old cloak in his hand. "What a disappointment. I was looking forward to that part."

That smile made her very uncomfortable. She would admit defeat, but not surrender. "Unfortunately," she said regretfully, "I cannot go with you. It is a rule. None of us can be with a man alone."

Joan nodded her head vigorously in support.

"Lady Idonia is gone, and unfortunately Joan has to meet with her brother soon," she added.

Joan continued nodding even though she had no such plans.

"It is a most serious prohibition," she emphasized. "As you can imagine, the consequences for disobeying are dire."

"Dire," Joan echoed helpfully.

David gave them both a look that indicated he thought that consequences had not been nearly dire enough for the two of them over the years.

"I might risk it, except that the Queen is most strict and . . ." She threw up her hands.

David flipped the cloak out and around her shoulders. He bent to pin the brooch under her neck. His closeness, and his hands working near her body, made her yet more uncomfortable.

"I am not just a man, I am your betrothed. What is the worst that can happen? If I ravish you, it simply means that the marriage is finalized that much earlier. Perhaps they would thank me for taking you off their hands. Besides, it is for me to punish your future bad behavior and not Lady Idonia and the Queen."

He was talking to her like a child again. In fact, he was dressing her like a child. Furthermore, this was his second reference to *that*, and she really could do without his innuendos. They prodded at something inside her that she didn't want to think about. Since they insinuated a familiarity that simply wasn't going to develop, she thought that it would be nice if they didn't even jest about it.

This merchant's presumptions indicated that he was taking his betrothal rights far too seriously. She did not want to be alone with David de Abyndon any longer than necessary, and she had ruined the chance of getting Joan to come with them. While he put on his own cloak, she caught Joan's attention.

Idonia, she mouthed.

She stood up to leave. With a smooth movement David bent and scooped her into his arms. She cried a startled "Oh!" and stared at him.

"I can walk." She fumed when he laughed.

"There are steps. If you get dizzy again, you might fall and break your neck."

"It is more likely that you will drop me."

"Nonsense. You are very light."

"Oh, dear saints," she groaned, letting her head fall back in exasperation. "Well, at least go down the back stairs to the entrance there. I don't want the whole court to see this."

As he carried her out, she turned her head and looked desperately back at Joan.

Send Idonia, she mouthed again.

He set her down at the back entrance that led to a small courtyard beneath Isabele's windows.

"There are some benches here and the sun is warm against that wall," she suggested. "Let us sit here."

"I think that we would prefer to take a ride."

Idonia would never find them and rescue her then. "*I* would prefer to sit here."

"Soon the shadows will move over that wall, and then you will get chilled. A ride in the sun will be better."

Walking beside him around the corner of the manor, she wondered if all men got so willful after one got betrothed to them. Would Stephen stop speaking pretty words when they were married? Was that just something done beforehand to lure women? The chansons weren't much help with this question. The couples in those romantic songs were never married. She immediately felt guilty for equating Stephen with this merchant. Stephen was a chivalrous knight, and poetry and romance flowed in his blood.

David took the reins of his horse from the young groom who had been holding them.

"I will send for a mount from the stables," she said.

"You will ride with me. One of the problems with being dizzy is that you cannot ride a horse unattended for a while." He lifted her up to the front of the saddle and swung up behind her.

She had never sat on a horse with a man before. The perch up front was a little precarious, especially if one leaned forward as she strained to do. This promised to be backbreaking and her mood did not improve.

They rode out the castle gate and turned upriver. The road grew deserted once they moved away from the castle and town. A few carts straggled past, and in the river an occasional barge drifted by. They were less than two miles from London's wall, but suddenly a world away.

They rode in silence for about a quarter of a mile. Christiana focused her attention on avoiding any contact with the man a hair's breadth behind her. Her back ached from the effort.

Suddenly and without warning, David pushed the horse to a faster walk. That did it. The gait threw her backward against his chest and shoulders. His arm slid around her waist. She tensed in surprise as that peculiar intensity flowed and embraced her more surely than his arm.

She noticed the solidity of his support and became acutely aware of his arm resting lightly across her waist. She looked down at the beautiful masculine hand gently holding her, and felt the soft pressure of his fingers as he steadied her. There was something tantalizing about his warmth along her back.

The oddest tremor swept through her. She tensed again.

"Are you afraid of me, Christiana?" he asked.

His face was very close to her head, and his voice barely louder than a whisper. His breath drifted over her temple, carrying his words. The warm sound mixed with the warm air and caressed her as surely as if fingers had touched her. Despite that warmth, a chill trembled down her neck and back. A very peculiar chill.

"Of course not."

"You act as if you are."

He had noticed the tremors, she thought, a little horrified but not sure why.

"I am a bit cold is all."

In response he drew the edges of his own cloak around her.

He seemed closer now. She could feel the muscles of his chest all along her back. His breath grazed her hair, making her scalp tingle. He was virtually a stranger, and the subtle intimacy of being cocooned inside his cloak with him did make her a little fearful now, but of what she couldn't say. She squirmed to let him know that she wanted him to let go.

He did not release her. Instead he bent his body over hers. Soft hair brushed against her cheek before he turned his head to kiss her neck.

The heat of his lips against her skin produced an incredible shock. He kissed her again, increasing the pressure, and the warmth of that mouth penetrated her skin, flowed down her neck and arms, and streaked through her chest and belly. The pure physicality of the sensation stunned her.

His arm pulled her tighter. His lips moved up her neck. Quivering, delicious tremors coursed through her. He nipped lightly along the edge of her ear. A hollow tension exploded, shaking her, and she gasped.

The sound woke her from the sensual daze. She turned her head away from his mouth. "Now I am afraid of you," she said.

"That was not fear."

She pushed against his arm. "I want to get down. This familiarity is wrong."

"We are betrothed."

"Not really."

"Very really."

"Not in my mind, and you know it. I want to get down. Now. I want to walk for a while."

He stopped the horse and swung off. She braced herself for his anger as she turned to be lifted down, but he only smiled and fell into step beside her.

Even walking apart from him, she could still feel the pull of that unsettling intimacy. This man had made her feel uncomfortable and vulnerable from the first time she had seen him, and it wasn't getting any better.

She felt an urgent need to banish the last few minutes from their memories, and took refuge in conversation to do so.

"Lady Idonia told me that the Abyndons are an aldermanic family in London."

"My uncle Stephen was an alderman about ten years ago, at the time that he died. I have an uncle Gilbert who would like to be."

"He did not come Saturday."

"We are estranged."

"And your parents did not come. Are they dead or are you estranged from them too?"

He didn't answer right away. "They did not tell you much about me, did they? My mother is dead. I do not know my father. Abyndon is my mother's name."

He was a bastard. Of all of the topics to choose for conversation, this had probably been the worst.

"Your brother knows of this," he added.

"It is a common thing. He would not find it worthwhile to comment upon it to me." That was a courteous lie, of course. It wasn't *that* common.

"Is there anything else you want to know about me?"

She thought a moment. "How old are you?"

"Twenty-nine."

"And you were an apprentice until twenty-five?"

"Actually, twenty-four."

"So how did you get so rich so fast?"

He laughed a little. A nice laugh. Quiet. "It is a long story."

"Not too long, if you are only twenty-nine."

He laughed again. "My master, David Constantyn, bought his goods from traders who came to England. Italians mostly, from Genoa and Venice. When I was about Andrew's age, twenty, I convinced him to send me to Flanders to purchase some wool directly. The prices at which we sell are regulated, so the only way to make more profit is to buy more cheaply."

"Your trip was successful?"

"Very much so. We did that for a year. Then, one day he came to me and agreed on another idea I had proposed. He gave me a large amount of money to try my luck elsewhere. I was gone for three years, and visited many of the ports around the Inland Sea. I sent back goods, became friends with men who became our agents, and established a trading network. We had a large advantage after that."

He told his tale as if men did this all of the time, but of course they did not and even a girl like her knew it. "You were still his apprentice then?"

"In the eyes of law. But he had been more like a father to me for years. As soon as I received the city's freedom and citizenship, he made me his partner. He was a widower and had no children, and left me his property upon his death. His wealth went to charity and for prayers for his soul."

She hadn't thought of a merchant as an adventurer. In her world only a knight errant or crusader might wander thus. "Where are some of the places that you traveled to?"

"I went by ship down the coast of the Aquitane and Castile and into the Inland Sea through the Pillars of Hercules. Then along the coast of the Dark Continent first."

"Saracen lands!"

"One must trade with Saracens to get anything from the East."

"It must have been dangerous."

"Only once. In Egypt. I stayed too long there. The ports welcome traders and depend on them. No one wants to discourage commerce by killing merchants. After Egypt, I went up to Tripoli and Constantinople, then sailed to Genoa. I came back through France."

She pictured the maps of the Inland Sea that she had seen. She imagined him riding through deserts and passing over the Alps. She glanced at the daggers he wore. One was a decorative eating tool, but the other was large and lethal looking.

"It still sounds dangerous. And very risky." Actually it sounded wonderfully exciting and adventurous.

"The risk was real enough, but mostly financial. David Constantyn was probably a bit of a fool to agree to it. Only as I see Andrew approaching the same age do I see the faith that he had."

"Will you have Andrew do as you did?"

"Nay. But I will send him to Genoa soon, where the agents send their goods for shipment here. I need a man there, I think, so that I do not have to travel down every other year."

There were many Florentine bankers and Italian traders in London, and tales of that sunny land had filtered through the court over the years. She felt a little envious of Andrew. The idea of spending her years embroidering in one of Stephen's drafty castles suddenly seemed very dull.

"I came to speak with you about something, Christiana," he said. "I was at Westminster to discuss the wedding. The spring and early summer are out of the question. There will be times when I will be out of London unexpectedly."

Spring and summer were the times when many trading fairs were held. Presumably he would need to attend some.

"Next fall, then," she offered. "October or November."

"I think not. Before Lent. The end of February."

"Five weeks hence! That is too soon!"

"How so?"

She glared at him. They had been having such a nice talk, too. He knew "how so." She marched on a little quicker, her gaze fixed on the road ahead.

He kept up by simply lengthening his stride. Finally his quiet voice flowed around her. "I said that I would step aside if this man comes, but you cannot expect me to arrange my life for his convenience. If he wants you, he will be here very soon."

She turned on him. "You are conceited and arrogant and I hate you. You are deliberately doing this to make things difficult for me."

"Nay. I only seek to avoid difficulties for myself that might complicate my business affairs. Five weeks is enough time for a man to decide that he wants a woman. I made my decision in a matter of days. A man in love should be even quicker."

He didn't think that Stephen would come, and now he had created a test for him. How dare he claim to know the heart of a chivalrous knight! How dare he compare himself to him! Stephen was as different from this mercer as a destrier from a palfrey. The same animal, but different breeds with different duties.

"Five weeks, my lady," he repeated firmly. He glanced up at the sun. "Now we must ride back. I have a meeting this afternoon."

He brought up the horse and lifted her up. She kept

her back very straight all of the way home to West-minster.

In the back courtyard they found Lady Idonia sitting by the wall. She rose at once and came toward them.

David dismounted and brought Christiana down. He turned to the guardian. "You decided to take some air, too, my lady? The day is fair, is it not?"

Lady Idonia did her best. "You should not have taken Christiana out with her illness. Her dizziness was most severe."

David slung an arm around Christiana's shoulders. It was a casual gesture, but it very effectively kept her from bolting. "Your solicitous concern for my betrothed moves me, my lady. But I have something to say to Christiana in private. Perhaps you would wait inside the entrance for her."

Idonia flustered in response to this blunt dismissal, glanced sharply at Christiana, and stomped off.

David dropped his arm and turned to her. "I will visit you next week."

Stephen would come soon, but not that soon. She really did not want to spend more time with David. It felt like a betrayal of her love. "That is not necessary," she said.

"It may not be necessary, but for your sake it is prudent. You expect your lover to come, but what if he does not?"

"He will come."

"And if not?"

His insistence irritated her. "What of it?"

"Then in five weeks you wed me, my girl. Just in case, shouldn't we spend this time getting to know one another? It is what betrothals are for."

But I am not really betrothed, she thought, eyeing him obstinately. *Not in my heart or mind.*

"Christiana, if you do not want to meet again until the wedding, that is how it will be. Yet think about it, girl. Going to bed with a stranger will not bother me at all, but you may find the experience distressing."

Her mouth fell open in shock at this blunt reminder of the marriage bed. Memories of herself with Stephen flew rapidly through her mind. He had not been a stranger, and she quickly relived the shock of his ferocious passion, the crushing insistence of his kisses, the almost horrible intimacy of his hand on her nakedness.

She stared up at David de Abyndon, noting the frank and open way that he watched her. It was cruel of him to make her think about this and face the possible conclusion of this betrothal. All the same, her mind involuntarily began to substitute him for Stephen in those memories. She was appalled that it had no trouble doing so and that the strange feelings that he summoned tried to attach themselves to the ghostlike fantasy. She shook those thoughts away. The whole notion was indeed distressing. And very frightening.

Five weeks.

"Am I supposed to wait upstairs for you to come and 'bid me to attend'?" she asked sarcastically.

"Let us say that I will come on Mondays. If I cannot, I will send word. If you are ill again, send a message to me."

She nodded and turned toward the door. She wanted to be done with this man today. She wanted to cleanse her mind of what it had just imagined.

He caught her arm and pulled her back. With gentle but firm movements he clasped her in an embrace.

A surging desperation claimed her. She remembered the betrothal ceremony and she knew, she just knew, that it was vital, essential, that he not kiss her again. She struggled against his arms and almost cried out for Idonia. As his head bent to hers, she twisted to avoid him.

His lips found hers anyway and connected with a grazing brush that wasn't even a kiss. She felt that same, warm soothing lightness again and again on her cheek and brow and neck. In spite of her love for Stephen, in spite of her anger at this man's intrusion into her life, she calmed beneath the repeated caress of his mouth as ripples of sensation flowed through her. Her awareness dulled to everything but those compelling feelings.

When he finally stopped, she wasn't struggling anymore. A little dazed, she looked up at him. The perfect planes of his face appeared tighter than usual, and he looked in her eyes with a commanding gaze that seemed to speak a language that she didn't understand. She knew that he was going to kiss her and that she should get away, but when he lowered his mouth to hers, she couldn't resist at all.

It was a beautiful kiss, full of warmth and promise. It deepened slowly and he held her head in one hand, the other arm lifting her into it. The waves of sensation flowed higher and stronger, carrying her toward a delicious oblivion.

He released the pressure on her mouth and took one lip, then the other, gently between his teeth. A sharper warmth shot down the center of her body. It was a stunning quiver of pleasurable discomfort that seemed to reach completely through her. Less gently, he kissed each pulse point on her neck, and it happened again and again, each time stronger, the compelling discomfort growing.

He lifted his head and looked down at her, his mouth set in a hard line with the lips slightly parted. He looked gloriously handsome like that.

"You make me forget myself," he said, his fingers stretching through her hair.

Their surroundings slowly intruded. Her position,

arching acceptingly into his embrace, suddenly became apparent, too.

Horrified, she abruptly disentangled herself. He let her go. With a very red face she hurried to the door.

Lady Idonia waited there. She looked up sharply. " 'Send Idonia to save me,' " she mimicked. "I sat out there almost an hour, worried for you, although why I don't know, since you are marrying the man. Then you return and what do I see? Keep that up, girl, and there will be no need for a wedding at all."

Christiana blushed deeper. A profound sense of guilt swept through her. She loved Stephen. How could she be so faithless? How could she let this man kiss her like that? Even if he forced her to it, how could she let those feelings undo her so outrageously?

She followed Idonia up the stairs, more confused and frightened than she had been on her betrothal day. This was wrong. She must never let it happen again. She must be sure that she was never again alone with this merchant.

At the second-level landing, she paused and looked out the small window to the courtyard below. David was just mounting his horse to leave. As he began riding away, a movement at the end of the courtyard caught her attention. A man stepped away from the building and toward David's approaching horse.

David stopped and spoke with the man for a moment, then made to move on. But the man followed alongside, speaking and gesturing. Finally David dismounted. He tied his reins to a post and disappeared behind the building, following the man.

Christiana frowned. They had been some distance away, but she felt sure that she recognized the man. He was the French-speaking diplomat who had passed her alcove in the King's passageway the morning after she had met David.

CHAPTER 4

DAVID STOOD AT the threshold between the solar and the bedchamber and studied the woman whom Sieg had just brought upstairs. She was still an attractive lady, but thirteen years take their toll on anyone. He hadn't realized back then how young she must have been. No more than twenty-five at the time, he would judge now. Still, he would remember her anywhere.

She hadn't noticed him, and he watched her glide around the solar, fingering the carving on the chairs and examining the tapestry on the wall. She touched the glazing in the windows much as Christiana had done that first night.

He would not think about Christiana now. If he did, he suspected that he might not go through with this. He had already spent more time the last week thinking of those diamond eyes than about the carefully planned harvest of justice that he would reap this afternoon. The last thing he wanted now was the thought of a good woman making him weak with a bad one.

The woman's face looked paler than her hands, and he could tell that she used wheat flour to make it so. An artful touch of paint flushed her cheeks and colored her lips. If he gave a damn, he would find a kind way to tell her that the coloring was a bit too strong for the honey hair that had begun to dull with age. He suspected that this was one of those women who looks in the mirror a lot but never really sees what is reflected there.

He shifted his weight silently but it drew her attention anyway. Amber cat eyes turned and regarded him. He saw the brief scrutiny and then the slow relief. *Aye*, he thought, *if this woman whores for a man, she prefers him young and handsome.* She continued looking at him and he noticed the total absence of recognition.

"David de Abyndon?" she asked. Her eyes narrowed and a thin smile stretched her mouth.

"Lady Catherine. I'm sorry that I could not see you sooner."

She misunderstood and, flattered, smiled more naturally.

He gestured and she joined him at the doorway. When she saw it was a bedchamber, she glanced at him, reproving him for his lack of subtlety.

She entered slowly and again she took in the details of the room, calculating their value. Time and again her gaze rested on the large tub set before the hearth. It had been brought in by the servants before David dismissed all of them for the afternoon. If they wondered why he wanted it here and not in the wardrobe where it belonged, they hadn't said so.

It had been filled with water, and more water was heating by the hearth. David lifted the buckets and poured them into the tub.

She watched him with amusement. "Perhaps I came too early."

"This is for you."

"You thought that I would be unclean?"

You are so unclean that all of the water in the world would not cleanse you. "Nay. But I remember how much you enjoy baths and sought to indulge you."

She frowned and looked at him more closely. A spark of memory tried to catch flame, but he watched it die.

"My husband assumed . . ."

"I know what your husband assumed. But we do it this way or not at all." He leaned against the hearth wall and waited.

A little flustered, but not too much so, she began to remove her clothing. She carefully folded the bejeweled sur-coat and placed it on the nearby stool. The beautiful cote-hardie followed. Rich fabrics. He had no trouble calculating how many of her husband's debts were devoted to her wardrobe.

She untied her garters and peeled off her hose. He noted her lack of embarrassment. He was by far not the first stranger she had stripped for.

The shift dropped to the floor and she looked at him boldly. He gestured to the tub and she stepped in with clear irritation.

She settled down. She was childless and her body was still youthful. Her full breasts bobbed in the high water.

"Well?" she asked.

"Your husband sent you here to ask something of me. To negotiate for him, did he not?"

She gestured with exasperation at the tub.

David smiled. "I only do this to give you every advantage, my lady. I remember that you negotiate best when you are thus."

Again that scrutiny. Again the flame of recognition that died before it caught fire. She became all business.

"My husband says that you have bought up all of his debts."

The man had amassed debts to merchants and bankers over the last few years. When he had resorted to borrowing from one to pay another, when the financial market in London had realized that he tottered on the edge of ruin, David had bought the loans at a deep discount. He had not even gone looking for today's justice. It had simply fallen into his lap, one of Fortune's many gifts to him.

"He needs time to repay them."

"They are long overdue, as I have explained to him."

"He thought that you might be more reasonable with me. I have come to ask for an extension. The properties have been less productive of late, but that should improve."

"They are less productive because they are neglected and mismanaged. Already the ones that I hold have improved."

"The loans were made with the promise that the property you hold now would be returned to us."

"Only if the loans are repaid." He paused. "I think that we might be able to work something out about the loans and the property, however. Is there anything else that you require?"

Her face lightened. It was going better than she thought it would. "Aye. We need a further loan. A small one. As a bridge until things work out."

This husband placed a high value indeed on his wife's favors. "You are asking me to throw good money after bad."

"You will be repaid in full."

"Madam, your husband gambles. You are extravagant. Both vices are rarely conquered. I will consider the extension of the old loans, but in truth you will never repay them. Why would I now give you more?"

She looked at him boldly and a small smile formed on her tinted lips. Slowly, expertly, she shifted in the tub so that he had a full view of her body.

The years fell away. He was in another chamber standing in front of a younger woman. She was a frequent visitor to the shop, but when she had come this day, David Constantyn had not been in. She bought expensive cloths and paid with a tally as was the habit of such women, but then insisted that the young apprentice deliver the goods that afternoon to her manor in Hampstead where the tally would be made good.

He had gone. Like others before him, he had innocently ridden the five miles north to Hampstead.

She had received him in her chamber, lying in a tub much as she did now. Pretending to ignore his presence, she had demanded that her servants open and examine the purchases while he waited. All the while she had bathed herself, slowly and languidly, occasionally looking at him with a challenging stare that dared him to react to her nakedness.

He did not. He was randy enough at sixteen and not inexperienced, but he held his body in check. At first his dismay and shock helped him. His knowledge of females consisted of the happy servant girls with whom coupling was a form of joyful play. Instinctively he knew that this woman was nothing like that and that she tempted him to something other than pleasure.

But as she continued displaying herself, it was anger that kept him in control. He turned away from her. He did not like playing the mouse to this cat woman. He resented her using her position and degree to humiliate him.

Finally he could tell that she grew angry too. She addressed him directly and began to renegotiate the price of the goods. She pursued the subject a long while, refusing to pay the whole tally, demanding his attention. Finally, he had to look at her, and as he did she raised one leg to the side of the tub and exposed herself.

He lost control then, but not in the way that she expected. He let his face show what he thought, but it was not the desire she demanded. He looked down at her and let her see his utter disgust before he walked out.

He had almost reached the road before her men came and dragged him back. They tied him to a metal ring set in the trunk of an oak tree in the garden. Before the lash fell, he looked over his shoulder and saw her honey hair at a window.

"You do not remember me," he said. "But then, there were a number of us, why would you remember one?"

Over the years, they had found each other, the boys now grown to men whom she had ensnared in her web. The woman's unhealthy appetite was not discussed openly, but it was not unknown. It was why David Constantyn had never let his apprentices serve her or deliver goods.

But he was the one who had not played her game as she wanted it, and so the lash fell harder on him than those others whose only crime had been to show the lust that she demanded and then punished while she watched from her bower window. He had been flogged once in Egypt, but it was this first time that had scarred his back. His youth had been beaten out of him that day.

He regarded her impassively, watching her study him hard. This time the spark of memory caught hold and her eyes flamed with recognition. Her gaze slowly swept the room as she calculated her danger. She collected herself.

"You were compensated," she said coolly.

Aye, he had been compensated. When he staggered back home and his master saw his condition, that good man had done what no other master or father had done. Going to the city courts the next day, he petitioned against this woman and forced the mayor to address the issue. After a long while, the husband had been made to pay fifty pounds. David had refused to touch the money.

"The others were not. And it is not a debt that money settles anyway."

She glared at him angrily before calming herself. She glanced at the bed and then eyed him with a question.

"Aye, that too. But if you want this extension, I have other terms. I will extend the loans in return for the Hampstead manor and property, and for one hour of your time."

"The Hampstead lands belong to me, not my husband. They were not pledged as surety for any loans."

"I know that they are yours. In return for them, however, I will in fact forgive the loans, not just extend them." He smiled. "See how well you negotiate? Already I have conceded much more than I had planned."

He saw her weighing certain ruin against the property. If he called the loans, she would have to sell it anyway.

"Why do you want that house? Why not another? Are you going to burn it or something?"

"Nay. We merchants are very practical people. We rarely destroy property. It is a very beautiful house and I have admired it. I will have need of a country home near London soon. I hold no grudge against a building."

"And the hour of my time?"

"That is for the other debt. You will go to a place that I tell you. There a man will flog you just as you watched others flogged for your pleasure. Ten lashes."

Her eyes flew open in shock. He noted her reaction with relief. Those who took pleasure in pain often went both ways, and he did not want her to get perverse enjoyment out of this.

"I didn't realize that we had so much in common," she finally said.

"We have nothing in common. I will not be there, although some of the others might be. They will be told of this and may want to see it. I would demand your husband do it, as he should have long ago, but he knows what he has in you, and if he started he might not stop. It is justice we seek, not revenge or your husband's satisfaction."

She abruptly rose from the tub. She stepped out and began to dry herself. Her hurried, angry movements gradually slowed, however, and the expression on her face changed. He saw her considering, calculating, planning the final negotiation that, if executed well enough, might change everything.

He realized with surprise that he had totally lost interest in taking her humiliation any further.

He removed a small purse from the front of his pourpoint. It contained exactly the difference between the value of the loans and the Hampstead property. He dropped the purse on top of her garments. "It is the money that you seek but not a loan. That would be bad business. However, I always pay for my whores whether I use them or not."

He walked to the door. "A week hence, madam. The time and place will be sent to you. Afterward husband can contact me about settling the loans and property."

Her voice, harsh and ugly, ripped across the chamber. "There will be a new debt to settle after this, you bastard son of a whore!"

He paused. Justice, not revenge, he reminded himself. Still . . .

"Fifteen lashes, I think now, my lady. The last five for the insult to my mother."

He strode out through the solar and hall and left the house.

✦   ✦   ✦

The sky had clouded over and a light snow was falling by the time David reined in his horse outside the tavern. To his right, along the Southwark docks, small craft of all types bobbed. Stretched out in front of them rose the small houses where the prostitutes of the Stews plied their trade. Even at night these docks would be full, for the city discouraged crossing the river after dark and it was traditional for these women to have their customers stay until dawn.

The rude tavern was dark and musty with river damp. David let his eyes adjust, and then walked to a corner table.

"You are late," the man sitting there said.

David slid onto the bench. "Oliver, you are the most punctual whoremonger I have ever met."

Oliver passed him a cup of ale, drank some of his own, and wiped his black mustache and beard on his sleeve. "I am a busy man, David. Time is money."

"Your woman's time is money, Oliver, not yours. How is Anne?"

Oliver shrugged. "She doesn't like the winter. The nights are too long in her opinion."

She would probably move to Cock Lane soon. It was right outside the city wall and the women there worked differently than here in Southwark. But then, they also had to deal with the city laws. Southwark, across the Thames from London, was a town apart and close to lawless.

He looked at Oliver's wiry thin body and long black hair. They had known each other since boyhood, when they had played and scrapped in the streets and alleys together. On occasion during those carefree days, they had met danger side by side. But then Oliver's poor family had moved up to Hull and David had been plucked from those alleys and sent to school and into trade.

They had met again when Oliver returned to London several years ago. David had recognized at once that he had found a man whom he could trust. Like Sieg, Oliver might do a criminal's deeds sometimes, but he lived by a code of loyalty and fairness that would put most knights to shame. Since then, they had again on occasion met danger side by side.

The decision for Anne to become a prostitute had simply been the easiest of several choices available to them when they had come back to London. Anne had already decided that the winter nights were too long when he had met them a short while later. Still, she probably earned three times as much on her back than she and Oliver could together through honest labor. The odd jobs Oliver did for him and others helped some.

He wondered how he was going to explain Oliver and Anne to Christiana. Sieg's story would be strange enough when she finally realized that he wasn't a typical servant.

"Has he spoken to you?" Oliver asked.

"Twice. The last time just this morning."

"I have followed him like you said. He spoke to a ship's master yesterday. I think that he will sail back soon."

"He will need to. I expect that he will seek me out one more time, though, and delay his trip until I will talk to him at length. He has only felt me out so far, and has not achieved what he came for."

"You think that it is set, then?"

"I think so. I refused him, but I left the door open."

Oliver shook his head. "I am not convinced. His actions have been very normal. He goes to merchants and other places of business. That is all."

"His offer to me has been subtle so far but unmistakable. He appears to be a merchant because he is one. Except for the letter for Edward and his mission with me, he is here for trade. It is the whole point. Whenever

I go to France or Flanders, I go for trade, too." He stretched out his legs beneath the table. "Speaking of which, tell Albin that I will need to go over in about a week or so."

"Running from your duel?" Oliver asked with a grin.

"Before that. After he talks with me but before my wedding. I want to sail along the coast."

"You are pushing things, my friend," Oliver said, laughing. "Wait until after you marry this princess. Tempt fate and you might find yourself caught in bad seas for a week and miss the ceremony. That will take some explaining, I'll warrant."

David looked away. Sieg had been right. It was a bad time to be getting married. Oliver was right, too. He should wait until after the wedding to sail the coast. But it needed to be done soon, and he had no intention of leaving Christiana for a while after she came to him. This girl, and the growing desire he felt for her, were complicating things.

Her eyes were faceted jewels full of bright reflections. A man could lose his soul in eyes like that.

For one thing, he had begun to lose interest in these subtle and dangerous plans that he had laid and in which Oliver played a role. He had finally admitted that to himself as he rode over here today, and had been astonished to discover it. After all, he had been slowly planting this particular field for almost two years. A piece of information here, a deliberate slip there. It had worked because people like himself were quick to notice mistakes and weakness and potential advantage, and he knew that he dealt with a man very much like himself. In fact, matching wits with him should be a pleasure in itself, and the final justice much more satisfying than the rather thin contentment he had felt with Lady Catherine today.

Instead, he was losing interest and even considering cutting things short just as they reached the critical moves. His own plans and Edward's had become so intertwined that he had pondered at length whether it would be possible to extricate one from the other. That he even considered such a thing had to do with Christiana. She had him thinking of the future more than the past. He already felt responsibility for her. He considered far too often what it would mean for her if in the end he lost this game.

He had changed his testament so that she would be a wealthy widow if something went wrong. Funds would be on account with Florentine bankers too. When the time came, he would give Sieg and Oliver instructions for getting her out of the country if that became necessary. But all of that would never compensate her if he failed.

Her gestures were full of elegance and poise, her hands and arms beautifully angled like a dancer's. It was the way that she moved that made her appear fragile.

She still expected that her lover would come for her. He didn't doubt her resolve on that for one moment.

Stephen Percy. Learning the man's name and something of his character had been easy enough, but the knowledge only confirmed David's initial instincts about the affair. Christiana was in for a bad disappointment.

That her heart would break soon went without saying, but when would she see the truth behind illusions? Two weeks? A month? Never? The last possible. A girl's first love could be a blind thing, and she was convinced that she was in love with this man. Accepting the truth could well be impossible. God knew he had seen that before.

So young Percy doesn't come for her. Then what? A marriage full of cold duty? He smiled thinly at the thought. He knew well what happened in such unions. The men found mistresses quickly or spent too many nights with the prostitutes on Cock Lane. The more honest wives absorbed themselves with religion or their children.

And the braver and bolder women . . . well, they eventually found their ways to the beds of men like David de Abyndon.

He felt her thin, lithe body against his. He sensed her responses to him, and her fear of them. A tremor flowed through her and into him, and he had wanted to kiss her again and again.

He had enough experience to recognize the possibilities which those tremors had revealed. But then, he had already sensed them that night in his solar.

In his memory's eye he saw her sparkling eyes and pale skin and the wide mouth that he couldn't see without wanting to kiss. He imagined her walking toward him, naked and inviting, that beautiful face and mouth finally turned up willingly to his.

But then her image grew hazy and dim, and another woman's face replaced it. Gaunt and tired, this face was beautiful too despite its weariness. Resting on a pillow with golden brown hair encircling it like a halo, its eyes were finally closed to disappointment and disillusion.

The image fell away and he could see the entire chamber with its flickering candles and the white sheets on the bed. Clothes hung on pegs along a wall and a fire burned too hotly in the hearth. And sitting on the bed, his graying head buried in that lifeless breast, bent the anguished figure of David Constantyn.

He hadn't realized until then how much the man had loved her. At night when the house was dark, did he go to her? Did she go to him? Had she slept with him? God, but he hoped so.

He firmly set aside consideration of the risks that had meant nothing before he met Christiana.

For both of them, then, he thought.

"If you refuse this merchant, do you think the other will come?" Oliver asked.

"He will come," David said. "I would come. Keep your ears and those of your listeners open, Oliver. Not just for that, by the way. Stay around the pilgrims' taverns. I seek news from Northumberland."

"Any particular news?"

"There is a knight named Stephen Percy. If he comes to Westminster, I want to know right away. Or if you hear anything else about that family."

Oliver raised an eyebrow. "And if this man comes?"

David saw the look and knew at once that Sieg had already told Oliver of his interest in Sir Stephen. No doubt they guessed that he had something to do with Christiana.

He remembered Sieg's offer to deal with Morvan, and knew that Oliver was making the same suggestion now. It was not in their natures to do such things, but out of friendship for him they would do them anyway. Their loyalty could be burdensome at times. He had enough trouble battling his own inclinations without having to worry about the souls of the men who served him.

He thought about his promise to step aside. It had been a moment of weakness while gazing at a lovely face. His eye for beauty drove him from one bad bargain to another sometimes, especially when he negotiated for something that he wanted to keep for himself. Fortunately, Percy would not return and test his honesty to that promise. All the same . . .

"Just let me know at once," he said. "I will decide then."

CHAPTER 5

CHRISTIANA REMAINED FIRM in her decision not to be alone again with David. The next Monday she insisted that they sit in the garden, where Lady Idonia just happened to find and join them. It was a pleasant visit as he entertained them with stories from his travels.

During dinner a few days later, Sir Walter Manny stopped by her table. Sir Walter was one of the Queen's men from Philippa's native land of Hainault. During their conversation he mentioned that he knew David and had even introduced him to the King two years ago when Edward had a letter for the mayor of Ghent and David was planning a trip to Flanders.

"Are you saying that David delivered the letter for the King?" she asked.

"It is done all the time, my lady. Why send a messenger if a trusted merchant makes the trip? Sometimes it is even better this way, especially if you do not want to draw attention to the communication. For example, everyone knows that there is currently a Flemish trader in

Westminster who is partial to the French alliance of the Count of Flanders, unlike his fellow burghers who support England. We just assume that he might have brought a private letter from the Count to our King. A formal exchange would be awkward since they are adversaries, but still negotiations occur." He scanned the hall and pointed. "There he is with Lady Catherine. His name is Frans van Horlst."

Christiana looked to where a gray-haired man fawned over Catherine. It was her "diplomat," the one she had seen speak with David that first Tuesday after the betrothal.

And then, out of the corner of her mind came another memory, of the first time that she had seen that man in the King's private corridor. Two voices speaking Parisian French. One soft and low and barely a whisper.

David? The voice had been too quiet to tell. He knew the King well enough to offer for the daughter of Hugh Fitzwaryn, and yet no one had ever seen him around court. The access of that private passageway would explain that contradiction. Had it been David there that day? If so, what was he to the King that he entered and left by that special route? And what had Frans van Horlst wanted of him?

"Do you know if David still performs such favors for the King?"

Sir Walter shrugged. "I suggested him that once and introduced them. Whether the relationship continued I cannot say."

"How did you come to know my betrothed?"

Sir Walter grinned and bent his fair head conspiratorially. "You no doubt know that he is an accomplished musician? Taught himself, too."

She nodded dutifully, although she didn't know that at all.

"We both belong to the Pui," he confided.

The Pui was one of many secret fraternities in London. The only thing truly secret about it was the date and location of its annual meetings. Besides drinking all night, the men of the Pui performed songs that they had composed, and one of the songs was chosen to be "crowned." Sometimes when a jongleur played a new chanson, one might hear references to it being from the Pui.

"Has he played the lute for you? His preferred instrument is that ancient Celtic harp of his, but it often doesn't suit the songs and so he has had to learn the lute. Still, two years ago he beat me out for the crown, and I still swear it was only because of the novelty of that damned harp," Walter said.

Christiana suddenly thought of the perfect way to be the exact opposite of alone with David that upcoming Monday. She confessed that her dear betrothed had never had the chance to play for her. Would Sir Walter be willing to help remedy the situation?

When David arrived Monday morning, she greeted him happily. She even smiled when he kissed her.

"I have called for a mount from the stables for you," he said. "We will go to my house for dinner. You should meet the servants, and the boys need to get to know you."

The last thing she wanted was to go to his house and meet the people involved in his life. They would be greeting her as their future mistress, while she would know that she would never see them again.

"Let us go out through the hall," she suggested. "I need to see if Morvan is there. I have something to tell him."

Of course Morvan wasn't there as she knew he wouldn't be. But Sir Walter was, sitting in a corner surrounded by seven young girls. He sang a plucky love song as he played his lute, raising his eyebrows comically at the more romantic parts. The girls giggled at his exaggerated expressions.

"David!" he called, breaking off his playing as they crossed the hall.

"Walter," David greeted him warmly. He glanced down at the girls sitting on the floor. "I see that you are living an Englishman's fantasy."

The girls turned and assessed him. Christiana watched them react to his handsome face. They were all unmarried and younger than her.

"I am trying out a new lute," Walter explained, holding up the instrument. He gestured to another on the bench beside him. "But I think that I prefer the old one."

"It is always thus at first," David said. He took Christiana's arm and began to guide her away.

Christiana glared at Walter.

"Let us see how they sound together, David," Walter said quickly.

The girls clapped their hands in encouragement. David looked at Walter. He looked at the second lute. He looked at Christiana.

She smiled and tried to make her expression glitter like Joan's. She let her eyes plead a little.

With a sigh of resignation he stepped through the girls and sat beside Walter, taking the lute on his lap. Walter mumbled something and they both began playing a song about spring.

They played a long while, until the hall began filling for dinner. Whenever David attempted to finish, the girls would whine and cajole. There came a point when Christiana could tell that he had given up, that he knew that he was trapped for the duration. After that he even enjoyed himself, trading jokes with Walter and finally singing a song on his own.

It was a love song that she had never heard before. The melody was lyrical and slow and a little sad. Christiana closed her eyes and felt her own sadness stirred by it.

Her thoughts turned to Stephen and the melancholy swelled. She lost track of the next few songs as her heart and worry dwelled on him. Then the girls moved around her and she became alert again. The merry group broke up and Walter insisted that David dine with him. David accepted and then helped her to her feet. Briefly he looked at her, then smiled and shook his head in amusement.

They did not go to his house. She did not meet the people there. More importantly, they were not alone all day. When she finally returned to Isabele's apartment, Idonia and Joan had returned, and so his departing kiss was as light and discreet as his greeting.

Christiana stepped out of the silvery pink wedding gown and handed it to the tailor, who managed adroitly not to see her standing in her shift.

This marriage business did wonders for a girl's wardrobe. She could not feel excited about this new cotehardie, however. The cost made her feel guilty because she knew that it would never be worn. It would be in extremely poor taste to run off with Stephen in defiance of the Queen but still take the gown that the Queen had purchased.

What really bothered her about this gown, however, was its relentless progress toward completion. These fittings had become unwelcome but unavoidable reminders that time kept passing far too quickly. Half of the five weeks had passed, and still she had no word from Stephen Percy.

A servant helped her into her plain purple cotehardie

and blue surcoat. She sent the woman off to find Joan while she slipped on some low boots.

It was Friday, almost three weeks since her betrothal, and she would be seeing David this afternoon instead of next Monday because he would be out of the city then. They were going to the horse fair and races at Smithfield, which she thought might be fun.

Before they got there, however, she had a thing to two to say to Master David de Abyndon.

David rode into Westminster flanked by Sieg and Andrew.

Sieg was frowning. "Now, if pretty young Joan comes out with her, I leave and Andrew stays," he said. "But if the little bit of fire from hell, that Lady Idonia, shows up, it's the other way around."

"I'm afraid so, Sieg," David said. On his left Andrew smirked.

Sieg frowned some more. "And whoever stays is to distract the other female so she's not in the way."

David nodded. He had used Christiana's own lie about the Queen insisting that the girls not be alone with men to explain his need of Sieg and Andrew today. He was almost thirty years old, but this girl had reduced him to games that he'd given up at eighteen. She had avoided being alone with him since that first Tuesday and had been very clever about it. He was amused and not annoyed, but then he was growing fascinated with her and would probably excuse anything.

Their mutual attraction simply did not fit in with her plans. Her response to his kiss and embrace had badly frightened her. She acted as confused and inexperienced as an untouched virgin. That effect of innocence had charmed him almost as much as her quick passion had enflamed him.

He could avoid this game. Eventually, soon in fact, she would be his. But he found himself picturing those eyes and tasting those lips in his memory far too often for complete retreat. Besides, he did not want her rebuilding her defenses too well. He didn't relish the notion of having to choose between continence or rape on his wedding night.

"The problem as I see it," Sieg continued, "is what if Lady Idonia won't be distracted? She's like a lioness protecting her cubs."

"Hell, Sieg, you're three times her size, for heaven's sake," Andrew muttered. "Just pick her up under your arm and walk off with her."

Sieg's frown disappeared. "*Ja?* That was how I did it back home, of course, but I thought that here in England . . ."

"Andrew is jesting, Sieg."

The frown returned. "Oh. *Ja.*"

David had agreed to meet Christiana in the back courtyard. She and Joan stood by two horses being held by grooms. Sieg turned his horse away and David slipped a delighted Andrew some coins. "Keep Lady Joan busy at the races and the stalls."

The grooms got the girls mounted. Christiana looked meaningfully in Andrew's direction.

"He will ride with us. He needs to see a man at the fair for me," David explained.

She seemed to accept that, and they rode together in silence. By the time that they reached the Strand, Joan and Andrew were four horse lengths ahead and Christiana didn't seem to mind.

"People have been talking about you," she said at last. David got the impression that she had waited for exactly the moment when Joan was too far ahead to hear what she said.

"People?"

"At court. Talking about you. Us. Everything."

"It was bound to happen, Christiana."

"Not these things. They weren't bound to be talked about because they are very unusual."

"You needn't turn to the court gossips. I will tell you anything you want to know."

She raised her eyebrows. "Will you? Well, first of all, some ladies have spoken to me on your behalf. Told me how wonderful you are."

"Which ladies?" he asked cautiously.

"Lady Elizabeth for one."

That surprised him. He and Elizabeth had an old friendship, but it was not her style to interfere in such things. "I am honored if Lady Elizabeth speaks well of me."

"And Alicia."

Hell.

Christiana's face was a picture of careful indifference. "Are you Lady Alicia's lover?"

"Did she say that?"

"Nay. There was something in the way that she spoke, however."

When he had offered to tell her anything, this was not what he had in mind. "I do not think that we want to pursue this, do you? I did not press you for the names of your lovers. You should not ask me for mine."

She twisted toward him abruptly. "Lovers! How dare you suggest that I have had lovers! I told you of one man."

"You told me of a current man. There may have been others, but as I said, I have been open-minded and not asked."

"Of course there were no others!"

"There is no of course to it. But it matters not." He

smiled inwardly at her dismay. "Christiana, I am almost thirty years old and I have not been a monk. I do not plan on being unfaithful to you. However, if our marriage is cold, I imagine that I will do as men have always done and find warmth elsewhere."

He had deliberately broached a topic that she would not want to talk about. As he expected, she had no response. So much for Lady Alicia. She would change the subject now. He waited.

"That is the least of what I have heard," she said.

"Somehow I thought so."

Her lids lowered. "Did you buy me?"

He had been wondering when she would hear of it. "Nay."

"Nay? I heard that Edward demanded a bride price. A big one. Morvan says it is true."

He had been waiting for this. He was ready. "A bride price is not the same as buying someone. Bride prices have an ancient tradition in England. Women were honored thus in the old days. With dowries, the woman is secondary to the property. It is as if a family pays someone to take her off their hands. If you think about it, dowries are much more insulting than bride prices."

"Then it is true?"

He chose his words carefully. If she found out the truth twenty years from now, he wanted to be able to say that he hadn't lied. "Your brother has seen the contract, as you will soon. There is no point in denying that there is a bride price in it."

"And instead of being insulted, you say that I should feel honored."

"Absolutely. Would you prefer if the King had just given you to me?"

"I would prefer if the King had continued to forget that I existed," she snapped.

They rode in silence for a minute. "How big is it? This honorable bride price?" she finally asked.

So Morvan had not told her. She would see the contract soon. David thought of the complicated formula it contained.

"How good are you at ciphering?" he asked casually.

"Excellent."

She would be. "One thousand pounds."

She stopped her horse and gaped at him. "One thousand pounds! An earl's income? Why?"

"Edward would hear of no less. I assure you that I bargained very hard. I personally thought that three hundred would be generous."

Her eyes narrowed suspiciously. "Morvan is right. This marriage never made any sense. Now it makes less."

"Aren't you worth one thousand pounds?"

"You must have been drunk when you made this offer. You will no doubt be relieved when I get you off the hook."

"He has come then?"

She ignored that. "Just as well for your health, too, that I will end this betrothal soon. I have heard about my brother's threat to you."

"Ah. That."

"Wednesday, they say."

"I expect Thursday," he corrected calmly. "Does your brother know that you have heard of this?"

"Of course. I went to him at once and told him that I wouldn't have it."

"Your concern touches me."

"Aye. Well, he wouldn't hear me. But, of course, you won't meet him."

"Of course I will."

She stopped her horse again. Joan and Andrew were far in the distance now. "You cannot be serious."

"What choice do I have?"

"You will not be in town Monday. Can't you extend your trip?"

"Eventually I must come back."

"Oh dear." She frowned fretfully.

He looked at her pretty puckered brow. "He will not kill me."

"Oh, it isn't that," she replied with ruthless honesty. "This just makes a messy situation messier. First a duel, then an abduction, then an annulment . . . well, it will make a terrific scandal."

"Perhaps someone will write a song about it."

"This is not humorous, David. You really should withdraw or leave. Morvan's sword is not a laughing matter. He may not kill you, but he may hurt you very badly."

"Aye. One thousand pounds is one thing. An arm or a leg is another. I certainly hope that you are worth it."

"How can you jest?"

"I am not jesting. But let me worry about Morvan, my lady. Are there any other rumors and gossip that you need to discuss?"

They had approached the city and began circling around its wall to the north. "Aye. Not all of the ladies who know you were so complimentary. Lady Catherine spoke with me. And with Morvan."

David waited. He would not assume what story Lady Catherine had given them.

"She told me that you are a moneylender," Christiana said quietly, as if she didn't want to be overheard by passing riders.

He almost laughed at her circumspection. The girl lived in a world that didn't exist anymore, full of virtuous knights and honored duty and stories of King Arthur's roundtable. King Edward carefully nurtured these illusions at his court with his pageants and festivals and tournaments. A mile away, within the gates of London, time moved on.

"It is true. Most merchants loan money."

"Usury is a sin."

"Perhaps so, but moneylending is a business. It is widely done, Christiana, and none think twice about it anymore. England could not survive without it. One of my sinful loans is to the King at his demand. Two others are to abbeys."

"So you just loan to the King and abbeys?"

"With others I purchase property and resell it back later at an agreed-upon time and price."

"At a profit?"

"Why else would I do it? I have no kinship or friendship with these people. However, often when I sell it back, my management has improved the income, so perhaps the profit is theirs."

"When the time is up, what if they cannot repurchase it?"

He had been trying to put a better face on this for her sake, and he cursed himself now. He had sworn he would not make excuses to this girl for being what he was. "I sell it elsewhere," he said bluntly.

She chewed on that awhile. "Why not keep it?"

It wasn't the argument he had expected. He thought that she would upbraid him for unkindness and chant sentimental pleas for the poor borrowers.

"I don't keep it because of King Edward's damned decrees saying any man with income from land over forty pounds a year has to be knighted. He has almost caught me twice."

"What do you mean, caught you? To be a knight is a wonderful thing. They are more respected than merchants, and of higher degree. You would better yourself if you were knighted."

She said it simply and innocently, stating a basic fact of life. She was oblivious to the insult and so he chose to ignore it. This time.

"Well, I am a merchant, and content as such."

One would have thought that he told her that he would rather be a devil than a saint. "You mean this, don't you?" she asked curiously. "You really don't want to be a knight."

"No one does, Christiana, except those born to it. Even many born to it avoid it. It is why Edward issues those decrees. The realm doesn't have enough knights for his ambitions. The position holds less and less appeal, so Edward plays up the chivalry and elevates the knights higher to compensate." He paused. He would be marrying this girl. He would try to explain. "It is not cowardice or fear of arms. Every London citizen swears to protect the city and realm. We must practice at arms and own what armor we can afford. I have a whole suit of the damn plate. We defend our city and send troops on Edward's wars. Many apprentices are excellent bowmen and Andrew has even mastered the longbow. But if you think about the military life honestly, it has little to recommend it."

"It is a glorious life! Full of honor and strength."

"It is a life of killing, girl. For good causes or personal gain, in honor or in murder, knights live to kill. In the end, for all of the pretty words in the songs, that is what they do. Their wars disrupt trade, ruin agriculture, and burn towns and villages. When they are victorious they rape and they steal all that they can move."

He had lost his patience and this tirade simply poured out. She stared at him as if he had slapped her, and he regretted the outburst. She was young and had lived a sheltered life. It shouldn't surprise him that she had never questioned the small protected world in which she had dwelled.

He had been too hard on her. It was her father and brother whom he described, after all. "I have no doubt that there are still many knights who are true to their honor and their vows," he said by way of a peace offering. "It is said that your brother is such a man."

That seemed to release her from the brutal reality he had thrown at her.

"Did Lady Catherine say anything else that concerns you?"

"Not to me. She said that she told Morvan something important. He said that it was nothing of significance, and then lectured me about not being friends with her."

"Good instruction, Christiana. I do not want you having anything to do with the woman."

"I think that I am old enough to choose my own friends."

"Not this one. When we are married, you are to avoid her."

Her irritation with him was visible, but she held her tongue. She turned her attention to the road as they approached Smithfield.

CHAPTER 6

SMITHFIELD ABUTTED LONDON'S north
wall. Around the periphery of the racing area, horse
traders had their animals tethered and lively bargaining
was underway. Buyers often asked to have the horse run
before purchasing, and that was how the informal
races had developed. The crowds attracted to this
spectacle in turn drew hawkers, food vendors, and
entertainers, and so, every Friday, Smithfield, the site of
London's livestock markets, was transformed into a
festival site.

They found a man with whom to leave the horses and
plunged into the crowd. Andrew immediately guided Joan
off in a separate direction. Christiana, still thoughtful over
their discussion, did not notice. She walked with her hands
and arms under her cloak, her pale face flushed from the
cold.

"Let us look at the horses," David said. "You will need
one once you leave the castle."

"I don't want you to buy me a horse, David."

"You will not be using the royal stables after we are wed. We will find a suitable horse today."

"After I am wed, I will not be riding your suitable horse, since I will not be wed to *you*."

"Then I will sell it. For convenience, we will see if there is one while you are here to choose. Just in case."

She suppressed the urge to get stubborn and fell into step beside him as they went to survey the animals.

As they walked around the field examining and discussing the horses, they found several possibilities. Toward the end of their circuit they came upon a most suitable horse, a beautiful small black palfrey. The owner produced a saddle, and Christiana tried him out. While David came to terms with the man and arranged for delivery to Westminster's stables, she scanned the crowd for signs of the long-absent Joan and Andrew. The field was too big and busy for her to find them. Just like Joan to forget the reason for coming in the first place.

A bear baiter and some dancers arrived to entertain. Christiana had no interest in the bear, but the dancers fascinated her. At court she tried never to miss dancers of any kind. This group was fairly rustic and unschooled compared to others she had seen, but still she followed their movements to the simple music for a long while. A part of her envied these women who were permitted to let the music entrance them, whose bodies swayed and curved and angled like moving pictures.

"I would have liked to be a dancer."

"You dance at banquets and feasts, do you not?" David asked.

She blushed. She hadn't even realized that she had spoken out loud. "Aye. But that is different. That is like a dinner conversation." She gestured to the women. "This is like a meditation, I think. Sometimes I will see one who looks to be in ecstasy, who is not even aware of the world anymore."

She felt his gaze and tore her eyes away from the performance to look at him. His face held that penetrating expression that he directed at her sometimes. There was something invasive about this focused awareness, and it never failed to make her uncomfortable.

It is like I am made of glass, she thought. It wasn't fair that he could do this. He knew how to remain forever opaque to her.

"I think that you would be a beautiful dancer," he said. "If you think that dancing thus will give you pleasure, then you should do it."

Finally the dancers took a break and the crowd that had formed drifted away.

"We should find Joan," she said, peering at the crowd.

"I'm sure that we will cross paths. If not, we will meet at the horses."

She joined him and they examined the wares that the vendors sold. She wondered what Joan was up to with that apprentice, and what Lady Idonia would say if she found out that Christiana had lost track of her.

One of the vendors offered savories of fried bread dipped in honey. The smell coming from the hot oil was delicious, and she glanced over longingly as they walked by. It was messy food and just the sort of thing that Lady Idonia had never let her buy when they went to festivals.

David noticed and went to purchase some.

"It is sure to stain my clothing," she said, echoing the reason Idonia had always given for avoiding such food.

"We will manage."

He took one of the doughy savories, and gestured for her to follow him behind the stall to some trees. The vendors edged the crowd and field, and there was no one back here.

He broke off a piece of the honey-covered bread and held it out. She reached for it but he pulled it away.

"There is no reason for us both to get covered with it," he said, and placed the dough near her lips.

It smelled warm and yeasty and sweet and wonderful. Baring her teeth to avoid the fingers that held it, she stretched her neck forward and took the morsel in her mouth. It tasted heavenly and she rolled her eyes at the pleasure.

He laughed and broke off another small piece. She stretched for it. "I must look like a chicken," she giggled with her mouth full.

Those long fingers fed her again. She felt some honey dripping down her lip and licked to catch it. He gently flicked it away, the pad of his finger grazing the edge of her mouth. Her lower lip quivered at the sensation, and her face and neck tingled.

The last piece was too big and she had to bite into it. Her teeth nipped his fingertips and she blushed, awkwardly conscious of the contact. He still held out the rest of it, and her gaze stayed on that beautiful hand as she chewed quickly and then hesitantly took the last of the savory.

His hand did not move away this time, but followed her head back. His fingertips brushed her lips and rested there. The dough suddenly felt very thick in her mouth.

She looked up at his face and saw the slight hardness around his mouth. His lids lowered as he watched her lips move beneath his hand. An odd stillness descended, and she swallowed the last of the sweet dough with difficulty.

With a deliberate movement and watchful eyes, he ran his finger around the edge of her mouth, collecting the errant honey, and then wiped the sweetness onto her lips.

She had a sudden shocking urge to lick the last of the

honey off those fingers. He looked in her eyes as if he understood. One by one, he wiped his fingers across her mouth like a repeated invitation to her impulse, layering the sticky remains on her lips.

The gesture mesmerized her. The sounds of the field and races receded to a distant roar. In the still silence that engulfed her, she could hear her heart beat harder with the light pressure of each small caress. The exciting intensity that she always sensed in him spread to surround her.

He looked at her a long moment when he finished. Then he abruptly took her hand and pulled her back amongst the trees. She stumbled after him, not really cooperating but not resisting either. Breathless anticipation claimed her as they left the sanctuary of the field. She told herself that she did not want to do this, that she would not go with him, but she went anyway.

He dragged her behind a large oak. With his arm, around her shoulders he pulled her into an embrace. The other arm slid under her cloak and around her waist, pressing her body to his body as he kissed her.

Those new sensations that had snuck up on her so insidiously the last time suddenly exploded all at once. It was if they had been carefully corralled for two weeks but now he had opened the gate and waved them to a frenzy. The intimacy of the embrace felt exhilarating, and a thundering tremor full of sharp sensual spikes shook her from her neck to her thighs.

He gentled his kiss and began biting and licking the honey off her lips in an unhurried way, pulling her yet closer to him. She became very alert but only to him and each touch of warmth on her mouth. Awareness of everything else washed away beneath the stunning waves of slow, tight heat that coursed over and over through her body.

His tongue grazed against her lips, inviting her to open to him. With the one thread of reason still left, she kept her mouth resolutely closed. He smiled before moving his mouth down.

Did she deliberately throw her head back so that he could reach the hollow at the base of her neck? She didn't know for sure, but his mouth was there suddenly and her arms were up and around his shoulders, and both of his hands grasped her beneath her cloak, holding her, bending her up to his kisses.

She grew acutely aware of every touch, every kiss, every wonderful strange reaction that she felt. Her upraised arms brought her body closer to his, and through the stretched fabric of her clothing she could feel his muscles and warmth tingling her breasts. The pressure of his hands around her felt both dangerous and comforting. Her awareness became full of something else, too, something commanding and expectant and connected to the hollow tension that spread through her belly. It was that as much as the exquisite feelings that kept her from stopping him. Vaguely, dully, her mind considered that he was luring her toward something that she did not really understand.

He kissed her mouth again, and his hands moved. Slowly, gently, he caressed down and up her sides beneath her cloak, his fingers splaying around the outer swells of her breasts. Shockingly, insistently, they moved down her back and over her buttocks and up her hips. The tightness in her belly ached and somewhere low inside her a throbbing demand pounded.

One hand stayed on her hips but the other moved up. She knew what he was going to do. She remembered Stephen's crushing grip and tensed, almost finding her senses, almost finding the strength to push him away.

But he did not crush her. His fingers stroked around

the edge of her breast in a gentle, delicate way, tantalizing her to an excruciating anticipation of she knew not what. Her breath quickened to a series of short gasps as her whole body waited.

When he finally caressed her breast, she bit back a moan. The pleasure startled her. She tried to pull away.

He would not let her go. Kissing her beautifully, caressing her softly, he summoned delicious feelings. His fingers touched her as if no cloth lay between them and her skin, finding her nipple and playing with it until that throbbing sensation low by her thighs became almost unbearable. He took the yearning hard bud between his thumb and finger and rubbed gently. This time she could not catch the small cry before it escaped her.

His mouth went to her ear and kissed and probed before his quiet voice flowed into her.

"Come back to my house with me. It is but a few minutes from here through the gate."

"Why?" she muttered, still floating in the sensual stupor that his hand created.

"Why? For one thing you should visit and meet the people who live there," he said, lifting his head to kiss her temple and brow. His hand still caressed her and she found it hard to pay attention to what he said. "For another, I am too old to make love behind trees and hedges."

Naming what they were doing intruded like a loud noise on a dream. The sounds of the races instantly thundered around her. His hand on her body suddenly felt scandalous. Burning with shame, she looked away.

"This is wrong," she said.

"Nay. It is very right."

"You know what I mean."

His hand fell away from her breast, but still he held her.

"Did your lover give you such pleasure?" he asked softly.

She blushed deeper. She could not look at him.

"I thought not."

"It was different," she said accusingly. "We are in love. This is . . . is . . ." What? What was this horrible, wonderful thing?

"Desire," he said.

So this was desire. No wonder the priests always preached against it. Desire seemed a very dangerous thing indeed.

"Well, girl, if I had to have one without the other, I would choose this," he said. "Desire can grow into something more, but if it isn't there at the beginning it never comes, and love dies without it."

He was lecturing her like a child again. She truly resented when he did that. "This is wrong," she repeated firmly, pushing a little, putting some distance between their bodies. "You know it is. You are luring me. It isn't fair."

"Luring you? Why would I do that?"

"Who knows why you do any of this? Why offer for me in the first place? Why pay the bride price?" She studied him. "Maybe you want to bed me so that when he comes, the betrothal cannot be annulled."

"It is a good idea. But that never occurred to me, because I know that he is not coming."

He had said that since the first night. Calmly, relentlessly he had repeated it. "You cannot know that," she snapped. But there had been something in his voice this time that terrified her. As if he did know. Somehow.

"He is not here, Christiana. He has had your message a long time now."

"Perhaps not. Maybe the messenger couldn't find him."

"I have spoken with the messenger whom you hired. He delivered the letter into the hands of the man to whom you sent it ten days after you wrote it."

"You spoke . . . you interfered in this? How dare you!"

"It is well that I did. Your messenger had no intention of leaving at once for your mission. He planned to wait until other business took him north. It could have been weeks. Even then he might have handed it off to any number of other people along the way and spared himself the trip."

"But he went at once for you? And delivered it directly?"

"I paid him a lot of money to do so. And to offer to bring a letter back."

She had been given no return letter. A frightening sadness tried to overwhelm her. She didn't want to hear what David was saying, didn't want to consider the implications. The messenger had been back for a while. If he could return in this time, so could Stephen. He could have at least sent a note. But perhaps the messenger had admitted doing her betrothed's bidding and Stephen did not want to risk it.

Fortunately her anger at David defeated her forebodings, or she might have been undone right there. She glared up at him. "Do you enjoy this? Destroying people's lives?"

He gave her a very hard look, but it quickly softened. His hand left her side and stroked her face. "In truth, it will pain me to see you hurt."

"Then help me," she cried impulsively. "Set me free and help me to go to him."

He looked at her in that way that made her feel transparent. "Nay. Because he does not want you enough to hold on to you, girl, and I find that I do."

For an instant, while he looked at her, she had

thought that she saw wavering, that he might actually do what she asked. His words crushed the small hope. Petulantly she shook off his arms and moved away. "I want to go back to Westminster now."

Wordlessly he led her back to the vendors and over to a woman selling little bits of lace. He spoke a few words to the woman, and then turned to her. "This is Goodwife Mary. Stay with her while I go and find Andrew and Lady Joan. Do not move from here," he ordered before walking away into the crowd.

She got the impression that he wanted to get away from her, and she was glad that he was gone, too. He gave her commands the way that Morvan did, and she resented it. *We will ride north. We will buy a horse. Stand here and do not move.* She was glad that they would not be marrying. Living with him would be like having her brother around all of the time, picking at her behavior. Lady Idonia could always be tricked and subverted. This man would be too shrewd for that.

She was glad that he had left for another reason. She never had any peace with him nearby. She knew now that it had to do with what had just occurred beneath the tree. Something of that excitement, of that anticipation, was there between them even when they just rode down the Strand and talked. Merely thinking about those wonderful feelings could call up her tingling responses again.

Desire, he had called it. She did not much like this desire. She did not like the invisible ties it wove between them. The excitement she had felt with Stephen seemed a thin and childish thing in comparison, and she didn't like that either.

Stephen. He had not come yet, had not sent a letter back. . . . A horrible, vacant ache gripped her chest. She would not think about that, would not doubt him. She especially would not contemplate what it might imply about her and David de Abyndon.

"There you are!" Joan came skipping toward her with Andrew.

Christiana glanced at her friend. Joan looked flush-faced and beautiful. A piece of hay stuck out of her hair.

"Aye, here I am. David has gone looking for you and ordered me to wait here like a child." She eyed the hay and plucked it out. "Where have you been?"

"Oh, everywhere," Joan cried. "This is much more fun if Lady Idonia isn't with us."

"I can only imagine." She held up the hay and raised her eyebrows. Andrew flushed and moved away.

Joan shrugged. "There was a hay wagon beneath a tree and we climbed the tree and jumped in. It was a lot of fun."

"I thought that you were in love with Thomas Holland."

"I am. We just played."

"Joan! He is an apprentice!"

"Oh, you are as bad as Idonia. We only kissed once."

"You kissed . . . for heaven's sake!"

Joan's eyes narrowed. "It was only one kiss. It isn't as if I am going to marry him."

She said it lightly, but the warning was unmistakable. David had been an apprentice like Andrew, and Christiana *was* going to marry *him*. *I love you*, the voice and eyes said, *but you are in no position to criticize me*.

A new, sad emotion surged. Joan pitied her. They all pitied her, didn't they? All of the desire and pleasure in the world could not balance that out, could it?

David emerged from the crowd then. He silently collected them and led the way to the horses.

"He looks angry," Joan whispered. "What did you do?"

It was more a matter of what she didn't do, Christiana suspected. Still, she found herself rather pleased that he was angry. Maybe because this was the first clear emotion that she had ever seen in him. It was the first time that she knew what he was thinking.

They retrieved the horses and headed toward Westminster. Joan and Andrew fell back and began talking again, but David tried to move at a fast pace. At first Christiana kept up with him, but then she simply slowed her horse and let him pull ahead. Shortly he slowed as well and rode beside her. She rather enjoyed making him do that.

His silence became oppressive, and after noting with a sigh that he brooded when angry just like Morvan, she stopped paying him any attention. She occupied herself with speculation about Stephen's home in Northumberland. The worry that David had given her about Stephen quickly disappeared as she found a variety of excuses for his delay in writing or coming back.

"You are thinking about him again, aren't you?" His voice, hard and quiet, intruded on her.

"What makes you say that?" she asked guiltily.

"The look on your face, girl. It is written all over you."

She was very sure that her expression showed nothing when she thought about Stephen. In fact, she worked at it. But then, David always seemed to see and know more than she wanted him to.

"You are a coward, Christiana," he said quietly, but the angry edge was unmistakable. "It would seem that I am too real for you. You refuse to see the truth. Not just about your lover not coming and this marriage really happening, but about us."

"There is no reality to face about us."

"I want you and you want me. That is very real. But it doesn't rhyme with the song that you have composed, does it? You continue to live the lyrics that you wrote in ignorance about this man and yourself."

"I do not live according to some song."

"Of course you do. Duels and abductions are the stuff of songs, not life. Do lutes play when you think of the man who used you? Are your memories colored like the images on painted cloth and tapestries?"

She looked away, trembling at these harsh words that spoke an understanding of her mind that no one should have. She suddenly felt helpless again against the fears those words raised in her. He was horrible to say that Stephen only used her. Cruel. She hated him.

His voice sounded raw and angry when he spoke again. "I should send you to him and let you see how your song ends."

"Why don't you then?" she cried.

He stopped both their horses. His hand came over and took her chin. She resisted its guiding turn.

"Look at me," he ordered.

She deliberately turned away. His hand forced her head around to him. His blue eyes flashed with something dangerous.

"Because he would use you again before he is honest with you. The past is one thing, but you belong to me now. I will let no one else have you so easily. Do not ever forget that."

She suddenly realized that his mood had to do with more than her refusing him. It involved something bigger. It was about her and him and Stephen.

Was he jealous? Of Stephen? It was so unlike him to show his reactions, and this anger flamed hot and alive and visible. Was this emotion one that he was not accustomed to controlling?

Anger unleashed something frightening in this man, and it made her especially unsettled that the fear itself seemed touched with that other tension that always seemed to exist between them.

Westminster looked like a haven from a storm when they finally arrived. She hopped off her horse before anyone could help her and ran inside without so much as glancing back at David de Abyndon.

CHAPTER 7

CHRISTIANA LIFTED HER knees and rested her head on the edge of the large wooden tub. The warm water almost reached the top, and positioned like this, she could float a little in the soothing heat. A circular tent of linen enclosed the tub and held in the steam, creating a humid, sultry environment that loosened her tense muscles.

The castle had been practically empty when she called for the servants to prepare this bath. A rumor spreading through Westminster that Morvan was to meet David on London Bridge had drawn the bored courtiers like flies to a savory. Idonia had stayed behind with her, but Isabele and Joan had attached themselves to a group including young Prince John and Thomas Holland.

Not everyone approved of this duel. Some of the older knights considered it unchivalrous to challenge a mere merchant, but even they understood Morvan's anger. Since the duel was to be so public, everyone assumed that Morvan meant only to humiliate David, and that made it more acceptable, too. After all, these merchants often forgot their place. In overwhelming David, Morvan would be reminding all of London that wealth could never replace breeding and nobility when it really mattered.

She closed her eyes and tried to get the knot in her stomach to untie. She prayed that David had delayed his return to London as she had advised. She had offered a number of such prayers during the last few days as this duel approached. She wouldn't want to see David harmed. He had become a friend of sorts, and she had rather grown to depend on his presence.

She had been thinking about him a lot since that day at Smithfield. Sometimes she listened to the remembered quiet voice in the King's private corridor. The more she thought about it, the more it sounded like David who had been approached by Frans van Horlst that day. Other times her mind drifted to the two of them under the oak tree. Those memories were both compelling and disturbing, and tended to sneak up on her when she least expected them.

Which would be worse? If David had returned from his journey, he would face her brother in front of hundreds of people and be made to look a fool. If he had not returned, the whole world would know him for a coward. Morvan and the court would probably prefer the latter. The lesson would be taught without a sword ever being raised.

Her brother did this out of love for her and concern for the family's honor, but she really wished he had stayed out of things. He was only making a complicated situation worse, and he might well ruin her plans completely. Did Morvan think that the humiliation would make David withdraw? In all likelihood it would only make him more stubborn. He might even refuse to honor his promise to let her go with Stephen.

Of course, Stephen wasn't here and the wedding was only twelve days away. She tried not to think about that, but it was becoming difficult. It was one thing to wait patiently and another to see the sun relentlessly set every day on your unfulfilled dreams. Lately she had found herself listening for horses whenever she went outside. Perhaps he planned some dramatic abduction soon. She imagined him riding down the river road with his boon companions in attendance, maybe on the day before the wedding itself. Would he wait that long? How would he get to her and get her out? There were always so many people about.

She sat up abruptly.

There were hardly any people about right now.

Morvan had been nowhere to be found this morning as the rumor of his duel on London Bridge spread. Who had started those whispers? Morvan himself? Or someone else who wanted Westminster emptied of all but the essential guard?

A heady excitement gripped her. Was Stephen coming for her today? If so, the plan was audacious and brilliant. She couldn't be sure, but it suddenly all made sense. If he had learned of the duel and its location from one of his friends here, he might well make use of it in this way. She hadn't realized that he was that clever.

Smiling happily, she quickly washed herself. She felt the knot of hair piled high on her head and considered whether she had time to wash and dry it.

Her arm froze at the sound of boot steps entering the wardrobe where the tub sat in front of a hearth.

She couldn't believe it! Finally! She eagerly parted the drape to greet her love.

Her gaze fell on beautiful leather boots and a starkly plain blue pourpoint. A sword hung from one belt and two daggers from another. Deep blue eyes regarded her, reading her thoughts like she was made of glass.

"You were expecting someone else?" David asked. He undid the sword belt and placed the weapon on the top of one of the chests that lined that walls of the wardrobe.

She let the drape fall closed and sank into the water.

"Nay. I just wasn't expecting you," she responded through the curtain of cloth.

"I said that I would come. But perhaps you thought that I would be dead."

"Badly wounded at least, if you were fool enough to meet him. Why aren't you?" That didn't come out the way she had planned, and she grimaced. It sounded like she was annoyed that he was whole.

"Edward stopped it as I knew he would. He is counting on that bride price, you see."

She heard him walk over to the wall by the door. He didn't leave.

What if she was right and Stephen came now? He would find David here. Morvan may not have drawn blood, but Stephen just might.

"You have to go, David."

"I think not."

"I must finish my bath. I will attend on you in the hall shortly."

"I will stay here. It is warm and very pleasant."

She splashed the water angrily.

"You are giving him too much credit for drama and intelligence, my girl. Stephen Percy is not in London or Westminster. His is not coming today or any day for a long while."

She sank her shoulders down under the water. *He knows what I am thinking. He knows Stephen's name. Is there anything that he doesn't know?*

"I sent the court to London Bridge, Christiana. I

wanted no one to follow your brother to the place where we really met."

"Why? So that no one would see him best you?"

"Nay. So if he forced me to kill him, I could lie to you and you would never know the truth of it."

The chamber became very still. It was absurd, of course. David could never hurt Morvan. When it came to skill at arms . . . and yet . . .

Footsteps came over to the tub. The drape parted and he handed her a towel through the slit. "Enough of this for now. The water must be cooling. Get out and dry yourself."

She grabbed the towel and jerked the drape closed. She waited as he walked away.

The water was indeed cooling and the steam had disappeared. It was getting chilly in the bath.

"Call the servant, please. She is in the chamber."

"I sent her away."

She looked down at her nakedness. She listened to the silence of the empty castle. She thought of her clothes piled on a stool by the hearth. The bath was losing its warmth quickly, but the chill that shook her had nothing to do with the water.

"Idonia should be returning soon, David. It will embarrass me if she finds you in here."

"Lady Idonia decided to take a ride with Sieg. A very long ride, I should think."

Her annoyance flared at this game he played with her. She grabbed the towel and stood in the water, drying her arms and body with hurried movements.

She would show this merchant what noblewomen were made of.

She draped the large linen towel around her, catching its ends under her arm. She stepped out of the tub and kicked aside the drape. Water from her legs began pooling on the wooden floor.

He sat atop a high chest next to the hearth, his back against the wall and one arm resting on a raised knee. His cool gaze met hers and then drifted down in a lazy way. She fought down the alarm that rose in her chest.

He had placed another log on the fire, and the small wardrobe, crowded with chests that held Isabele's gowns and furs, felt warm enough. She sat on a stool by the tub and patted the ends of the long towel against her legs to dry them.

She did not look at him but she knew that he watched her. She worked hard not to let him see that it unsettled her.

"How did you know his name?" she asked, proud of how casual her voice sounded. Almost as casual and placid as his did all of the time. Except when he was jealous. She groaned inwardly at her stupidity. Perhaps it would be best to avoid talk of Stephen Percy under the circumstances.

"I've known who he was from the beginning. Don't look so surprised. You all but told me his name that first night. I also know that you are not the first innocent girl whom he has seduced, nor will you be the last. Some men have a taste for such things, and he is one of them."

His words probed at forbidden thoughts buried deep in her heart, thoughts that tried to surface late at night as she lay in her bed and counted days passing and days left. She had walled those worries into a dark corner, and she rebelled at this man going near them.

She glared at him. *He sits there so damned calmly*, she thought. *He looks at me like he has a right to be here. Like he owns me.* She braced herself against the feelings of vulnerability and tension which that look summoned.

"I hate you," she muttered.

His lids lowered. "Careful, girl. I may decide to encourage your hatred. I find that I prefer it to your indifference."

He hopped off the chest. The movement made her tense.

"You still wait for him," he said. "After all of this time and when the truth is so clear. It is well that Edward gave you to me. You would have spent your whole life waiting and living in a faded dream."

"Perhaps I still will." She spoke the words like a bold threat.

"Nay. You wake up today."

He stepped toward her. She rose from her stool at once, clutching the towel around her and backing up. He stopped.

She didn't like the way he watched her. Even worse, she didn't like the way that she was reacting to it. For all of her annoyance, that exquisite expectation branched through her. Sharp and vivid memories of the pleasure she had felt at Smithfield forced themselves onto her thoughts and her body.

"I demand that you leave," she said.

He shook his head. "Your brother is out of this now. So is Stephen Percy. There was no duel and there will be no abduction. Finally it is just you and me."

Her heart pounded desperately. "You are frightening me, David."

"At least I have your attention for a change. Besides, I told you before. It is not fear that you feel with me."

"It is now." And it was. A horrible, wonderful combination of fear and anticipation and attraction and denial. Like the lines of a rope twined in on each other, they twisted and twisted together, pulling and stretching her soul. If he didn't leave, she was sure that something would snap.

"If you won't leave, I shall." Somehow she found enough composure to speak calmly.

He gestured to the clothes on the stool to his right and the door to his left. "I will not stop you, Christiana."

She had to pass him to leave. Was it her imagination that his blue eyes dared her to approach? *He is enjoying this*, she thought, and the vexation surged in her again, vanquishing those other feelings for a moment and making her brave.

The daughter of Hugh Fitzwaryn need not be afraid of a tradesman, she thought firmly. A noblewoman could walk naked down the Strand and her status would protect her and clothe her as surely as steel. How many tailors and haberdashers of David's degree had seen her dressed in no more than a shift as they waited upon the princess and her friends? This towel covered her more. Such men did not exist if one chose to have it so.

Aye. It would even be thus with David de Abyndon.

She lowered her eyes and collected herself. She imagined that he was a mercer who had come to show his wares. She let her spirit withdraw from him and from those strange feelings that he summoned so easily, and she wrapped herself in the knowledge of who she was and what he was.

Lifting her gaze, she looked more to the hearth than to him. Holding the towel around her, she calmly walked over to the stool and bent her knees so as to reach the garments.

Fingers stroked firmly into her hair and twisted. The clothes fell from her hand as he yanked her up. Gasping with shock, she found her face inches away from flaming blue eyes.

"Do not do that again," he warned. "Ever."

She was looking into the face of danger and she knew it. She did not move. She barely breathed.

Slowly, as he held her and looked at her, the flames cooled and the hardness left his eyes and mouth. She could see when he regained control and the anger fell from his perfect face.

The expression that replaced it was just as dangerous in its own way, though. His hand did not release her hair. If anything, it gripped a little tighter.

He looked over her face slowly and then down at her bare shoulders and neck. She watched his gaze drift to the damp towel clutched against her body. She had never been so thoroughly looked at in her life. His unhurried possessive inspection left her as breathless and tingling as a caress.

He pulled her toward him. A tremor of fearful anticipation quaked through her. Her legs almost wouldn't support her as her body followed her head. He lowered his mouth to hers.

She fought the emotions. She battled them valiantly with every bit of her strength of will. But her defenses had never been very strong against his kisses, and as this one deepened and his other arm embraced her, she melted against him as those wonderful sensations took control of her.

His mouth moved beautifully over her face and neck and ears and shoulders, kissing and biting gently, drawing softly at the pulse points. He played at the lines of tension stretching through her like they were the strings on a lute, luring her toward acceptance. She knew what was happening, but the pleasure of the heated shocks that spiraled from each kiss made her want more, and the gentle waves flowing through her from his caress on her back promised an ocean of oblivious delight.

He tugged gently at the back of the towel. She fought to the surface of her sensual sea.

"Nay," she whispered.

"Aye," he said.

The towel's edge dislodged from under her arm and fell away from her back. That fear that wasn't fear shrieked and she clutched the edge of the linen tighter to her chest, her arms crossing her breasts.

He did not try to remove it. Untangling his hand from her hair, he embraced her tightly so that her arms were imprisoned between their bodies. He lowered his mouth to the skin just above her hands while his embrace moved down her back.

The feel of his warm hands on her bare skin exhilarated her. Even her awareness of his kisses dimmed as all of her senses focused on those heated caresses. Her whole being waited and felt and savored the progress of that touch. Low and deep in her body that strange pulse began throbbing.

He took her mouth again and his hands went lower, down to her hips and lower back, down finally to her bottom. She started in surprise but he kissed her harder and his hands stayed there, following the swells of her body. That secret pulse grew aching and hot, and she dully realized that it was deep in her belly near her thighs and his hands were very close to it.

The feelings were too exquisite, too delicious to stop him. The voice of her mind grew very quiet and weak. That rational awareness only observed, noticing the scent of the man who held her and the sound of her gasping breaths. The waiting expectation she had first felt at Smithfield obliterated any real thought and grew now into something demanding and impatient and slightly painful.

His hands drifted lower. He cupped her lower buttocks

in a caress of commanding intimacy. She gasped aloud as that throbbing center of pleasure exploded with a white heat.

His fingers rested at the very top of her thighs where they joined. She felt as she had when she waited for him to touch her breast, only the anticipation had a frantic, desperate quality to it and the pulsing expectation possessed a physical reality that stunned her.

Suddenly the fear that had always been there when he kissed and touched her rose from the depths where the pleasure had banished it. The small voice of her mind considered that something was occurring here that had never happened with Stephen.

"David . . ." she whispered, beginning a feeble protest.

He lifted his head and looked at her with a face transformed and more handsome than ever. The glowing warmth in those eyes left her speechless.

He pulled her hips closer to his. Her arms still held the towel to her chest, and she didn't stand of her own will now. The fingers near her thighs shifted as he moved her closer yet.

Her belly pressed against him. She felt warmth and hardness. That hidden place, so full of ache and yearning and so close to his hand, responded forcefully.

Her eyes flew open wide.

He bent to kiss her again. "Aye," he said quietly.

A very peculiar notion teased at her mind and then forced itself on her.

Outrageous, really.

Impossible.

As if reading her thoughts, he slid his hand between the back of her thighs and gently touched her. Effortlessly his fingers found that hungry ache.

She cried out from the shock of the pleasure. Twisting

violently, she jumped out of his arms and just stared at him.

His own reaction was just as strong. She watched breathlessly as surprise gave way to perplexity and then finally to anger. Pulling the towel back around her, she moved away, trying desperately to sort her confused thoughts and emotions.

She didn't want him angry. She wanted to explain. But explain what? That a bizarre, unnatural idea of what he wanted from her had unaccountably lodged in her mind and suddenly seemed . . . logical? She was probably wrong, and if she spoke of this to him, he would think her perverted. All the same, she didn't want him touching her again, especially like that, until she found out for sure that she hadn't grossly misunderstood everything.

He just looked at her, the beautiful warmth dimming from his eyes and the placid expression reclaiming him. She felt like a fool standing there in her towel, but she didn't know what to say.

"Very well, Christiana. If you do not want to give yourself to me now, I will wait," he finally said, walking over to pick up his sword.

Her mind reeled. *Give yourself to me*, Stephen had pleaded that day on the bed. She thought he meant in marriage. But it meant something else, didn't it? Had she gotten absolutely everything wrong?

She needed to talk to someone. Now. Soon. Who? Joan. Would Joan know?

David walked back over to the door. *Today you wake up*, he had said. Dear God, but she felt awake now. Horribly so.

"I will not return here, Christiana. We will do it your way. Today I learned that Edward will attend our wedding. Your brother and the King will deliver you to me two

Tuesdays hence. If you have need of me before that, you know where to find me."

He turned to go. Out of the jumbled confusion of her mind a question that she had pondered leapt forward. Without thinking, she blurted it out. "Who is Frans van Horlst to you?"

Perhaps because it was so unexpected and so irrelevant to what had just occurred, it startled him. He quickly composed himself.

"He is a Flemish merchant. We have business together."

He was lying. She just sensed it. *Dear God, I don't know him at all. Twelve days and I don't know him.*

The shock to her emotions had made her very alert, very awake. Inconsistencies about David suddenly presented themselves. She had never noticed them before. She had never paid attention.

There were a lot, and her suspicions about Frans van Horlst only added to them. What were these trips he took? How did he have access to Edward? Why offer for her and pay a huge bride price? Why did he have a servant who looked like a soldier? How did he know that Stephen was not coming?

He knew that for sure. She just felt it.

Finally she spoke. "Who are you? Really?"

The question startled him anew. For the briefest instant the mask dropped, and in those eyes of lapis lazuli she saw layer upon layer of shadowed emotions. Then his careful expression returned and he smiled at her. It was a faint smile that revealed nothing.

He opened the door. "You know who I am, my lady. I am the merchant who paid a fortune for the right to take you to my bed."

She stood with her arms embracing herself in the

towel and listened to his steps recede through the ante-room.

He had responded to the last question just as she had asked it, in perfect Parisian French.

Christiana waited until the deep of night when the apartment and the castle were silent before slipping out of her bed. At the end of the room, Lady Idonia slept the sleep of the dead. Christiana wasn't surprised. Idonia had returned from her ride with Sieg flush faced and bright eyed, looking very young for her thirty-eight years. Kerchief gone and hair disarrayed, she had only halfheartedly mumbled some criticisms of David's presumptuous servant and of David himself, who had ordered Sieg to carry her off.

She padded the few steps to Joan's bed and slipped between the curtains. She sat on the bed and jostled her shoulder. Total darkness wrapped the bed, and that suited her just fine. She felt like an idiot and didn't need to see Joan's amusement during this conversation.

She sensed Joan jolt wake and heard her sit up.

"It is I," Christiana whispered. "I need to speak with you. It is very important."

Little stretches and yawns filled the tented space. Joan shifted over to make more room. Christiana crossed her legs and pulled part of the coverlet over them.

"Joan, I need you to tell me what happens between a man and a woman when they are married."

"Oh my goodness," Joan said. "You mean . . . no one ever . . . Idonia didn't . . ."

"Idonia did. When I was about ten. But I think that I misunderstood." Christiana remembered well what Idonia had said to her. In its own way it had been quite straightforward, up to a point, and had struck her at the time as very peculiar and not very interesting. She suspected that Idonia had assumed that over the years common sense would fill in the essential gaps, but until this afternoon her imagination had failed her.

"You marry in less than two weeks, Christiana."

"Which is why I need to know now."

"I would say so. The notion usually takes a while to get used to."

"How long?"

"For me, about three years."

Wonderful.

"So tell me."

Joan sighed. "Let's see. Well, haven't you ever seen animals mating?"

"I have lived at court since I was seven. Where in these crowded castles and palaces do animals mate? The stables? The kennels? Not the dinner hall or the garden. I didn't grow up on a country estate like you, Joan."

"Dear saints."

"Tell me bluntly, Joan. Plain language. No gaps."

Joan took a deep breath and then explained quickly. Christiana felt more the fool with each word that she heard. Deep in her heart she had known since David touched her that it was thus, but her mind simply wouldn't accept the appalling logic of it.

Jokes suddenly made sense. Vague lines in songs abruptly became clear. Stephen's hand pushing apart her thighs . . .

He had not done this thing to her, but he had planned to. Only Idonia's arrival had saved her from that brutal shock. She hadn't even known what he was about.

David . . . good heavens.

"Can a man tell if you have done this before?" she asked cautiously.

She could feel Joan's eyes boring through the blackness. "Usually." Joan explained how they could tell. Christiana winced at the description of pain and blood.

"Are you saying that you did this and didn't know it, Christiana? That doesn't make sense."

"Nay. I thought that I had . . . I told David that I had."

Joan barely suppressed a giggle. "Well, that is a switch. Normally girls need to make excuses why there *isn't* evidence of virginity. You, on the other hand . . ."

"Don't laugh at me, Joan. This is serious."

"Aye. He may think that you lied to get out of the marriage, mayn't he?"

Aye, he may, Christiana thought dully.

Joan's hand touched her arm. "Who was it? I didn't realize there was someone. No wonder that you have been so unhappy about this betrothal. I never saw you even speak with a man more than once or twice, except maybe . . ." Her hand gripped tighter. "Is that who it was? Stephen Percy? Oh, Christiana."

She neither agreed nor disagreed. Joan knew she had guessed right, though, and in a way she was glad. It felt good to finally share that agony, even if the pain had been dulling for some time now.

Joan's hand sought hers in the dark. When she spoke, her voice was low and sympathetic. "I must tell you something. You will hear it soon, for it will be all around the court in the next day or so. Stephen's uncle was on the bridge, and Thomas and I spoke with him. He received a messenger today from Northumberland." She squeezed Christiana's hand. "Stephen was betrothed ten days ago. The match had been made when he was just a youth."

A huge, deep fissure opened up inside her, slicing through her soul as if it were carved by hot steel. It reached down to the deepest reaches, releasing at last all of those fears and suspicions and forbidden doubts. They surged and overwhelmed her.

"I am sure that he loves you," Joan said soothingly. "His family no doubt forced him to this. It is common enough when early matches are made."

Aye, common enough. Men married women they did not love or want and amused themselves elsewhere as they pleased. She suddenly and clearly saw Stephen's wooing of her as the insincere, dishonorable thing it had been. A game of seduction to pass the time even while he knew his future wife waited back home. Had Morvan's threats made the siege more interesting, more exciting?

She thought of the letter she had sent him. Had he laughed? Her ignorance about men and women had been making her feel like a fool this evening, but that was nothing compared to the devastating desolation this news of Stephen caused. Her body shook and her heart began burning and shattering. She released Joan's hand and scooted off the bed.

"I'm so sorry, Christiana," Joan said.

Controlling her emotions by a hairbreadth, she pushed through the drapery and rushed to her own bed. She threw herself on her stomach and, biting a pillow to muffle the sound, cried out her humiliation and bitter disappointment.

CHAPTER 8

SHE REMAINED IN bed for two days. During the first one, she wallowed in a bitter pain full of memories suddenly seen anew. Stephen's words and face had not changed in them, but different meanings now became terribly clear. The truth mortified her, and by day's end she was close to hating Stephen Percy for having used and humiliated her.

The next day she lay in a dumb stupor, floating mindlessly through time. The numb daze was soothing and she considered staying forever in it.

On Sunday she rose from her bed and dressed. She managed not to think about Stephen much at all, but on the few occasions that she did, a raw sore of pain and anger reopened before she pushed his memory out of her mind.

By Tuesday she felt much better and more herself again. She even laughed at a little joke that Isabele made while they dressed in the morning. The glances of relief that Idonia and Joan exchanged made her laugh again.

And then, right after dinner, the tailor arrived for the final fitting of her wedding gown, reminding her abruptly that in exactly one week she would marry David de Abyndon.

That reality had been neatly obscured by the violent emotions that had ripped through her upon hearing the news about Stephen. As she stood motionlessly in the silvery pink gown, however, she knew that it was time to face the facts about this marriage.

It was going to happen. In a week Morvan would literally hand her over to him. She would live in the house that she had refused to visit, and be mistress to a household whom she had refused to meet. The center of her life would move from Westminster's court to the merchant community of London. Her life would be tied to and owned by this man forever.

Nothing would be the same. She looked at Joan and Isabele. Would they remain her friends? Perhaps, but they would drift apart because her life would not be here. She thought about the animosity between Morvan and David. Would her husband let her see her brother again? It would be in his power to refuse it.

During her years at court, she had always been a little adrift, but her brother and her few friends had served as anchors for her. After she married, she would have only David for a long while. Without him she would be completely alone in that new life that awaited.

As she turned this way and that while the tailor inspected his work, she contemplated David. She desperately wanted to hate him for being right about Stephen, but she could not. If David had not pointed the way to the truth, would she have ever seen it? How much easier to make excuses for Stephen like Joan had done. How reassuring to avoid the real pain and continue the illusion of a true love thwarted.

She didn't know David very well, but she had come very close to not knowing him at all. In the face of her indifference to him and blind loyalty to Stephen, he had tried to prepare her.

She had left things badly with him. True to his word, he had not come back to Westminster. She had insulted him that day in ways that she didn't fully understand.

The tailor left, and she walked over to a window and gazed down into the courtyard. She pictured David riding in and dismounting, and imagined his steps coming toward the apartment. In her mind he kissed her and her skin awoke with the warmth of his lips. She let the memories fuse and progress, and she felt his firm hand on her breast. She clenched her teeth against the desire that phantom touch awakened. Finally she forced herself to picture the joining that Joan had described.

Her imagination failed her and the image disappeared as if a drape had dropped in front of it. Pain and blood the first time, according to Joan. Lured by pleasure into horror.

He would not come. *You know where to find me,* he had said. An invitation. To what, though? His company or his bed?

It surprised her what these thoughts were doing. Her heart yearned to indeed see him appear in the courtyard below. She missed him, and the knowledge that he waited for her went far to ease the pain of these last days. The fear of what he awaited could not obscure the images of his kind attention to her. Thinking of Stephen still opened hollows in her soul, but David's memory soothed the devastation.

It was whispered that he wanted her so much he had paid that bride price to have her. The idea of the marriage bed filled her with dismay, but at least David had pursued her honorably. He hadn't tried to steal what he wanted in a dusty room in a deserted passageway as Stephen had.

He had a right to know about Stephen. More importantly, she needed to explain the stupid mistake that she had made about that other thing. The world treated virginity as very important, and so she suspected that such things mattered much to men.

It would not be easy to go to him. She steeled her will. They faced a life together. She could not meet him at the wedding with what stood between them unresolved.

Tomorrow she would go and find him. She would ride her black horse and wear her red cloak. She would also deal with one other problem as well.

That evening she went down to the hall well before supper and sought out Morvan. She found him with a young widow who had recently come down from the Midlands to visit Philippa. His black eyes sparkled with their dark fire. The poor girl looked like a stunned animal caught in the light of a torch. Christiana knew well this feminine reaction to him. Now, however, she understood exactly what he was about. Marching over, she interrupted his seduction with a loud greeting and a rude dismissal of the woman.

"Later, Christiana," he snapped.

"Now, brother," she replied. "In the garden, where we can be alone, please."

Fuming silently he took leave of his helpless prey and followed her through the passageways to the garden. The sun had set and twilight dimmed.

He was still annoyed. She didn't care. The stories about her brother were some of those things that made far too much sense all of a sudden. He was little better than Stephen from what she could tell, except that he didn't ruin virgins.

"Tomorrow I want to go and see David in the city," she explained. "I want you to take me to him."

"Send word to him and let him come here."

"He will not come. I left things badly when last we met."

"Then let him wait until the wedding to see you."

"I must speak with him, Morvan. There are things that I need to discuss."

"You will have years to talk, thanks to the King. I will not take you to him." He turned to leave.

She stomped her foot and grabbed his arm. "He thinks that I am not a virgin, Morvan."

That stopped him. He regarded her carefully. "Why?"

She faced him bravely. She understood her brother now, and his overbearing protection. Like David, he knew men well. He protected her from such as himself.

"Because I told him that I was not."

"You lied about such a thing? Even to avoid this marriage, Christiana, such a lie . . ."

"I thought it was the truth."

The implications sank in. "Who?" he asked quietly. Too quietly.

"I will not say. Do not think to bully me, Morvan. It is over and done with and thanks to Idonia I am whole. It is partly your fault, brother. If you had not scared off every boy, I might have had some experience in knowing a man's intentions. As it was, I was helpless against them and, until three days ago, didn't even know what he wanted from me."

He stood silently in the gray light. "Good God," he finally said.

"Aye. Eighteen and as ignorant as a babe. I came close to learning the hard way, didn't I? And almost went to my marriage bed a complete innocent."

"Hell."

"So, I did not lie to David. What had occurred between me and this other man seemed to fit all of the requirements as I stupidly understood them."

"And this merchant, knowing this, still took your hand?"

"Aye. I told him before the betrothal. He said that repudiation would ruin me."

He shook his head thoughtfully. "This marriage never made any sense."

"Nay, but I cannot worry about that now. I must see him before the wedding. I want to explain this."

He brought his arm around her shoulders and began guiding her back toward the castle door. "It is well that you explain. He might hurt you more than he has to if he doesn't know."

The very frank way he said this surprised her. So did this new ambiguous piece of information. Perhaps she should have talked to Morvan instead of Joan. She smiled, picturing her brother's distress as she demanded blunt descriptions with no gaps.

"If you go to him, he will misunderstand why you have come," he said. "It is said that he wants you badly. Perhaps that is the explanation for everything after all."

"Then I wish I had not been so unworldly. I might have traded my body for my freedom that night."

"It doesn't work that way, Christiana."

How does it work? she wanted to ask. "Well, I marry him in less than a week. When he hears what I have to say, he will not misunderstand why I have come. I must go, and I want you to bring me."

A torch by the doorway illuminated his handsome face. "So you go to him before the wedding, and I take you there? Of your own will, prior to the King's command? Having just learned what this man expects from you?"

"I face a life with him, Morvan. I want to see him and start it well. And I want him to know that you accept it, so that perhaps he will not stand between us. Aye, I go of my own will and I want him to see that I do."

He sighed with resignation. "In the morning then. Although it will kill me. Never have I brought such a precious gift to a man I disliked so much."

They stopped their horses at the end of the lane and looked up at David's shop. A large cart stood outside laden with large cylinders wrapped in rough cloth. Sieg pulled strenuously on a rope running up to a round wheel projecting from the beam of the attic. One of the cylinders dangled from the other end of the rope while he hauled it up the side of the building, his large muscles rippling under the strain as he yanked the rope hand over hand.

The cylinder reached the open attic window. Christiana caught a brief glimpse of golden brown hair as a strong arm reached out and grabbed the rope, pulling the load in.

Her courage had been slowly leaking away since yesterday evening and now she debated turning back. If David was busy today . . .

"He will stop his work when you come," Morvan said. He moved his horse forward.

She fell in beside him. "I don't know, Morvan. Perhaps. . . ."

"He wants you and nothing else will matter. Trust me on this, sister. I know of what I speak." He gave her a wink.

Morvan helped her to dismount. Sieg was busy

tying another cylinder to the rope and did not notice her.

"I will come back in a few hours. Early afternoon," Morvan said.

"Maybe tomorrow would be better."

He kissed her brow. "You made your decision with a clear head and an honest heart, Christiana. You were right. This marriage cannot be stopped and it is best that you see him. Courage now."

She nodded and entered the shop.

Two apprentices served patrons inside. The younger, dark-haired one, a youth of perhaps fourteen years, approached her.

"My name is Michael, my lady. How can I serve you?"

"I am Christiana Fitzwaryn. I have come to see your master. He is upstairs?"

Michael nodded, his expression awestruck.

"My horse is in the lane," she said, handing her cloak to him. "Perhaps when you are free you will move him for me."

She marched valiantly down the passageway. She climbed the steep steps to the second level and the sounds of tailors talking and working in the front chamber. Along the wall of this passage rose another set of steps, very steep and open like a ladder. She walked down to their base and, gathering her tattered courage, lifted her skirt to mount them.

She held on to the wall to keep her balance. The treads were narrow and treacherous. Her concentration distracted her and so she was almost at the top before she realized that her way was blocked. A little sound caught her attention.

On the third step from the top perched a small black kitten. It wailed faintly and helplessly as it surveyed its precarious position. Somehow it had gotten itself here, but it knew not how to get back up or down.

She tottered on the stair. She hadn't seen many cats before. Most people were afraid of them. This one, with its puny little sounds, was adorable. And in her way.

She lifted the kitten into her arms. At first it curled against her chest as if grateful for the security. But when she tried to climb the next step, it shrieked in terror and stretched up, clawing into her chest. She gasped as tiny spikes dug into her skin.

Footsteps approached the top of the stairs. Andrew, stripped to the waist, gazed down at her.

"David," he called over his shoulder.

David walked into view. Like Andrew he was naked to the waist, and a slight sheen of sweat glistened on his shoulders from his labors in the warm attic. She noticed with surprise the taut definition of the muscles of his broad shoulders and arms and chest. He looked lean and hard and athletic.

She was unaccustomed to seeing men undressed. In the summer, knights and soldiers stripped thus when they used the practice yards, and some of the girls made it a point to walk by, but Lady Idonia had forbidden it and lectured them about impure thoughts. David's very apparent flesh stunned her. She stared speechlessly up at that handsome face and body.

The kitten decided to move. She cried and tottered as the little paws dug their way up until the furry body straddled her shoulder.

"Steady now," David said. He stepped down and sat on the landing, reaching toward the kitten. He pried its claws out of her skin, removing them carefully so that the fabric of her surcoat and gown would not snag. He lifted the howling animal away.

It curled up contentedly, soft and furry against his chest. He stroked it absently and turned his blue eyes to her. Those beautiful hands holding that black fur against the hard chest struck her as incredibly alluring.

"You are busy. I should have sent word first," she said.

He twisted and placed the kitten on the floor behind him. The action made his muscles stretch with sinuous elegance. "Go find your mother," he told the cat. The little black face closed its eyes and rubbed against his back before scampering off.

He looked at her again and smiled. "I am not so busy. I am glad that you came."

He rose and stepped down toward her. "I will help you back down." He squeezed past and aided her as her feet blindly sought each step. Halfway down he jumped to the floor and plucked her off by her waist, setting her beside him.

"Go downstairs and wait for me."

There had been no greeting. No courtly pleasantries. He had not asked why she had come, and simply acted as if he knew. She scurried down to the invisibility of the lower passageway.

David watched her hurry away. She had surprised him by coming here. He had underestimated her.

Andrew hopped down the steps, carrying both of their shirts. He glanced at Christiana's disappearing skirt. "She's going to bolt," he observed casually.

David took his shirt.

Andrew gestured to the stairs. "By the time you are washed and dressed, she'll be gone."

"Are you giving me advice on women now?"

Andrew laughed. "Women? Hell, no, I wouldn't think of it. But then, she's not a woman, is she? She's just a girl.

I wager I've had more experience with them than you have recently." He pulled his shirt over his head. "One moment they are brave, the next they are shy. First it's aye, then nay. Remember? She used all of her courage to come, and now she is telling herself to leave. Unless, of course, your warm welcome reassured her. Smooth, that."

David looked at the empty stairs. Andrew's sarcasm was justified. He hadn't greeted her well and it *had* taken a lot of courage for her to come.

He went into the counting room and grabbed Andrew's pourpoint and threw it at him. "Then get your-self down there, boy, and stall her until I come," he said. "Block the damn door with a sword if you have to."

Andrew grinned and pulled the garment on. "Aye. And I'll tell Sieg that we'll take a break with the last car-pets. He and I can get it done before dinner without you." He sidled to the doorway. "I assume this means that we will forget about that last nightwalking fine."

"Go!"

He followed Andrew down the stairs and watched him head in search of Christiana. He slipped out the back to the well and began washing off the dust in the crisp air.

She had heard about Percy's betrothal, of course. Almost a week ago probably. How bad had it been for her? He didn't like to think of her hurt, but he didn't want her making excuses for the man either. A woman could fill a lifetime with excuses to avoid the truth.

His head had been full of her since he had left her last Thursday. He rarely second-guessed himself, but during the days and long into the nights as he thought about her, he had considered how he had handled this girl and whether he hadn't made some miscalculations. He wasn't

used to them so young, of course. He forgot sometimes
that there was still something of the child in her. Even his
greeting today . . . an Alicia would have welcomed his
frank acceptance of her arrival. But Christiana was not like
Alicia.

He had visited Westminster on Monday and almost
gone to that apartment. He felt pulled there, and only a
long inner debate had kept him away. *Let her come to me*,
he had decided. *Either on her own or for the wedding*. He
had stuck to that resolve until last night, when Oliver had
appeared late at the house with some news. And then he
had known that he couldn't wait for her to come any
longer.

He dried himself as he went back upstairs to dress.
But for the early arrival of that ship from Spain and its
cargo of carpets, he would have spared her this cost to
her pride. He had planned to fetch her from Westminster this morning, and only this work had delayed him.
She had come to him first, however. A small gift to
him from Lady Fortune. It was better for Christiana this
way, too.

He went back downstairs. He could see a bit of
red near the entrance of the shoproom. She had already
reclaimed her cloak. Andrew's body stretched casually against the threshold, his foot resting across the
space on the opposite jamb. He hadn't blocked the
way with a sword exactly, but the red cloak could not
pass.

He walked toward them and Andrew looked up in a
meaningful way. Dropping his leg, he let the cloak ease
into the passageway, right into David's arms.

"You are ready to go then?" David asked.

"Go?" she asked, flustered by his sudden presence.

"We will go to the house. John Constantyn is coming

for dinner but first we need to get some salve for the cat scratches. They might make you ill if you aren't careful."

She smiled weakly. "Your house . . . aye, I would like to see it."

There had been the possibility, small but real, that she had come to ask for the annulment. He allowed himself one breath of relief that the request would not come and that he would not have to refuse it.

"How did you get here?"

"My horse is in the alley, I think. Morvan brought me. He comes back in three hours or so."

Interesting. "We will walk. Let me tell the boys to bring the horse."

He went back into the shop and gave the apprentices instructions, then returned to her. He guided her up the lane with his arm about her shoulders, enjoying her warmth beside him and the feel of her arm beneath his hand.

Nothing could hide in this sunlight and he studied her face. She looked as exquisitely beautiful as ever, but subtle changes were apparent. He knew her face well, had memorized its details and nuances, and could read the anguish of the last days in it.

She turned her head and her sparkling eyes regarded him. He saw a change in those dark diamonds as well. Their glitter had dimmed very slightly, as if one facet of trust and innocence had dulled.

I will obliterate your memory of him.

She kept glancing at him and parting her lips as if she planned to speak. Finally the words poured out.

"You were right. About Stephen. He is betrothed as well. An old match. But you knew that, didn't you? You knew on Thursday that I would hear of it soon."

How long before she could read him as clearly as he

did her? She was by nature intelligent and perceptive. The girl often misunderstood what she saw, but the woman would not.

"I knew."

"Why didn't you tell me?"

"It was not for me to do so."

"You knew before the court. Even his uncle only heard that morning."

"Merchants and pilgrims arrive every day from the north. They bring gossip and news."

"You were asking them?"

"Aye."

"I feel like an idiot," she said forcefully. "You must think women are fools and that I am one of the worst."

"I do not think that. And if it makes you feel like an idiot, let us not speak of it."

They turned onto the lane with his house. She stopped and turned to him. Her brow puckered as she looked in his eyes.

"Will you tell me now? Why you marry me?"

He glanced away from her confused curiosity. Sore and wounded, she thought she had nothing to lose from blunt questions and frank answers. How would she react if he told her the truth?

What was the truth?

It had been weeks since he had thought about the bizarre bargain that had given her to him. In his mind, Edward's story had become real, and the license and its payment the deception. He had indeed seen her and wanted her and offered a fortune for her. The money had been for her and the license had become the gift and not the other way around. If the King tomorrow demanded another thousand pounds to let him keep her, he would pay it without a second thought.

He wanted her. Not for one night or a few months. He did not think of her that way and never had. Perhaps the inevitable permanence of marriage had woken this deeper desire in him. He wanted her body and her soul and her loyalty and her joy. He did not question why he wanted her. It just *was*.

"I marry you because I want to," he said.

CHAPTER 9

THE GATE TO the courtyard stood open. She paused in the passageway and then walked bravely into the sunny yard full of laughing women and fluttering cloth. Two large tubs stood side by side, one over a low fire.

Laundry day.

David strolled into the melee. A thin old woman with a kerchief on her hair hustled in their direction. He embraced the crone and kissed her cheek.

"They said you was out for a shipment, and I didn't expect to see you," the woman said, smiling.

"Slow down so you can have dinner with us, Meg," he said. "John is coming." He turned and pulled Christiana forward. "This is Christiana, Meg. My wife."

Meg peered at her with filmy eyes. Her toothless mouth gaped in a grin. "A beauty, David." She winked at Christiana. "Watch yourself. He's been nothing but trouble and mischief since he could walk."

David led Christiana away. "You and the women will stay, Meg. I will tell Vittorio."

Christiana followed him into the hall. "The laundress Meg has known you a long time," she said as she took in the large chamber's furnishings. Nice chairs. A handsome tapestry. Beautiful copper sconces to hold the wall torches.

"My mother worked for her when I was a child."

A middle-aged woman opened a door at the far end, and tumultuous sounds of pots banging and male cursing poured out at them. The plump woman carried a stack of silver plates in her arms. She looked Christiana up and down. David introduced her as Geva, the housekeeper. Geva smiled, but Christiana saw criticism in her sharp gray eyes.

David pushed open the door to the kitchen attached to the side of the hall. "And this is Vittorio." He gestured to a rotund, round-eyed man barking accented orders to a girl and man who assisted him. Worktables laden with knives and chopped food lined the room, and copper pots hung in the immense hearth. Vittorio bent his head to one of the pots, sniffed, and raised his thick black eyebrows in an expression of reluctant approval.

"Vittorio," David called.

The fat man straightened and looked over. "Ah! *La ragazza! La sposa!*" he announced to the assistants. They stopped their chores and smiled greetings.

He clasped his hands effusively. "*Finalmente!* Signorina Christiana, eh? Beautiful name. *Bellissima*, David." He made a comical look of approval.

"Lady Christiana will dine with us, Vittorio. And Meg and her women as well."

Vittorio nodded. "*Si, si.*" He turned back to the kitchen and gestured for the assistants.

David took her into the building across from the gate. She knew from her last visit that the solar was upstairs, but he led her past the steps to a simple bedchamber. "I will have Geva get the salves," he explained before leaving.

She removed her cloak. This chamber held some items of a personal nature. A simple cloak hung on a wall peg. A silver comb lay on a table. She sat on the bed and waited for Geva.

It was David who returned, however, and not the housekeeper. He carried a bowl of water and a rag and a small jar. He placed them on the table.

His long fingers pushed aside the shoulder of her surcoat. She glanced down at that hand and the scratches it uncovered. He moved to her other side and began unlacing the back neckline of the sleeveless outer garment. She glanced up at him in surprise.

"The salve will stain it," he explained, gesturing for her to stand and helping her to step out of it. The intimacy of the simple, practical action unsettled her.

"Is this Geva's chamber?"

The neck of her cotehardie was cut low and broad and exposed the scratches. He dipped a rag in the water and began wiping the little streaks of blood from her skin. "Geva lives in the city with her family and comes by day. This was my mother's chamber. She was David Constantyn's housekeeper for ten years before her death. He met her through Meg. She did laundry here with the others, and when his housekeeper died he gave her the position."

"And later made you his apprentice?"

"Aye."

He carefully cleaned the scratches on the back of her shoulder. She tried to ignore his closeness and the attention he gave his ministrations. She noticed again the objects on the table. They seemed to still hold something of the dead woman's presence.

He picked up the jar. "Don't worry. You are not intruding on a shrine. This chamber is used by visitors."

He soothed some of the salve over the scratches, and she sat very still with the warmth of his fingertips on her skin and the slight sting of the medicine in the sores. She lifted her gaze and saw him looking down at her. She thought that she knew that look.

She had better explain why she had come. Soon. They needed a place to talk alone, but not here in this room.

"Is there a garden?" she asked, rising.

He lifted her cloak to her shoulders. "This way."

The garden stretched behind the building and the kitchen. A high wall enclosed it. It was barren now except for some hedges and ivy, but she could tell that in summer it would be lush. Flower beds, crisscrossed with paths, flowed back to a little orchard of fruit trees. A larger bed near the kitchen would be planted with vegetables.

"There is a smaller garden back here," he said, leading her to a door in the wall.

The tiny second garden charmed her. Ivy grew everywhere, covering the walls and ground and creeping up to form a roof on a small arbor set in one corner. Two tall trees filled the space. In summer this enclosure would be cool and silent. An outer stairway led from the garden to the second level of the building.

She doubted that she would find anyplace more private than this. "Can we sit down? I need to tell you something."

They sat on a stone bench nestled deep inside the ivy covered arbor. Sunlight broke through the dense covering, mottling the shadows with little pools of yellow light.

She bent over and plucked a sprig of ivy from the carpet at her feet. She nervously pulled the little points off the leaves. Probably best to just plunge in.

"When we first met, I told you . . . I indicated that I was not . . . that Stephen and I had . . ."

"That does not matter now."

"It does, though. I must explain something." She tried to remember the exact words that she had rehearsed.

His voice came low and quiet. "Are you saying that there were others?"

"Heavens, nay! I did not lie about that. I am trying to say that there was no one, not even Stephen. It seems that I was wrong. I made a mistake." She thought that she would feel less awkward once it was said. It didn't work that way.

For a long while he didn't move or speak. She concentrated on pulling the ivy leaves off their branch.

"It is a difficult mistake for a girl to make, Christiana. Impossible, I would think," he finally said.

Saints, but she felt like a fool. "Not if she doesn't know what she is talking about, David."

His motionless silence stretched longer this time. She suffered it for a while, and then snuck a glance at him.

"Are you angry?"

"You have it backwards. A man is supposed to get angry when he learns of his new wife's experience, not her innocence."

"You might be angry if you thought that I lied on purpose. To discourage you."

"I don't think that. In fact, what you have told me explains much. When did you realize your mistake?"

She had assumed that she could just blurt this out and be done with it. She hadn't expected a conversation.

"Last Thursday night."

He stayed silent and she knew that he was remembering the two of them in the wardrobe. His body pressed to hers. That intimate caress. Her cry of shock.

"I must have frightened you very badly."

He regarded her with a warm and concerned expression. He could be a very kind man sometimes. Perhaps he even understood how distressing all of this had been. Maybe . . .

"Nay," he said with a small smile.

"Nay what?"

"You are wondering if, under the circumstances, we might put off the wedding or at least that part of it. I think not."

She blushed from her hair to her neck. It really was discomforting to have him read her thoughts like that.

He reached over and lightly touched her hair. "Although, considering this stunning revelation, I probably won't seduce you today as I had planned."

She almost gushed relief and gratitude before she caught herself. Her face burned hotter yet. His fingers on her hair and head felt very nice, though. Comforting.

"Who spoke with you?"

"I asked Joan."

"She is unmarried herself. Are you sure she got it right? That you know what I expect from you?"

"I doubt that Joan gets much wrong where men are concerned."

He laughed. "Aye, I suspect not."

Never in her life had she felt this awkward and embarrassed. She wished that someone would come and announce that John Constantyn had arrived.

"How often were you with him?"

Dear saints. She stared at her lap, covered now with little bits of ivy leaves and branches. She brushed them off.

"Just that once. Do not be too hard on him, David. He had reason to believe that I agreed. My misunderstanding of his intentions and actions was boundless."

"Were you unclothed?"

Her mouth fell open. She continued staring at her lap,

and as she did, his hand appeared and he placed another sprig of ivy there. The gesture and its understanding of her embarrassment touched her. All the same he waited for her answer. It seemed odd that when he thought her experienced, he had requested no information, but now that he knew her not to be, he wanted these details. She had opened a door and he seemed determined to examine the entire chamber behind it.

"Partly. He ripped one of my surcoats." Stephen's carelessness there had assumed a symbolic quality these last few days.

His hand still gently touched her head, brushing a few feathery hairs away from her temple. "Did he touch you?"

"We were on a bed together. He couldn't avoid touching me," she sharply. "I don't want to talk about this. Why do you ask me these things?"

"So I know how careful I must be with you."

She took a deep breath. She realized that there was such a thing as being so embarrassed that it couldn't get any deeper and that she had reached that point. There was a certain freedom in knowing that it wouldn't get any worse.

"Not the way that you did . . . last time. Idonia came in first. Just in time, according to her. He touched my breast, though. He hurt me." It felt good accusing Stephen of that. She had thought at the time that it was the only way.

"I didn't like it," she added, honestly remembering her reaction to that crushing body. "I decided that I was one of those women who . . . who . . ."

"Is cold?"

"Aye. One of those."

"We both know that is not so, Christiana. Besides, I do not think that there are many cold women. There are, however, many men who are ignorant, selfish, or impatient. You will find that I am none of those things."

Deep in her heart, she knew that. It was what kept her from panicking when she thought about this marriage, so inevitable and close now. It was that which had given her the courage to come despite Morvan's warnings of what it might lead to. Still, she was glad that he had decided not to seduce her today.

She waited for his next question as he touched her in that soothing, vaguely exciting way. Her scalp tingled from the light pressure of his fingers. She gazed at her lap and the destruction she had absently wrought on the second sprig of ivy.

There were other things that she needed to say. She wanted to tell him that she accepted the marriage. He deserved to hear it after all of the times she had smugly insisted it would never happen. She needed to promise that she would try to be a good wife to him, whatever that meant. She would like to thank him for being so patient with her. She had expected all of those things to be easier to explain than this first admission, but she found now that they were much harder.

As she groped to phrase these other things and sought the courage to say them, his right hand came into her view and settled on her lap beside her own. He turned it palm up.

She smiled down at that beautiful hand waiting for her. Her gaze locked on its exciting, elegant strength. No kinsman or priest would join them today, but there was an offer and promise in his gesture far more meaningful than the official betrothal.

He understood. He was making it easier for her. Today is the real beginning, that hand said.

Forever. The immensity of it tried to suffocate her for an instant, but she pushed the fear away.

It was why she had come, wasn't it?

She placed her own hand in his. Of her own will.

He pulled gently and lifted her, turning her so that he could set her on his lap. The devastated ivy scattered down her cloak.

She looked into deep blue eyes full of kindness and warmth. It occurred to her that maybe she didn't have to say anything else at all.

Tentatively she placed her arm around his shoulders. A little awkwardly, she reached out and touched his face. It was the first time that she had touched him instead of the other way around. It felt different this way, and she marveled at the sensation of his skin beneath her fingertips.

She let her fingers caress the planes of his handsome face. They came to rest on his lips, and she lightly stroked their warmth.

He did not move. She lifted her gaze to his eyes and collected her bravery. After a little false start she leaned forward and kissed him.

She had never done this before, with him or anyone, and once her lips were on his she really didn't know what to do. It felt very nice though, and she pressed a little harder. His mouth smiled beneath hers.

She pulled away sheepishly. "You are laughing at me because I don't know how to do it."

His hand rose up and cradled her head. "Nay. I am thinking that was the most wonderful kiss I have ever had."

She blushed and kissed him again. He took over this time, responding to her artless start.

She loved the way that he kissed her. She always had. The sensations he awoke in her were always so powerful and sweet and heady. This time she didn't completely lose herself, though, but followed his lead, doing as he did, learning from him. Finally, when he gently bit the corner of her mouth, she parted her lips to him.

He did not choke and gag her as Stephen had, but instead gently stroked the inside of her mouth at first, sending chill upon chill down her spine. The intimacy startled her, and when he deepened the kiss she sensed a change in him and a rising passion that excited her as much as his warmth and touch. She had always been so caught up in her own reactions that she hadn't noticed his. Sharing the pleasure was much richer than just accepting it, and in a way this kiss moved her more than anything they had ever done before.

"Oh my," she gasped when they separated.

"Surely you have kissed like that before."

"It wasn't so nice."

"Ah. Well, perhaps it helps now that you know that it won't get you with child."

She closed her eyes and groaned in mortification. Burying her face into his shoulder, she muttered miserably, "How did you know?"

He began laughing. "You have always kept your lips locked like they were the gate to paradise itself, Christiana. I thought that you simply didn't like it. But it is the only misunderstanding that has any logic."

She laughed too. She lifted her head and wiped the tears brimming at her eyes. "Oh, dear saints. I assure you, it made perfect sense in light of what Idonia had told me when I was younger. You must think that I am the most stupid girl you have ever met."

He shook his head. "I think that you are the most beautiful girl whom I have ever met."

It was sweet of him to say that, but he had no doubt known many beautiful women. Still, it felt nice to be wooed with pretty words. He had never done that before.

"You don't believe me."

"I am pretty enough, David. I know that. But not really beautiful. Not like Joan."

"Lady Joan is like a sunbeam and is a beautiful girl, Christiana. You, however, are the velvet night. Dark sky"—he touched her hair—"Pale light"—his fingers stroked her skin—"Stars"—he kissed the side of her eye.

The sounds of voices intruded from the outer garden. She glanced resentfully in their direction. She wanted to stay in this hidden arbor longer, laughing and talking with David. Maybe kissing again.

"We must go back," he said regretfully. "John will be here by now."

They found John talking loudly with Sieg and peering around the garden for signs of the alerted lovers. He gave David a very male look as the couple emerged through the garden door and greeted him.

CHAPTER 10

CHRISTIANA ASSUMED THAT the dinner was more lavish than the household's usual midday meal. The visit of John Constantyn probably accounted for most of the extra dishes and savories, but she suspected that her own presence had inspired Vittorio to some last minute delicacies.

"He's one of the best cooks in London, I'll wager," John confided. "I wrangle an invitation to eat here whenever I can." He patted his thickening girth. "Better not let him cook for your wedding, David. The King will take him from you."

Vittorio made sure that everything was perfect on the table, and then took a seat with the apprentices and Sieg. Soon that whole table chattered in Italian.

"It is easiest for them to learn it at table," David explained. "They will need it for trade."

Christiana watched the boys. Andrew was older than her and Roger just two years younger. They would not find it odd, though, that a girl their own age married their master. Actually, child brides were more common and she was a bit old for the role.

John helped himself to some salmon. "I heard that you received a shipment today, David."

"Carpets from Castile."

"You have been taking a lot of winter cargo."

"They come when they come."

"Like hell. You expect trade to be disrupted in the spring or summer, don't you?" He lowered his voice. "He's going to do it, isn't he? Another damn campaign. Another army to France and every ship in sight requisitioned for it. I'm glad that I only deal in wool. He'll never interfere with that."

"If Edward keeps borrowing money, there will be no silver in the realm even to buy your wool, John, let alone Spanish carpets."

"You always sell your luxuries, David. You always know what they want." He leaned toward Christiana. "He has golden instincts, my lady. Wouldn't touch the King's monopoly for exporting raw wool a few years back and talked me out of it too. Saved my ass. Most everyone involved lost their shirt."

The meal was long, friendly, and relaxed. David and John chatted about business and politics, and they discussed Edward's policies more bluntly than the courtiers. On occasion certain opinions even sounded faintly disloyal. Barons and knights probably spoke thus amongst themselves, too, she realized, but not in the King's hall.

She surveyed the people sitting at the other three tables. In addition to Sieg, Vittorio, Geva, and the apprentices, four other servants worked here on a regular basis. David's household appeared large, well run, and efficient. He certainly didn't need a wife to manage things. She suspected uncomfortably that her own presence would be superfluous at best and maybe even disruptive.

Throughout the entire meal, David let her know that he had not forgotten her presence. His gestures and glances suggested that despite his attention to his guest, most of his mind dwelled on her. When they had both finished eating, his hand rested permanently over hers atop the table, the long fingers absently caressing the back of her palm while he conversed. In subtle ways he maintained the intimacy they had shared in the ivy garden.

She became very conscious of his touch and looks as the meal drew to a close. As the hall began emptying, the apprentices heading back to the shop and the servants to their duties, she sensed his awareness of her heighten even though nothing changed in his behavior or actions.

John Constantyn did not linger long after the other tables had cleared. They accompanied him into the courtyard.

"I will see you at the wedding, my lady," John said. "Is it true that the King attends, David?"

"So I have been told. Christiana is his ward."

"I hear that the mayor convinced you to move the banquet to the Guildhall."

Christiana tried not to embarrass David by letting it show that she knew nothing of the plans for her own wedding. They had never spoken of it. She had never asked, because she had never expected to be there herself.

She could not blame him if he thoroughly disliked her by now. Maybe he did. He would never let her know. He was trapped as completely as she, but would try to make the best of the situation. Is that all they were? Two people accommodating themselves to the inevitable?

"Aye. And the mayor made clear that if the royal family attended, all of the aldermen should be invited," David said. "We will have the mayor's dull, official banquet, and then another one here for the ward and household. Save your appetite, John. Vittorio cooks for the second one."

John laughed. "And your uncle Gilbert, David? Will he come?"

"I invited him. I borrowed a royal page to send the message, in fact. Gilbert's wife is a good woman and I would not insult her. She will make him attend." His eyes sparkled mischievously. "The decision will drive him mad. Decline and he misses the King. Accept and he honors me."

"Aye," John said, grinning. "His dilemma might be cause enough to get married if the best reason didn't stand by your side now."

She decided not to think about how David came to have use of a royal page.

John left then. The courtyard suddenly seemed very quiet.

David's arm slid around her waist. "Come. I'll show you the house."

They visited the stable first. Her black horse, unsaddled and brushed, stood in a stall beside David's two mounts. The groom was nowhere to be seen. She reached up and petted the black nose. She supposed that she could name him now that she would be keeping him.

In the building facing the street she saw the chambers used by Michael, Roger, and some of the servants. Andrew slept at the shop, she knew. It impressed her that each person had his own small room. The servants of this mercer possessed more privacy than the noble wards of the King.

Silence greeted them as they reentered the hall. Even the kitchen echoed empty. Vittorio was just leaving with a basket on his arm to shop for the evening meal. He smiled indulgently and slipped away.

As David opened the door to the last building, Christiana thought that there should probably be a little more household bustle going on. She realized with a jolt that everyone had left the premises.

She followed David to the storage rooms filled with wooden crates on the first level, beyond his mother's old chamber. The scent of cinnamon and cloves wafted toward her. Carpets and spices and silks. Luxuries. John's observation had been correct. David would always sell these things. They defined status and honor and many people would eat only soup in order to purchase them.

His arm circled her shoulders as he led her back toward the kitchen. The simple gesture suddenly seemed less casual than before. Had he dismissed the whole household, or had natural discretion made them all decide to become scarce so that the master could be alone with his lady?

They were alone, that was certain. The resonating silence had imbued this simple tour with a creeping intimacy. By the time they returned to the stairs leading to the upper level and David's chambers, her caution was fully alerted.

David began guiding her up. She balked on the second step.

His smile of amusement made her feel childish. He took her hand. "Come now, girl. You should see your house."

Her mind chastised her instincts. After all, she had been in the solar before. They would marry soon and, despite Morvan's warnings, he had not misunderstood her reason for coming. She let herself be cajoled upwards.

In the light of day she could see the solar's beauty. The glazed windows on one side looked down on the garden, and in summer the flowers' scents would drift into the square high chamber. David built up the fire and she walked around, admiring the furnishings. Each carved chair, each tapestry, every item down to the silver candleholders, possessed an individual and distinctive beauty.

She fingered the relief of ivy edging the chair on which she had sat that first night. What had this man thought of the child who faced him, her feet dangling as she announced her love for someone else?

Stephen. The thought of him could still open a hollow ache.

She looked up to see David regarding her. "Did these lovely things come to you with the house?" she asked.

"Nay."

She hadn't thought so. Like the severe cut of his clothes, they were, in their own ways, perfect.

"You must spend a lot of time looking for such things."

"Rarely. Something catches my eye and I buy it. It doesn't take long at all."

She gazed at one of the tapestries hanging beside the windows. Superb. She thought about Elizabeth's dependence on his taste. He had a natural eye for beauty. It must give him a tremendous advantage in his trade.

I think that you are the most beautiful girl whom I have ever met.

Her eyes slowly followed the sinuous lead tracery that held the pieces of glass together in the windows. She felt him watching her.

He saw her and wanted her and offered the King a fortune for her.

A small book rested on a low table near the hearth. She knew that if she opened it, she would find richly painted illuminations. Like everything else in this room, it would be exquisite.

Something catches my eye and I buy it. It doesn't take long at all.

Two doors flanked the hearth. She drifted to the one on the right and opened it. She found herself on the threshold to his bedchamber. Ignoring a qualm of misgiving at the way he watched her, she went inside.

The hearth in this chamber backed on the solar's and the windows also overlooked the garden. The chamber was simply furnished, with one chair near the fire and a large bed on a low dais in the center of the room. Heavy blue drapes surrounded the bed and formed a canopy, and one side was tied open to reveal a rich matching coverlet. A fire burned in the hearth.

She walked along the wall overlooking the garden and passed through a door at the far end of the chamber. She entered a wardrobe with chests and pegs for clothes. It included a small hearth and wooden tub just like Isabele's, and a door at its end led to a garderobe and privy. A spout in a wall niche, similar to ones seen elsewhere in the house, provided piped water.

She opened a door cut in the wall and found herself at the top of the stairs leading down to the small ivy garden. Besides the solar, this was the only other way into the apartment.

Back in the bedchamber, she looked around, trying to grow accustomed to this space. David stood at the threshold, his shoulder resting casually against the doorjamb. She smiled weakly at him, feeling like an intruder.

"Where is my chamber?"

"You mean the lady's bower? There is none. Merchants do not live that way. Your place is here with me."

He walked to the hearth. There was no need to build up this fire. It sparked and crackled with new logs. She stared at the hot bright flames and read their flickering significance.

Who had come and prepared this room? Geva? He

would not expose his intentions to a woman. Sieg, then. The big Swede had been the first to leave the hall. She doubted that David had said a word to him. It had simply been done. She managed not to glance at that big bed dominating the room. Of course, Sieg would not know of David's reassurances in the garden.

She could not just stand here forever. She searched for something to look at.

The solar stretched the width of the building and had windows over both the garden and the courtyard. This chamber was not so wide, and its court wall was solid. She spied a door at its end and strode toward it.

As soon as she saw the side chamber she stopped in her tracks. It was a study. She quickly surveyed the objects filling it and knew that now she definitely intruded. She began backing out and bumped into David's chest. His hand came to rest over hers on the door and he pushed it forward.

"This is your home," he said. "There are no doors closed to you here."

Home. She had not had a home since Harclow. Not really. As the royal household moved from one castle or manor to the next, she had never felt at home, not even at Westminster. For eleven years she had been something of a permanent guest.

This small chamber might not be closed to her today, but it obviously was to everyone else. No housekeeper tended this room, and a thin layer of dust covered some of the items on the shelves flanking the high window. Her gaze took in a stack of books and some scrolls of paper. A small painting in the Byzantine style and a beautiful ivory carving were propped at one end beside an ancient hand harp whose frame was inlaid with intricate twining lines of silver.

The only furniture was a large table covered with

parchment papers and documents. A chair angled behind it, and underneath she saw a small locked chest on the floor.

From the corner of her eye she noticed that the wall behind the door also bore shelves. She turned and gasped as a man's face peered back at her.

David laughed and stepped past her to the shelf.

"It is remarkable, isn't it?"

She approached in amazement. The man's face was carved in marble and its realism astonished her. Whichever mason had done this work possessed a god's touch. Subtle shadows modeled the skin so accurately that one believed one could touch flesh and feel bone beneath it.

"I found it in Rome," he explained. "Just lying there in the ancient ruins. I picked up a small section of a column and this was underneath. There are many such statues there. Whole bodies just as real, and stone caskets covered with figures that are used now to hold water at fountains. I saw some statues at the Cathedral of Reims recently that come close, but nothing else similar north of the Alps."

Reims. Near Paris. What was he doing there recently? Stupid question. He was a merchant, after all.

"You carried it all of the way home?"

"Nay. I bribed Sieg to," he said, laughing.

"You seem to like carvings and paintings a lot. Why didn't you become a limner or a mason?"

"Because David Constantyn was a mercer and it was he who gave me an apprenticeship. As a boy I sometimes dawdled around a limner's shop and watched them work, mixing their colors and painting the images in books. The master tolerated me and even showed me how to burn wood to make drawing tools. Fate had other plans for me, however, and I do not regret it."

She stepped behind the table. On its corner were some new parchments folded and closed with a seal showing three entwined serpents. Strewn across it were papers with oddly drawn marks. The top one simply showed jagged lines connected by sweeping numbered curves. Little squares and circles lined up along snaking borders. She glanced away carefully. It was a map. Why did David make maps?

Not today, she reminded herself.

She turned and examined the books on the high shelf. "Can I look at one?"

"Which one do you want?"

"The biggest one."

He lifted the large folio down, placing it on the table, covering the cryptic drawings. Christiana sat in the chair and carefully opened it. She stared in surprise at the lines and dots spread out in front of her.

"It is Saracen, David."

"Aye. The pictures are wonderful. Keep turning."

She flipped the large sheets of parchment. "Can you read this?"

"Some of it. I never learned to write the language well, though."

"Is this forbidden?" she asked skeptically. She knew that the church frowned on certain books.

"Probably."

She came to one of the pictures, and it was indeed wonderful and strange. Little men in turbans and odd clothes moved across a world drawn to look like a carpet.

"Will you teach me to read this?"

"If you wish."

He took down the harp and leaned against the table's edge beside her, looking down at the book while he plucked absently on the strings. The instrument gave a lovely lyrical sound. She continued turning the pages, glancing on occasion at the man resting close to her now and the compelling fingers creating a haunting melody.

Toward the back of the book she found some loose sheets covered with chalk drawings. Spare lines described tents on a desert and a town by the sea. She knew without asking that David had drawn them.

Beneath them, on smaller sheets, lay the faces of two women.

One of them riveted her attention. The face, beautiful and melancholy, appeared vaguely familiar. She realized that she studied an image of his mother. It felt eerie to be facing a dead person thus, but she examined the face closely.

"Will you tell me about her?" she asked quietly.

"Someday."

She turned her attention to the other face. "Who is she?" She gazed at the sloe-eyed exotic beauty captured forever with careful, fine lines. She knew that she pried but she could not ignore the worldly way this woman's face looked at her.

"A woman whom I met in Alexandria."

As with the likeness of his mother, there was much of the artist's feelings in the sensitive way this woman was drawn.

"Did you love her?" she asked, a little shocked by her own boldness but not too much so. He had become much less a stranger since she stepped into this chamber.

"Nay. In fact, she almost got me killed. But I was enchanted by her beauty, as I am by yours."

Something in his quiet tone made her go very still. She lifted her gaze and found him looking at her and not at the book and its drawings. Looking and waiting. He was good at that. Something in his eyes and in the set of his mouth told her that he contemplated waiting no longer.

He saw her and wanted her and paid the King a fortune to have her.

He had stopped playing the harp. Her pulses pounded a little harder in the renewed silence. Total silence. Not a sound in the whole house.

She returned to the book and very carefully turned the page, burying the drawings. Another painting loomed but she didn't really see it.

"Do you know that I have only seen your hair down once, at the betrothal," he said. She sensed his hand reach toward her even before his fingers fell on her head. "Even in the bath it was bound up."

The light pressure of his caress sent a tremor through her. The bath. The wardrobe. His hands and his touch.

"Take down your hair for me, Christiana."

His tone fell somewhere between a request and a command. She leaned back in the chair, away from him.

She would marry this man very soon. She shouldn't be afraid of him. But her quickening blood and unworldly spirit shouted to her that she should get away from him now.

She looked at him, silently asking him to remember their conversation in the garden and to understand and wait a little longer. "Morvan is probably at the shop, David. I should go and meet him."

"I left word that we were coming here."

"Then he most likely waits outside. He will not enter. I should not leave him there."

He gestured to the window. "It looks out on the courtyard. See if he awaits you."

She eased out of the chair and past him, and turned on her tiptoes to glance down at the deserted courtyard.

His quiet voice flowed over her back and shoulders. "He will not come. He accepts that you belong to me now. As you do."

She went down from her toes and looked up at the clear afternoon sky. A part of her wanted desperately to fly out that window. But his touch and words and the expectant silence of this house had awakened those other feelings, and that exquisite anticipation licked through her.

"You frighten me sometimes," she said. "I know that you should not and that you have said that it isn't fear, but a part of it truly is."

He was quiet for a moment. The house seemed to quake with its emptiness. "Aye," he finally said. "For a virgin, part of it truly is."

She sensed him move. She felt his presence behind her. She both awaited and dreaded his touch, her spirit stretched with tension like a string pulled taut.

His hands gently took her waist and she sighed at the feel of each finger. His head bent to her bare shoulder. He kissed the little scratches, and then her neck. She closed her eyes, savoring the delicious closeness of him.

"Take down your hair, Christiana."

She raised her arms and clumsily fumbled for the pins that held her hair. She pulled out the intricate twists and plaits, terribly conscious of how weak and vulnerable she felt, wonderfully aware of those fingers splayed around her.

The heavy waves fell section by section down her neck and back, all the way to his hands. She shook her head to release the last of them, placing the pins on the windowsill.

He nuzzled his face in her unbound hair, and his breath tingled her scalp and neck through the tresses.

His hands turned her to him and took her face, cradling

it gently like something precious and fragile. He kissed her tenderly, beautifully, and fully, and she trembled as his mouth made the low tension and excitement sharpen and rise.

He prolonged the kiss, taking her in an embrace that pulled her to his warmth. She held her arms open at his sides for one worried moment before accepting him.

She sensed a change in him after that. His kiss deepened, commanding her desire. His hand cupped her breast. She gasped and closed her eyes, waiting for the delicious sensations.

They undid her completely. Her limbs went languid as heat poured through her body. His soft hair brushed her face as he lowered his mouth to the skin exposed by her low-cut cotehardie, kissing the top swell of the breasts that his fingers caressed into peaks of yearning.

Fear told her to stop him but the desire would not let her. Rivulets of pleasure merged into a fast-running river, and struggling against its current seemed futile and impossible.

His fingers played at her and the pleasure became a little frantic. *I am drowning in it*, she thought as his mouth claimed hers again.

He lifted his head and looked down at her, watching her responses to his touch. She gazed at the parted lips and deep eyes and knew that there would be no help from him this day.

He began guiding her toward the chamber door.

She thought about where they were going and what he wanted. "I don't . . ." she whispered even as she took another step.

"It is why you came, is it not? For reassurance that this marriage need not be so terrible?"

She resisted at the threshold. His hand returned to her breast and his lips to her neck.

"You said . . . you said that today you wouldn't . . ."

"I said probably," he murmured. "And I lied."

He took her face in his hands again. "His shadow is between us and I would banish that ghost. Today we even the accounts and turn the page. It will be easier for you this way, too."

She read the decision in his eyes.

"Do not be afraid. I will wait until you are ready and until you want me. It will be all right. I will make it so," he promised.

I am helpless against these feelings, she thought. *It is unnecessary to fight them. This is inevitable anyway. I am his forever.*

She turned her face and kissed his hand.

He lifted her in his arms and carried her into the chamber.

CHAPTER 11

HER THIN ARMS encircled his neck and tightened as he approached the bed.

It will be all right. I will make it so. Brave words from a man who hadn't taken a virgin since he was sixteen. Still, he would indeed make it so. Whatever lies he told her today, that would not be one of them.

He should have known. *She's just a girl,* Andrew had said. *One moment they are brave and the next shy. Remember?*

He sat on the side of the bed and settled her into his lap. He kissed her until the arm grasping his neck loosened a bit.

Innocent and ignorant. All during dinner it had been all he could do not to stare in astonishment. While he ate and spoke, his mind had recalculated what this revelation meant. Perhaps it made today unnecessary and he should wait. Perhaps it made it essential. In the end his own desire chose the course. He would not let her leave without claiming her. He wanted her and there was only one way to possess her securely.

She touched his face in that tentative way, and his desire surged. He took her mouth hungrily and fought back the cataclysmic storm that threatened to thunder through him. Slowly and simply, he reminded himself again.

He caressed her breasts and when her arms tightened this time it was not in fear. Her body relaxed into his. She tried to imitate his deep kiss and probed cautiously and delicately. The artless effort almost undid him.

The joy he found in her innocent passion surprised him. He had never sought it in other women. It shouldn't matter with Christiana either, but it did. He felt her body responding to him and listened to her sharpened breathing. He delighted in her awkward embrace and in her startled gasps when his hands raised a new pleasure. He reveled in the knowledge that despite what had occurred with Percy, no man but himself had ever aroused her.

He kissed her again, savoring the soft taste of her and the compliant arch of her back. His hand sought the lacing of her cotehardie, and he began undressing her.

The virgin stiffened for an instant as the garment loosened, but then those glittering eyes watched his hands ease the gown off her arms and down to her waist. Her mouth trembled open and her eyes closed as he touched her breast through the thin batiste of her shift.

A small hand left his shoulders and caressed down his chest, and the thunder tried to erupt again. Her fingers slid under the flap hiding the closures to his pourpoint. He watched her earnest expression as that hand fumbled down his chest. Aye. Having chosen to yield, the sister of Morvan Fitzwaryn would not play the reluctant victim.

He slid the straps of the shift down and uncovered her beautiful breasts. His gaze followed the path of his fingers as he traced their high, round swells. Her breath quickened and she buried her face shyly in his shoulder.

She was beautifully formed, pale and flawless. Her skin was not translucent and white like so many Englishwomen, but rather had the opaque tint of new ivory. It was the color of the bleached beaches along the Inland Sea. He caressed her, whisking and grazing the tight nipples, and her whole body reacted. With a faint moan she arched into his touch. The light brown tips beckoned like an offering. He lowered his head and gently kissed one before taking it into his mouth.

She almost jumped out of his arms.

He held her firmly and looked at the startled shock in her eyes. He kissed her cheek reassuringly.

He lowered his kisses until that sweet breast was in his mouth again. Jesus, the man must have barely touched her. No thought to her at all. If Idonia hadn't found them, he would have brutalized her.

A picture of that formed in his mind, and his spirit reacted with a surge of protective anger followed by a wave of tenderness. He played at her with his tongue and teeth until her bottom pressed against his thigh in her search for relief. He reached back and pulled down the bed coverings. Slowly and simply, but before she left him he would show her the glory of the pleasure. She was all that mattered this time.

He rose with her in his arms and turned and laid her down. Dark eyes, liquid with passion, regarded him cautiously. He gazed down at her lying there, naked to the waist with her clothes falling around her hips, and he considered leaving her thus. She looked sweet and fresh and reminded him of the girls of his youth lying back in hay and grass. He thought of the carpet of ivy in the small garden below. If he lived until summer, the warm starlit nights promised a special ecstasy.

Gently he pulled the cotehardie and shift down her slender curves.

Christiana bit her lower lip as shock and excitement merged at the sight of him undressing her. She watched her naked body emerge. When the gown and shift were gone, he untied the garters at her knees and slid off her hose.

A prickly expectation twisted in her. The fear had not completely disappeared. It acted like a spice in the stew of emotions and sensations that boiled inside her.

He shook off his pourpoint and removed his shirt before lowering down beside her. She watched his hard body come to her, and sighed with relief when he was in her arms again.

She let her hands feel his shoulders and back, and she noted the ridges of scars there. He moved into her caress. The heady warmth and closeness overwhelmed her. That strange pounding need went all through her now, shaking her from shoulders to toes.

He kissed her deeply while his hand followed the tremor, sliding down her stomach and belly, reaching down her thighs and legs. Possessive, hot and confident, his caress took control of every inch of her. Her body arched into his touch and rocked to the rhythm of that hollow hidden pulse. Everything began to spiral into the need now. Her breathing, her blood, her awareness, even the pleasure flowed to and from it.

He cupped her breast in his hand and rubbed the tip with his thumb. "I am going to kiss all of you now," he said. "Do not be shy. Nothing is forbidden if it gives us both pleasure."

And he did kiss all of her, his mouth pressing and biting and drawing down her body, creating new pleasures and surprises and leaving her breathless. Down her stomach and belly, down even to her legs. Several kisses even shockingly landed on the flesh of her thighs and then on the soft mound above them and she cried out as long, hot streaks shot through her.

His lips closed on one breast while he caressed the other and the excitement rose to a frantic level. She grabbed desperately at his back and hair. His muscles felt tense beneath her fingers, and his breath sounded ragged to her ears.

He rose up and loosened the rest of his clothing. She reached down to help and her hand brushed his arousal. She felt a reaction all through him, and she bravely touched him again as he kicked off his clothes.

Fear spiked through the oblivion of desire.

Impossible . . .

He returned her hand to his shoulder and then stroked down her body to her legs. Teasing her thighs apart, he slid his hand up and under to her buttocks. His arm pressed up against her while his tongue and lips aroused her breasts.

The pounding need exploded, obliterating the renewed fear. She pushed down against the pressure of that arm offering relief but only bringing torture. Her whole body wanted to move in abandoned, base ways, and she controlled it with difficulty. Over and over she bit back wanton cries that threatened to fill the room.

The warm water of his voice flowed over her. "Do not fight it, Christiana. The sounds and moves of your desire are beautiful to me."

Gratefully she submitted to the delirium. When his hand came forward, she opened her legs without encouragement. She felt no shyness or shock as he caressed her, only a torturous desire that would surely explode into flames if it was not fulfilled.

The sensations of his magic touch led her into madness. Gentle caresses created streaks of concentrated pleasure. Deliberate touches summoned a wild and desperate excitement.

His quiet voice penetrated the wonderful anguish. "Do you want me now, Christiana?"

He touched her differently and she cried out. She managed to nod.

"Then tell me so. Say my name and tell me so."

In the distance somewhere she heard her voice say it. The frantic need completely took over and her hips rose to meet the body coming over hers.

She reveled in the feel of his long length along her and the total closeness of their bodies. She delighted in the concentrated passion transforming his face as he looked at her.

He took her slowly and carefully and she marveled at the beauty of it. With gentle pressure and measured thrusts he seduced her open. The feared pain was not really pain at all but only a stretching tightness lost in the wonderful relief of him filling that aching need. Without thinking, she rocked up to meet his gentle invasion.

She froze as a burning shock stopped her.

He kissed her softly and pulled back. "It cannot be helped, darling." He thrust and a sharp pain eclipsed the pleasure for a flashing instant.

His body didn't stop and the hurt and its memory quickly disappeared as he withdrew slowly and slid in again. It felt desperately good. Instinctively she embraced him with her legs, holding him closer, taking all of him to herself. She found his rhythm and rocked with it in a soundless chant of acceptance.

Nothing, not the songs or his touch or Joan's lesson, had prepared her for the intimacy that engulfed them. Skin on skin, breath on breath, limbs entwined and bodies joined . . . the physical connections overwhelmed her senses. Each time he withdrew, it was a loss. Each time he filled her, it was a renewed completion. It awed her and she sighed her amazement each time they rocked together.

He paused and she opened her eyes to see him looking at her. The careful mask was gone and those blue eyes showed the depths that he never let people see. She moved her hand and touched the perfect face, then let her caress drift down to his neck and chest.

He moved again and it was less gentle this time. He closed his eyes as if he sought to contain something, but if he fought a battle he lost it. "Aye," she whispered when he moved hard again. It hurt a little but the power of it awoke something in her soul. She wanted to absorb his strength and his need. She wanted to know him thus without his careful defenses.

He looked straight in her eyes and then kissed her as he surrendered. As his passion rose in a series of strong, deep thrusts and peaked in a long, hard release, she felt that she touched his essence and he hers.

She held him to her, her arms splayed across his back and her legs around his waist, and she floated in the emotion-laden silence, feeling his heartbeat against her breast. Her body felt bruised and alive and pulsing where they were still joined.

Slowly the chamber surrounded her again. She felt the reality of his weight and strength above her and his soft hair on her cheek.

Still half a stranger, she thought, wondering at this thing that could connect her in indescribable ways to a man whom she barely knew. Amazing and frightening to touch the soul when you did not know the mind.

Her awareness of the unknown half of him seeped around her. She suddenly felt very shy.

He rose up on his arms and kissed her gently. "You are wonderful," he said.

She didn't know what that meant but she was glad he was pleased. "It is much nicer than I thought it would be," she confided.

"Did I hurt you at the end?"

"Nay. In fact, I'm a little sorry it is over."

He caressed down her leg and removed it from his waist. He shifted off her. "That is because you are not done."

She thought of his almost violent ending. "I would say that we are most done, David."

He shook his head and touched her breast. Her eyes flew open at her immediate forceful response. His hand ventured between her legs. She grabbed onto him in surprise.

"I would have given this to you earlier, darling, but you needed to need me this first time," he said as the frenzy slammed into her again.

He touched and stroked at flesh still sensitive from the fullness of him, and a frantic wildness unhinged her. She called out to him, saying his name over and over as her mind and senses folded in on themselves and she lost hold of everything except the ascending pleasurable oblivion.

And then, when she thought that she couldn't bear it anymore and that she would die or faint, the tension snapped in a marvelous way and she screamed in the ecstasy of release rushing through her body.

She rode the eddies with stunned astonishment until they slowly flowed away.

"Oh my," she sighed as she lay breathless and trembling in his arms.

"Aye. Oh my," he said, laughing and pulling her closer. He reached for the bedclothes and covered them both, molding her against his body. His face rested on her hair, his lips against her temple. They lay together in a lulling peace.

The intimacy of their lovemaking had been stunning and poignant. This quiet closeness felt sweet and full and a little awkward. In the matter of an hour a connection had been forged forever. He had taken possession of her in ways she hadn't expected.

She slept and awoke to a darkened room, the twilight eking through the windows. Distant sounds of voices and activity drifted toward her. She turned and found David up on his arm, looking at her.

He liked looking at her. Like his carvings and books? It was something at least. It could have been a man who cared not for her at all.

"I should be going back," she said.

"You will stay here tonight. I will bring you in the morning."

"Idonia . . ."

"I sent a message that you were with me. She will not worry."

"She will know."

"Perhaps, but no one else will. I will get you back by dawn."

A shout from Vittorio echoed through the garden and into the windows. Everyone here probably knew, or would soon when she didn't leave. She thought of the sidelong glances that she faced from these servants and apprentices, from Idonia and even the whole court if word got out.

"You will stay here with me," he repeated. It wasn't a request.

He rose from the bed and walked to the hearth. His sculpted muscles moved as he stretched for a log and placed it on the fire. In the sudden bright illumination she studied his body, casual and unashamed of its nakedness, and noticed the lines on his back that her fingers had felt. Flogging scars. How had he come by them? His dead master did not sound like a man to do this. He returned to her and she watched him come, surprised by the thrilling pleasure she found in looking at him.

Pulling down the coverlet, he gazed at her body. He caressed her curves languidly. She watched that exciting hand move.

"Are you sore, darling? I would have you again, but not if it would hurt you."

Again? How often did people do this? For all of Joan's bluntness, a lot of information had been left out.

His frank statement of desire sent a tremor through her. She didn't doubt his concern for her, but she knew that his question also offered her a choice. "I am not hurt." She raised her arms to embrace him and the wonder.

Throughout the evening and night he forged an invisible chain of steel tying her to him. She felt it happening and wondered if it was something that he controlled. Links of passion and intimacy joined by pleasure and tenderness encircled her.

Late at night, while they basked in the hearth's warmth, she asked him about the wedding and learned that the ceremony had also been moved. They would wed in the cathedral with the bishop in attendance instead of in David's parish church.

"It is getting very elaborate," she mused.

"It couldn't be helped. Once the mayor found out that Edward was coming, the fat was in the fire. I had hoped no one would know and he could just show up."

He spoke of the King in a casual way. Why did she hesitate to just ask him about that relationship? Why did she feel that the topic was forbidden and that to pursue it would be prying?

She sensed that it would be, though, and tonight she did not want to knock on doors that he might not open. She changed the subject. "David, what else do you expect of me?"

The question surprised him. "What do you mean?"

"Considering how stupid I was about this, it won't surprise you to learn that I know little about marriage. I haven't had a very practical education."

"I expect you to be faithful to me. No other man touches you now."

His firm tone stunned her.

"Do you understand this, Christiana?"

"Of course. I'm not *that* stupid, David. I was referring to household things. Everything here is so organized."

"I hadn't really thought about it."

Then why did you go looking for a wife if you hadn't realized that you needed one.

"Isabele thinks that you expect me to work for you," she said, grinning.

"Does she now? I confess that it hadn't occurred to me, but it is a good idea. I shall have to thank the princess. A wife provides excellent free labor. We will get you a loom."

"I can't weave."

"You can learn."

"How much can you earn off of me after I learn?"

"At least five pounds a year, I would guess."

"That means that in two hundred years I will earn back my bride price."

"Aye. A shrewd bargain for me, isn't it?"

They laughed at that and then he added, "Well, the household is yours. Geva will be glad for it, I think. And the boys need a mother sometimes."

"One of the boys is older than me, David."

"It will not always be so, and Michael and Roger are far from home and could use a woman's understanding sometimes. And you will have your own children, too, in time."

Children. Everything he had mentioned could have been provided by some merchant's daughter who brought a large dowry. Children, too. But her sons would be the grandchildren of Hugh Fitzwaryn.

Morvan suspected that David sought their bloodline for his children with this marriage. Could he be right? She found that she hoped it was true. It would explain much, and mean that she brought something to him that another woman could not.

Late that night she awoke in his sleeping embrace. It seemed normal to be in his arms. She lay motionless, alert to his reality and warmth. How odd to feel so close to someone so quickly.

True to his word, he brought her back to Westminster by dawn. She walked through the corridors of a building that felt slightly foreign to her. She slipped into the hidden privacy of her bed while Joan and Idonia still slept.

A firm hand jostled her awake and she looked up into Joan's beaming face. "Aren't you coming to dinner? You sleep the sleep of the dead," Joan said.

Christiana thought that skipping dinner and just sleeping all day sounded like a wonderful idea, but she pulled herself up and asked Joan to call for a servant.

An hour later, dressed and coiffed, she sat beside Joan on a bench in the large hall, picking at food and watching the familiar scene that now looked slightly strange. Her senses were both alerted and dulled at the same time and she knew that those hours with David had caused this. Joan asked her some questions about David's house, and she answered halfheartedly, not wanting to share any of those memories right now.

Toward the end of the meal, Lady Catherine approached their table, her cat eyes gleaming. She chatted with Joan for a while and then turned a gracious face on Christiana.

"You marry quite soon, don't you, dear?"

Christiana nodded. Joan glanced at Catherine sharply, as if it was rude to mention this marriage.

"I have a small gift for you. I will send it to your chamber," Catherine said before leaving.

She wondered why Lady Catherine would do such a thing. After all, they weren't good friends. Still, the gesture touched her and left her thinking that Morvan, as usual, had overreacted to something in warning her off Catherine.

Thomas Holland spirited Joan away and left Christiana on her own. She returned to Isabele's deserted apartment, glad for the privacy. The court routine seemed intrusive when her thoughts dwelled on yesterday and the future.

She went into Isabele's chamber. *Four days and I leave here forever,* she thought, looking out the window. She no longer feared that. A part of her had already departed.

The sound of a door opening reached her ears. Joan or Idonia returning. She hadn't seen the guardian since her return. She wondered what that little woman would say to her.

The footsteps that advanced through the anteroom were not a woman's, however. Morvan had come. One look at her and he would know. Was she brave enough to say "Aye, you were right and it was magic and I liked it?" His strength had stood for years between her and all men, and now she had given herself to one whom he hated.

The steps came forward. They stopped at the threshold to the bedchamber.

"Darling," a familiar voice said.

Shock screamed through her. She swung around.

There in the doorway stood none other than Stephen Percy.

CHAPTER 12

"STEPHEN," SHE GASPED.

He smiled and advanced toward her, his arms inviting an embrace. She watched him come with an odd combination of astonished dismay, warm delight, and cold objectivity. She noticed the thick muscles beneath his pourpoint. She observed the harsh handsomeness of his features. His blond hair and fair skin struck her as blanched and vague compared to David's golden coloring.

She couldn't move. Confused, horrified, and yearning emotions paralyzed her. *Not now*, her soul shrieked. *A month ago or a month hence, but not now. Especially not today.*

Strong arms surrounded her. A hard mouth crushed hers.

She pushed him off. His green eyes expressed surprise and then, briefly, something else. Annoyance?

"You are angry with me, my love," he said with a sigh. "I cannot blame you."

She turned away, grasping the edge of the window for support. Dear God, was she to have no peace? She had found acceptance and contentment and even the hope of something more, and now this.

"Why are you here?"

"To see you, of course."

"You returned to Westminster to see me?"

"Aye, darling. Why else? I used the excuse of the pre-Lenten tournament."

The tournament was scheduled to begin the day after her wedding. Stephen loved those contests. She suspected that was his true reason for coming, but her broken heart, not yet totally healed, lurched at the notion that he came for her.

The pain was still too raw, the humiliation still too new, for her to completely reject the hope that he indeed loved her. The girl who had been faithful to this man desperately still wanted to believe it. Her heart yearned for that reassurance.

Her mind, however, had learned a thing or two from its agony. "When did you arrive?"

"Two days ago. I did not seek you immediately because I was with my friend Geoffrey. He is in a bad way with a fever. He lies in Lady Catherine's house in London."

"You are friends with Catherine?"

"Not really. Geoffrey is, however." He stepped toward her. "She told me all about your marriage to this merchant," he said sympathetically. "If Edward were not my king, I would challenge him for degrading you thus."

She glanced at the concern in his expression. It struck her as a little exaggerated, like a mask one puts on for a festival.

He reached out and caressed her face. The broken heart, aching for the balm of renewed illusions, sighed.

The spirit and mind, remembering last night's passion and David's rights, made her move away.

"You already knew of my marriage, did you not? I wrote you a letter."

"I knew. I received it, darling. But I never imagined that the King would go through with this. And Catherine has told me of your unhappiness and humiliation."

How kind of Lady Catherine, Christiana thought bitterly. Why did this woman meddle in her affairs? And how had Catherine known about Stephen and her?

Joan. Joan had gossiped. Did everyone know now? Probably. They would all be watching and waiting the next few days, maybe the next few years, to see how this drama unfolded.

"Perhaps I should not have come," Stephen muttered. "Catherine assured me that you would want to see me."

"I am glad to see you, Stephen. At the least I can congratulate you on your own betrothal."

He made a face of resignation. "She was my father and uncle's choice, my sweet. She does not suit me, in truth."

"All the same, she is your wife. As David is my husband."

"Aye, and it tears me apart that there is nought we can do about that, my sweet."

A candle inside her snuffed out then, and she knew that it was the last flame of her illusions and childish dreams. It did not hurt much, but something of her innocence died with it, and she felt that loss bitterly.

Through it all, she had saved a little bit of hope, despite knowing and seeing the truth. If he had not returned, it would have slowly disappeared as she lived her life and spent her passion with David, much as a small pool of water will disappear in the heat of a summer afternoon.

What if Stephen had spoken differently? What if he had come to plead with her to run away together and petition to have both of their betrothals annulled? It was what that reserve of hope had wanted, after all.

A week ago she would have done it, despite the disgrace that would fall on her. Even last weekend, such an offer might have instantly healed her pain and banished her doubts about him.

Now, however, it would have been impossible. Now . . .

A horrible comprehension dawned. Stephen's presence receded as her mind grasped the implications.

Impossible now. David had seen to that, hadn't he?

Last night had consummated their marriage. No annulment would be possible now, unless David himself denied what had occurred. And she knew, she just knew, that he would not, despite his promise that first night.

I expect you to be faithful to me. No other man touches you now.

All of those witnesses . . . even Idonia and her brother.

An eerie chill shook her.

David had known Stephen was coming. He had been asking the pilgrims and merchants. He could not know if Stephen came to claim her, however. Nonetheless, he had still covered that eventuality. Methodically, carefully, he had made sure that she could not leave with Stephen. If she did anyway, despite the invisible chains forged last night, despite the dishonor and disgrace, he possessed the proof necessary to get her back.

The ruthlessness of it stunned her.

She remembered the poignant emotions she had felt last night. Twice a fool. More childish illusions. Her stupid trust of men must be laughable to them.

A warm presence near her shoulder interrupted her thoughts. Stephen hovered closely, his face near hers.

"There is nought that we can do about these marriages, darling, but in life there is duty and then there is love."

"What are you saying, Stephen?"

"You cannot love this man, Christiana. It will never happen. He is base and his very touch will insult you. I would spare you that if I could, but I cannot. But I can soothe your hurt, darling. Our love can do that. Give this merchant your duty, but keep our love in your heart."

She wanted to tell him how wrong he was, how David's touch never insulted. But what words could she use to explain that? Besides, she wasn't at all sure that the magic would return now that she knew why he had seduced her. Perhaps the next time, on their wedding night, she would indeed feel insulted and used.

Well, what had she expected? David was a merchant and she was property. Very expensive property. She doubted that King Edward gave refunds.

Love, she thought sadly. She had thought that there was some love in it. Her ignorance was amazing. David was right. She did live her life like she expected it to be some love song. But life was not like that. Men were not like that.

"I am a married woman, Stephen. What you are suggesting is dishonorable."

He smiled at her much the way one might smile at an innocent child. "Love has nothing to do with honor and dishonor. It has to do with feeling alive instead of dead. You will realize that soon enough."

"I hope that you are not so bold as to ask for the proof of my love now. I wed in several days."

"Nay. I would not give a merchant reason to upbraid or harm you, although the thought of him having you first angers me. Marry your mercer as you must, darling. But know that I am here."

"I am an honest woman, Stephen. And I do not think that you love me at all. I think that this was a game to you, and still is. A game in which you lose nothing but I risk everything. I will not play in the future."

He began protesting and reaching for her. Footsteps in the anteroom stopped him. She turned to the new presence at the threshold.

Good Lord, was there no mercy?

Morvan filled the doorway, gazing at them both. For one horrible moment an acute tension filled the room.

"Percy, it is good to see you," Morvan said, advancing into the chamber. "You have come for the tournament?"

"Aye," Stephen said, easing away from her.

Morvan eyed them both again. "I assume that you are wishing each other happiness in your upcoming marriages."

She nodded numbly. There was no point in trying to explain away Stephen's presence. She saw in her brother's eyes that he had heard the gossip.

"It is a strange thing about my sister's marriage, Stephen," Morvan said as he paced to the hearth. "It is said that the King sold her for money, and I believed that too. But I have lately wondered if this didn't come about for another reason. Perhaps he sought to salvage her reputation and my family's honor, and not disgrace it."

She watched them consider each other. *Not now, Morvan,* she urged silently. *It doesn't matter anymore.*

"I must be going, my lady," Stephen said, turning a

warm smile on her. She gestured helplessly and watched him stride across the chamber.

"Sir Stephen," Morvan called from the hearth. "It would be unwise for you to pursue this."

"Do you threaten me?" Stephen hissed.

"Nay. It is no longer for me to do so. I simply tell you as a friend that it would be a mistake. Her husband is not your typical merchant. And I have reason to think that he knows well how to use the daggers that he wears."

Stephen smirked in a condescending way before leaving the apartment.

She faced her brother's dark scrutiny. He looked her up and down, and searched her eyes with his own.

"It is customary, sister, to wait a decent interval after the wedding before meeting with one's old lovers."

She had no response to that calm scolding.

"And since you spent the night in that man's bed, you are indeed truly wed now."

"David. His name is David. You always call him 'that merchant' or 'that man,' Morvan. He has a name."

He regarded her with lowered lids. "I am right, am I not? You slept with him. With *David*."

It was pointless to lie. She knew he could tell. She nodded, feeling much less secure about that decision now that she understood David's motivations.

"You must not see Percy again for a long while."

"I did not arrange to meet Stephen."

"Still, you should be careful. Such things are taken in stride if the woman is discreet or if the husband does not care, but you have no experience in such deceptions and your merchant does not strike me as a willing cuckold."

"I told Stephen that I am not interested in him anymore."

"He does not believe you."

He was just trying to help her. In this his advice was probably as sound as any man's. He'd certainly bedded his share of married women.

"Do you despise me?" she whispered.

A strained expression covered his face. He strode across the space and gathered her into his arms. "Nay. But I would not have you be this man's wife, and I would not have you be Percy's whore. Can you understand that? And I blame myself because I did not find a way to take you away from here."

She looked into his dark eyes. She read the worry there and thought that she understood part of it.

"I do not think that being David's wife will be so bad, Morvan. He can be very kind."

A small smile teased at his mouth. "Well, that at least is good news. I am glad that he is accomplished at something besides making money."

She giggled. He tightened his embrace and then released her. "Take your meals with me these last days," he said. "I would have this time with you."

She nodded and watched sadly as he walked away.

She never doubted that her brother had requested her attendance at meals because he wanted her company. She would be leaving him soon, and a subtle nostalgia hung between them at those dinners and suppers, even when they conversed merrily with the other young people at their table.

Morvan's presence beside her had other benefits, however, and she suspected that he had thought of them. Stephen did not dare approach her in the hall while Morvan stayed nearby, and the peering, glancing courtiers received no satisfaction to their curiosity about the status of that love affair.

Everyone knew. Stephen had only to rise from his bench and sidelong looks would watch to see if he would speak with her. It became abundantly clear that the court believed an adulterous affair with Stephen was probably inevitable at some point. She got the impression that many of these nobles accepted the notion with relief, as if such an affair would be a form of redemption for her. The marriage to the merchant would just be a formality, then, and much easier to swallow and even ignore.

Aye, Joan had gossiped. When Christiana confronted her, she tearfully admitted it. Just one girl, she insisted. Christiana had no trouble imagining that small leak turning into a river of whispers within hours.

She filled the next days with preparations for the wedding. Philippa came to the apartment to survey her wardrobe on Saturday and immediately ordered more shifts and hose made for her. A new surcoat was fitted as well. Haberdashers descended so that she could choose two new headdresses. Trunks arrived to be filled with linens and household goods for her to bring to her new home.

She spent most of her time in the apartment managing this accumulation, but her mind dwelled on David. They had agreed that he would not come before the wedding because of their time-consuming preparations and because he had his own affairs to put in order. All the same, she expected him to surprise her with a visit. It would be the romantic thing to do, but when he came it would not be for that reason, although he might pretend that it was. She expected him to check that Stephen had not persuaded her to run away or do anything dishonorable. He would want to make sure that his plan had worked.

He did not come. Saturday turned into Sunday and stretched into Monday. She began to get annoyed.

She felt positive that David knew that Stephen had returned. How could he just leave her here to her own devices when another man drifted about who wanted to seduce her? A man, furthermore, with whom she had been in love? Was he that sure of himself? That sure that one night could balance the ledger sheet of a woman's heart? Didn't he worry about what Stephen's presence might be doing to her?

She pondered this sporadically during the days. At night she chewed it over resentfully. But in the dark silence of her curtained bed, her recriminations always managed to flow away as other thoughts of David would flood her like some inexorable incoming tide. Images of his blue eyes and straight shoulders above her. The power of his passion overwhelming his thoughtful restraint. Her breasts would grow sensitive and her thighs moist and the thoughts would merge into wakeful dreams during a fitful sleep.

She awoke each morning feeling as though she had been ravished by a phantom but had found no release.

David did not come, but others did. Singly or in twos or threes, the women of the court approached her.

Aye, Joan had gossiped, and not just about Stephen. It seemed every lady felt obliged to advise the motherless girl who, rumor had it, was unbelievably ignorant about procreation.

Some of the servants joined in. While she bathed on her wedding day, the girl who attended her boldly described how to make a man mad with desire. Christiana blushed from her hairline to her toes. She seriously doubted that noblewomen did most of these things, but she tucked the tamer tidbits away in her mind.

Getting her dressed turned into a merry party with all of her friends there. They gave her presents and chatted as the servants prepared her. Philippa arrived to escort her down to the hall. The Queen examined her closely and reset the red cloak on her shoulders. Then with her daughters beside her, and with Idonia, Joan, and several other women in attendance, Queen Philippa brought her down to the hall.

Morvan awaited them. He wore a formal robe that reached to mid-calf. His knight's belt bound his waist but no sword hung there. "Come now," he said, taking her arm. "The King already awaits."

The doors swung open. She stepped outside.

She froze. "Oh, dear saints," she gasped.

"Quite a sight, isn't it?" Morvan muttered dryly.

The yard was full of horses and people and transport vehicles. She saw Lady Elizabeth entering one of the painted covered wagons, and other feminine arms dangling from its windows. Knights and lords waited on horses decked out for a pageant. King Edward, resplendent in a gold-embroidered red robe, paced his stallion near the doorway. A long line of royal guards stood waiting.

The presence of so many knights and nobles touched her. They came to honor her family and, perhaps, to reassure her. They also came for her brother's sake, and she was grateful.

The extensive royal entourage, and the obvious instructions that everyone should follow the King in parade, were another matter.

The King gestured and three golden chariots drove forward.

"Oh, dear saints," she gasped again, watching this final grandiose touch arrive.

"Aye, one is for you. The Queen herself will ride with you," Morvan explained.

"This retinue will stretch for blocks. All of London will watch this."

"The King honors you, Christiana."

She turned away from Edward's smiling gaze and spoke lowly into her brother's shoulder. "I am not stupid, Morvan. The King does not honor me, he honors London. He does not bring Christiana Fitzwaryn to wed David de Abyndon. He brings a daughter of the nobility to marry a son of the city. He turns me into a gift to London and a symbol of his generosity to her."

He grasped her elbow and eased her forward. "It cannot be undone. You must be our mother's daughter in this and handle it as she would have. I will ride beside you."

She let him guide her to the front chariot and lift her in. She bent and whispered in his ear. "I will think the whole time how I am not the virgin sacrifice they expect."

The parade filed out of the yard, led by the King and his sons. By the time they reached the Strand, thick crowds had formed. Inside the city gates it got worse. The guards used their horses to keep the people back. Slowly, with excruciating visibility, they made their way through to St. Paul's Cathedral.

Morvan lifted her off the chariot. "Well, brother, don't you have anything to say to me?" she asked as they approached the entrance. "No words of advice? No lectures on being a dutiful and obedient wife? There is no father to admonish me, so it falls to you, doesn't it?"

He paused on the porch and glanced through the open portal into the cavernous nave filled with noisy courtiers and curious townspeople.

"Aye, I have words for you, but no lectures." He bent to her ear. "You are a very beautiful girl. There is power for a woman in a man's desire, little sister. Use it well and you will own him and not the other way around."

She laughed. Smiling, he sped her down the nave.

David waited near the altar. Her heart lurched at the sight of him. He looked magnificent, perfect, the equal of any lord in attendance. The narrow cut of his long, belted, blue velvet robe enhanced his height. The fitted sleeves made the exaggerated lengths and widths of the other men's fashions look ridiculous and unmanly. Beautiful gold embroidery decorated the edges and center of the garment. She wondered who had convinced him to agree to that. The heavy gold chain stretched from shoulder to shoulder.

Morvan handed her over. Idonia fluttered by, took her cloak, and disappeared. David gazed down at her while the noise of the crowd echoed off the high stone ceiling.

"You are the most beautiful girl whom I have ever met," he said, repeating the words he had spoken in the ivy garden.

She had a long list of things to upbraid him about, and some deep hurts and misgivings that worried her heart. But the warmth in those blue eyes softened her, and the sound of his beautiful voice soothed her. There would be time enough for worry and hurt. This was her wedding and the whole world watched.

An hour later she emerged from the cathedral with a gold ring around her finger and David de Abyndon's arm around her waist. The chariot awaited but Sieg, looking almost civilized in a handsome gray robe, brought over a horse.

"You will ride with me, darling. With these crowds, those chariots may never make it to the Guildhall."

"You might have warned me about all of this, David," she said as pandemonium spilled into the cathedral yard and surrounding streets. "It was like the prelude to an ancient sacrifice."

"I did not know, but perhaps I should have expected something like this. Edward loves ceremony and pageantry, doesn't he?"

She wasn't convinced. He always seemed to know

everything. She glanced askance at his face as he lifted her onto the saddle and swung up behind. His bland acceptance of Edward's behavior irked her, but then he hadn't been the girl on public display.

"The King must think very highly of you to have brought such an entourage," she remarked dryly.

"I would be a fool to think so. This had nothing to do with you or me."

They joined the flow of mounted knights and lords inching toward the Cheap. David's arm encircled her waist, his hand resting beneath her cloak. She reached up and touched the diamond hanging from a silver chain around her neck. It had been delivered while she dressed. "Thank you for the necklace. It went perfectly with the gown."

"Edmund assured me that it would. I'm pleased that you like it."

"Edmund?"

"The tailor who made your wedding garments, Christiana. And your betrothal gown. And most of your cotehardies and surcoats over the last few years. His name is Edmund. He is one of the leading citizens of the town of Westminster and an important man in his world."

She felt herself blush. She knew the tailor's name. She had simply forgotten it just now. But David was telling her that she should know the people who served her and not think of them as nonentities.

Her chagrin quickly gave way to annoyance. She didn't like it that one of the first things her new husband had said to her had been this oblique scolding.

Other reasons for annoyance marched forward in her mind.

"I thought that you would come to see me," she said.

"We agreed that I would not."

"All the same, I thought that you would come."

She felt him looking at her, but he said nothing.

"He is back at court," she added. "But, of course, you know that, don't you?"

"I know."

That was it. No questions. Nothing else.

"Didn't you wonder what would happen?" she blurted angrily. "Are you that damn sure of yourself?"

"To have come would have insulted you. I assumed that the daughter of Hugh Fitzwaryn had too much pride and honor to leave her marriage bed and go to another man, especially after she had seen the truth about him."

"All the same . . ."

"Christiana," he interrupted quietly, lowering his mouth to her ear and running his lips along its edge, "we will not speak of this now. I did not come because my days were filled making ready for this wedding. In the time I could steal, I settled business affairs so that I could spend the next three days in bed with you. And my nights were spent thinking about what I would do when I had you there."

She would have liked to ignore the shiver of excitement that his lips and words summoned, but her body had been betraying her during the nights too and now it responded against her will.

She forced herself to remember his calculating seduction to claim his property. She resented self-confidence.

"What makes you think that I will choose to spend the next three days that way?" she asked.

"You are my wife now, girl. Surely you know that you only have choices if I give them to you." He pressed his lips to her temple and spoke more gently. "You will find that I am a reasonable master, darling. I have always preferred persuasion to command."

Beneath the full flow of her cloak, he reached up and caressed her breast.

Her body shook with a startling release of pleasure.

She glanced around nervously at the faces turned up to them in smiling curiosity.

He stroked at her nipple and kissed her cheek. She felt the urge to turn and bite his neck. She twisted her head and accepted the deep kiss waiting for her and those wonderful sensations flowed through her like a delicious sigh of relief.

All of London watched.

"David, people . . . they can see . . ." she whispered breathlessly when he lifted his head but did not move his hand. His fingers were driving her mad.

"They cannot. Some might suspect, but none can know for sure," he whispered. "If you are angry with me, you can upbraid me at will after the banquets. I promise to listen very seriously and take all of your criticisms to heart." He kissed her neck again. "Even as I lick your breasts and kiss your thighs, I will be paying close attention to your scolding. We can discuss my bad behavior between your cries of pleasure."

She was already having a very hard time remembering what she wanted to scold or discuss.

At about the point when she felt an unrelenting urge to squirm against the saddle, they arrived at the Guildhall. She worried that she would not be able to stand on her languid legs when he lifted her to the ground.

"That wasn't fair," she hissed.

He took her hand and led her into the Guildhall. "I only play to win, Christiana, and I make my own rules. Haven't you learned that by now?"

CHAPTER 13

DAVID LEANED IN the shadows against the threshold of the hall, watching the dancers whirl around the huge bonfire in the center of the courtyard. Couples romped together in a round dance on the periphery of the circle, but near the center a group of women performed an energetic exhibition alone. Oliver's woman Anne led the group, since she danced professionally on occasion when the opportunity and pay were convenient. Serving girls and women from the ward surrounded her. In the thick of it, her face flushed with delight and her eyes sparkling with pleasure, swung the elegant figure of Christiana Fitzwaryn.

The lights from the bonfire seemed to flame over the women in a rhythm that matched the beating drums. The whole courtyard and house glowed from that huge blaze and from the many torches lining the buildings and the back garden. The fires tinted the night sky orange, and from a distance it probably appeared that the house was burning. No doubt the priests would insist that the scene, with revelers giving themselves over to all of the deadly sins, resembled the inferno of hell itself.

People filled the courtyard, the gardens, and the rooms of the house. Men and woman perched on the roof of the stable. To his left several couples embraced in a dark corner.

A loud laugh caught his attention and he leaned back and glanced into the hall. The milling bodies parted for a moment and he saw the laughing man sitting by the fire with a girl on each knee. The gold embroidery on the red robe was the only proof that this man was a king, for Edward had shed his royal persona as soon as he slipped through the gate with his two guards after sending his wife and family home after the Guildhall banquet. He was well into his cups now, and long ago the party had stopped treating him like the sovereign and simply absorbed him into their merriment.

David returned his attention to his wife. He enjoyed watching her even when she didn't move at all, but her freedom and pleasure in this dance mesmerized him. Like her King, she had quickly succumbed to the unrestrained mood of this second party, and David had delighted in watching her joy as she feasted and drank and traded jests with the neighbors from the ward.

She moved beautifully, languidly, imbuing even this base dance with a noble elegance. Her lips parted in a sensual smile as she twirled around, enjoying at last the ecstasy of movement that she had vicariously felt so often before.

He watched and waited, suppressing the urge to walk to that fire and pick her up and carry her away.

He wanted her. Badly. He had wanted her for weeks, and their night together had only made the wanting more fierce. He had spent the last days in a state of perpetual desire.

Her innocence that day had disarmed him in a dangerous way. Her passion had no defenses, and her total giving and taking had burned down his own. Unlike the experienced women he usually bedded, she knew nothing about protecting herself from the deeper intimacies that could emerge in lovemaking, knew nothing about holding her essence separate from the joining, knew nothing about keeping the act one of simple physical pleasure. She had felt the closeness for what it could be and had simply let the power come and wash over them both. He had seen the wonder of it in her eyes and felt her amazement of it in her grasping embrace and had almost warned her to be careful, for there could be danger and pain in it for her, too. But he had not warned her, for that deep intimacy brought a knowing of her that something inside him craved and in the end he also proved defenseless against the magic that he hadn't felt in so many years.

His gaze followed her, his body responding to the seductive moves of her dance. In his mind's eye she looked up at him and touched his face and his chest and sighed an "aye" that asked for all of himself.

A figure strolled in front of him, mercifully distracting his heated thoughts. Morvan drank some wine as he walked, casually surveying the dancers.

The drums and timbrels beat out a frenzied finale and then the dance ended abruptly. All around the fire, bodies stopped and heaved deep breaths from their exertions. Christiana and Anne embraced with a laugh.

She thought that Anne was Oliver's wife. He would have to tell her the truth, he supposed.

Morvan caught Christiana's eye and gestured for her. She skipped over to him with a broad smile. He bent and said something, and David watched the happiness and pleasure fall from her face and her body like someone had stripped it off.

She threw her arms around him and spoke earnestly, entreating him no doubt to stay longer. Morvan shook his head, caressed her face, and pulled away.

He walked toward the gate. Christiana gazed after him, her straight body suddenly alone and isolated despite the crowd milling around her. David could see her composed expression but he had no trouble reading the sadness in her.

Her whole life, her whole family, her whole past was leaving the house now.

He pushed away from the threshold and went to her. He draped her cloak over her shoulders, and she glanced up with a weak smile before her gaze returned to the retreating tall man.

He smiled and shook his head. He strode after Morvan, calling his name. A part of him couldn't believe that he was going to do this for her.

The young knight stopped and turned. He came back and met David partway. They faced each other in the fire glow.

"You are leaving, Morvan?"

"Aye. It is best if I go now." He glanced at his sister.

"You must come and visit her soon. She will want to see you."

Morvan looked over in surprise.

"Her life will be much changed and it may be hard on her," David continued. "I would not have her unhappy. Come when you will. This house is always open to you."

Morvan looked more surprised yet. He nodded and smiled a little. "I thank you for that, David. For both our sakes."

David walked back to Christiana. The cloak was falling off and he wrapped her in it more warmly, embracing her shoulder.

"What did you say to him?" she asked, her gaze still on her brother.

"I told him that he must visit you whenever he wants."

"Did you, David? Did you really?" She turned to him with a bright smile. Her unaffected surprise and gratitude wrenched something inside him.

"I know that he is all that you have, darling. He only sought to protect you, and I can blame no man for that. I would not stand between you."

She nestled closer to him and looked into his eyes with an almost childish innocence. "Not all that I have, David. Not anymore. There is you now, isn't there? We have each other, don't we?"

He embraced her and she placed her head on his chest, her face turned to the shadows that swallowed her brother's tall body. David laid his face on the silky cloud of her hair.

All that she was, all that she was supposed to be, left through that gate. The life she had led and had been born to live, the position assured her by her blood, returned to Westminster tonight without her. He didn't doubt that she understood that. She knew what this marriage had taken from her.

He kissed her hair and closed his eyes. He could give it back to her. All that she was losing and more. It was in his power to do so. The offer still stood and would be made again, of that he was sure. He had only to play out the game as planned but change the final move. He knew exactly how to do it. He had been considering the possibility for weeks.

As if reading his thoughts, she tilted her head and looked up at him. "You are very good to me, David. I know that you will take care of me and do all that you can for me."

He bent to kiss her and her parted lips rose to meet

his. A tremor shook her and she pressed herself against him as she embraced him tightly. His mind clouded and the restraint of the last hours cracked.

She grasped him as desperately as he did her, her mouth inviting his deep kiss. Perhaps it was the wine and the dance. Maybe it was her gratitude over Morvan. He didn't care. He would accept her passion any way that it came to him.

They stood thus at the edge of the fire glow, two bodies molded together, banishing the separateness, the sounds of revelry echoing around them. He kissed her again and again, wanting to consume her and absorb her into himself.

He found the sanity to pull his mouth away. "Come upstairs with me now," he whispered, his face buried in her neck, her scent driving him mad.

"Aye," she said. "Now."

He turned her under his arm while he kissed her again. Somehow he found his way blindly across the courtyard, into the building, and up the stairs. A group of revelers discreetly poured out of the solar when they arrived, and he kicked the door closed behind them.

In his chamber he threw off their cloaks and fell on the bed with her, covering her with his body, feeling her pliant length bend up into him. His head emptied to everything but the feel and smell of her. He tried to check himself, tried to calm the thundering storm that controlled him, but the deep, probing kiss he gave her turned fierce and needful when she took his head between her hands and pressed him closer.

He managed to remove her surcoat without tearing it, but the cotehardie's lacing defied his practiced fingers. He plucked at the knot as he kissed and bit the tops of her breasts. Finally, in a fury of frustration, he moved aside, turned her on her stomach, and stared at the recalcitrant closure.

"Hold still," he muttered, pulling out his dining dagger and blinking away the obscuring passion. He rose on his knees and slid the blade under the lacings. "It is an old wedding trick. Your servants tied a knot that cannot be undone."

She laughed beautifully, lyrically, and then turned on her back, joyfully helping him push down the gown. When it was gone, she got to her knees and flew to him as if the separation had lasted an eternity.

He lost himself then. In a frantic whirlwind of caresses and kisses, they managed to pull off his clothes. With cries and gasps and little ecstatic laughs, her hands met his on his belt and shirt and finally poured heatedly over his skin. He pushed her shift down from her shoulders, uncovering her breasts, and bent her back so that he could revel in their sweet softness.

Her cries undid him and unraveled his last thread of control. He pushed the shift up her hips and felt for the moisture of her arousal.

"I promise that I will give you slow pleasure later," he said as he laid her down. "All night if you want. But right now I cannot wait, darling."

He spread her legs and knelt between them. She looked up at him, her dark eyes full of stars.

He gazed at her lovely face and her round white breasts. The shift bunched at her waist and the hose were still gartered at her knees. He pushed the bottom of the shift up higher, exposing her hips and stomach. He touched the pulsing, swollen flesh between her thighs and watched the pleasure quake through her.

The fantasies of his desire pressed on him relentlessly. Despite her ignorance and his need, he could not resist them all. He bent her legs so that she was raised and open to him. Her ragged breathing broke through his fog, and he glanced and saw the flicker of wariness and surprise in her eyes.

"Do not be afraid," he said as he lifted her hips. "I want to kiss all of you. That is all."

He knew that he could not indulge himself thus for long. His own body would not let him. Nor, it turned out, would hers. She writhed and cried out from the shock and intensity of this new pleasure, and soon he felt the first flexes of her release.

He left her and came up over her, bringing her legs with him, settling them on his shoulders. She thrashed in frustration that he had brought her to the edge of the precipice but no further.

"Soon, darling. I promise. When we are together," he said soothingly, and he rose up and entered her with one thrust.

His whole body shook from the torturous pleasure of it, but the tremor itself gave him back some of his control. Extending his arms, he stroked into her, his consciousness filling with the exquisite sensation that came from tottering on the edge of his own release.

She watched him as he moved, her hands caressing his shoulders and chest in that open, accepting way of hers, her sparkling eyes and soft sighs telling him that he filled other needs besides those of her body. The emotions seeped out of her and around him and embraced them both as surely as their arms had entwined moments ago.

He felt her tensing, stretching, for her climax. His own control began crumbling. He reached down between their bodies to give her release. As the frenzy possessed her she grabbed fiercely for him, arching her hips up against his thrusts, pulling him with her into the delicious oblivion.

He rarely sought a mutual release. In fact he avoided

them. Now, as their passion peaked and shattered together, he felt her ecstasy even as his own split through him. For an unearthly instant the lightning of the storm melted them into one sharing completeness.

When they were done, he stayed with her, kissing her softly while he moved her legs down, letting himself enjoy the glorious expression on her beautiful face. He rolled over to his back, bringing her with him so that she lay on him. He held her there, her head on his chest and her knees straddling his hips, and watched his hand caress her pale back and hips.

After a long while she lifted her head and cocked it thoughtfully. "I hear lutes," she said.

"You flatter me."

She giggled and thumped his shoulder playfully. "Nay, David. I really do. Listen."

He focused his awareness and heard the lyrical tones amidst the distant noise of the party. He moved her off, got out of bed, and disappeared into the wardrobe.

Christiana waited, still floating in the wonder and magic of their passion. It seemed that the lutes got louder.

He returned and pulled the coverlet off the bed. "They are for you. You should acknowledge them." He draped the warm cover over his shoulders, and she got up and joined him in its cozy cocoon.

The door to the stairs leading to the ivy garden was open, and they went out on the stone landing. David lifted her up and sat her on the low surrounding wall, tucking the coverlet securely around her legs.

Below in the tiny garden she could see four men with lutes. They sang the poetic lines of a love song. She recognized the deep bass of Walter Manny.

"Who are the others?" she whispered.

"They are all from the Pui. It is a tradition when one of them marries."

They began another song. Torches lit the larger garden, but here the singers were only dark forms in the shadows. Above them the clear night sky glittered with a hundred stars. David stood beside her, holding her under their cover, nuzzling her hair. There was something incredibly romantic about being with him in the cold night with the intimacy of their joining still hanging on them while the music played.

Walter sang the next song alone. It possessed a slow, quiet melody that she had heard only once before. It was the song that David had sung that day in the hall, the one she had found so sad at the time. Now she realized that it wasn't sad at all, just soft and beautiful. It had sent her off thinking of Stephen that day, and she hadn't really noticed the words, but this time she listened carefully.

It wasn't really a love song, but more a song that praised a woman and her beauty. The words spoke of elegant limbs and noble bearing. Her hair was described as black as the velvet night, her skin pale as moonlight, and her eyes like the diamonds of the stars. . . .

She grew very still. She listened to the rest of the lovely song that described her. David had written this. He had played it in the hall for her that day, and she hadn't even heard it.

Walter's voice and lute closed the melody. She looked up at the shadow of the man beside her. Her heart glowed warm and proud that he had honored her in this way, so long ago, even as she treated him so badly.

"Thank you," she whispered, stretching up to kiss his face.

They listened to several more songs, and then the four musicians walked forward and bowed to her. "Thank you, Walter," she called quietly.

"My lady," he replied, and the shadows swallowed him.

"What a marvelous tradition," she said to David as they returned to their bed. "Have you done that?"

"Aye, I've spent my share of cold winter nights in gardens singing to new brides. We stay until she acknowledges that she has heard us. On occasion the groom is so enraptured in bed that it takes hours. We give him hell afterwards then."

She laughed and rested her head on his shoulder.

"It was a wonderful wedding, David." A din still leaked through the windows from the continued revelry outside and below. "I had so much fun. Anne says that I dance very well for an amateur. She said that she will teach me more if I want."

"If it pleases you, you should do it."

"I like her. I like Oliver, too. He is an old friend?"

"From when we were boys."

"Have they been married a long time?"

A peculiar expression passed over his face. He looked so handsome now, his golden brown hair falling over his forehead, his deep blue eyes regarding her.

"Christiana, Oliver sells women. Anne lives with him but is not his wife. She is one of his women."

"You mean she is his whore? Anne is a whore? She does this with strangers, for pay? He lets her, and even brings the men to her?"

"Aye."

"How can he? He seemed to care for her, David. How . . ."

"In truth, I do not know."

She pictured Anne, with her pretty brown curls and sweet but worldly face. "It must be horrible for her."

"I suspect that most of her isn't really there with them."

Could people do that? Join like this and not even care about it, not feel anything? Or just take the pleasure and close their eyes to the person giving it? It struck her as a sad and frightening thought.

She turned her head and gazed up at the billowing canopy of blue cloth above them, feeling sorry for Anne and not much liking Oliver for expecting such things of her. They were poor, true, but surely there must be some other way.

And yet, she had to admit that this lovemaking obviously happened in all kinds of ways and for all kinds of reasons. In fact, she suspected that often love had nothing to do with it at all, especially for men. After all, the desire that she and David shared was mostly physical, wasn't it? For him, that was all that it was. And other women had been here, where she was now, experiencing the same thing. He had wanted them and now he wanted her. Whom would he want next?

The magic and wonder suddenly seemed a lot less special.

Did it last long, this desire? Perhaps if a man paid a thousand pounds for a woman, he felt obligated to desire her for a long time. But when the desire faded, what would be left for her? A home and maybe children. Not small things, but she wanted more.

The admission startled her and she didn't understand the feelings that it revealed. She realized, however, that there could be danger in this bed with this man, and the chance of disappointments far worse than she had known with Stephen Percy.

A strange emptiness opened inside her. It felt like a desolate loneliness, despite the man who held her. She had been having a wonderful time these last hours, laughing and dancing and being overwhelmed by their mutual passion. Nestling with him outside while the love songs played had been so romantic. She bleakly realized that she had been foolishly building another illusion, another dream.

She felt him shift and then those blue eyes were above her, studying her.

"What are you thinking about?" he asked.

Don't you know? she wanted to say. *You always know.*

She met his gaze and realized that he did know. At least part of it.

"I am thinking that there is more to all of this than I understand." She made a little gesture that covered the bed. "You must find me very childish and ignorant compared to the other women whom you have known."

Beautiful women. Worldly women. Experienced women. She could never compete with them. She didn't even know how. Why in God's name had he married her?

His hand caressed her cheek and turned her face to his. "I am most pleased with you, Christiana."

She felt a little better then, but not much.

"Alicia was your lover, wasn't she?" she blurted.

"Aye. But it is over."

"There were others, too, others whom I know and who know me," she said blankly.

He just looked at her.

"Elizabeth?" she asked, thinking of that exquisitely lovely woman and feeling a spike of infuriating jealousy. No one could ever compete with Elizabeth.

"Elizabeth is an old friend, but we were never lovers."

Protective indignation instantly replaced the jealousy. "Why not! You are better than most of the men she has been linked with. And that lord she married is old and ugly."

He laughed. "Now you are angry with her because we didn't sleep together? Nay, there was no insult in it. Elizabeth likes her lovers very young."

"You are young."

"Not young enough. She likes them still partly unformed. She wants to influence them."

"Young like Morvan?"

"Aye."

She thought about that, and those months when Morvan had attended on Elizabeth. A long time for him. Worrying about her brother relieved her of the worries about herself.

"Do you know about the two of them, and what happened? Some at court thought that they would marry, but then it just ended. Morvan would never speak to me about it."

He looked down at the pillow for a moment and she could tell that he did know.

"Oh, please, David, tell me," she cajoled. "He is my brother, after all. I am very discreet, you know. I am the only female at court who didn't gossip."

"A rare virtue that I should not corrupt."

"I always *listened*. I just never repeated what I heard," she said.

"Elizabeth didn't marry your brother because he never asked her to. Also, she loved him and he didn't love her. Not the way she wanted. Elizabeth would never bind herself to such an uneven love. Then there is the fact that she is barren. She has known it since girlhood. It is why only old men offer for her. They already have their heirs. One day your brother will be lord of Harclow again and he will want a son."

"Nay, David, I do not think he ever will be. The King swore to see it happen, but he has forgotten."

"Men do not forget the oaths that they swear."

She wondered what else David knew about the people with whom she had spent her life. Perhaps, if she proved very discreet, he would tell her sometime. This felt very pleasant and cozy, talking like this in the warmth of the bed. When he was up and walking about, he still remained a mystery to her, but the intimacy here temporarily banished that.

"I was surprised that the King came here this evening," she said, wondering how far she could push the mood.

"Even kings like to have some fun. Being regal can get tedious, and Edward is still a young man. He isn't much older than I am."

"He seems to know you well."

"We are of similar age, and he is more comfortable with me than with the city officials who are very formal with him. And I have done some favors for him. He sends me on errands. To Flanders mostly. I carried letters to the governor of Ghent on several trips."

"Do you still do this? These errands?"

"Aye. Some of the trips that I take are for Edward."

That was that. She smiled at her foolish hesitation. She should have just asked earlier. It all made perfect and innocent sense. Still . . .

"Are they ever dangerous? These trips?"

"They haven't been."

That wasn't the same as saying that they weren't. She decided to leave it, however.

She snuggled closer, enjoying the feel of his arm around her. She thought about some of the people she had met at the Guildhall banquet. In particular, she remembered the thin-lipped, gray-haired Gilbert de Abyndon, who had tried to ignore David's presence even while David introduced her.

"I liked Margaret, Gilbert's wife. I think that she and I could be friends. Do you think that he would permit that?"

Actually, she wanted to know if David would permit

it. Margaret was not much older than herself, and a friendly blond-haired woman. They had enjoyed their brief meeting and chat, even if their two husbands had stood there like frozen sentinels.

"Most likely. Gilbert is very ambitious. He will overlook your marriage to me because of your nobility and connections at court. Like most of the wealthier merchants, he wants to lift his family into the gentry."

"Still, he may object to her visiting me. It is clear that you and he hate each other very much."

Her comment was met with a long silence. She turned and found him gazing at the blue canopy much as she had done earlier. He glanced at her with a glint in his eyes. Had simply mentioning this uncle angered him? He kissed her hair as if to reassure her.

"I hate him for what he did to my mother, and he hates me because I am alive and use the Abyndon name. He is the worst of our breed, my girl. Judgmental and unbending. He is full of self-righteousness and attends church each morning before he spends his day damning people. If he had been at this house today, he would have seen nothing of the joy and pleasure but only sin and weakness. If you are going to befriend Margaret, you should know this, because that is the man she is tied to. Hopefully, for her sake, her old husband will die soon."

She blinked at his last words. Wishing someone dead was a dreadful thing. The dispassionate way he said it stunned her even more.

"We need to find a servant to help you with your clothes and such," he added. "Geva said that you would want to choose the girl yourself. In a few days, go and visit Margaret and ask for her help in this. See if Gilbert permits it."

He stroked her hair and her shoulder and she stretched against him as the tingling warmth of his caress awoke her skin. She suspected that he wanted to make love again. She waited for him to start, and was surprised when he began speaking, his quiet voice flowing into her ear.

"My uncles Gilbert and Stephen were already in their twenties when my mother was still a girl. Old enough, when she turned fourteen, to know what they had in her. She was beautiful. Perfect. Even when she died, despite everything, she was still beautiful. Her brothers saw her marriage for the opportunity it was. They had it all planned. A nobleman for her. Second choice, a merchant with the Hanseatic League. Third, a husband from the gentry. They settled a fat dowry on her and began pushing her in front of such men. Every banquet, they brought her with them, dressed like a lady."

"And did it work?"

"Aye, it worked. John Constantyn has told me what she did not. The offers poured in. Gilbert and Stephen debated the marriage that would be best for them, of course, and not her. They became too clever and played one man off against the other."

"Did she refuse their choice? Is that why . . ."

"Worse than that, as my body beside you proves. They had not been careful enough with her. Their parents were dead, and the servants who supervised her indulged her. She fell in love. The man was gone by the time she found herself with child."

"Was it one of her suitors?"

"Apparently not. Still, her brothers sought to solve the disaster in the usual ways. They demanded to know his name so they could force a marriage, but she would not give it to them. Gilbert tried to beat it out of her, and still she would not say. And so they found another husband who would accept her under those circumstances and sought to have a quick wedding."

Christiana grimaced inwardly. She remembered that first night in David's solar, and him asking if she was with child. He had thought that it was the same story, and that he was the other man whose quick wedding would cover up a girl's mistake.

"She would not have him," he continued. "She was certain that her lover would return for her. She went to the priest and declared that she was unwilling."

Braver than me, Christiana thought. *My God, what must have been running through David's mind that night as he faced me so impassively in front of the fire?*

"What did they do?"

"They sent her away. There are some relatives in Hastings and she went there. Gilbert told her to give up the child when it was born. If she did not, all of their support of her would cease and she would be as if dead to them. Under no circumstances was she to return to London."

"But she kept you. And she came back."

"She was sure that her lover would come, and she knew that he would not know where to find her if she wasn't here. And so she returned quickly. Somehow she found Meg and began working with the laundresses. Meg served as midwife when I was born. Those early years, we lived in a small chamber behind a stable near the river. Besides Meg and the other workers, I was my mother's only companion. Gilbert and Stephen never saw her, and true to their threat, did not so much as give her a shilling. She could have starved for all they knew or cared."

"And you? Did you know who she was and who they were?"

"Not until I was about seven. And then I would hear

of these men with my mother's name and I began to figure some of it out. Stephen began rising in city politics
then. And I knew by then that I was a bastard. The other
boys made sure I knew that. Several years later she became
David Constantyn's housekeeper and things got better for
her, although Gilbert and Stephen never forgave him for
helping her. In their minds she deserved all that had happened to her. Her misery was the price of her sin against
God and them. Mostly them."

He had told this story simply and evenly, as was his
way. But she sensed that many other thoughts were tied to
this tale, and that some of them concerned herself.

She remembered the drawing of this woman's face
which she had seen, and looking at his perfect bones now,
she could see his mother in him. But another face had
contributed to these planes and deep eyes. An unknown
face.

"What was her name? Your mother's name?"

"Joanna."

"And your father? Do you know him?"

"The only father I ever knew was my master. The first
time I saw him, he scolded me for stealing one of his
apples. He came out of the ivy garden as I sat beneath the
tree eating it while my mother helped with the laundry in
the courtyard. I talked fast and hard to get out of a beating, I'll tell you that. He gave me a good wallop anyway
and dragged me back to my mother. A few weeks later he
showed up while we were here and took me into the city
to see a thief hang. On the way back he told me that there
were two ways for clever men to get rich. One was
through stealing and the other was through trade, but that
the thieves lived shorter lives. By age eight I had done my
share of stealing, and the lesson was not lost on me."

She pictured the urchins whom she sometimes saw on
the city streets sidling up to carts and windows, running

off with food and goods. She imagined a little David amongst them. Never getting caught, of course.

"He offered to marry her, I think," he added thoughtfully. "I remember coming upon them one day when I was about twelve. They were sitting in the hall. Something important was being discussed, I could tell. I sensed what it was."

"She refused him, you think?"

"Aye. I assumed then that he offered because he wanted me. We had become close by then, much like father and son. We even shared a name. She had chosen mine from the Bible, but it is an unusual name in England and I knew from the start that it fascinated him that I had it. Even her position here— I thought he had accepted the mother to get the son. But I think now that maybe it was the other way around."

"Did she refuse him because of the other man, your real father?"

"Aye. Her heart waited long after her mind gave up. I despised her for that when I was a youth, but by the time she died I understood a little."

She thought of David's patient understanding during their betrothal, but also of his cruel, relentless prods about Stephen.

You still wait for him, after all of this time and when the truth is so clear. It is well that Edward gave you to me. You would have spent your whole life waiting, living in some faded dream.

In not repudiating her, he had taken a horrible, painful chance.

She pressed herself against the warm comfort of his body, feeling the texture of his skin against her length. It touched her that he had told her about Joanna and his early life. Little by little, in ways like this, perhaps he would cease to be a stranger to her. She also knew that it was not in his nature to make such confidences and that only the intimacy of their marriage and passion had permitted it.

Without thinking, she rubbed her face against his chest and then turned and kissed it. She tasted the skin and kissed again. Her desire to give and take comfort and revel in their new closeness changed to something else as she kissed him, and impulsively she turned her head and gently licked his nipple. He touched her head and held it, encouraging her. A languid sensuality spread through her, and she felt the change in him, too. Only then did she remember that this was one of the things that the servant girl had told her about during her bath this morning.

He let her lips and tongue caress him a while longer, and then gently turned her on her back.

"I think that I promised you slow pleasure," he said. "Let us see how slow we can make it."

Much later, for David could make the pleasure very slow when he chose to, they lay together on the darkened bed, the curtains pulled against the dimming sounds and lights from the wedding party. Christiana began drifting into sleep in his arms.

She felt him move, and sensed him looking at her nearly invisible profile.

"Did you speak with him?" he asked quietly.

She had forgotten about that. Had forgotten about Stephen Percy and her anger and hurt with David. This day and night had obscured her suspicions about his motivations with her, and she really wished now that he hadn't reminded her.

He lives with realities, she thought. *You are the one who constructs dreams and songs.* But he had written that song about her, hadn't he? Not a love song, though. He thought her beautiful and had written about it. Perhaps he composes such melodies about sunsets and forest glens too.

"Aye, I spoke with him."

"What did he want?"

"Nothing honorable."

He was silent awhile.

"I do not want you seeing him," he finally said.

"He is at court often. Are you saying that I cannot go back to Westminster again?"

"I do not mean that. You know what I am saying."

"It is over, David. Like you and Alicia. It is the same."

"It is not. I never loved Alicia."

She turned her head to his. He had opened this door and she felt a compulsion to walk through it now.

"You never planned to let me go with him, did you?"

"I did not lie when I said it, but I was sure it would not come up."

"And if it had?"

His fingers touched her face in the darkness. "I would not have let you go. Early on I knew it."

Why? Your pride? Your investment? To save me from your mother's fate? She could not ask the question. She did not want to know the true answer. A girl should be allowed some illusions and ambiguities if she had to live with a man. There was such a thing as too much reality.

"How did you know that I would come that day?"

"I did not expect it. I planned to go and get you."

"And if I wouldn't come and agree to your seduction?"

"I would not have given you much choice."

She thought about that.

"You were very clever, David, I will grant you that. Very careful. Lots of witnesses. Your whole household. Idonia. How thorough were you? Did you even save the sheets? Did you leave them on the bed until Geva had seen them the next day?" Her tone came out more petulantly than she felt.

He kissed her temple and pulled her into the curve of his body. "The first time I met you and every time after you told me that you loved him, Christiana. Up until last Wednesday itself. Despite what happened between us when I kissed you, despite his misuse of you. Aye, darling, I was thorough. And calculating and clever. I deliberately made this marriage a fact and bound you to me. I took no chances that he might tell the lies that your heart wanted to hear so that he could misuse you again. Would you have had me do otherwise? Should I have stood back from this knight like the merchant I am? Would honoring my promise to let you go have pleased you?"

She trembled a little at the blunt force of his words. It sounded very different when he put it that way, when she saw it through his eyes. It had been so easy to forget how she had been before last Wednesday.

"Nay," she whispered, and it was true. She would not have been pleased at all if he had proven indifferent and had simply let Stephen lure her away. Another reaction that she feared to examine too closely.

The silence descended again, and after a time she relaxed in his embrace. Sleep had almost claimed her when she heard him laugh quietly in her ear.

"Aye, my girl, I was thorough and took no chances. I saved the sheets."

CHAPTER 14

DAVID WAS DROWSILY aware of the curtains being pushed back. He turned his face away from the flooding light.

"Hell," a man's voice said, pulling him awake.

He opened one eye a slit. Unless he was still dreaming, his wife was gone and the King of England stood beside his bed.

"Damnation, David."

Not dreaming.

"My lord?" He rose up on his elbows.

The King stared down with a frown. "Will you be wanting to repudiate her? Philippa assured me the girl was whole, I swear. I told her we should have her examined, but she and Idonia . . ."

David looked to where the King gazed. The coverlet and sheets were bunched over to reveal a bloodless marriage bed.

Hell. The last thing he had expected was someone

looking for evidence of Christiana's virginity. What was Edward doing here, anyway?

"Do not let it concern you, my lord. There will be no repudiation."

Edward's frown relaxed. "Damn chivalrous of you, David."

"I am a merchant and we are apart from chivalry. That is reserved for your knights. I assure you that my wife came to me a virgin, though. If I had thought that someone would seek the evidence this morning, I would have bled a chicken."

Edward looked at him blankly.

The man was still half besotted. David noted the red robe. The King had been here all night. Where and with whom? David decided that he didn't want to know.

"Do you need to see the original sheets? I have them," he offered with a laugh, but as soon as he said it he realized that Edward's mind had moved on.

"I want to speak with you. It will save you a ride to Westminster."

David glanced around the bed. Christiana's and his clothes were still strewn around the posts and floor. "Perhaps in the solar?"

Edward nodded and drifted off.

David grabbed a robe off a peg in the wardrobe, threw it on, and followed. Edward stood by the solar windows with a speculative, hooded expression on his face. David joined him and glanced down at the courtyard. A red-haired serving woman from a nearby house lounged against the well, surrounded by the litter of the night's revelry.

Edward sighed. "I suppose I have to give her something, eh? Hell, I can't even remember." He patted his robe for evidence of a purse or coins.

"She is not a whore," David said. "Wait one moment."

He went back to the wardrobe and returned with a purple silk veil embroidered with gold thread.

Edward examined it. "Awfully nice, David. Don't you have something plainer? I don't even know if I enjoyed myself. This would be good for Philippa, though. Peace offering . . ."

David went to the wardrobe once again and fetched a blue veil with no embroidery.

"What, do you keep a whole box of them to give to your women?" the King teased as he stuffed them in his robe. "Best hide them from your wife. See my wardrobe treasurer about them."

David pictured himself arriving at Westminster without a debenture or tally to claim payment for two veils purchased by the King for his slut and his neglected wife.

"Consider them gifts," he said dryly. "You wanted to speak with me about something?"

"Aye. The council met two days ago. It was decided to embark right after Easter. I'll summon the barons shortly."

David waited patiently for the rest of it.

"We received word that Grossmont engaged with the French and has secured Gascony," the King continued.

David nodded. Gascony, below England's Aquitaine on the west coast of the continent, was territory held by Edward in fief to the French king. Among the many points of contention between the two monarchs had been the degree of control which France wanted to exert there. Henry Grossmont had been sent to stabilize the area.

"Furthermore, he has pushed as far north as Poitiers," Edward said. "The port of Bordeaux is secure now. We will go in that way, join with him, and head northeast. I'll not be needing that last bit of information from you after all."

"Poitiers is a long way from Paris. The spring rains will make movement difficult."

"The council considered all of that. Still, our army and Grossmont's will be a formidable force. And debarking at Bordeaux will be riskless."

Presumably the council of barons knew what they were doing. They were experienced soldiers. But it struck him as a fruitless strategy.

Edward watched him with an amused expression. "You do not approve. Speak your mind."

He knew that a merchant's mind was irrelevant, but he spoke it anyway. "Bordeaux is a seven-day sea voyage. A long way to take an army by boat, and you risk bad winds. The French already await you at Poitiers. Even with a decisive victory you will be a long way from Paris. If the French crown is your goal, you must take that city and the royal demesne, must you not?"

"I will have twenty thousand with me," Edward replied jovially. "We will cut through France like a hot blade through butter."

Like all armies paid with spoils, yours will slog through France like a feather through cream, David silently replied.

"Those weapons you offered me," Edward mused. "Where are they?"

"Nowhere near Poitiers. I have one here, outside the city. If you have room on one of your ships, it is yours. Send me some men and I will train them in its use."

"Ah well, one toy is probably enough. I will need the maps that you have been making of that region. Do you have them ready? We will want to know all of the possible routes and the best roads. Especially where to cross the Loire river during spring floods."

"They are in my study." The King followed him through the door by the hearth into the small chamber.

He took some rolled parchments off the shelf and placed them on the table. "This one is of the north. This other is Brittany, from Brest to the marches of Normandy. The large one shows the routes out from Bordeaux." He unrolled the largest parchment. "Remember that I was there in November, and the marked river crossings are based on conversations that I had with the people in the area, and not on what I saw for myself. The conditions of the roads were obvious even in late autumn, however." He pointed to one line. "This road is fairly direct for your purposes and lies on high ground, so it should be in better condition than the main one. It passes through farmland, and there are few towns along it." Few opportunities for looting. The barons would press for the muddy low road so that they could pay their retinues.

Edward admired the drawing. "You have a knack for this sort of thing. I told the council that you would do the job and none would be the wiser."

"Do you want them all?"

"You can bring the others later. This one I will take now. We are itching to begin our plans." He took the parchment and tucked it under his arm. "A clever idea, to have you map out three possibilities. I know your own mind on this, but it will be Bordeaux."

Aye, David thought. *The army will land and engage. Battles will be fought and towns besieged, and knights and soldiers will grow rich from the looting. And after a summer of fighting, you will come back and nothing will have been resolved. Until you take Paris, this will never end.*

What this decision meant to him and his own plans was another matter, and one that he would consider carefully later.

A sound behind made them both turn. Christiana

stood at the threshold to the bedchamber with a startled expression on her face. She carried a tray with food and ale.

"My lord," she said, stepping in quickly and placing the tray on the table. "My apologies."

They watched her go.

"Do you think that she heard?" Edward asked, frowning.

"If so, she will say nothing." It really didn't matter. One could hardly sail hundreds of ships down the coast of Brittany and France and not be noticed. There would be little surprise when this invasion finally happened.

Was it over? He smiled at his King, but already his mind began recalculating.

On the fourth morning after their wedding, David told Christiana that they would ride north of the city a ways.

"I recently acquired a property in Hampstead," he explained as they headed out the city gate side by side. "We will go there so that you can see it. I have to speak with some workers, and there are other matters to attend."

"Is it a farm?"

"There are farms attached to it, but it is the house that you should see."

"Many farms?"

"Ten, as I remember."

"Aren't you afraid that the income will put you over the forty-pound limit? That Edward will force knighthood on you?" she teased.

"Aye. That is why I put the property in your name."

"My name!"

"Yours. It belongs to you, as do the farms' rents."

She absorbed this startling news. Married women

almost never owned their own property. It went with them to their husbands. The only woman she knew who owned land outright was Lady Elizabeth. Joan had told her that Elizabeth always demanded property in her name as part of her marriage settlements to those old men.

"The dowry manor that Edward settled on you is yours as well, Christiana."

"Why, David?"

"I want you to know that you are secure, and without land you never will feel thus. I am comfortable with wealth based on credits and coin, but you never will be. Also, I take risks in my trade, sometimes big ones. I want to know that should my judgment fail, you will not suffer."

It made a certain sense, but still it astonished her.

"There is something that you should know about this house," he said later as they turned off the road onto a lane. "It came to me through moneylending. You should also know that it was owned by Lady Catherine. If you do not like that, you can sell it and purchase elsewhere. Near London, though. I want you to have someplace to go when the summer illnesses spread in the city."

The twinge of guilt that she felt at this news disappeared as soon as she saw the house. Wide and tall, its base built of stone and its upper level of timber and plaster, it sat beautifully inside a stone wall at the end of the lane, surrounded by outbuildings and gardens. A bank of glazed windows on the second level indicated its recent construction.

Workers were laying tiles on the hall floor when they entered, and David went over to speak with them. She explored the other chambers. Very little furniture had been left, and the building echoed with their footsteps. David explained that he would leave furnishing the house to her.

"We need to ride out onto the property," he said as they reclaimed their horses. "There are some men awaiting me."

The men worked half a mile away on an open field. Three of them stood around a big metal cylinder, narrower at the top than the bottom, propped and angled up on logs. A bulky man with black hair explained something to the others as they approached.

"What is that?" she asked.

"A toy. You will see how it works."

He tied the horses to a tree and walked over to the men. She wrapped her cloak more tightly around her and sat down on the dried grass near a small fire that had been built. David and the others fiddled and fussed with the toy a long time, and the black-haired man kept crouching behind the low end of the cylinder and spying along its length. Her eyes followed the man's line of sight, and in the distance she saw an old wooden building.

David poured some sand in it from a leather bag and stuck a stick down after it. He lifted a large stone from in front of it. A mason had clearly worked it, for the stone was perfectly round. He rolled the stone into the cylinder.

He came over to the fire and lifted a flaming torch.

"Cover your ears," he said. He lit a line of the sand snaking along the lower end of the toy.

A moment later the loudest clap of thunder that she had ever heard cracked the winter silence. Smoke spewed out of the cylinder and it jumped back. Across the deep field, a few seconds after the toy was fired, the farm building's roof burst into pieces.

She jumped up and crossed over to the smoking cylinder. The black-haired man drew the other two aside and began to explain something that sounded a lot like geometry.

"What is this?" she asked, peering into the hot hollow.

"The future. It is called a gonne."

She walked along its length, and noted the stack of round stones nearby. "It is a siege machine, isn't it?"

"Aye, that it is."

She knew more than she wanted about siege machines. As a child she had watched the towers and catapults built outside Harclow. She had seen the horrible damage that they wrought and had lived in fear of those flying missiles and baskets of fire. She looked at the farm building. Only the shells of its side walls remained. It had been old, and built of wood, but this toy possessed more force in hurling its small stones than any of the machines which she had seen at Harclow.

"Do you plan to make and sell these?"

"Nay. But they will be made by others. It is inevitable. I first saw them on my way home on my first trip. There was a demonstration near Pisa. They didn't work well, and never hit their mark then, but already they improve. They fascinate me, that is all. This one is for Edward. Other kings will have them, so he must." He walked toward the horses. "I am going to check the building. You can come if you want to."

She wasn't at all sure that she wanted to, but she went nonetheless.

She gazed at the tatters of the building. No wonder David did not want to be a knight. Of what use were armor and shields against war machines like this?

There were other buildings nearby, all neglected. This had once been a horse farm with many stables.

"I should tell you that this section of the property is not yours," he explained as he dismounted.

She saw no signs of labor here. It appeared that David had kept the poorest portion for himself. "You need a field with old buildings to play with your toys?"

"Aye. And to collect that which makes them work." He led the way into one of the stables.

The roof of this structure was in disrepair, and splotches of sunlight leaked through its holes. David went into one of the stalls and crouched down. He wiped his fingers across the dried dirt and lifted his hand. A sandy substance glittered.

"It is found in stables like this that have been used a long time, and other places where animals live. The powder that makes the machine work requires it. It is said that the secret was brought back overland from Cathay in the Far East. It has no English name, although some translate it to saltpeter."

"Are those men back there from the King?"

"Two are. The other brought the machine from Italy."

"Will Edward use it? Will he take it with him to France? To Bordeaux?"

He did not answer her. They remounted and rode back to the men who had already prepared the machine again. David spoke in Italian to the black-haired one and then led her away.

"I know that you overheard Edward in my study, Christiana," he finally said. "You know, I'm sure, that you cannot repeat such things. Even when everyone else suspects and talks of it, you should pretend ignorance."

It was true, then. She had heard the King mention Bordeaux and had seen the rolled parchment under his arm. It was one of those maps she had noticed that day in David's study. Her husband did not just deliver messages. He did other things for Edward as well. Much more dangerous things. Dangerous enough and important enough that the King told him about Bordeaux.

She prayed that now that Edward had chosen his

course, David would be out of it. He wasn't a knight or noble. It wasn't fair for the King to use him thus when he would see little profit and significant loss from such wars.

They approached the house from the rear. The tilers' wagon had left. A new horse was tethered by the side of the house, however, and a man stood beside it.

David stopped his horse. He gazed hard at the newcomer.

The stranger was a tall man with long white hair and a short beard. A dull brown cloak, no more than a shapeless mantle, hung to the ground. The horse beside him looked bony and old.

David dismounted and lifted her off her horse.

"Wait outside while I speak with this man."

"It is cold."

"I am sorry for it, but do not come in."

They had been out most of the day, and the chill had long ago penetrated her cloak. "I will go up to the solar and you can use the hall," she suggested.

"You are not to come into the house while he is here," he ordered harshly. His gaze had not left the waiting man. "I insist that you obey me on this, my girl."

His tone stunned her. She watched his absorbed attention with the figure by the house. His awareness of her had essentially disappeared. The withdrawal was so complete that she had never felt more separate from him than she did at that moment, not even the night when she first met him as a total stranger in his solar. This sudden indifference, contrasting so vividly with the constant attention that he had shown her since their wedding, sickened her heart.

Giving the stranger a more thorough examination, she strolled toward the garden.

✦   ✦   ✦

David walked slowly toward the house, and with each step the eerie internal silence grew more absorbing. Scattered thoughts scrambled through his mind, and odd emotions welled inside his chest. Emotions that he could not afford to either acknowledge or examine now.

Nor could he afford to indulge himself in the usual fascination with the sound of Fortune's wheel turning yet again. He shook off the silence.

The man waited and watched. He stood too tall and proud to make the worker's cloak an effective disguise, but David doubted that anyone else had paid much attention.

He had expected this man eventually, but not today and not here. Oliver had received no report yet, for one thing. That must mean that he had come by way of a northern port, and not one along the southern or eastern coasts. A long detour, then, to ensure safety. It was the sort of refined and careful strategy that David could appreciate. He had come alone, too. Either he was very brave or very sure of himself. Probably both.

He tied the horses' reins to a post near the stable building and then walked over to the man. The white head rose as high as his own. Deep brown eyes regarded him carefully.

They did not greet each other but David suspected that the odd familiarity which he experienced was felt by the other, too.

"How did you find me?" David asked.

"Frans learned from its previous owner that you had acquired this property. I thought that you might bring your bride here. A beautiful girl, by the way. Worthy of her bloodline. Worthy of you."

He ignored the compliment, except to note that it was

not one which a man like this would normally give a merchant. "Frans has a friendship with Lady Catherine? Is she one of yours? A watcher?"

The man hesitated and David had his answer. No doubt Lady Catherine would do anything for a price.

"You should have waited until my wife was not with me. I do not want her involved in any way."

"I could not wait forever. I am here at great risk to myself. If you had left her side for a few hours . . ."

The man's voice drifted away and a full silence fell. It held for a long time. They faced each other, both knowing that whoever spoke first again would be at the disadvantage.

David calmly let the moments throb past. He had much more experience in waiting than his guest. A lifetime of it, in fact.

"Do you know who I am?" the man finally asked.

"I know who you are. I assume that you seek what Frans sought, and since I told him I would not help, I wonder about the reason for this meeting."

The man reached into the front of his mantle and withdrew a folded piece of parchment. "This is one of yours. It was found amongst the papers of Jacques van Artevelde."

"Your man and I have already discussed my relationship with Jacques. My letters to him were matters of trade, nothing else."

"His relationship with you and others like you got him killed."

Jacques van Artevelde, the leader of Ghent's pro-English burghers, had become a friend. His death last year at the hands of a mob had been more than a political loss for David, and he resented this offhand reference to it.

It went without saying that the Count of Flanders had been behind that mob's murder. Had this other man been involved, too?

"We met for business and nothing more," David said blandly.

"Let us skip the games, Master David. As Frans explained, we know about you. Not everything, I'm sure. But enough. Besides, it was not the content of this letter that made him bring it to me. It was the seal." His long fingers played with the parchment. "An unusual seal. Three entwined serpents. How did you come to use it?"

"It was on a piece of jewelry that my mother owned. It was as useful a device as any other."

"This item of jewelry. Was it a ring? With a gray stone?"

David let the silence pulse as he absorbed this astounding question and its unexpected implications.

"Aye. A ring."

The man sighed audibly. He stepped closer and scrutinized David's face. "Aye, I can see it. The eyes, but not their color. His were brown. The mouth. Even your voice."

David met that piercing gaze with his own. "I, of course, have no way of knowing if you are right or if you lie. You want something from me. It is in your interest to claim a resemblance."

"I do not come here to trick you into treason."

"Merely meeting with you might be construed as treason. Your presence here compromises me. You should have given me a choice."

"It was essential that I see you. I had to know. Surely you understand that."

"I'm not sure that I do."

"Why did you never come to us?"

"I had no need of you, and you none of me."

"We have need of you now."

David examined the man's serious, expectant expression. "You must want this very badly, to appeal to a stranger."

Shrewd eyes met David's own. "Aye, I want it badly. I want it for my country but I want it for myself, too. You are not such a stranger. I have made it my business to learn about you. Your accomplishments in trade will not satisfy you much longer. Already those small victories seem thin and shallow, do they not? Especially compared to the politics of monarchies."

David glanced away, knowing even as he did so that the reflex signaled a certain defeat.

He gestured for the man to follow him into the house.

Christiana huddled in her cloak on the bench under a tree in the garden. She was not at all pleased to be stuck out here while David held this secret meeting. She was even less pleased with the way he had dismissed her, and his tone when he ordered her obedience.

That tall man's presence had obviously surprised him, and that explained some of it. Still, she doubted that this meeting had anything to do with trade or finance. The stranger was no merchant, despite his simple cloak and humble horse. He could no more hide his true status than he could hide his height. She had recognized him for what he was. Any time, any place, nobles knew each other when they met.

They were talking a very long time. Her hands felt a little numb from the raw chill, and she wrapped them in the billows of her cloak.

If David didn't come and get her soon, she was going to disobey him and go inside. It was one thing to be a dutiful wife, and quite another to sit out here and freeze like an idiot who didn't know when to come in from the cold.

She stomped her feet and huddled smaller. She tried to distract herself by thinking about that strange invention David had shown her earlier. For someone who didn't like knights and war, David had a peculiar fascination with siege machines.

Her eyes scanned the house, looking for some sign of movement. They were probably in the solar in front. From her vantage point she could see the rump of the stranger's horse tied by the side of the building.

David had ordered her to stay outside. He hadn't said where.

She got up and walked through the garden, heading to the sorry-looking animal. Not much of a horse for a nobleman. Perhaps it was someone down on his luck seeking a loan.

A bag lay over the animal's hind quarters. Soothing him with her hands and voice, she eyed the loose flap.

She really shouldn't. It was definitely none of her business.

Asking for forgiveness, she lifted the flap and peered inside.

The bag held clothes. Rich clothes. Expensive fabrics. Garments not at all in keeping with this horse and that worn cloak. The man had disguised himself to look poor.

Voices startled her. She let the flap drop and hurried away.

She had just turned the corner of the house when she heard David's voice.

"We must not meet again in England."

That stopped her. She pressed against the stones of the house.

"I leave tomorrow. Do not worry. I know your risk. I have no desire to jeopardize you," the stranger said. He spoke English, but the accent was unmistakable. This man, this nobleman, was French.

"Frans is not to return to England until this is over. The man is careless, and his long stay last time was noticed. His woman friend is a complication that I will not accept. Sever ties with her," David said.

Frans van Horlst. A French noble. Dear saints!

"He will leave with me tomorrow and not return. The lady will be out of it as well."

"There is one final condition. I will want documents from you. Witnessed."

Only the sound of her heart broke the silence that ensued.

"You do not trust me," the stranger finally said. "I suppose I can't blame you. How will I get these documents to you?"

"You will not. I will come to you."

Her mind scrambled to make sense of these cryptic statements. Documents? Why was David meeting in secret with a French noble and discussing such things? Her heart heaved as one horrible possibility sprang to mind. But if that were the case, David would be providing the documents, and not the other way around.

The sounds of a saddle creaking and a horse stomping reached her ears. She began easing away.

"I look forward to knowing you better," the stranger said. "In France, then."

The horse walked away. David would come looking for her now. She plunged away from the house and ran into the garden.

CHAPTER 15

As soon as David returned to his trade, Christiana presented herself at the house of Gilbert de Abyndon. No one seemed surprised at her going alone. She marveled at this and other new freedoms, so in contrast to the close supervision of Westminster. A childish exhilaration gripped her as she walked along the city streets, pausing occasionally to inspect the activities and wares in the tradesmen's windows.

Margaret appeared both delighted and flustered to see her. Hesitation briefly clouded her pale, delicate face before a very mature resolve took its place. "Does your husband know that you are here?" she asked after she sent a servant for some wine.

"He knows. It was his suggestion that I come. I am in need of a servant and he thought that you might be able to help me."

Margaret tilted her head and raised her eyebrows. "You know that they hate each other. Our husbands."

"I know. And it is always deep when kinsmen feel like that with each other. If my visit will cause trouble for you, I will leave."

Margaret sat on a cushioned window seat and patted the space beside her. Christiana joined her. "I will handle Gilbert. I recently learned that I am with child. I will tell him that I was feeling poorly and that your visit healed me." She smiled conspiratorially. "This child has already changed much and will change more. He will be like clay in my hands now."

Christiana blinked at this bald admission of manipulation. Margaret appeared so frail and sweet, it was hard to believe that a steel rod of practicality held her upright in this marriage.

She felt sorry that Margaret had a marriage in which only her breeding potential was valued. Then she reminded herself that was the likely reason for her own match.

Over the next few hours they formed a bond. The next day Margaret sent a girl named Emma to enter service. Although the daughter of a merchant who had fallen on bad times, Emma proved to be a willing and excellent servant. She arrived daily at the house before dawn and helped Vittorio and Geva until Christiana called for her.

Christiana learned about the fall in Emma's fortunes. Her father had been wealthy one day and poor the next because of one shipping disaster. She wondered if David's wealth tottered so precariously. He had suggested as much when he told her about the lands he had put in her name. Her consideration of this and of the household which she now directed led her to a decision. It was time to acquire a practical education, for the day might come when she had no servants. She set about learning how to cook from Vittorio and how to sew from the women. She learned from Geva how to be a housekeeper.

She had visitors, too, those first few weeks. Morvan came several times to take her for rides and to reassure himself that she wasn't miserable. Isabele and Idonia came once so that Isabele could examine Christiana's new home. Margaret visited at least once a week and they formed a fast friendship.

Toward the end of Lent, troops began arriving to muster for the King's French campaign. Most of the men lived in camps on the surrounding fields. During the days, they descended on the crowded city to pass the time while they awaited embarkation. David curtailed her freedom then, and told her not to leave the house alone.

The Tuesday before Easter, she returned from a trip to the market with Vittorio to find Joan waiting for her. The King's purveyors had been busy the last weeks requisitioning food throughout the countryside to feed the army, and the stalls in London had been hawking depleted meats and produce at inflated prices. She began her conversation with Joan by complaining about this.

Joan laughed. "You are sounding like some bootmaker's goodwife, Christiana. It is well that I have come. We will go to your chamber and I will teach your servant a new hairstyle which I learned. You can show me the things that your rich husband has bought you while I tell you the court gossip."

"How is Thomas Holland?" Christiana asked as she led Joan upstairs.

"He has been sent to Southhampton to help with the ships there. Have you ever seen anything like it? There must be two hundred in harbor here alone, and they say it is the same in the Cinque Ports and up the east coast as well. And no one knows where Edward plans to land once he gets to the Continent."

Bordeaux, Christiana almost said. *He goes to relieve Grossmont at Poitiers.* The ships were merchant ships, requisitioned by the King. Overseas trade had stopped. But Joan would not want to hear about the hardships that would cause.

"With Thomas gone, it has been lonely, but fortunately William Montagu has been very attentive, so I do not feel too dour," Joan giggled. "In truth, it would be hard for any girl to feel sad at court right now. Westminster is bursting with knights and barons, all here without their ladies. The few females around are surrounded by men. It is delicious."

"If I were still there, it would not be delicious for me," Christiana said, laughing. "I would die of thirst in that lake of male attention. Morvan would probably stand up at a banquet and issue a general warning and challenge."

"But he has no say now. You have to come and visit," Joan cajoled as she began working Christiana's long hair into thin braids that she then looped around her head. "Before the fleet leaves, while it is still busy and gay."

"I am married, Joan. My place is here now."

"You can come for a few days, can't you? It really isn't as much fun without you. At least come for the Easter banquet. Bring David with you. He can keep the men away."

Christiana thought about the elaborate banquet and tournament held to celebrate Easter at court. It would be nice to attend as an adult rather than a child.

That night she told David about Joan's invitation. They were sitting in the solar while she practiced the Saracen letters that he had taught her.

"You must go if you want to," he said.

She stared down at the shallow box of sand in which she traced the letters with a stick. They had been married five weeks and David had never accompanied her to court, even when she attended a dinner.

"Joan says that she will arrange for us to have a chamber for a few nights if we want," she said. "You don't think the boys will mind if we are gone for Easter?"

"The household can celebrate without us."

"We will go then?"

"As it happens, I must be out of London then."

"And if not, you still would not come, would you?"

"You had and have a life and place there, and I would not deny you that. But it is not my world. I will not be the upstart merchant who enters the King's court by hanging on to the hem of his wife's veil."

His frank admission that he would not share that part of her life saddened her. She missed him when she was at Westminster. A part of her remained removed from the gaiety, thinking about him. Sometimes she would find herself turning to comment on some entertainment or jest and be a little startled not to find him beside her.

She enjoyed those visits to the court, but she always returned to the city eager to see David and relate the gossip and news which she had learned. She realized that there could be no joy in anything unless she could share it with him in some way.

She looked over at the man gazing thoughtfully into the hearth fire as his long body lounged in the wooden chair. She thought about how she filled her days with activities but how, through them all, a part of her was always waiting for something. Waiting for him, for the sound of his horse in the courtyard and his footsteps in the hall. She was always so happy to see him that sometimes, without thinking, she would run to him and he would laugh and sweep her up into a kiss. She thought about how his return to the house for dinner and again each evening filled her with comfort and relief as if, upon his leaving, she had taken a deep breath and only released it when he came back. He was the center of this household, its very heartbeat. His presence brought security and joy and excitement.

"I need to speak with you about this trip, Christiana."

"Will it be a long one?" she asked, returning to her letters. She wondered how she would get through the nights without him.

"It could be. Two weeks, maybe longer."

"Where do you go?"

"West. Towards Salisbury. The King has received reports of corruption among royal purveyors in that shire. He has asked me to find out what I can before he orders an official investigation."

Another favor for Edward? The thing about secret trips for the King was that no one could ever check on them.

"It is the first time that you have left since our marriage."

"That is why we must talk. All journeys have some danger in them. I should explain some things to you before I go."

She glanced up sharply. He faced her impassively, but she had learned much about him these last weeks, and that perfect face could never be a complete mask to her again. Now she noticed the thin veil of concern that diffused the warmth of his eyes. A strange numbness began slipping over her.

"Before I go, I will be giving you a key. It is for the box in my study. There is coin there. I will also show you a trunk in the wardrobe that contains papers regarding properties and banking credits. The mercery accounts are at the shop. Andrew is well familiar with them. Should you ever need help with anything, John Constantyn will aid you." He paused. "He is the executor of my testament."

Somehow she managed to draw another letter despite her shock. "You only ride to Salisbury, David."

"You should know what to do. I have seen too many women who did not."

"I do not want to speak of this."

"Nor do I, but we must nonetheless."

She gritted her teeth and tried to ignore the appalling realization that forced itself into her mind. She knew, she just knew, that David did not go to Salisbury. He was going someplace very dangerous to do something very risky.

For Edward? She wanted to believe that was so, but the memories of Frans van Horlst asking a man for help in the King's secret corridor, and of a French noble meeting David in Hampstead, boiled in her mind.

I have no desire to jeopardize you. In France then.

He watched her with that deep gaze that always saw too much. Could he read these thoughts as he could so many others?

She was surely wrong. The very notion was unworthy of her. But he knew about Bordeaux and he played to win and used his own rules.

He could not do this. He would not. Their gold and silver would not tempt him. He was not ruled by such hungers.

"I expect that with John's help I will be able to manage things," she said. "Do not concern yourself."

"If something ever happens to me, the shop can be either sold or liquidated. Andrew could help with that. The mercers' wardens will see to placing the boys with other masters."

"And me, David? Will they seek to place me with a new master as well?"

"They have no authority over your life. But they will no doubt offer advice and counsel you to remarry and join your property and business with another merchant's."

"Is that the advice that you gave women as a warden?"

"Often. You, of course, need not look to merchants. You will be very wealthy."

He spoke as though that should reassure her. He was telling her that if wealthy, widowed, and noble, she could have the husband she was born to have. It hurt her that he could so blithely talk about her going to another man.

"I assume that the properties in my name are well documented? And there will be money enough to buy more. Perhaps, then, I will not remarry at all."

He reached over and stroked her cheek. "The thought of you living your life alone gives me no pleasure."

"Let us be frank, David. We are speaking of your possible death. Your pleasure afterwards will not matter. Now, are we finished with this morbid topic? When do you leave?"

"Two days."

Holy Thursday. Joan had said that the rumors called for the fleet to embark for France soon after Easter. Two days and then two weeks of empty chambers. She knew that a part of her would simply cease to exist while he was gone. Maybe it would cease to exist forever. She wouldn't believe that, she couldn't accept its possibility, but he had as much as warned her so just now. He would not have spoken thus unless he thought his danger very real.

A ripping ache filled her chest. Wherever he went, he must go for Edward. Surely he would not risk giving her such pain for anything else.

She set aside her box and stared at her lap. She tried not to care. She argued valiantly that if he was involved in something dishonorable, she would not want to see him again anyway. She told herself that if the worst happened and she became a rich widow, that would not be so bad. None of it helped relieve the weight around her heart.

Her throat burned and she fought to hold on to her composure.

Suddenly he stood in front of her. He lifted her up into his arms. Before she buried her face in his chest, she saw surprise in his eyes.

"I did not mean to upset you, my girl."

The warmth of his embrace made the tears flow. "Did you not?" she mumbled. "You speak to me of dying and widowhood as if you speculated about next year's wool shipments."

"That is because I do not expect to be harmed. I am just being practical for your sake. I have survived many worse dangers than I could possibly face on this little adventure."

There was much in this man that remained a mystery to her, but the parts that she knew she had come to know very well. And she knew now that he lied to her. He did not do that too much anymore, mostly because she avoided asking the sorts of questions that led him to it. And his lies had rarely been true lies. Usually they were ambiguous statements like this one.

She nestled her head closer and his embrace tightened. "Can you not stay? Let another do this," she whispered.

"None other can do it," he said quietly. "I have committed myself."

"Then I care not where or why you go," she said. "You are a merchant, and there will be many trips, some of them very long. Go where you have to go, David, as long as you promise to come back."

David and Sieg left Thursday morning. Christiana threw herself into a whirlwind of packing in order to distract herself. She chose and rechose her clothes for court until Emma was frantic. She tried not to think too much about the poignancy that had imbued David's lovemaking the last two nights.

He had hired two men to guard the house in Sieg's absence, and in the afternoon she had one of them escort her to Westminster.

She reclaimed her bed in the anteroom, and tried hard to pretend that it was just like old times. Sometimes it was, but often, as Joan and she lay on Isabele's bed and shared gossip and talk, her mind would suddenly drift away as she wondered where David was and whether he was safe.

Her suspicions about what he might be doing played over in her mind, and more than once she forced herself to analyze the evidence suggesting treason. That's what it was, after all. Treason of the highest kind, that would put people whom she loved in danger. She told herself that there was no proof that David was selling the French information about the fleet's destination and that she had let some overheard phrases work evils in her mind.

At the Easter banquet the King formally announced the embarkation to France, and the cheers in the hall greeted it as joyous news. Word spread that the troops would board the ships on Wednesday.

On Tuesday morning Joan roused her out of bed early. "There is to be a big hunt, and then lots of private parties in the taverns and inns on the Strand before tonight's feast. One last celebration before all the knights leave," she said as she went to Christiana's trunks and began choosing clothes for her. "You must come with William and me and be my chaperon so Idonia won't interfere. It will be a day of play to last everyone through the summer."

Christiana had been enjoying her stay at court, even

if a part of her kept worrying about David. Joan had been right, and Westminster bulged with knights eager to pay any female attention. They practiced their poetic flattery even on unattainable women. It was expected for women at court to accept the milder attentions, and she did so, in part because they helped distract her from her concerns and suspicions about David.

Like most of the women, she merely rode to the hunt and watched the men demonstrate their prowess with arrow and spear. She stayed close to Joan and William Montagu the whole morning. The young earl acted besotted with the Fair Maid of Kent. Joan flirted back enough to give more hope than she ought. Christiana thought about Thomas Holland supervising the loading of ships in Southhampton. First Andrew and now William and who knew how many in between. Joan's constancy hadn't lasted very long.

The hunting parties made their way to the Strand at midday, and Joan's group descended on a large inn close to the city gates. Usually inns did not serve meals, but most had brought in cooks to deal with the large number of visitors to the area. This one's public room became so stuffed with tables and people that one could barely move, and Christiana soon lost track of Joan. She found herself standing against a wall, searching the crowd for friends to join.

"There you are," said a soft voice at her shoulder.

She turned to find Lady Catherine edging up close to her.

The older woman's cat eyes gleamed. "This is horrible, isn't it? I expected as much and took a large chamber upstairs. Come and join my party for dinner, Christiana."

She hesitated, remembering David and her brother telling her to avoid Catherine.

"I expect Morvan to eat with us," Lady Catherine said.

She hadn't seen much of her brother these last days. The King's knights had been managing the troops provided by the city. It seemed odd that Morvan would dine with Catherine, but maybe whatever he held against her had been resolved.

The crowd pressed against her. Catherine touched her arm and gestured with her head. Christiana debated the offer. It would be nice to spend some time with Morvan before he sailed.

"Thank you," she said, deciding quickly. There could be no harm in it, and surely David wouldn't mind if Morvan was there, too.

She followed Catherine through the throng to the stairs leading to the second level. Even up there the bodies were thick, because others had shown Catherine's foresight and taken chambers. Lady Catherine continued up to the inn's quiet third level, led her to a door, and ushered her in.

The chamber had been prepared for a party of fifteen. Two long tables cramped the space between the bed and the hearth. It was a warm April day and the narrow windows overlooking the courtyard had been opened, but the thick walls obscured the sounds from below.

Only one person waited in the chamber. Stephen Percy stood near the farthest window.

"I must go and collect the others," Lady Catherine said brightly, turning to leave. "We will be back shortly."

Christiana stared at Stephen. He smiled and walked to one of the tables and poured wine into two cups.

"A fortuitous coincidence, Christiana," he said as he handed her one of them. "I feared that I would not see you before we left."

She glanced at the tables awaiting the other diners. How long before some of them arrived?

"You will ride with your father?" she asked.

"Aye. The King has collected a huge army. It promises to be a glorious war. Come and sit with me awhile before the others come."

She thought of David's demand that she not see this man. By rights she should leave. But they would only be alone for a few moments and there could be no harm in wishing him well. She took a seat across from him at one of the tables.

"How is your merchant?" Stephen asked.

"David is well."

"He is not with you. He did not accompany you on this visit or on the others." His tone lacked subtlety. He assumed she returned to court to avoid David. That she sought solace amongst her friends.

"He is a busy man, Stephen, and is out of the city now."

"Still, I expected him to welcome the entry to court that you provided."

"He has little interest in such things."

Stephen raised his eyebrows in mock surprise. He leaned forward and his gaze drifted over her face.

His attention evoked an utter lack of feeling. In a strange way she felt as if she were seeing him for the first time. The face which she had once thought ruggedly handsome now appeared a bit coarse. There was something ill defined in the cheeks and jaws, especially compared to the precision of David's features. The blond hair, she felt quite sure, would not feel very soft if she touched it. Those thick eyebrows contrasted so little with the fair skin as to be almost invisible.

"You are so beautiful," he said softly. "I think that you grow more lovely each time that I see you."

She raised the cup of wine to her mouth and watched him over its rim. His hand reached toward her face.

In that instant before he touched her, she suddenly knew several things clearly and absolutely. She knew them as surely as she knew that day would follow night. Although they came as revelations, they did not surprise her at all. Rather she took a step and there they were, new facts of life to be reckoned with.

She knew, first of all, that no other diners would be joining them. No one, least of all Morvan, would arrive at that door. Stephen had arranged this with Lady Catherine's help, or maybe Catherine had done it herself. The tables, the cups, were all a ruse to get and keep her here so that she and Stephen could be alone.

She also knew, as she regarded that suddenly unfamiliar face, that she had never loved this man. Infatuated, giddy, and excited, she had been those things, but those feelings would have passed with time if he had not tried to seduce her and thus disrupted her life. She had decided that she loved him in order to assuage her guilt and humiliation after Idonia found them. She had clung to that illusion in hopes of rescue from the consequences. But she had never really been in love with him, nor he with her, and now she felt only a vacant indifference toward that hand reaching for her.

And finally she knew, with a peaceful acceptance that made her smile, that the daughter of Hugh Fitzwaryn had fallen in love with a common merchant. A glorious burst of tenderness for David flowed through her with the admission.

She leaned back out of reach.

"Nay."

He dropped his hand and sat upright, his green eyes examining her own. She let him search as long as he wanted, for he would not find what he sought. He smiled ruefully and poured some more wine.

"You have grown up quickly. It is a woman's face that I see now."

"I have had little choice. Perhaps I was overlong a child anyway."

"Innocence has its charm," he said, laughing.

"And its convenience."

He glanced at her and shrugged. "Your merchant is a very fortunate man, my sweet."

She felt a vague affection for Stephen. He was a rogue to be sure, but no longer dangerous to her heart. "I know that none at court will ever believe this, Stephen, but I think myself fortunate, too."

It felt good saying that. It felt wonderful standing up for her husband against the pity and sympathy of these people.

Stephen glanced at her sharply and then laughed in an artificial way. "Then my quest is indeed hopeless."

"Aye. Hopeless."

He made an exaggerated sigh. "First your brother's sword and now your husband's love. This story is a tragedy."

Nay, it was always a farce. Written by you and played by me who thought it real life. But she found that she could not hold that against him anymore. It really didn't matter. He didn't matter.

Dinner actually arrived, brought by two servants, and she stayed and ate with Stephen because being alone with him held no betrayal now. Her love for David felt like a suit of armor, and she was sure that Stephen recognized the futility of trying to penetrate it. They spoke casually about many things, and the hour passed pleasantly.

Toward the end of the meal, however, she suspected that he again began weighing her resolve against his skill at seduction. His smiles got warmer and his flattery more florid. His hand accidentally touched hers several times.

She calmly watched the unfolding of his final effort with surprise and amusement. She rose to leave before he could act on his intentions.

He rose more quickly and stepped between her and the door. His slow, insinuating smile filled her with sudden alarm.

"The meal was lovely, and it was good to share this time with an old friend, Stephen. But I must go now."

He shook his head, and his green eyes burned brightly. "The duty that says you must go was not chosen by you. In this world and this chamber, it does not bind you, my love."

She cursed herself for thinking that she could treat this man as a friend. "It is not duty that takes me away, but my love for my husband," she replied, hoping to kill any illusions he might have that she pined for him.

A spring breeze, light and free, blew through her heart with this more blatant admission of her feelings for David. How long had she loved him? Quite a while, she suspected.

How ironic that the first person to whom she admitted her love should be Stephen Percy. Ironic and also fair and just. Now she must tell David when he came back. If he came back. Then again, maybe she would not have to. Maybe he will just look at her and know. Of all her thoughts and emotions that he had read, this would probably be the most obvious.

Stephen had not moved out of her path, and he considered her closely, as if he judged her determination. She looked back firmly. Her response did not evoke the reaction she expected. Instead of backing down, a subtle ferocity entered his eyes and twisted his mouth.

He suddenly reached for her. She tried to duck his grasp, but he caught her shoulder and pulled her toward him. Surprised by his aggressive insistence, she squirmed to get free. He imprisoned her in his arms.

"A woman such as you cannot love such a man. One might as well try to mix oil and water. You have told yourself that you do in order to survive your fall, my love. That is all."

"You are wrong," she hissed, narrowing her eyes at him. "I love David, and I do not love you. Now *unhand me.*"

"You may think you do not love me, but you will see the truth of it." His face and lips came toward her.

She leaned back until she could lean no further. She desperately turned her face away, but that bruising mouth found her cheek and neck. He grasped her hair to steady her darting head and forced a crushing kiss on her lips. His other hand slid down to grab her bottom. Her stomach turned. To think that she had cried over this lout! She began using all of her strength to break free.

Stephen laughed. "You are spirited. That will soothe my regret that you are no longer innocent. The memory of the passion that I awoke in you last time has filled my memory ever since, begging for completion."

"Passion? I felt no passion with you, you conceited fool! You hurt and humiliated me that day and you will not do it again! Loose me or I will scream and the whole court will know that you force unwilling women!"

"You are not unwilling, just afraid," he murmured, pressing her against his warmth and forcing a caress down her back. "I will show you the pleasure that love can be when you are with a real man. When you scream, it will be with desire and none will hear you. The walls are thick and the building noisy, so do not be shy."

Good Lord, his arrogance knew no bounds. No wonder Idonia never wanted them to be alone with men.

His hands began wandering freely over her body. She gritted her teeth against the repulsion she felt, and took advantage of his loosening hold. Frantically she groped behind her back on the table, feeling for some weapon. Her hand closed on a crockery pitcher.

Just in time, too. Stephen's breathing had grown ragged and heavy. He began pressing her backward against the table, trying to lay her down. His hand started raising her skirt.

She stopped her fight and leveraged her hips against the table's edge. She smiled at him. Stephen paused, looked at her triumphantly, and readjusted his stance. With a snarl, she lifted her knee with all of her strength up between his legs. Then she crashed the pitcher down on his head.

His face shattered in pain and surprise while he bent over. She roughly pushed him away.

"I am an honest woman who loves her husband," she seethed. "Do not ever touch me again."

She strode to the door. As she left she glanced back at the man in whom she had believed during the last days of her childhood.

As she flew down the stairs she heard his step behind her. On the second level he caught up with her. She shook off the hand with which he tried to restrain her. Pushing her way through the throng of revelers, she hurried to the public room below.

She noticed Lady Catherine in the crowd, and those cat eyes glanced at her smugly. Stephen had said that he was not friends with Catherine, and yet this woman had gone out of her way to help him. She wondered why.

"You might at least bid me farewell, my sweet," Stephen said lowly in her ear. His attempt at lightness could not hide an underlying anger in his tone.

She turned on him, furious at his persistence. Before she could speak, he bent down and kissed her, then smiled and melted into the crowd.

CHAPTER 16

THE FLEET SET sail. Westminster and London, emptied not only of the visiting soldiers but also of many of their workers, grew strangely quiet. Christiana returned home and impatiently counted the days until David returned.

Spring storms arrived and soon the news spread that the fleet was returning. Long before the first masts reappeared on the Thames five days after embarkation, everyone knew that ill winds had forced King Edward to cancel his invasion.

The city filled with soldiers again, this time passing through as they began their return to towns and farms and castles inland. Edward could not hold the troops indefinitely for better sailing and had dispersed them.

Christiana was stunned by the relief that she experienced when the news of the aborted campaign reached her. She thought that she had convinced herself that David indeed had gone to Salisbury, but her reaction spoke the lie of that illusion. Now she just felt gratitude that Edward's plans had changed and made the possibility of David's betrayal irrelevant.

The chance that he had done this thing, or had even tried to, should appall her more than it did. The potential dishonor should disgust her. But all she cared about was his safety and the fact that this turn of events would preserve him from the horrible consequences of discovery.

She longed to see him. Memories of him hung on her every moment of the day and filled the hours of the night. She realized that she had probably loved him for a long while. She had refused to see it because of her obligation of loyalty to Stephen. And, she had to admit, she had long denied her feelings because David was a merchant. Noblewomen were not supposed to love such men. She had been raised to think such a thing contrary to nature.

Did he love her at all? His joy appeared to match her own at his homecomings each day, and he had seemed sad about leaving her for this trip. During their lovemaking she saw more in his eyes than simple pleasure, but in truth she did not know how he really felt. She had no experience in such things, and he remained an enigma in many ways.

It didn't matter. As the days slowly passed she knew that there could be no hope of hiding her feelings. Surely when she gave him a child, some type of love would grow for her. In the meantime she felt confident that he would accept her love kindly. She did not plan when she would tell him. It would simply happen in the warmth of their reunion.

He rode into the courtyard a day early. She heard the sounds of his arrival while she sewed in the solar. She threw aside her needle to run down the stairs. Bursting through the door, she flew to him and jumped into his arms.

He caught her as he always did, and swung her around

as he embraced and kissed her. She clung to him while his scent and touch reawoke her soul.

Her blood raced with joy. "I am so glad that you are back and safe. There is something that I must tell you . . ."

The expression in his eyes brought her up short. He examined her with a haunted scrutiny. No affection reached out to her, despite his embrace. In fact, those arms closed on her in a restrictive way as if he sought to hold her in place while he studied her.

She noticed with misgivings the hard line of his mouth. Something dark and disturbing emanated from him. She had never seen this expression and mood. Indeed, for a horrible instant, she felt as if she had never seen this man before.

"What is it?" Had he been discovered after all? Was he in danger?

He turned her in his arm and guided her toward the hall. The grip holding her shoulder felt hard and commanding. "I have had a bad journey and need a bath and some food, Christiana. We will talk later. Send a servant up to me."

His arm fell away and he walked across the hall toward their chambers. His words and manner made it clear that he did not expect her to follow.

Flustered and hurt, she set about seeing to his needs. She sent Emma and the manservant up to prepare the bath and warned Vittorio to serve dinner as soon as possible. Then she paced the hall, absorbed with concern over this change in him.

Could this be his reaction at having his plans thwarted? If he had gone to France, and risked what he risked, had the turn of events angered him? For there had been anger in those blue eyes, and a cold distance that chilled her.

He joined the household for dinner. He sat beside her

and received reports from Andrew as he ate. Nothing specific conveyed his displeasure, but she could sense it distinctly. At the end of the table, Sieg ate his meal with a methodical silence that suggested he at least recognized David's mood.

She had assumed that they would tumble into bed at the first chance upon his return, but under the circumstances she didn't mind too much when he moved his chair to the hearth after the meal. The others left and she sat across from him and watched him stare into the fire.

A very strange silence descended. She bore it awhile and then tried to fill it with conversation. She described small events in the household while he was gone, and the reaction when the fleet returned. Chattering on anxiously, she told him about her sad leave-taking of Morvan and then her relief upon his unexpected return.

He turned those haunted eyes on her while she spoke. His steady regard made her uncomfortable. She had imagined his homecoming many times, and it had been filled with elation and joy and her newly discovered love. She found all of those emotions retreating from the dark presence sitting near her.

She began telling him about the Easter joust, but he interrupted with an abruptness that suggested that he hadn't been listening to anything.

"You were seen," he said.

She jolted in confusion. The frightening realization struck her that this change in him had something to do with her.

"Seen? What do you mean?" She instinctively felt defensive.

He rose from his chair. Grabbing her arm, he lifted her and began pushing her in front of him through the hall.

"What are you talking about?" She glanced back at the stranger forcing her to scramble up the steps.

He dragged her to the bedchamber and slammed the door behind them. She sensed his anger spike dangerously. Some anger of her own rose in response and mixed with her worry and fear. She shook off his grip and backed up to the windows.

He faced her with tense hands on his hips. "You were seen, girl. With your lover."

"There were men at court who paid me attention, David, but it was harmless. No doubt many saw me, but not with any lover."

Her light response only made it worse. His anger surged. "Men paying you attention are inevitable. Stephen Percy, it seems, was inevitable, too, despite your vows and your assurances to me. It did not take you long to find your way back to that knight's bed."

His crisp words stunned her. She had actually forgotten about that dinner with Stephen these last few days. Stephen Percy had ceased to exist for her as she reveled in her love for David. She stared at him speechlessly and knew that the truth, that she had met with Stephen, was written on her face.

"That was harmless, too," she said, knowing that her denial would not matter. The meeting itself was the betrayal and he would assume the worst.

"You have no talent for adultery, darling. You don't even know when to lie and how to do it. Harmless? Lady Catherine was seen taking you up to a chamber in that inn and then returning without you. An hour later you emerged with Percy. I am told that your kiss of farewell was chaste enough, but he could afford restraint and discretion by then."

"What you were told is true, but I did nothing wrong in that chamber," she explained with a calm she did not feel at all. She could offer only her word against the damning evidence. "Who told you of this, David? Many saw, I am sure, and I am sorry that I did not think how it would appear to them and what it might cost your pride. But who felt the need to tell you? Was it Catherine? She helped Stephen in the ruse that brought me to him unknowingly."

"No doubt Lady Catherine eagerly awaits letting me know," he said bitterly.

"Then who?" but even as she asked it she knew the answer. He had just arrived back in London. Whoever had told him this was someone he trusted. Her indignation at the implications helped beat back the desperation.

"Oliver," she gasped. "You were having me followed. Dear saints! All of the time? When I walked about the city, was he always there? Did he hide in the shadows of Westminster and follow us into the forest for the hunt? Did you trust me so little . . ."

"He followed you for your protection, and not to catch you thus. In this one thing I surely trusted you, or I would not have let you go back to court where he could not follow."

"He was there? At the inn?"

He advanced toward her, dangerous and tense, and she backed up until she bumped against the window.

"He tried to hide the truth from me, but I can read him as I read you, and I forced it out." He reached out and laid his hand against her face. There was nothing soothing in his quiet voice or reassuring in that touch. "So you have finally had your knight, my lady. Was it all that you expected? Like the songs and poetry of chivalry on which you were raised? Did that knight's hands give you comfort that you are still who you were born to be? That you had not been debased beyond redemption in the bed of a merchant?"

Nay, she wanted to say, *it was the other way around*. But admitting that Stephen had touched her would only throw oil on this fire.

He neither crowded her nor restrained her, but she suddenly felt extremely helpless. A sensual edge in his soft tone made her wary.

"I did nothing wrong . . ." She repeated, searching his eyes for belief and understanding. She saw only shadows and fire and something else that alarmed her.

When he lowered his head, she tried to turn away. His hand twisted into her hair and held her as his mouth claimed hers.

She loved him and missed him and wanted him, and at first her body and spirit accepted him gratefully. But as she felt his passion rise and his kiss deepen, she knew that it was neither love nor affection driving him but rather pride and anger, and this reminded her too much of Stephen's assault. She jerked her head away and struggled as he pulled her into his arms.

"Nay. Do not . . ."

"Aye, my girl. I have been two weeks without a woman. That is the best thing about marriage. One need not waste time wooing and seducing when it waits for you at home." He imprisoned her with his embrace and cradled her head steady with a forceful grip. "This is the problem with adultery, and you might as well learn it today. The man can avoid his wife if he chooses, but the woman must return to a husband who still has his rights."

He held her firmly and kissed her again. She desperately squirmed against those strong arms. Her shock eclipsed every other emotion. He might have been a stranger handling her.

"I feared that you might repulse me, knowing where you had been and what you had been doing the first time I left the city," he said as his hands moved over her body.

He smiled faintly but she could tell that his anger hadn't abated at all. "It would be ironic, wouldn't it? To have paid all of that silver for property and then found that I no longer wanted the use of it."

Her mind clouded with horror at hearing him speak so coldly of their marriage. There had certainly been evidence that he thought of her thus and had even seduced her to lay claim to what was his, but to hear the words bluntly spoken and to have the confirmation thrown into the face of her love sickened her.

"Property . . ." she gasped.

"Aye. Bought and paid for."

Her eyes blurred and she thought that her heart would shatter. But his words also insulted her pride and her fury flared.

"I don't choose to be property to be used at your convenience," she cried, twisting and kicking to break free. "You will not do this in anger and punishment."

Her struggle only infuriated him. With two rough moves he pinned and immobilized her against the window.

"You are my wife. You have no choices."

She screamed as he lifted her and carried her to the bed as if she were a carpet. When he threw her down, she rolled away and tried to scramble free. He caught her and pulled her to him, pressing his chest into her back and throwing a leg over hers.

He held her until her thrashing stopped. She emerged from her delirium of rebellion. He softly stroked her hair and back as if she were a skittish animal.

Devastation flooded her. She bit her lower lip and fought back tears. She thought of the stupid and trusting joy which she had carried down to him just a few hours before. Love, alive but battered, searched for shelter somewhere inside her.

He shifted off of her and ran his hand down her back. His fingers pried at the knot of her cotehardie's lacing.

"I'm sorry if I frightened you, but I share you with no man, least of all that one." His voice came quietly and gently, but anger still radiated from him, mixing with the passion of his body. "You must never go to him again. If you do, I will kill him."

He said it simply and evenly, in the voice of the David she knew. The hands that she relished stroked her back through the loosened garment, their warmth flowing through the thin fabric of her shift. Her foolish love glowed in response. Her bludgeoned pride pushed it back into a corner.

She turned onto her back. His mood had not improved much although he tried to hide it now. She gazed at that handsome face that could so easily make her heart sigh. His expression softened, and he caressed her stomach and breast. A pleasurable yearning fluttered through her and it horrified her that she could respond under these conditions. Her love started stringing through her, offering to weave an illusion for escape.

His blunt words repeated themselves in her head. She grabbed his wrist and stayed his hand. Love or not, she could not delude herself about what was about to happen and why he did it and what it meant to him.

"So, we are down to base reality at last," she said, narrowing her eyes. "How tedious it must have been to have to pretend otherwise with the child whom you married."

He stared at her. His lack of response and denial turned her anguish to hateful spite. "The merchant has need of his property, much as he rides his horse when it suits him? Well, go ahead, husband. Reclaim your rights. Show that you are equal to any baron by using one of their daughters against her will. Will you hurt me, too? To make sure that the lesson of your ownership is well learned?"

Still he did not react. Her heart broke with a suffocating pain and she threw out whatever she could to hurt him, in turn. "Do not bother with seduction and pleasure, mercer. Soil feels nothing when it is tilled, nor wool when it is cut. I will think about who I am and what you are and feel nothing, too. But be quick about it so that I can go cleanse myself." And then she looked at him and through him the way she had that day after her bath.

She thought that he was going to hit her. In that brief moment of his renewed anger, as he drew up and his eyes darkened, she rolled frantically off the bed and half ran, half crawled to the door of the wardrobe.

She slammed and barred it just as he reached her. A vicious kick jarred the door and bolt. She pushed a heavy trunk over against them and stood back fearfully as he kicked again.

Then came only silence. She ran to the door leading to the exterior stairs and barred it too. She waited tensely a long time but the quiet held and he made no more attempts to enter.

Heaving breaths of relief, she sank down on a stool and finally let the tears flow. She cried long and hard, awash in misery and shock, his cruel words echoing in her ears. Her pathetic love fluttered out of hiding and added to the agony.

Eventually a numb stupor claimed her. Only one thought came clearly, over and over again. She had to get away and leave this house and this man. She would not, could not, live with the reality he had forced on her this day. Not now. Not for a long while. Maybe not ever.

✦   ✦   ✦

The rain pounded relentlessly, its blowing spray stinging David's face. He stood on the short dock and watched the patterns that the drops made in the muddy Thames. Beautiful, rhythmic splashes, full of faint highlights of purity, existed for split instants before the dirty flow absorbed them.

He let the rain wash over him. It soaked his clothes and plastered his hair to his head. After a long while it cleansed the black anger from his mind.

And then, with the madness gone, he faced the memory of what had occurred. That would never wash away and he lived it all again. His spiteful words. Her harsh insults. His vicious debasement of her.

Thank God she had gotten away.

They knew each other well enough to point the daggers expertly and draw blood from each other's weaknesses. He would never forget what she had said, but he couldn't blame her for admitting those feelings and thoughts. Since the day she had come to him, she had tried valiantly to ignore what this marriage meant to her life.

He had never been as cruel and hard to a woman as he had been with Christiana this day. Oliver and Sieg had been right. He should never have returned home and confronted her while the knowledge of her infidelity still flared like a fresh log tossed on a fire. He had known that they were right even as he ignored their advice and entreaties.

He pictured Oliver sitting across the tavern table from him and Sieg, listening with studied absorption to their tale of waiting on the Normandy coast for signs of the fleet passing. David described how the days had turned dark with storms and how he had realized that this month at least he would be spared the decision awaiting him in France.

And all the time that Oliver carefully listened and prolonged the tale with questions, he had watched the signs of ill ease on his old friend's face. They betrayed him worse when David asked after Christiana. Poor Oliver. He had tried to lie and then to equivocate when he probed for details. David knew that his own expression had turned dangerous when he felt Sieg's hand on his shoulder and that lilting voice urging him to stay away from the house for a few more days.

Impossible, of course. He had to see her at once and look into those diamonds knowing what he knew. He wanted and expected to feel dead to her, to be free of the love that was complicating his life and making him suddenly indecisive.

For when he had stepped off Albin's boat this morning after two treacherous days at sea, he had known that he loved her. He had recognized the feelings for a long time, but in Normandy he had put the name to them. He had sought out Oliver before returning home, because he knew that when he entered that house he would not want to leave again for a long while.

In his mind he saw her running to him, face flushed and eyes bright. He had watched her exuberant greeting with dark fascination. He had not expected her to be so good at deception. And mixed with that initial reaction had been the appalling realization that he still wanted her.

A dangerous mix, he thought now as he raised his face to the rain. Anger and desire and jealousy. Why had he let her play the game out? Why had he permitted those hours to pass as she pretended that nothing had changed and his own rancor grew? He grimaced and wiped the water from his face. He had been watching and waiting and, aye, hoping. Waiting for a confession and hoping it included the admission that her infidelity had been disillusioning.

Waiting for her to beg forgiveness and say that she now knew that she no longer loved Percy.

Fool. Unfaithful wives never did such things. Even when cornered with the evidence, the prudent course was to lie. Honesty was too dangerous. Men reacted too violently. He had certainly proven that today, hadn't he? He had forced her into lies born of her fear.

He closed his mind to the memory of her shock and terror.

She had denied it, but he didn't believe her. She loved Sir Stephen and her knight had been leaving for war. Her own testimony suggested that Stephen had no skill as a lover, but that did not reassure him in the least. A woman in love sought more than pleasure in bed and would forgive any clumsiness.

He contemplated that denial as he walked back to his horse. One part rang true. *Lady Catherine brought me to Stephen unknowingly*, she had said. He believed that, and it was something at least. Christiana had not arranged that meeting on her own, but had been lured there. Considering how she felt about Stephen, perhaps the rest had been so inevitable as to make her practically innocent.

As for Lady Catherine and her role in this . . . Well, when he settled this new account, he would permit himself the pleasure of revenge and not just justice.

He couldn't stay away from the house forever, and so he rode back, not knowing what he would say to Christiana when he got there. The temptation presented itself to pretend that the whole day had never happened, that he had never confronted her in his rage.

Would she accept their behaviors as an effective trade? One infidelity and betrayal for one attempted rape? If it had just been that, the accounts might be cleared, but his words and manner had insulted her more than any bodily assault could. To hurt her, he had told her that she was only a noble whore whom he had bought. She would not quickly forgive him that.

He rode into the wet courtyard and handed his reins to the groom. As soon as he entered the hall, a corner of his soul suspected.

The house felt as it had before their wedding. It had been his home for years and he had found contentment in it and so he had never noticed the voids that it held after his mother and master died. Only after Christiana filled those spaces with her smiles and joy had he realized their previous vacancy. Now he heard his footsteps echo in the large chamber as if all of the furniture had been removed. He paced to the hearth, avoiding the confirmation of his suspicion.

Geva entered from the kitchen with crockery plates in her arms. She glanced at him and shook her head.

"You be soaking wet, David. Best get out of those garments," she scolded.

He turned his back to the fire. Geva hummed as she set out the plates for supper. She acted as if nothing was amiss, and his foreboding retreated. With one final glance at him, she disappeared back into the kitchen.

He looked at the tables. He counted the plates. One short. The foreboding rushed back.

He slowly walked across the hall and up to his chambers, knowing what he would find.

In the wardrobe, hanging on their pegs and folded in trunks, were all of the garments that he had given her, including the red cloak. He flipped through them, noting that her other things, her old things, were mostly gone. Not all of them, however. One trunk still held some winter wools. He lifted them to his face and savored her scent, and an invisible hand squeezed his heart.

He left the wardrobe and passed quickly through the

bedchamber, not wanting to look at that space that still held the vivid images of the wounds they had inflicted on each other.

Sieg squatted in the solar, building the fire. He raised his eyebrows at the soaked garments.

"Did you throw yourself in the river then?"

David ignored him.

"Did you harm her?"

He shook his head.

Sieg finished with the fire and then rose. "I told you to wait, David. Your mood was blacker than night. I've not seen you like that, even when the Mamluks first threw you into that hell with me after that slut sold you out to them. Not even during our escape when you killed the one who had flogged us."

"I should have listened."

"*Ja*, well you never have where this girl goes, so this is no different."

David hesitated. With any other man he would not have asked, but Sieg had seen him weak before.

"Where is she?"

Sieg's eyes flashed and his posture straightened. "Hell! You don't know? I swear she told me that you'd agreed to it or I'd not have taken her . . ."

"Where?"

"Back to Westminster." He turned toward the door. "I go and get her now. Hell."

"Do not. Leave her stay awhile."

"Do you mean to say that you will stand down to this fool of a knight who steals your wife? You will permit this?"

"If it comes to that, I have driven her to it," he said. "Do you think that she plans to remain at court? Did you sense that she intended to continue on elsewhere?"

"She promised to remain there, which I found odd, since she owes me no explanation."

"Sir Stephen left for Northumberland several days ago. Oliver told me. She knows that I will know, or find out. Her promise was to assure me that she does not go to him." He smiled thinly. "I said that I would kill him if she did. My behavior gave her reason to believe me."

Sieg threw up his hands. "It makes no sense, David. If this man is up north, why does she just go to Westminster? If she doesn't go to him, why run away at all?"

David didn't reply, although the answer was obvious. *She does not run to Percy*, he thought. *She runs from me.*

Christiana sat in a garden redolent with the scent of late May flowers. She gazed at the pastel buds and smiled. Being a woman instead of a child wasn't all bad. Last year she would have taken the flowers' beauty for granted. Today she carefully admired their fresh purity.

David had taught her this. To pay attention to the fleeting beauties in the world. Not a small gift.

She sighed into the silence. The garden was empty despite the warm weather because the court attended dinner in the hall right now. She had avoided those crowded meals and all other events where she would be required to chat and make merry. She had escaped to Westminster for sanctuary and to heal her heart and soul.

She had found welcome and sympathy when she arrived. Lady Idonia had taken one look at her and known the reason for the visit. That little woman asked no questions and settled her in as if they had been expecting her. Joan and Isabele, warned by Idonia no doubt, sought no explanations either.

They were the only family she had known for years, and they surrounded her and protected her in her pain. Even Philippa, on hearing of her extended stay, had come to see her. Alone together in the ante-room, the Queen had tried to be a mother to her for once as she explained the difficulties of marriage. Upon leaving, she had offered to write to David and say that she requested his wife's continued attendance. He would not dare come for her then, and Christiana would have more time.

More time. For what? To reconcile herself to living her life with a man who at most wanted her available to satisfy his needs? Who had purchased a well-bred and well-formed bedmate, much as he carefully chose his horses? A man who did not believe her now after she had always been honest with him to the point of cruelty? A man who barely cared for her at all, but whom she loved despite everything?

There lay the real problem, of course. The rest she could manage and accept if she didn't love him. It was the lot of most women, and she had even ridden to her wedding assuming that it would be hers. Mutual indifference would make it bearable. Wasn't Margaret surviving?

Aye, she needed time. Time to stop loving him.

She had been working hard at that these last few weeks. She kept the memory of his harsh indifference and his attempted rape sharp in her brain. She reexamined the evidence implicating him in some treasonous game. It hadn't worked and she was in a quandary. The love wouldn't die and he had robbed her of the chance to build illusions out of ambiguities.

She looked up from the flowers. More time. How much would it take? How long before she could return to that house and that bed as indifferent to him as he was to her? How long before he could touch her and she would feel no more than simple pleasure or, if not that, remove herself from the experience? Hadn't David said that Anne handled her whoring that way? What was she but some incredibly expensive whore?

Surely just being away from him should kill these feelings eventually.

A palace door opened. Morvan paused in the threshold. He looked at her a moment before walking over. He sat down and stayed there in silence with his arm around her back. She let her head rest on his shoulder.

She hadn't spoken with him all of this time and had actually avoided him. When they briefly saw each other, she turned away from the questions in his eyes. Now he had deliberately sought her out and she felt grateful. He possessed so much strength that there always seemed to be extra to spare for her.

She turned and looked at his profile and saw his concern. She also saw something else and suspected with a numb resignation that her time was up.

"Why are you here, Christiana?" he finally asked, demanding the information that no one else had required.

"I could not stay there."

"Why not?"

Because my husband does not love me at all. She could not say it. It sounded too childish. Like most nobles, Morvan probably thought the issue of love irrelevant in marriages.

"Did he hurt you? Abuse you?"

"Nay." Not the way that Morvan meant. If he had, she would have lied. She did not want her brother killing David.

"Does he use you too hard?" he asked softly.

"Nay," she whispered.

"Has he gone to other women? If it is that, Christiana, I must tell you that with men . . ."

"To my knowledge he has not, Morvan. He thinks that I went to another man. To Stephen. He does not believe me when I deny it. He was mad with anger and jealousy. We argued and said things . . . ugly things."

"All couples argue. Our parents had terrible fights."

"This was different."

"Perhaps not."

"Did our father love our mother?"

The question surprised him. "It was a love match. I think they still loved each other at the end."

"Then it was different."

"That is a rare thing, Christiana. What they had. I do not think that it is given to most. Not really."

"Not you?"

"Nay. Not me. Like most men, I settle for brief simulacrums of it."

She thought that sad. She remembered David saying that Elizabeth would not marry Morvan because of their uneven love. She understood Elizabeth now and knew why Elizabeth had chosen instead that old baron for whom she felt nothing. Marriage to Morvan would have torn her heart daily.

"You cannot stay here," Morvan said gently. "Philippa spoke with me. Edward has become aware of your presence and questioned her about it. She does not think that David said anything, but the King has some affection for your husband, it seems, and interfered on his own."

"I cannot go back there."

"There is no place else to go."

She closed her eyes.

"God willing, Christiana, the day will come when I will have a home. If you still need to leave, I will take you in forever and keep him from getting you back. But for now, there is no choice." He paused and added carefully,

"Unless you want to go north to Percy. Did Stephen offer to keep you?"

She uttered a short laugh. "Nothing so formal or permanent, brother. Even if he had, I would not go, because I do not care for him now and would not dishonor you thus even if I did. Also I would not go because David has said that he will kill Stephen if I do, and I believe him." She smiled mischievously. "Would you have let me go?"

"Probably not."

"I did not think so."

He smiled kindly at her. "I have asked Idonia to pack your things. Horses await. I am taking you home now."

Her stomach twisted. "So soon?"

"Whatever is between you and David will only be a day worse tomorrow."

He rose and held out his hand.

"I do not know if I can bear this, Morvan. The last time I saw him . . ."

The last time she saw him, he was about to hit her because she had spoken to him noble to commoner and implied that his touch would debase and dirty her. The last sound she had heard him make was that kick trying to break down the wardrobe door.

"He will probably be happy and relieved to see you," Morvan said as he raised her to her feet. "It occurs to me that this is the third time that I have brought you to him. The man should have great affection for me by now."

She forced a laugh at her brother's attempt at levity, but she didn't think for one moment that David would be relieved to see her.

David heard the horses enter the courtyard just as dinner ended. Andrew was leaving the hall and he glanced over meaningfully, confirming the riders' identities.

Michael, crowding in behind Andrew at the door, announced happily to the servants that their mistress had returned.

David gestured for everyone to go about their business. He went to the door and stepped outside. The apprentices greeted Christiana as they passed her on their way to the gate. She rode forward slowly beside her brother.

She had been gone for almost three weeks. No messages or notes had passed between them, and his option of fetching her back had been cut off by the Queen's interference. Three weeks and before that two more. He'd only had that horrible afternoon with her in all of that time.

They stopped their horses right in front of him. Christiana looked down impassively. Morvan tried to appear casual and amiable. He swung off his saddle and walked around to lift his sister down.

"Christiana asked me to escort her home," he said as he began untying the small trunks on the saddle. "She was finding Westminster tedious."

David waited. Christiana walked a few steps and faced him.

"He is lying," she said quietly. "He made me come."

"All the same, it is good to have you back."

She glanced at him skeptically. "Did you keep Emma?"

"She is inside."

"I will go and rest now," she announced. "I find that I have a headache and am a bit dizzy."

He let her pass, nodding acknowledgment of her old excuse for avoiding him.

Morvan set the trunks down near the door.

"I thank you, Morvan."

Morvan's face hardened. "Do not thank me. She is pained about something, although I know not what. If there had been anywhere else to take her, I would have done so."

He mounted his horse. "I will come in a few days to see her," he said pointedly.

"I will not hurt her over this."

He turned his horse. "All the same, I will come."

David crossed the courtyard and entered the side building. As he approached the stairs he saw Emma emerge from his mother's old chamber. She softly closed the door and eased over to him.

"She is most poorly, I think. She said that she could not make the steps."

He glanced at the door behind which his young wife hid from him. Would she ever open it again of her own will, or would he eventually have to tear it down? He would wait and see. He was good at waiting.

"She will use that chamber until she feels better, then. Make her as comfortable as you can, Emma."

CHAPTER 17

THE BED FELT a little strange. Christiana snuggled under the covers even though the June night was warm enough to leave the windows open. She gazed up at the pleated blue drapery.

She did not have to be here, she reminded herself, and she still had time to change her mind. He would not be back for several nights. No one knew that their sick mistress had stolen up these stairs and entered this chamber while the household slept. She could return to Joanna's room before morning and continue her deception.

She doubted that anyone continued to be fooled by her illness, except maybe trusting Emma. The concern with which she had been treated those first days had long ago dissolved into silent curiosity.

Her arm stretched out and slid over the cool sheets where normally David slept. Perhaps it had been a mistake to come here tonight. Even if she left now and never returned, he would undoubtedly sense that she had been here. It had probably been foolish to steal up to this bed and try to imagine whether she could return to him without being devastated.

He had supported her claim of illness. For three weeks he had treated her with concern in front of the others. He greeted her warmly upon returning to the house and placed his hand over hers while the conversations continued after the meals.

When they were alone, she had seen other things in those blue eyes, however. The knowledge that she deliberately avoided him. A forbearing but not eternal patience. Sometimes, perhaps, an intelligent male mind calculating his options with her.

Since she ostensibly could not climb the stairs, she had taken to sewing in the hall after the evening meals. After the first few days, he began joining her there. A subtle tension underlaid the stilted conversations which they held across the hearth, but recently its tremoring pulse had gotten worse during the long silences. She would look up from her sewing and find him watching her and the look in his eyes would summon that old fear that wasn't fear. She would curse herself and pray that he would leave her alone in peace and not remind her with his presence and his gaze how much she still loved and wanted him.

It had been deliberate. Every touch, every gentle kiss good night when she left the hearth to return to Joanna's room, had been intended to remind her of the pleasure she felt with him. He had been playing a slow, methodical melody on the strings of her desire.

It had succeeded. The last week as she lay in her lonely bed, she had begun considering that maybe she could live this life in which she had been imprisoned. She could take the pleasure for what it was. Why deny herself? It had become clear that this special hunger, once awakened, did not sleep easily ever again.

Since the day she had returned, she had lain in that

bed every night, unable to sleep quickly, listening for the step outside her door that warned that he finally came to demand his rights and her duty.

Last night she had barely slept at all. He had intended to leave in the morning to attend one of the trade fairs inland. She did not doubt the truth of his destination this time, because John Constantyn was going with him. It would not be a long journey, but their silent evening by the hearth had been heavy with the knowledge of his impending departure. Did his memories turn as hers did to his last emotional leave-taking and what had occurred upon his return?

His kiss when she finally left him had been long and less chaste, and his hands had caressed her while he embraced her. Hungry, aching feelings long denied had flooded her before he drew away. If he had lifted her up and carried her back to his bed then, she could not have stopped him.

He did not, though. He let her leave him as he always had these last weeks. She went to the small chamber that had become her home. She waited, praying this time that he would indeed come and end this even as she dreaded that he would. Her need for his closeness overpowered her. Her insulted pride and her hurt at his indifference ceased to matter. That her desire was totally entwined with her love did not frighten her so much anymore. She would manage those feelings somehow.

He had come, but not during the night. At first light her door had opened and she had turned to find him standing there, looking down at her. She rose up against the headboard and pulled the sheet around her naked shoulders.

He sat down beside her and she saw signs of weariness in his face that suggested he had not slept much either.

"You are leaving now?" she asked.

"Aye. John awaits outside. Sieg will stay here. There are rumors that Edward has summoned the army again, Christiana. If men start arriving in the city, do not leave the house without Sieg or Vittorio."

She hadn't known that Edward had renewed his plans about France, but then she hadn't left this house in weeks because of her illness. Margaret had visited her several times, but Margaret had no interest in court gossip or politics and so had told her nothing. Nor had David until now.

Perhaps there were no rumors yet. Perhaps David only knew because the King had told him.

He only travels to a trade fair, she told herself firmly. *John Constantyn goes with him, not Sieg.*

He placed his hand on her knee. She looked down at it, so exciting in its elegant strength, so warm despite the sheet between their flesh. That quivering intensity that always emanated from him seemed especially apparent this morning.

"This cannot go on," he said. "You cannot stay here."

They had never spoken of that day nor of why she feigned this illness. A part of her had hoped that they never would.

"That is what Morvan said. He came to me at Westminster and said I could not stay there. Now you say it about this house."

"Nay. I say it about this chamber. I'll not see another woman buried alive in it."

"Then give me some money to pay servants and I will go live in Hampstead. I will repay you from the farm rents."

A glint of anger glowed in those blue eyes before he suppressed it. He slowly shook his head.

His hand still rested on her knee, beckoning her with its warmth, offering her its pleasures. Better if he had just carried her upstairs last night. Better to have never put words to what was happening.

"What are you saying, David? Are you ordering me to my duty?"

"I am asking you to return to our marriage and our bed."

"What about Stephen Percy?"

"We will put that behind us."

"You still do not believe me, do you? But you kindly forgive me. That is most generous of you, but I neither want nor need your forgiveness."

"Perhaps I want and need yours."

"I do not know if I can give it," she whispered, as memories of that day drifted into the space between them. "Even now, as you ask me to come back to you, I know that you just find that you have need of your property and resent being denied it. It may be the way these things always are, but I do not think many women have to hear it so frankly stated and then live with the truth in such a naked way. Perhaps that is the reason for dowries. To give women some other value in marriages so that their dignity is preserved."

That exciting hand rose from her knee and stroked her cheek above the bunched sheet with which she shielded herself. It rested there, and its warmth flowed into her and down her neck. "We both spoke harsh things to each other. I think of no person as property, Christiana. Least of all you."

He leaned toward her. She knew that it would not be a simple kiss of parting and that she should turn away, but she could not even though the connection would bring her anguish. The warm touch, the quiet voice, the intense blue eyes had made her defenseless. Sensual memories during the night had left her tired body half aroused. His kiss lingered and deepened and she could not fight it because something inside her, apart from her reason and her hurt, hungered for him.

He kissed her as if the world had ceased to exist. Gently, almost lazily, he bit along her lips. The nips and warmth stunned her. He slowly pried his tongue into her and she parted her mouth stiffly, accepting him with a hesitation her trembling, anxious body didn't feel at all. The heady intimacy of this small joining washed over her and submerged her resentment and hurt.

A small internal voice cried a warning, but her appalling, forceful longing ignored it. She released one hand's hold on the sheet and awkwardly embraced the shoulders leaning toward her.

They kissed again tentatively, like first-time lovers finding their way. Then slowly, carefully, as if each touch revealed something precious, he pressed his lips to her neck and shoulders. Her whole body tremored with grateful relief at the repeated warm contact of that mouth.

She opened her eyes and found him looking at her, and she guessed that he could, as always, see everything and knew that her traitorous body had vanquished her resolve. She silently begged him to stay and also prayed that he would not.

"Come here," he said, reaching for her. He lifted and turned her and set her on his lap, resting her head and shoulders on the support of one arm while his other one embraced her to him. She still clutched the sheet and it followed her, trailing over her body as it twisted from the bed. Despite the sheet and his clothing, she felt his warmth and strength and sighed at the closeness. Her buttocks pressed against the hard muscles of his thighs and her hip felt the hot ridge of his arousal. It had been months since he had held her, and she lost herself in a mindless fog of connected warmth.

Cradling her in his arms, he lifted her to a hungry,

probing kiss. She felt his passion overwhelm his restraint of the last weeks. Her barely controlled desire also broke loose of her tenuous hold. Her last clear thought was an indifferent awareness that she would pay for this pleasure with pain.

With her free hand she encircled his neck and pressed him closer, asking for more, encouraging him. Her long abstinence had made her shameless, and she would not let him end the deep, frantic kiss. His embracing arm loosened and she moaned into him as his wonderful hand caressed her bare back and hip.

He broke the kiss and looked down into her eyes. His gaze lowered and his fingers traced down to where she still grabbed the top of the sheet.

"It did not help you much that day in the wardrobe, darling," he said quietly. "Let go now."

He spoke of the sheet, but he also meant much more. He softly stroked her clutching hand until her fingers relaxed beneath his seductive touch. She turned her face into his shoulder as he eased the sheet from her grip and slid it away. Cool air alerted the skin of her entire body.

She knew that he looked at her as he so often had done, only now she felt suddenly shy and stunned by a furious anticipation. She gritted her teeth and buried her face harder in his shoulder.

He kissed her neck and his quiet voice flowed with his breath into her ear. "Do not hide your face from me, Christiana. The desire that we feel for each other is a wonderful thing. I want you to watch me as I give you pleasure."

Gently he turned her face to his and forced her to meet his gaze. He had not even touched her yet, but that aching need already tensed her belly and a hot insistence throbbed between her legs.

She watched as he demanded. Watched as he cradled

her and kissed her breasts and moistened their hard tips with his tongue. Watched as his fingers slowly traced along her breastbone and teased in a circle. Her breasts swelled beneath that wandering touch, anxious, begging, and her consciousness focused on nothing besides her silent, breathless urging. His fingers slid to one moist nipple. She saw her body arch toward that devastating touch, and then she saw little else. Incredible sensations and single-minded desire obliterated all thought.

He aroused her as if time didn't matter, as if no one awaited him in the courtyard and no journey beckoned. Her breasts had never been so sensitive, and his deliberate caresses raised excruciating pleasures. When his strong arm lifted her shoulders and his mouth replaced his hand, the delicious need he created with his lips and teeth became consuming and painful.

He lifted his head and looked down her body. Her own dazed eyes followed. His hand splayed over her belly, his light golden skin contrasting in a compelling way with her creamy whiteness. He pressed down, stilling the rock of her hips. He caressed her thighs and they both watched that hand's progress. Her breath shortened to a series of low sighs.

"I am thinking that it is in my interests to leave you ill contented," he said softly as his hand trailed over her body. "Abstinence is a powerful enhancement to passion. I do not think that you would remain ill too long after my return."

She barely heard this frank assessment of her condition and resolve. She watched and felt his hand follow the crevice where her legs joined. Stabs of heat distracted her.

"But I find that I cannot do it," he said, "I have missed your passion and would at least have that from you this day."

His gaze claimed her attention, and his words penetrated her stupor. He kissed her beautifully. "Open to me, darling," he said while his fingers touched the soft mound of hair.

She had been waiting for him to rise and turn and lay her down. She had been waiting for the intimacy of his body along hers and the obliteration of her choices. She realized that he had never intended to use her desire against her like that today.

She hesitated, and almost said, as he made her say that first time, that she wanted him.

"Open," he commanded gently. His fingers caressed so close to her need that her breathing stopped and that hidden flesh pulsed. "There is no defeat in taking pleasure from me thus."

She had no resistance. She closed her eyes and parted her legs and accepted the relief he offered. It did not take long. He touched her slowly and gently as if to prolong the ecstasy, but her body already cried for release and each touch sent lines of frantic sensations through her until soon she felt the incredible tension wind inside and she thrashed and stiffened and exhaled sounds of mounting desire. He pulled her shoulders to him and held her firmly, kissing her ferociously while he pushed her over the edge into fulfillment, taking her cries into himself when the violent climax finally crashed through her.

He held her in a tight embrace for a long while, his face buried in the angle of her neck and shoulder. She awoke from the delirium to find her hands clawing the garments at his chest. She doubted that he had found satisfaction in this.

He loosened his hold and looked down at her. She noticed a little blood on his lip where she must have bitten him.

Silently he rose and laid her down on the bed. He caressed her face and looked into her eyes. "I must go."

He had contented her, but her deeper desire still burned. She almost urged him to stay longer and to finish what had begun. The choice would not really be hers then.

He left. Left her with the proof that he possessed the power to seduce her back. Forcing would have never been necessary, this parting visit had said, because this gentler persuasion had always been available to him and would be in the future. For a while longer the choice would be squarely hers, though. He had left her to decide if she could live this marriage and come to him, once again, of her own will.

She gazed at the blue pleats billowing above the bed. Aye, maybe she could. During that brief submersion into pleasure she hadn't thought about anything else, not even what she meant to him. Only later, when he left, had the pain and doubts closed in. In time perhaps they would cease to torment her. In a few years maybe her love would only exist as an amusing memory.

She should leave this bed now, before she fell asleep. If Emma found her upstairs in the morning, the whole household would assume that her illness had ended and Joanna's room would cease to be an option. No choice then. She smiled at how greedily her soul grasped at the possibility for self-deception. *Stay here, fall asleep, and it is done. An accident rather than a decision.*

The bed had lost its strangeness and a delicious relaxation claimed her. Even as she admonished herself to leave, her lids lowered. She surrendered to the prideless love that would accept any pain to be close to him and would gratefully accept the small part of himself that he chose to give her.

She did not know how long she slept, but suddenly

her eyes flew open. A sound had penetrated her dream, prodding her out of her peace. She raised herself on an elbow.

A large dark shadow moved past the window nearest the wardrobe door.

"David?" she mumbled, wiping her eyes.

A strange presence filled the chamber. She heard soft, scuffling footsteps. The shadow moved, and two others joined it.

Suddenly alert with shock, she started to scream. The large shadow lunged toward her. Strong arms pinned her down while rough hands pried and shoved a cloth into her mouth.

She thrashed violently against the suffocating gag. More hands pressed on her until she became immobile. She stared up into strange faces barely visible in the moonlight while her heart pounded wildly in the renewed silence.

"Now you be calm, my lady, and no harm will come to you," a man's voice said softly, just inches from her ear. Not an English voice, she considered as she jerked motionlessly against the restraining hands. Scottish.

One hand released her and a glint of steel appeared in it and waved in front of her eyes. "Listen carefully. We will let you up, but there be three of us here and armed at that, so do as I say. You will go into the wardrobe and dress and pack some things for yourself."

Pack? These men planned to take her someplace. Where and for what possible purpose?

Her mind frantically assessed her danger. How had they gotten into this house with its surrounding wall? Where was Sieg?

"Do you understand? Don't raise your hands to the gag."

She dumbly nodded. The hands fell off her one by

one and the talking man eased away. Shaking with terror, she slid out of the bed, grateful that she had not lit a candle and that these men could not see her naked body very well in the moonlight.

She staggered on wobbly legs to the wardrobe, trying to control the panic that threatened to cloud her mind of all reason and sense. Despite their warnings, she wanted to run and run and let the terror consume her as she did. She rashly decided that in the blackness of the wardrobe she would remove the gag and scream for help.

Upon entering, she saw the door to the garden open. Enough light seeped through to make the lines of her shadow visible and her actions obvious.

They watched as she fumbled for a loose gown and pulled it on. One of the men found a small traveling trunk, and she stuffed clothing into it, not knowing what she grabbed.

Thrusting her feet into shoes, she turned to them. She tried to remain calm although the deathly panic still wanted to unhinge her. Her only hope was to keep her wits about her. If Sieg still lived, he would save her when they tried to leave. She would make as much noise as possible on the courtyard stones in hopes of awakening him and the others.

"Now we will walk down those steps out there and go to the back of the garden," the man said.

Her heart sank. They had come in over the wall, not through the gate. Sieg slept unknowingly in the front building. He and the others would never hear.

They surrounded her like a prisoner being moved and guided her down the stairs and out the gate to the main garden. At the back wall two of them disappeared up a crude ladder.

"Now you. There's another on the other side. Take care, my lady. The drop could hurt you," the Scot said.

She tottered up, turned her body blindly, and felt for the wooden slats on the other side. Hands plucked her off halfway down and set her on the ground. They walked up the alley to where horses waited. Someone tied her hands before lifting her onto a saddle. Being bound made her feel even more helpless. They trailed out through the city lanes, towing her along.

She watched the streets anxiously, hoping to see the flames of torches that indicated other night travelers or the ward constable. If they were stopped, would the constable notice her gag? Would these men use their steel if they were challenged?

No challenge came. Her fear grew as she noted their approach to the city's gate. To her anguished dismay, the gate guard let them pass.

The lead man continued straight ahead after they passed through the wall. She straightened in shock. They headed for the northern road.

North. Northumberland. *Stephen?*

The Percy family held lands in Scotland and on England's border in Northumberland. Was this Scot one of their retainers?

Stephen abducting her? Now? It would be madness. Nay, not Stephen. Unless his pride had been wounded because he had lost his game to a mercer. During tournaments, Stephen had never been especially gracious in defeat. And if not Stephen, then who? She could think of no other possibility.

As they rode silently through the night, she told herself that Stephen would never do something so absurd, but a part of her worried that in fact he might. He might even consider it chivalrous and romantic and a grand gesture of salvation.

Duels and abductions are the stuff of songs, not life. Unless you were dealing with some childish girl and a foolish knight. Stephen, she suspected, could be very foolish.

He had seemed in the end to accept her refusal at that dinner. Had he later reconsidered her resolve? Had his conceit led him to conclude that she fought him against her heart's true desire?

Dear saints. David would kill them both.

Her misgivings flared when, some miles north of London, she spied shadows on the road ahead. Her small group approached two other figures on horses and stopped.

"You made quick work of it," a woman's voice said.

Christiana's eyes widened and she peered in the dark toward the hooded cloak. She knew this voice. This *was* Stephen's doing. And once again he had enlisted Lady Catherine's help.

Catherine's arm stretched out. "Here is the coin you will need. Do it exactly as I told you, and do not delay. The man will pay you your fee. And remember, she is not to be harmed."

Christiana made a loud sound from behind her gag. Lady Catherine turned toward her. "You want to speak, child? Remove her gag."

Dirty fingers pried the wadded cloth out of her mouth. She gasped deep breaths of air before speaking.

"Where do you take me?" she demanded.

"You will find out soon enough."

"If you abduct me for ransom, tell me now. Name your price and return me home. I will pay it."

"A generous offer, but there will be no ransom," Catherine said.

"Then why? Who bids you do this? Stephen Percy?"

Catherine laughed lightly. "All will be explained in good time, my dear. In the end you will thank me for this."

Did Catherine assume, like so many others at court, that she must welcome redemption in Stephen's arms?

"My husband will kill you for this," she hissed toward the men who waited. She realized that it was the first time she had claimed David's protection instead of Morvan's. But David *would* kill them. The thing about property was that one didn't like it stolen.

"By the time he finds you, it may not matter so much to him," Catherine said. "He will have bigger concerns. Take her now, and remember that she is not to be molested or handled. Do not try to run away, Christiana, for they have their orders to deliver you and will tie you to the horse if they have to."

"This is madness—" she began to protest, but the gag suddenly filled her mouth again and she choked on the words.

Lady Catherine and her silent companion turned south while her captors tugged the reins and started north. Christiana held the front of the saddle with bound hands and swayed into the animal's quicker walk.

North. Of all of the times for Stephen Percy to finally decide to live out some chanson!

Didn't he remember that violent deaths and jealous murders often ended those long love songs?

CHAPTER 18

DAVID LET HIS father's blood flow. He unblocked it from the recesses and fissures in which he kept it dammed and controlled. He permitted all of its dark strength to wash through him.

Sieg walked beside him as he rode across the courtyard. He looked down on the Swede's furrowed brow. Sieg blamed his own negligence for Christiana's disappearance and would not rest contented until he had helped bring her back. David would welcome his friend's help in the end, but not right now.

"The swords, Sieg. Don't forget to pack them," he said. Sieg nodded and David passed to the gate. It was possible that he wouldn't need the preparations that he was leaving Sieg to make. Possibly he would find her elsewhere. He doubted it, however. Still, he would have to check.

He paused and looked back at the buildings where he had lived his youth and manhood. If things turned out as he expected, he would never see this home again.

His father's blood didn't give a damn. He smiled thinly. Nay, no sentiment there. Not when faced with a quest or a goal. Or revenge.

He had known for years that it was in him and what it could do. As a youth he had examined his face and soul to know what came from the Abyndons and what came from the other side. He had tried to reconstruct the image of his absent father from the disconnected pieces that bore no Abyndon legacy. The love of beauty. The emotional restraint. The dark calculations. The ability to kill. Even Gilbert's self-righteous cruelty could not match his own inclinations to cold ruthlessness. That in particular had always been in him, a strength to be used and a weakness to be feared, and it went far beyond the shrewd analysis taught as part of a mercer's trade. His mother's blood had tempered it some, but the real lessons in controlling it had been David Constantyn's greatest gift to him.

It had been his father's half that had hurt Christiana.

He would check London and Westminster first, just to be sure.

A short while later he rode into the courtyard of Gilbert de Abyndon's house for the first time in his life. A groom approached for his horse but he ignored the man and tied the reins to a post.

The household sat to dinner when he entered the hall. He had planned it this way. He did not want Margaret to have to confront her husband's wrath if he came when Gilbert wasn't home, and he wanted plenty of people around so that maybe he wouldn't smash his fist into Gilbert's face when his uncle insulted him, as the man was sure to do.

Gilbert looked up from his conversation as David approached his table, and one would have thought that the man had seen an apparition, so complete was his shock. Margaret visibly paled.

David simply nodded acknowledgment of his uncle and turned his attention to Margaret.

"I am seeking Christiana, Margaret."

She frowned. "Seeking?"

"She has left the house."

"She is better then?"

So Christiana had not confided in her new friend. "Aye. But she is two days gone, Margaret. Did she come to you?"

Realization took hold, but Margaret hid it from her expression. Gilbert proved less discreet.

"So your noble wife has left you so soon?" he jeered softly.

"Is she here, Margaret?"

She shook her head.

"You have never known your place, boy," Gilbert snarled. "The conceit of marrying such a woman! Of course she is gone. It is a wonder she stayed this long."

David managed to ignore him. "Do you know where she is, Margaret?"

Poor Margaret shook her head again. Distressed eyes flickered up to his. Her hand rested protectively on her slightly swelled belly.

Gilbert laughed. "It is a pleasure to see great pride humbled. Such are the wages of that sin. Look you to the beds in the castles of the realm for her, nephew. Those women have no morals."

His hand shot out and he grabbed his uncle by the neck. Gilbert cried out and fell back in his chair. David let his arm and hand follow until he had the man pinned against the wooden back. The hall fell silent and a dozen pairs of eyes watched.

"You will say no more, Uncle, or I will release your young wife from the misery of this marriage," he said. "Now, you will permit Margaret to accompany me to the door and you will not follow. Do you agree to this?"

Gilbert glared at him. David squeezed. Gilbert nodded.

Margaret eased off her bench and came around the table. David dropped his hand.

"I am sorry," he said as they walked across the hall. "There was nothing for it but to come here."

"I understand. Do not worry. He will sputter for a few days and speak ill of you to all he meets, but that is nothing new, is it?"

David paused at the door. "Did she ever speak of Sir Stephen Percy to you?"

Margaret's surprise and shock were genuine. "Nay, David. She spoke of no man to me except you and her brother. Even when she described a humorous event at court, the players had no significance."

He nodded and turned to go. "Be well, Margaret."

She stopped him, and stepped out into the courtyard so that she could speak privately. "Why do you ask me about this man, David? Do you think Christiana has run away?"

"It is possible."

"With this man?" She looked at him incredulously. "I always thought that you were the exception to the rule that men were fools, David. If she held another in her heart, then I did not know her at all. She spoke only of you, and with warmth and affection and respect. If she is gone, it is not of her will, I am sure." She frowned with distress. "She is in danger, isn't she? Oh dear God . . ."

"I do not think that she is in danger," he said soothingly. "Go back to your husband now. Tell him that I would not let you leave me until you answered my questions."

"You must find her . . ."

"I will find her."

David stood against the wall of the practice yard and watched Morvan Fitzwaryn swing his battle-ax and land it against his opponent's shield. A bright sheen of sweat glistened on Morvan's naked chest and shoulders.

David sensed a movement behind him and turned to see two women peering over the wall as they strolled past. They eyed the tall knight appreciatively and giggled some comments to each other behind raised hands before they moved on.

He waited. Morvan had noticed him already. Eventually this practice must end.

Soon it did. Morvan's opponent gestured a finish. The two knights walked over to a water trough and sluiced themselves. Morvan came over as he shook the water from his head.

"You want me?" he asked, his voice still a little breathless from his exertions.

"Aye. Three nights ago Christiana left the house. None saw her and she told no one where she was going."

Morvan had been in the process of wiping his brow. His hand froze there.

"Did she come here, Morvan?"

"Nay."

"You said that you would have taken her elsewhere if possible. Have you done so now?"

Morvan glared at him. "If I had taken her from you, I would have let you see me do it."

David began walking away.

"She has not gone to him," Morvan called after him. He pivoted. "How do you know?"

"Because she told me she would not."

"Then you received more assurances than I did."

"Why give assurances to a man who does not believe them?" Morvan asked tightly as he walked up to him.

"I will know the truth of it soon enough, I suppose."

Morvan stared thoughtfully at the ground. "The last time she left and came here, she let you know where she was."

"Aye."

"But not this time. And she told me that she no longer cares for him. If she is with Percy, David, I do not think that it is her choice."

"I thought of that. You know the man better than me. Is it in his nature to do this? To abduct her?"

Morvan glanced blindly around the practice yard. "Hell if I know. He is vain and conceited and, I always thought, a little dull in the wits. The women say that he does not take rejection well. The men know that he is quick with a challenge if he thinks himself slighted."

David absorbed this. He should have met Sir Stephen or at least learned more about him. Pride had prevented it, but that had been a mistake. One should always know one's competitors' strengths and weaknesses. Even a green apprentice knew that.

"I will let you know when I find her."

"Do you ride north, then?" Morvan asked cautiously.

"Aye."

"I will come with you."

"I will go alone. For one thing, the King will need you here as the army musters. For another, I do not plan to do this in a knight's way."

He turned to leave, but Morvan gripped his arm. He looked into sparkling, troubled eyes so like those others.

"You must promise me, if you find her there, that you will give her a chance to speak. If there is an explanation, you must hear it," Morvan said.

David glanced down on the hand restraining him, and then at the intense bright eyes studying his face. Did he look as dangerous as Morvan's worry suggested?

"I will hear her out, brother."

He left then, to meet Sieg and Oliver and begin the journey to Northumberland. First, however, he made his way to the stone stairs that led to Edward's private chambers.

David and Oliver eased along the gutter of the inn, their backs pressed against the steep roof. Below them the lane that led to this hostelry appeared deserted except for the large shadow of a man resting casually against a fence rail. The shadow's head looked up to check their progress.

It went without saying that Sieg could not join them up here. He weight would have broken the tiles. He would wait below and then enter the normal way, dispatching in his wake any inconvenient squires or companions who might try to interfere.

"This reminds me of the old days," Oliver whispered cheerfully as they carefully set their steps into the gutter tiles. "Remember that time we boys got into the grocer's loft through the roof? Filled our pockets with salt."

"Nothing so practical, Oliver. It was cinnamon, and worth more than gold. They'd have hung us if they caught us, children or not."

"A great adventure, though."

"At least your mother used what you took. Mine knew it was stolen, gave it away, and dragged me to the priest."

"Her sensitivities on such things are no doubt why your life took a turn for the worse when you got older," Oliver said. "School and all."

"No doubt."

Oliver's foot slipped and a tile crashed to the ground. Both men froze and waited for the sounds that indicated someone had heard.

"I've a good mind to slit this knight's throat just to express my annoyance that he was so hard to find," Oliver muttered in the silence.

David smiled thinly. Percy had certainly been hard to find, and the length of their search had not improved David's own humor much. The man seemed to be hiding. Not a good sign.

They had ridden first to his father's estate, then his uncle's, and finally to the properties which Stephen himself managed. There had been no need to approach the castles and manor houses. A few hours in the nearest town or village gave them the information they sought. Young Sir Stephen had not been seen for at least a week. Finally, on the road south, a chance conversation with a passing jongleur had revealed that Percy had been resting at length at this public inn several miles north of Newcastle.

David surveyed the ground below him, dimly lit by one torch. Sieg glanced up and nodded. They were just above the window to Stephen's chamber on the top level of the inn. The warm June night had caused the window to be left open.

It was the dead of night and no sounds came from the inn or the chamber below. David turned to the roof, crouched, and grasped the eaves. He lowered his body down, slowly unbending his arms. His feet found the opening and he angled in, dropping with the slightest thud on the floor of the chamber.

He peered around at the flickering shadows cast by one night candle. Curtains surrounded the beds in this expensive inn, but here they had been left open. He saw a man's naked back and blond hair, and a strong arm slung over another body. Long dark tresses poured over the sheet.

His stomach clenched. A bloody fury obscured his sight. He unsheathed the dagger on his hip.

Oliver swung in the window and landed beside him. He gestured for David to be still, and then eased over to the door. Sieg waited on the other side.

With Sieg's arrival there could be little hope of keeping their presence a secret. The Swede stomped in, unsheathing his sword. Stephen Percy's head jerked up.

Sieg reached him before he had fully turned over. He placed a silencing finger to Percy's lips and the sword to his throat. Stephen froze. The woman still slept.

David found a taper near the hearth and bent it to the guttering night candle. He walked over and inspected the man who had caused him so much trouble.

Bright green eyes stared back warily over the shining blade. Stephen had rugged features and his skin appeared very pale, especially with all of the blood gone out of it now. David grudgingly admitted that women might find this man attractive.

"Who are you?" Stephen asked hoarsely in a voice that tried to sound indignant.

David leaned into better view. "I am Christiana's husband. The merchant."

Stephen's gaze slid over David, then angled up at Sieg and over to Oliver. "Thank God," he sighed with relief.

Sieg frowned at David. David gestured to Oliver. The wiry man moved to the other side of the bed.

Oliver pushed back the raven tresses spilling over a thin back. The girl jolted awake and turned. She managed one low shriek before Oliver's hand clamped down over her mouth.

Oliver stared. "Hell, David, it isn't her!"

"Nay. I never really thought it would be. She would not come on her own, and he never cared enough to abduct her. But I had to be sure."

The girl had noticed the sword at Percy's throat, its point not far from her own neck. She huddled herself into a ball and stared around wild-eyed.

David smiled down at Sir Stephen. "You thought we might be her kinsmen?"

Stephen gave a little shrug.

"Another virgin sacrifice to your vanity, Sir Stephen?"

Stephen's eyes narrowed. "Have you lost something, merchant? You can see she is not here, so be gone."

"Do you have her elsewhere?"

Stephen laughed. "She was sweet, but not worth that much trouble."

Dangerous anger seeped into David's mind. "Sweet, was she?"

A sneer played on Stephen's face. Sieg lifted the blade a bit, forcing Percy's chin to rise with it. Stephen glowered down at the sword and hesitated, but conceit won out.

"Aye," he smirked. "Very sweet. Well worth the wait."

"I kill him now, David," Sieg said matter-of-factly.

"Nay. If he dies, he is mine."

The girl had begun crying into her knees. Oliver sat beside her and patted her shoulder. She muttered something between her sobs.

"Considering your position, you are either very brave or very stupid to taunt me thus," David said.

Stephen laughed. "You are no threat to me, mercer.

Harm a hair on my head and you had best leave the realm. If the law doesn't hang you, my family will."

"A good point. Except that I had already planned to leave the realm, and so it appears that I have nothing to lose."

The smug smile fell from Stephen's face.

"David," Oliver said, "this girl is little more than a child. Look at how small she is. How old are you, girl?"

"Just fourteen this summer," she sobbed miserably. She glared at Stephen. "He was going to take me to London, wasn't he?"

Stephen rolled his eyes. "We will go, my sweet. After it is safe . . ."

"Nay, you won't," Oliver said to her. "He will leave you to the wrath of your kinsmen, and you'll be lucky to end up in a convent. What are you? Gentry? Aye, well, they won't press case against a Percy, will they? Nay, girl, it's a convent or whoring for you, I'm afraid."

The girl wailed. Percy cursed.

"So do we kill him now?" Sieg asked.

Quick. Easy. So tempting. David gazed impassively at the rugged face trying to remain brave and cool.

"I think not," he finally said.

Stephen's eyes closed in relief as Sieg cursed and sheathed his sword.

"Give me your dagger, David," Sieg said, holding out his hand. "The Mamluk one."

"What for?"

Sieg sniffed. "In honor of the love I feel for this country and in protection of the few virgins left in it, I'm going to fix this man."

Stephen frowned in perplexity.

"Remember that physician in prison, David? The one who had once worked at the palace? Well, he told me how they made eunuchs. It is a simple thing, really. Just a quick cut . . ."

Stephen's eyes widened in horror.

"Sieg . . ." David began.

"The dagger, David. You always keep it sharp. We'll be out of here as quick as a nick."

David looked at Sir Stephen's sweating brow. He looked at the crying girl and Oliver's gentle comfort. He thought about Christiana's pain over this man.

"If you insist," he said blandly.

"Aye. Oliver, help hold him down for me."

The girl saw the dagger approach and began a series of low, hoarse screams. Sir Stephen practically jumped out of his skin. He inched back on the bed, staring at the looming, implacable Sieg. He turned to David. "Good God, man, you can't be serious!"

"As I said, I have nothing to lose."

Stephen laughed nervously and held up a hand as if to ward off the dagger. "Listen. Seriously. What I said before about Christiana . . . I was lying. I never had her. In truth I never did."

"It is more likely that you are lying now."

"I swear to you, I never . . . I barely touched her! I tried, I'll admit, but, hell, we all try, don't we?" He turned wildly to Sieg and Oliver, seeking confirmation.

"Let's see. Kneel on his legs, David. Oliver, climb over and put your weight on his chest," Sieg said as he reached for the sheet.

"*Jesus!*" Stephen yelled. "I swear it on my soul, she wouldn't have me."

David smiled. "I already knew that."

Sieg took another step forward. Stephen looked ready to faint.

"How?" Stephen croaked while he stared at the ugly length of steel.

"She told me." He placed a hand on Sieg's shoulder. "Let us go, Sieg. Leave this man."

"Hell, David, he is disgusting . . ."

"Let us go."

Oliver got up from the bed and fetched some garments from a stool. "You wait outside, we will be down soon."

"We?"

"We can't leave her here, can we? He's ruined her if she's found. I told her that we'd take her to Newcastle and leave her at an abbey. She'll say that she got knocked on the head and lost her memory and wandered for days until some kind soul brought her to the city."

"Ah. The knocked-on-the-head-and-wandered-for-days explanation. A bit overused, don't you think?"

"Her family will believe it because they will want to. On the way, I'll tell her how to fake the evidence when she gets married."

"Oliver . . ."

"She's just a child, David. Too trusting, that is all."

"You are a whoremonger, Oliver. You are supposed to recruit girls who have fallen, not save them." He looked at the girl not much younger than Joanna had been. He sighed and went to the door with Sieg.

Hell. At this rate, he'd never get out of England.

But, then, that had been the whole point of forcing him to make this search in the first place.

CHAPTER 19

CHRISTIANA PULLED THE knotted sheets and towels tautly to be sure they held together. She slid her arm through the center of the coiled rope of cloth and draped her light cloak over all of it.

It will work, she decided. It has to.

Leaving the chamber and building, she walked across the courtyard to the hall. She sought out Heloise sewing with her servants and three daughters. Beautiful, blond Heloise looked up kindly as she approached.

"The evening is fair," Christiana said in the distant tone she had maintained since her arrival. "I will sit in the garden for a while, I think."

"The breeze is cooling," Heloise said.

"I have brought my cloak if I need it."

The woman nodded and returned to her conversation.

Christiana forced her steps to slow indifferently. Outside she nipped into the walled garden behind the hall. She meandered through the plantings so that her progress would appear accidental. Slowly, deliberately, she worked her way toward the tall tree in the back corner of the garden.

Five days. Five days she had been a prisoner, and she still did not know why they had brought her here. She doubted that Heloise knew either. Perhaps her husband, the mayor of Caen, in whose palatial home she now found herself, had the answer, but he had explained nothing. Since the day she had stumbled into that hall, filthy and disheveled from her journey on horse and sea, furiously indignant and ready to kill or be killed, no one had told her anything. They had welcomed her as a guest, however, and shown her every honor and hospitality.

Except one. She could not leave.

Well, she would leave now. Yesterday she had found this tree. It grew higher than the wall, and she had eagerly climbed it, praying that some structure to which she could jump abutted the wall on the other side. Hovering amongst the obscuring branches and leaves, she had looked down at the sheer twenty-foot drop awaiting her. Even as disappointment flooded her, however, she had laid her plans.

She glanced around cautiously while she backed up into the shadow of the tree. At least two hours before nightfall. Enough time to get away from this city and find shelter somewhere.

Hoisting the line of sheets up her arm, she climbed the tree. She found a strong branch overhanging the wall's crest and settled herself on it. Easing off the sheets, she tied one end to the branch and threw the rest over the wall.

She shimmied out over the precipice and looked down. The dangling white line reached within ten feet of the ground. If she hung near the end and dropped, she should be safe enough.

She eyed the sheets and their knots. If they failed to support her weight, this could maim her. She prayed that the mayor of Caen bought top-quality linen for his bedding.

Lowering her feet to the top of the wall, she grabbed the first knot. She stepped back.

She had hoped that she could basically walk down the wall, but it didn't work that way. She found herself dangling against it, her hands clawing at the white line that supported her. The muscles in her arms and shoulders immediately rebelled.

Only one way to go now. Grasping with all of her strength, she began to jerk her way down, hand over hand. Halfway to the ground, she began to hear a distant commotion. It grew and moved toward her.

Noises and voices resonated through the stone wall. A lot of people were in the garden, thrashing around. She continued her painful progress and stared up at the tree limb fearfully, waiting for the face that would discover her. The leaves must have hidden her rope's end, because the noises retreated.

She had tied some towels at the end to lengthen the rope, and she reached them now. The knot stretched against her weight. Just as her hands were about to give out anyway, she heard the rip that sent her crashing to the ground.

It had only been a drop of eight feet, but it still stunned her. She cautiously rose to her feet and glanced around.

Another wall, of another house, stretched in front of her. Between the two ran a very narrow alley where she now stood. At one end she saw a jumble of roofs that suggested it gave out on a city lane. The other way looked clearer.

Staying in the wall's shadow, she quickly walked

up the alley with a triumphant elation pounding through her. Whatever the mayor of Caen had planned for her, he could find another Englishwoman for the role.

She would cross the river and and stay off the roads and make her way to the coast and a port town. Maybe she would find an English fisherman or merchant there who would help her.

She stopped near the end of the wall and strained her ears for the sounds of the searchers. All was silent. She started forward again.

Suddenly a man stepped from behind the wall's end. He stood twenty yards in front of her with his arms crossed over his chest. She paused and stared at him in the evening light.

Definitely not the portly, short mayor. Too tall and lean, although the long hair was just as white and the clothing just as rich. Not one of his retainers either. She carefully walked forward, hoping that this man's presence had nothing to do with her, despite the concentrated way that he watched her approach.

She had just decided to smile sweetly and pretend that she belonged in this alley and neighborhood when she drew near enough to see his face.

She recognized him and, she knew, he recognized her. Her heart sank as her feet continued bringing her closer to the French noble who had disguised himself to meet with David at Hampstead.

She had not met him up close that day, but she stopped only a few paces away and faced him squarely now. She remembered more about his appearance than she had thought, for he looked very familiar to her in unspecified ways. Hooded brown eyes gazed down examining her. Between the white mustache and short beard, a slow smile formed.

"You have spirit," he said. "A good sign." He looked

down the alley to the swaying white line of sheets and towels. "You might have hurt yourself."

"Does it matter?"

"It matters a great deal."

"Well, that at least is good news."

He stepped aside. With a flourishing gesture, he pointed her back toward her prison.

Christiana plied her needle in the twilight eking through the open window. A low fire burned in the hearth, but the early July evening was very warm and the fire would not be built up when the daylight faded.

She glanced at the women and girls sitting around her, speaking lowly to each other as they bent to their own needlework. Occasionally one would look at her curiously. They still did not know why she had been foisted on them to befriend and entertain, and nothing beyond the previous polite courtesy had developed over the seven days since her attempted escape.

She looked down the hall to the other hearth and the four men gathered around it. Two of them were local barons from the region who had arrived during the last few days with their retinues at the French king's command. Others had come before them. The city was filling with knights and soldiers. Some camped across the river that served as a natural defense to this Norman city. A few had entered the castle, but most came here, to the mayor's house, and consulted with the tall white-haired man sitting by the other hearth.

She knew his name now. Theobald, the Comte of Senlis. Not just a noble, as she had surmised that day in Hampstead, but an important baron equal in rank to an English earl, and an advisor to the French king.

He had only spoken to her enough to ascertain that she had not been harmed or molested. He had ignored her demanding questions. She suspected, however, that she had been brought here at his initiative and command, and not the mayor's.

A prisoner still. *His prisoner*. To what end and what purpose? The women did not know. The Comte would not say. She sat in this house day after day, keeping to herself, refusing all but the barest hospitality, and watched the lords' arrivals and the daily consultations at the other end of the hall.

The light had faded. She rose and went to a bench below a window on the long wall of the hall. She would sit alone for a while and give the ladies time to gossip and speculate about her. Her unnatural and strained social situation did nothing to alleviate the chilling fear that she had carried inside her ever since those men had pulled her from her home. She admitted that the chill had gotten colder since she had faced the Comte at the end of the alley.

She had imagined during her first days here that David would come to rescue her. Perhaps he would bring Morvan and Walter Manny and some of the other knights to help. They would ride up to the river and across the bridge and into the city and demand her release. Like something out of a chanson.

She grimaced at her foolishness. If David were coming, he would have been here by now. In fact, he could have arrived before her. Returning home and finding her gone, he could have sailed from London and reached France before her own boat. Her captors had dragged her all the way north, almost to Scotland, before securing passage at a seaside port. A waste of time that made no sense, but then none of this did.

She had closed her eyes as she contemplated her situation, and the hall had receded from her awareness. A slight commotion intruded on her reverie now.

At the far hearth the Comte had risen from his chair and bent his ear to a gesturing man-at-arms. A broad smile broke over his face. He turned and said something to the mayor. One of the barons clapped his hand merrily on the other's shoulder.

The entrance to the hall swung open and she had a view of the anteroom beyond. Through the threshold to the courtyard she saw a man approach. Torchlight reflected off armor before the darkness of the anteroom swallowed him.

Another baron. They came to prepare for King Edward's invasion, of course. No doubt similar councils and musterings were taking place all over France.

One of the Comte's squires entered first, carrying a helmet and shield. She glanced at the newly painted and unscarred blue and gold coat of arms on it. Five gold disks over three entwined serpents, and the bar sinister of a bastard son.

Three entwined serpents . . . shocked alertness shook her. She sat upright and stared.

The knight entered the chamber. Tall and lean, he looked around placidly as he removed his gauntlets. His body moved fluidly in the clumsy armor as if he wore a second skin. He stood proudly with a touch of arrogance. Mussed brown hair hung around his perfect, weather-bronzed face. Blue eyes met her intently.

She watched speechlessly. To her right, the women turned to regard the strong and handsome new man. To her left, the Comte strode forward, smiling, his hands outstretched.

"Welcome to France, nephew."

David de Abyndon, her David, her merchant, turned to the Comte de Senlis.

Nephew! Stunned, she looked from him to the Comt
and then back again. She suddenly understood the od
familiarity she had felt when she looked in that olde
man's face.

She glared at David, standing there so casually an
naturally in his damn armor, looking for all the world lik
a knight, accepting a kinsman's welcome from this Frencl
baron.

Of course. Of course. Why hadn't she seen it before? Th
height. The strength. The lack of deference. He hadn'
told her. He had never even hinted. The urge to strangl
her husband assaulted her.

The Comte spoke quietly and gestured David towar
the hearth.

"I will see to my wife first," David said, and dismiss
ing his uncle's interest, he crossed the space to her.

She glanced up the molded metal plates and looke
him accusingly straight in the eyes. He looked straigh
back. Placid. Inscrutable. Cool.

"You are well and unharmed?"

"Aside from feeling like an ignorant and stupid foo
who is married to a lying stranger, I am well."

He bent to kiss her. "I will explain all when w
are alone," he said quietly. "Come now, and sit witl
me. Do not take to heart what I say to him, darling.
would have the Comte think that we are not conten
together."

"I should be able to help you with that."

The Comte wanted to speak with David alone. H
had dismissed the barons and mayor, and frowned ir
annoyance when David led Christiana to the hearth.

"Thanks to you, I gamble with her life now as well a
my own," David said. "She has a right to know my situation."

She sat in a chair. David stood near the hearth and she

watched him with confusion and shock and anger. In a strange way, however, a small part of her nodded with understanding. Something seemed appallingly *right* about seeing him like this, as if a shadow that had always floated behind him had suddenly taken substance and form. *Who are you really?*

She glanced at the Comte and could tell from that old man's approving gaze that he saw what she saw.

David turned to his uncle and let his annoyance flare. "I told you that she was not to be involved."

The Comte raised his hands. "You did not come in April. I sought to encourage you."

"I did not come because the storms rose as soon as I reached Normandy. Why deliver news that would have no value? The fleet barely made it back to England."

So he had come to France at Easter. But then, she had known that as soon as she saw him enter the hall.

"I had men waiting for you at Calais and St. Malo. You did not come."

"Do you think that I am so stupid as to put in at a major trading port where I might be recognized? Would you be so careless?"

The Comte considered this and made a face of tentative acceptance. "Still, you are late. I expected you weeks ago. The army is ready to move."

"I am late because my wife disappeared and I sought to find her."

"You knew where she was."

"I did not. I could hardly leave England without knowing her fate."

The Comte flushed. "They were to leave—"

"No note or word was left." David stared hard at the Comte. "You sent Frans to do this, didn't you? Against our agreement."

"He knew the people. He knows your habits."

"Aye. But he relied on Lady Catherine, who holds no love for me. Also against our agreement. And she had her own plans for me. I was lucky to get out of England alive."

The Comte reddened. "She endangered you?"

"You probably assumed that I would know, note or not, that you had taken Christiana. What other explanation could there be? What you did not know is that my wife has a lover who lives in the north country."

The Comte glanced in scathing disappointment at her. She faced him down. David had better have a damn good reason for telling his uncle that.

"Lady Catherine knew this, however," David continued. "And so she had the men whom she and Frans hired leave no note or sign, so I would wonder if Christiana had gone to this man. They even took her out of the country by way of a northern port, so that I could follow her trail toward her lover. All the while, time is passing and I am still in England." He paused and smiled unpleasantly. "And during that time, Catherine went to King Edward and told him about me. She had a lot to tell, because Frans had let her know of my relationship to you."

A very hard expression masked the Comte's face. Christiana drew back in alarm. She had seen that expression before, but not on this Frenchman's face.

"I will deal with them both. The woman and Frans."

"I have already done so."

"If the woman betrayed you to Edward, what you know may be useless. He may change the port."

She had been correct in her suspicions then. David planned to give the port's location to the Comte and the French. But not in exchange for silver and gold. And, as a son of Senlis, not even in treason. Every noble knew and respected the loyalties of blood ties. An oath of fealty bound one just as strongly, but a wise king or lord never asked his liegemen to make a choice between the two obligations.

"I thought of that," David said. "And it may happen. But before I slipped out, I learned that, even two weeks after hearing Catherine's tale, he had not changed his mind. He had already sent word to the English forces on the Continent, and there was no time to undo that. But he may hope that you expect him to, so that you resist committing all of your forces to the one place. I wonder if he did not let me escape with the news of Lady Catherine's betrayal in order to cast doubt on the value of this information in the event that I had managed to send it to you earlier."

All of David's attention was concentrated on his uncle, and those blue eyes never wavered in their scrutiny of the older man's face. The Comte's own eyes, brown rather than blue but so similar nonetheless, appeared just as piercing whenever he studied David.

Who are you really? Well, now she knew. She was too numb and confused to decipher how she felt about this startling revelation. She should be relieved. Her husband was not common. His father's blood, the important blood, had been noble.

So why did this anger unaccountably want to unhinge her?

The Comte paced and nodded to himself. "I think that you are right. The summer is passing quickly. If he comes at all, he must do so now. His army has been mustered. It is too late to change course." He pivoted toward David. "Do you have it, then?"

"I have it. More than he knows that I have. The roads he will take and the direction he will head. The size of his force. I have it all."

The Comte waited expectantly.

David smiled faintly. "Do you have the documents?"

The Comte gave an exasperated sigh. "Mine is here and witnessed. The constable brings that from the King when he arrives. But we waste time . . ."

"You have already broken most of our spoken agreement. And because of that, I have been left no choice but to do this. I cannot return to England, and although Edward may one day acknowledge Christiana's innocence and welcome her back, she is forced now to a future that she did not choose either. I do not plan to start life over with the little gold I brought with me. I go no further without the documents."

A very ugly tension seemed to paralyze the two men, and something threatening and dark flowed out of the Comte. Christiana sucked in her breath. She had felt this dangerous presence before, too. She wondered what the Comte contemplated. He was as unreadable as David.

Except to David.

"I was tortured once in Egypt," David said calmly. "The French mind cannot compete with Saracen invention on that. You will buy no time that way, and will have an heir who waits to see you dead."

Beneath hooded lids, brown eyes slid subtly in her direction. A horrible chill prickled her neck.

David's eyes narrowed. "Do not shame your name and your blood by even considering it. She knows absolutely nothing, as your wife would not under the circumstances."

But I do know, she thought frantically. She suspected that this uncle could read people as well as David. She lowered her eyes from his inspection and prayed that he saw only her palpable fear in her face.

The Comte considered her a moment and then laughed lightly.

"When do you expect the constable?" David asked.

"By early morning."

"You are too impatient then, and too quickly consider

dishonor. Is it any wonder that I demand written assurances?"

A dangerous scolding for a merchant to give a baron, kinsman or not. Laden with distrust and insult. But the Comte seemed more impressed than angry.

"All men consider things that they would never do, nephew. Recognizing one's options is not the same as choosing them."

David frowned thoughtfully and then nodded, as if he completely understood the Comte's explanation and had reason to accept it as sound.

The tension slowly unwound.

"I promise that there will be time enough to move your forces. The ships were not even half ready to sail when I left," David said.

That seemed to lighten the mood even more. The Comte smiled pleasantly, even warmly.

David walked over and took her hand. "Show me our chamber, Christiana. I want to get out of this steel that has broiled my body under the hot sun all day."

"I will send my squires to help you," the Comte said. "And tell the mistress to have servants prepare a bath for you."

Christiana wordlessly led David out of the hall and toward the tall side building that held the chambers.

"The man drains me," David muttered as they walked through the warm night. "It is like negotiating with the image I see in a mirror."

CHAPTER 20

THE TWO SQUIRES removed David's armor. They kept calling him "my lord." Christiana glanced with annoyance at her husband's tall body standing spread legged while the plate came off. One would think he had done this a thousand times.

Near the low-burning hearth fire, servants prepared the water in a deep wooden hip bath. One girl kept looking at David and smiling sweetly whenever she caught his eye. Christiana grabbed her by the scruff of the neck when the last pail had been poured.

"Out. I will attend my husband."

The servants scurried away. The squires finished their long chore and, calling merry farewells, drifted off. David stripped off his inner garments and settled into the tub.

The sight of his body stirred her more than she cared to admit. She cursed silently at her weakness and at her traitorous heart's independence from her will and mind. *Our life together has been one long illusion*, she fumed. *It was a mistake to think that I could find contentment in pleasure alone. He will always be a stranger. I will always be the play-thing who shares his bed but not his life. I will have it out with him once and for all and then demand another chamber.*

She pulled over a stool, sat down, and faced him.

"Aren't you going to attend me?" he asked.

"Wash," she ordered dangerously, throwing him a chunk of soap. "And talk."

"Ah," he said thoughtfully.

"And no 'ahs,' David. One more 'ah' and I will drown you."

"I understand that you are angry, darling. Believe me, I went through great trouble not to involve you. I intended you to know nothing. Edward would never have blamed you for my sins. The Comte surprised me with this abduction. Frankly, I am disappointed in him."

"Are you indeed?"

"Aye. I expected more chivalry of him. To abduct and endanger an innocent woman . . . It is really very churlish."

"He wants the name of the port, David. He would probably kill me if he thought it would make you give it to him a minute sooner."

"Which is why I want him to think that we are not content together. I do not want him debating whether he can use you against me. Once the Constable d'Eu arrives, I will get his assurance of your safety before I speak with them. The constable is reputed to be honorable to the point of stupidity."

She rolled her eyes. "Let us start at the beginning. Is the Comte in fact your kinsman?"

"It would seem so."

"How long have you known?

"Almost my whole life. My mother told me of my father when I was a child. So I would know that I was not an ordinary, gutter variety bastard."

"Why didn't you tell me?"

"It is a claim easily made but hard to prove, Christiana. And unless a bastard is recognized, it has no value." He watched himself lather an arm. "Would it have helped, darling?"

She sorely wished that she could say not. "It might have. At the beginning."

"Then I am sorry that I didn't tell you."

"Nay, you are not. Your pride wanted me to accept you as the merchant, not the son of Senlis. You can be very strange, David. Not many men would think noble blood makes them less than they are instead of more."

He glanced at her sharply. She let him see her anger.

"You lied to me," she said. "Over and over."

"Only to protect you. This began long before we met. I sought to keep you out of it, ignorant of it, so that you would be spared if something went wrong."

"I am your wife. No one would believe my ignorance."

"You are the daughter of Hugh Fitzwaryn and were a ward of the King. All would believe it. Neither Edward nor his barons would have blamed you for the actions of your merchant husband."

His bland excuses infuriated her. She raised her fists and slammed them down on her lap. "I am your *wife*! If something went wrong, I would have had to watch them tear your body apart even if I was spared. I still may have to, for all that I know. But worse, you hid yourself from me, hid your true nature, who you are."

That hardness played around his mouth and eyes. "You have not been my wife for months now. Should I have trusted the girl who lived in my home like a guest or a cousin?"

"Better a guest than some precious artwork. Better a

cousin than a piece of noble property purchased to salve the forgotten son's wounded pride."

His eyes flashed. "If you truly believe that, then there is no point in explaining anything to you. No matter what I said that day, you should know better of me."

"Know better of you? Right now I don't think that I know you at all, damn you. And do not insinuate that our separation led you to maintain your deception. You had no intention of telling me anything until this was over, no matter how dutiful I might have been. What then? Would you have stayed in France and sent for me? Written a letter that bid me to attend on you here?"

"It always was and still is my intention to give you a choice."

"Indeed? Well, your uncle has closed that door!"

"That remains to be seen."

She looked away until she regained control. She smoothed the skirt of her gown. "I want you to tell me all of it. Now. I would know my situation and my choices. From the beginning."

He told his tale while he washed. "It began simply enough. Edward had asked me to make the maps. It occurred to me that when the time came, I might learn the port that he chose from the questions that he asked me about them. I have never really forgiven my father for what he did to Joanna. He destroyed her and left her to the mercy of the world. Perhaps I also resented his ignorance and neglect of me. Anyway, not really expecting it to work, I began making enough mistakes in France so that anyone paying attention might suspect what I did there. And I began using the three serpents as the device on my seal. They were carved into a ring my father left with my mother. She thought it like a wedding ring, but I suspect he had intended it as payment for her favors."

He paused and lathered the soap between his hands. The gesture distracted him. Christiana watched him examine the white foam and then the cake itself. She had to smile. The merchant's wife had been similarly distracted during her first bath here.

"It comes from a town on the Loire," she said.

David smelled the foam. "Superior, isn't it? I wonder . . ."

"Twenty large cakes for a mark."

He raised his eyebrows. She watched him silently begin calculating the cost of importation and the potential profit.

"David," she said, calling him back.

"Aye. Well, my plan was to let the Comte know of me, realize our connection, and then approach me for the port. I would resist and let him cajole me by playing on the bonds of kinship. I would relent, accepting no payment so he thought that I did it for my blood and so trusted me. But I would give him the wrong port. The French army would go in one direction, Edward would come from the other, and the way would be clear for an English victory."

She looked at his expression. Matter-of-fact. Blasé. As if men calculated such elaborate schemes all of the time and spent years manipulating the pieces.

He enjoys this, she realized. He traveled to the Dark Continent and he crosses the Alps every other year. He needs the adventure, the planning, the challenge.

"And you would have punished that family for your mother's fate," she added.

"That too. I doubt that the Comte de Senlis would remain on the King's council after giving such bad advice. A loss of status and honor, but no real harm. Unlike Joanna's fall. Still, some justice."

"So what went wrong?"

"Nothing. It unfolded as planned. Except for a few surprises. Early on, Honoré, the last Comte, died, and his brother Theobald took his place. A more dangerous man, Theobald."

She stood up and paced slowly around the chamber. She waited for the rest. David waited longer.

"What did you mean when you said that about his heir wanting him dead?" she blurted.

"The other surprise. A very big one. He did not offer me silver. He offered me recognition and Senlis itself. Honoré's and Theobald's other sons are dead. He offered to swear that his brother had made secret vows with my mother. It would be a lie, but it would secure my right to inherit."

She stared at him.

David. Her merchant. The Comte de Senlis.

"Men have been tempted to treason by much less, my girl."

"You said that you had no interest in being a knight."

He laughed. "Darling, a knight is one thing. A leading baron and councilor to the King of France is quite another."

"You are going to do it then?"

"I have not yet decided. What would you have me do?"

"Nay, David. You began this long ago. You do not foist the choice on me now."

She began pacing again, thinking out loud. "There are many men who owe fealty to two kings or lords. Many English barons also have lands in France. Everyone understands that loyalties conflict sometimes."

He reached out and caught her arm as she passed. His grasp held her firmly and he looked up at her, shaking his head. "Let us not pretend that I face other than I do.

What you say is true, but there are rules that decide which way a man goes in those cases. This is different. If I help the Comte and France, if I do this, I betray a trust and a friendship and my country. For the prize that is offered, I am not above doing it, but I will not pretend it is prettier than it is."

Damn him. *Damn him*. There were enough ambiguities here for a bishop to rationalize his actions. He could at least let her find some comfort in them.

"France is your country, David," she pointed out. "Your father was French."

"In truth, I find that it is not England that concerns me. Or even Edward. He has had barons do worse by him, and he possesses a large capacity for understanding and even forgiving such things. Nay, it is London that has been on my mind. If not for my city, I do not think that I would hesitate."

He held up the soap. "Since you sent the servants away, you could at least wash my back."

She knelt behind him and smoothed the lather over his muscles. Despite her inner turmoil, she couldn't help but notice that it was the first time that she had touched his body in months. A slight tensing beneath her palm told her of his awareness of it, too.

"You lied to me in April. You came to France and did not go to Salisbury."

"I could hardly implicate you with the truth." He glanced over his shoulder. "That day in the wardrobe. Your questions. How much did you suspect?"

"Most of it eventually, but not about your father. I heard Frans's first approach to you. I was hiding in the passageway. But I wasn't sure that it had been you there. I learned that he was an agent for the French cause. I saw you meet with him again at Westminster. When the

Comte came to Hampstead, I heard his voice before he left. I knew that he was French and a noble."

"You thought that I might be selling Edward's plans for silver?"

"It was one explanation for these things. Actually, it was the silver that didn't make sense. You enjoy your wealth, but are too generous to be a man who would do anything out of greed."

He twisted around and looked down at her. "If you knew so much, I am surprised that you did not leave sooner, while I was gone, for your own safety and the honor of your family. You might have gone to Edward with your suspicions. Why didn't you?"

She looked away from his knowing eyes. She did not want the vulnerability that answering would expose. Besides, it was her turn for questions.

"You had said that you would come back in April and I believed you. Did you lie about that, too?"

He shook his head. "I had not decided what I would do once I got here, but I expected to come back in either case. If I had given the Comte the port of Bordeaux, and he had gone there, Edward would never have suspected me or anyone else even if the whole of France waited for him. Half of their army is already in the south dealing with Grossmont. The rest might have received reports of the ships sailing down the coast, or have gone to reinforce the siege at Angiullon down there. I fully expected to return, assuming that Theobald would permit it."

His steady gaze and quiet voice, his face so close to hers, disconcerted her. Her resolve began loosening. She pushed his shoulder so that she could rinse off the soap, and he turned away.

"But now Lady Catherine has told Edward about you,

and so you cannot go back. Why would she do this? Is she angry about the property in Hampstead?"

He didn't respond for several moments. She suspected that he debated his answer. She braced herself for more lies.

"Lady Catherine and I have a long history. The property is a small and recent part of it. She did me an injury when I was a youth. The evidence is beneath your fingers now. Some months ago I responded in kind."

She rocked back on her heels in shock. She looked down at the strong back and the diagonal scars on it. Despite her determination to treat him with the same indifference he felt for her, her heart tore.

She didn't need to hear the story, because she could imagine it. Her fingertips traced the thin, permanent welts. She pictured him being flogged as a boy. She saw Lady Catherine, secure in the immunity that her nobility gave her, ordering it for some perceived slight or crime. Not in London, of course. Even as an apprentice, he would have been protected there.

He had responded in kind. Did that mean Catherine's own skin bore scars now? She hoped so.

She felt a wave of tenderness for the youth who had been so harshly abused. She barely resisted the urge to kiss those welts.

This is madness, she admonished herself. *He wants no sympathy or tenderness from me. I am no part of his history or his revenge. I have no role in the pageant unfolding now, either. At best I am an inconvenience with which the Comte has complicated his plans.*

"You say that you have not decided what to do, David. What will happen if you will not give the port tomorrow?"

She was glad that she couldn't see his face. If he lied to her, she didn't want to know.

"The Comte has done everything possible to ensure that that isn't much of a choice anymore. Catherine did go to Edward as I said, but the Comte's surprise at the news was false. He sent her to betray me, to force my hand in this. Her plan to keep me in England so that Edward could capture me was all her own, however. Still, he sought to force me out of England, and he took you so that I would have to come here. With my life endangered in England, he knows that his offer becomes very attractive." He paused. "However, kin or not, I do not think that he will allow me to leave here alive if I refuse him."

She wished that he had indeed lied. "Then you have no choice."

"Of course I do."

She felt sick. On the one hand, status and wealth awaited. More than he had ever expected in life. Senlis was his right and his due and he should take it. But, dear God, men whom she knew and loved would ride those ships to France. Her brother, her King, Thomas and others . . . and now he had all but said that Theobald would kill him if he did not cooperate.

It should not matter to her. He should not matter.

She almost embraced him and begged him to find a way to take both choices and thus none at all.

She returned to the stool. "Were you truly almost captured?"

"No one challenged or questioned me. The armor proved a good disguise, since there are knights moving everywhere in England. Even here, it helped me travel without suspicion."

"The coat of arms on your shield?"

"Do you like it? I could hardly pass myself off as a knight with a blank shield. Fortunately, I met no heralds who would know it was new and unofficial."

"You followed me north, then?"

"Aye." He shot her a piercing look. "Do not worry. He was not harmed. Although when Sieg threatened to make him a eunuch, I thought he might die of fright. Since I saved him from that, he will probably be glad to lay down his life for me now."

She glanced to the hearth, not much caring if Sieg had made Stephen a eunuch, whatever that was.

"We were further delayed when Oliver insisted on taking the girl with Stephen under his wing and trying to save her from her family's wrath."

She barely heard him. She went over to the hearth. A bucket of water warmed there and she picked it up and carried it the few steps to the tub.

She noticed David looking at her.

"What?" she asked.

"Didn't you hear me? Aren't you jealous? I said he had a girl with him."

She narrowed her eyes. "For a clever man, you can be an idiot!" she shrieked, pouring the water over his head. She upturned the bucket, slammed it down to his ears, and stomped away.

She stared at the wall, blind with fury. She heard him leave the tub and dry himself. A few moments later he came up behind her.

He touched her shoulder lightly.

"You still do not believe me," she spat, shrugging off his hand. "You have told me lie after lie, while I gave you nothing but the truth from the beginning. Do you assume that everyone lives the kind of deceptions that you do?"

"I believe you. But I wonder if you still love him. You never said that you had stopped."

"I told you it was over."

"That is not the same thing."

"You should have just asked me, then, if you wondered."

He stepped closer and spoke quietly. "I did not ask you about this, just as you did not ask me about France, and for the same reasons. We have not spoken to each other about the things which might pain us. I never asked you, because I feared the answer. I hoped that time would deal with it. But we have run out of time and I am asking you now. Do you still love him?"

She closed her eyes and savored the sound of his beautiful voice and wished that its quiet tones were not asking questions which led down this path. She feared where it might lead.

Still, he was right. Finally, today, he had given her honesty. She should not start her own deceptions now. But honesty about them, the two of them, could well leave her bereft of everything even as it destroyed the fragile resolve with which her anger had conquered her passion and love.

"I no longer care for him at all and doubt that I ever loved him."

"Why do you doubt it?"

Because I know what love feels like now, she almost said.

The silence pulsed as he awaited her answer. She suddenly felt terribly vulnerable. This was the second question that if answered honestly would demand an admission of love from her.

Why not just tell him? Admit the truth, and then walk out the door. She grimaced. A grand gesture totally lacking the hoped-for drama and impact. He would simply let her go, and then proceed to live the life he chose for himself. He did not care enough to be touched by either the admission or the rejection.

"Why do you believe me now about that meeting, David? Did Stephen tell you the truth? Did you believe that fool when you hadn't believed me?"

"He told me, but he would have sworn to being chaste from birth under the circumstances. It did not matter because I already believed you. Whenever I thought about that day, I kept seeing a beautiful girl running into my arms. Full of joy, not guilt or fear." His hands gently took her shoulders. "What was it you wanted to tell me then?"

Again a probing question.

He suspects, she realized with shock. *His mind's reflection has seen what his anger did not.*

She became acutely conscious of his warmth and scent behind her. The silence tightened as something else flowed from him. Something expectant and impatient.

She ached to say it, but she thought about the things she had thrown at him that afternoon in their chamber. She remembered how she had avoided him and his affections during their betrothal. She imagined the apprentice being tortured at the will of the noble Lady Catherine.

She certainly could not tell him now. Even if he put some small value on her feelings for him, he would think that his change in fortune from merchant to baronial heir had made her find sudden love.

"I do not remember," she muttered.

He stayed silent, softly stroking her arms. She closed her eyes and absorbed his touch and closeness. His exciting intensity surrounded her in a luring, seductive way. Despite the knot into which the day's revelations had tied her emotions, despite her decision to leave this stranger, she drew amazing comfort from his slow caress.

"I need to know some things from you now," he finally said.

"No story I can tell will be nearly as interesting as yours."

"Were you harmed at all?"

"Nay. Not really. We rode for days and my rump

got sore from the saddle and my skin red from the summer sun, but that is all. At nights we stayed in rude inns and all shared one hot chamber, but the men did not bother me, although one looked at me too boldly for comfort. The food was horrible and the sea trip frightening, and I arrived looking like the worst peasant, and smelling too ripe for decent company, but I was not harmed."

He turned her around. He had thrown on a loose, long robe, like something a Saracen might wear. She looked up into his face and saw things hiding beneath his calm expression that she had never witnessed in him before. Worry. Indecision. Doubt. He looked much less contained than he had in the bath.

He touched her face. "If I do this thing, you need not stay. Very soon Edward will accept that you were no part of it. You can return home."

She gazed at him, her love twisting her heart. This small contact of skin on skin was enough to awaken all of her senses to him. "That is why you put the properties in my name, isn't it? So they could not be confiscated."

"Aye. There was always the chance that Edward would learn enough to suspect me, no matter what my intentions. I did not want you left dependent if this dangerous game went wrong."

"Why didn't you wait? To marry? You said that this began long before we met. Long before you offered for me. Why complicate things thus for yourself?"

Even as she said it, an eerie sensation swept through her. A knowledge that she did not want to face stretched and stood tall and presented itself squarely. An explanation for one of the first and most enduring questions she had ever had about this man stared at her.

Dear God. *Dear God.* Even that had been a lie, an illusion! It hadn't been much, but at least, as her love sought a compromise with her life, it had been something to hold on to.

His fingers still rested on her face. She looked desperately into his blue eyes and sought all the awareness she had ever had of him during their closest intimacy. She gazed through the veils and intensity, trying to see his soul.

"You never offered for me, did you?" she said. "It was Edward's idea. He proposed this marriage, for my sake perhaps, but also to get money out of you. You could not refuse him."

He took her face in his hands and bent closer. He looked straight back at her. The control and restraint fell away and he permitted her to see what she sought. He let her look through the shadows and layers, down to his depths. Naked of all defenses and armor he met her inspection. Her breath caught at the emotions suddenly exposed to her.

"Nay," he said quietly. "I saw you and wanted you and paid Edward a fortune to have you. And I did not wait because I could not. It was selfish of me." His thumbs stroked her cheekbones. "I am out of time, Christiana. I need to know my true choices, and what I gain and what I lose. If I do this thing, are you going to stay with me?"

She barely heard his words because the stunning truth written inside him made the events which had created this marriage suddenly irrelevant. She could not turn from his warm, binding gaze. She did not want to lose this soulful connection, this total knowing that he offered her. She doubted that he had ever before let anyone, even his mother, see him thus.

Everything was reflected in those deep eyes. Everything. His guilt at endangering her. His fear of himself. His hard hungers and conflicting needs and dark inclinations. But illuminating all of those shadows, warming their chilly depths, flowed a sparkling emotion that she recognized for its beauty and joy and salvation. Her own love spread and reached out to meet it gratefully. His lips parted and a glorious warmth suffused his gaze. An exquisite, anguished relief poured out of him.

"Will you stay?" he repeated, his face inches from hers.

"I will not leave," she whispered, for there could be no other answer after what she had just seen. "Noble or merchant, I will stay with you."

He pulled her into an embracing kiss. She grasped his shoulders and lost herself in a warm rush of poignant intimacy. For a breathless, eternal moment, their bodies seemed to dissolve within the dazzling brilliance flowing between them.

The connection and knowing was so complete that she felt no need to speak of it. But David did.

"What did you want to say to me that day, Christiana?"

"Couldn't you tell? I was sure that you would see it at once."

"My anger and pain blinded me to everything else. I stepped off that boat with a head and heart full of love for you, and Oliver's tale cut me like a dagger and made me a madman."

She lifted her eyes to his, rendered speechless by this calm articulation of what she had just seen and felt in him. In speaking first, he made it easier for her. He had always done that, every step of the way. Out of sympathy and understanding at first maybe, but later because of his love.

She touched his face. She let her fingers drift over the tanned ridges of his cheekbones and jaw, and caress his lips. "I wanted to tell you that day that I was in love with you. I realized it when Catherine delivered me to Stephen. The love was just there, very obvious and completely real. I knew that I have loved you a long while."

He kissed her again, so gently and sweetly that her awareness of his love filled her to the point of weightlessness.

His lips moved to her ear. "They took you from my chamber. Upstairs. Geva had touched nothing when I returned."

His quiet, beautiful voice warmed her as much as his breath and touch. A delicious peace flowed through her like a breeze. She was grateful that he knew that she had loved David the mercer long before she learned the whole truth about him. Glad that he knew that she had returned to him of her own will.

"Do you want me, Christiana? Will you come to bed with me now?"

"You know that I do. You know that I will."

He held her and let her innocent love and joy overwhelm him. Ever since he had returned to the house and seen that disheveled bed, his physical desire for her had beat a low, constant rhythm in his soul and body. Now, however, he resisted the movements that would take her to bed. Her loving embrace soothed him as no passion would.

Noble or merchant, I will stay with you. More than he had asked for or expected. Far more than he deserved.

She broke his long kiss and smiled up at him. "Has it been so long that you have forgotten how to do it?"

He laughed. "Aye. Perhaps I should have kept in practice."

Her brows rose in surprise and he laughed again. "There has been no one else. I found sitting near you at

the hearth more compelling than seducing my way into
some strange bed."

She frowned. "It is strange, David. I sat there loving
you and you sat loving me and we didn't see it. Why not?
You see everything. Can thoughtless, cruel words build
such walls?"

"It is over. We do not have to—"

"I want to. I spoke to hurt you, and you did the same.
We threw the other's fears and illusions at each other and
we each believed the words even though the truth stared
us in the face." She gazed intently at him. "If I had
thought clearly then, as I have since, I would have known
that you never thought of me as property. In fact, you
behaved just the opposite. If you had bought yourself a
noble whore, you certainly did not make much use of her,
did you? Why?"

She surprised him. She was growing up fast, and her
sharp intelligence, freed of its isolating shelter, had
already learned to see to the heart of things.

He loved the girl. He suspected that he would wor-
ship the woman.

"You were very innocent, darling."

"Not so innocent. Women speak to girls before they
marry. I knew that men usually expected more than you
ever asked of me. I knew there could be more to lovemaking than you ever sought."

"We were not together very long, Christiana."

She bit her lower lip thoughtfully. "I do not think it
was that. You knew your blood, but I did not. I think that
you worried that I would indeed feel debased and used.
For all of your pride, David, you did not meet me as an
equal in our bed."

She astonished him. He had been very careful with
her. He had never gone beyond the impulsive acts of their
wedding night. The restraint had come naturally to him

and he had never thought about it, but now he had to admit some truth in what she said.

A very worldly and determined expression flickered in those diamonds. "I have been jealous, you know. I do not like knowing that you did things with Alicia and others that we never did. Noble or merchant, I will stay with you, David, but not as some precious vessel that you fear to break."

Playfully, she pushed him back, up against the post of the bed. She leaned up into him, pressed her body along his, lowered his head with her hand, and kissed him. He accepted her erotic little assault. Lightning flashed through him and the tightness grew and spread.

She glanced up, very pleased with herself. He grasped her hips and pulled her closer and she deliberately rubbed against him. Weeks of need and waiting responded forcefully and he lifted her into a devouring, obscuring kiss. She gave herself over to it and their passion melted them together. But then her hands smoothed over his shoulders and down to his chest and she subtly pushed away.

"On my wedding a day, a servant gave me some very explicit lessons," she said, looking more to his chest than his face. "She said that men like to watch women undress. Would it please my merchant husband if I undressed now?"

She looked up at him and blushed. He thought his heart would tear his chest open. She turned and walked away, her hands plucking at the knot on her gown's laces. The simple gesture almost undid him. He leaned against the bedpost and crossed his arms over his chest.

He had seen her undress many times, of course, but not like this. She moved so beautifully, so elegantly, that her sudden awkwardness at finding herself watched thus almost wasn't apparent. But he could tell that she immediately found it harder than she had thought. He managed not to smile at the slight flush on her face and the hot look in her eyes as she turned to him and let the gown slide to the floor. She bent to her hose.

"Nay," he said. "The shift first."

She straightened. Crossing her arms over her chest, and appearing very much the shy virgin she had so recently been, she slid the shift off her shoulders. Her hands and arms followed its descent, unfolding to reveal first her breasts and then her hips and thighs.

The thin garment fluttered to her feet and she stepped out of it. She looked at the floor a moment before raising her eyes to his. The glint in those diamonds told him that she had discovered that this could arouse the woman as much as the man.

Her beauty mesmerized him as always. Her frank desire to give him pleasure transformed the pleasure itself. His storm of need subdued itself into a threatening but controllable gale. He knew that he could ride its wind indefinitely.

"Now the hose."

She bent and her graceful arms reached for the garter of one forward-stepping leg. He glimpsed the taper of her shoulder to her waist and the gentle flair of hips beyond. Her breasts, tight with need, hung for a moment like two perfect half globes as she rolled the hose off her leg.

"Turn for the other."

She glanced over in surprise, but then did as he asked.

The graceful curves of her hips and buttocks fell into erotic swells as she bent to untie the garter. She must have sensed her vulnerability, because her bravery deserted her and she made quick work with the hose.

She straightened and faced him with eyes like liquid stars. He let his memory be branded with her image. Not short and not even small, but beautifully formed in her slender fullness.

"Your hair, Christiana. Take down your hair for me."

Her arms rose as she sought the pins. The movement brought her breasts high and their hard tips angled upward. She unplaited her raven locks and they began spilling around her. He made no effort to hide what he felt from her gaze.

"Come here, my girl, and kiss me the way a bride in love should."

She walked slowly toward him, her expression a heart-stopping combination of passion and love and joy and invitation.

More than he ever expected. Far more than he deserved.

The morning was a lifetime away.

She stepped up to him and placed her hands on his chest. She stretched up toward him. He lowered his head and took her kiss with more restraint than he felt. He let her lead, biting gently around his mouth. Delicately, but not so artlessly, her tongue grazed his lips and then flickered more intimately.

He embraced her with one arm, reveling in the sensation of her skin beneath his hand. A slight sheen of sweat covered her and the warmth and moisture sent a flare through his whole body.

He caressed her face, and broke their kiss so he could watch his hand and her body as it traced down. His embrace arched her back, and her breasts rose to him. Her tremor when he touched her taut nipple flowed right into his hips and thighs.

Neither one of them succumbed to the waiting frenzy. They both sought to prolong the exquisite anticipation she had begun.

Her hands still lay on his chest and now they caressed at the loose lacing down the front of the long robe.

"It looks very exotic. Very handsome."

"Saracens know how to dress for hot weather."

She stroked his chest lazily. "The servant said that men like to be undressed by women, too."

He didn't answer, but watched as she carefully untied and pulled out the laces down to his waist.

She caressed him through the gap. He closed his eyes to the heat of that small hand. It had been too long since he had even this small connection and affection from her.

She pushed the garment open, almost off his shoulders, and laid her face against him. Languidly, deliciously, with a slow care that only increased the tension between them, she rubbed her cheek against his chest and watched her hand follow his muscles.

"You were right," she said as she turned to kiss him. "Abstinence is a powerful enhancement to passion. A part of me cannot wait and already screams for you, but another part wants to prolong this forever."

"You know how it will end. I have never failed you there. Let us enjoy the journey. We will never take quite the same path again."

She smiled sensually and nodded. Running both hands up his chest, she slid the robe off his shoulders and guided it down his back.

His control threatened to dissolve when she extended her caresses to his hips and thighs.

"What else did the servant tell you?" he asked, touching her as she did him, feeling tremors quake subtly through her.

"That men like to be kissed and touched, but I have already learned that is true." She proved it by mouthing at his chest. Rumbling shocks rocked through him with each kiss and nip. "Other things. I thought them shocking at the time. I do not find them so now."

The robe still hung from his hips. She gently shook

off his embrace. She caressed and kissed down his body as she lowered herself.

He watched and waited, his breath barely coming to him. An obscuring haze of passion clouded his mind and he saw both nothing and everything. Saw her hands push the robe to his feet. Felt her fluttering caress on his thighs and legs. Saw her fingers stroke his hard phallus while her lips pressed to his belly and hip. Her boldness both touched and stunned him. He wondered at the deceptive calm his body maintained, because desire began splitting him apart.

She caressed the back of his thighs and moved her head away. Questioning eyes glanced up at him. He bent and reached down for her and drew her up to his embrace. "Only if you want to, darling. And never on your knees."

She nestled into his arms. "Then take me to bed, merchant, so I can show you my love and honor."

He lifted her into a kiss that removed her feet from the floor. He turned and laid her down and lowered himself next to her.

The warm night air flowing through the window felt cool against the heat of their entwined bodies. He lost himself in the intimacy of her scent and swells and slick sweat.

He would show her such a journey as she had never imagined.

Slowly, deliberately, using all of his knowledge of her, he obliterated her shaky control. Never touching her below her hips, he drew her toward completion. Caresses on her inner arm, biting teeth on her nipples, consuming mouth on her neck—her passion rose with each knowing demand. She tried, despite her growing mindlessness, to give him pleasure in return, but he would not let her. He listened to her low sounds of abandon and felt her body climbing, shaking, toward its peak of sensation.

She grasped his shoulders. "David, I . . . please . . ."

He stilled his hands and mouth and held her. She twisted against him in rebellious frustration. Her eyes flew open.

"David!" she cried accusingly.

"Hush, darling. I said that I have never failed you."

"You mean to torture me to death first?" She pummeled his shoulder none too playfully.

He laughed lightly. "It is only torture if you think only about the release. Take the pleasure of the climbs for themselves, knowing that eventually you will fly."

Her passion had receded and the frenzy had passed. Her arms surrounded his shoulders and he turned his head to kiss the bend of her arm while his hand stroked down her body. "Again, then," he said.

She clung to him and opened her legs and accepted his touch. Her folds and passage already throbbed with her arousal, and he deliberately caressed her in ways that would bring pleasure but not fulfillment. She rebelled at first, and tried to move toward more productive touches, but then she relaxed and took the streaks of pleasure with joyful gasps and low moans.

He saw the glorious ecstasy on her face and nearly lost control himself. He touched her differently and watched her climb again, higher this time, as it would be every time. He took her to the peak and kept her there, tottering on its exquisite contracting edge, and let her taste the first tremor before he withdrew his hand.

Her nails had dug into his arm and shoulder. He kissed her and soothed her with soft caresses.

"That was wonderful," she whispered. "Does it keep getting better each time?"

"Up to a point."

"Do you plan to do this all night?"

He laughed. "I seriously doubt it. Love has made me very noble and chivalrous, but I have my limits."

She regarded him. "I think that two can play this game of yours, David. Would that please you?"

"Very much, if you desire it."

She rose up and pushed his shoulders down on the bed. She gave him a smug little smile full of unwarranted self-confidence. She kissed him fully before moving her hands and her mouth down his chest. He closed his eyes and stroked her back.

"Nay, David. You did not let me touch you, so you cannot touch me."

The luxurious spots of heat she created moved lower. He sensed her pause to consider the situation. Then he felt her turn and draw up her legs and lean against his stomach.

He had taught her to please him with her hands, and her caresses drove him close to delirium. When she paused again he opened his eyes just as she lowered her head.

He knew no thought after that. He looked through a cloud of engulfing sensation and pleasure at the erotic lines of her back and buttocks and the two delicate feet tucked beneath her.

He knew his limits but she did not. As he neared them he reached down and slid his fingers along the cleft of her bottom.

She groaned and shifted and accepted his touch. He rearranged their bodies so that his mouth could reach her. Bracing himself for control, he let them share the ecstatic pleasure a while longer as he brought her as far as she had him, to the very edge. Finally it was too much for them both and she sensed it. She released him and turned toward him and as she did he lifted her body and brought her down straddling his hips.

For an instant she seemed surprised to find hersel
there. Then wordlessly, instinctively, she rose up and took
him into herself.

His sigh met hers in the space between them. She
closed her eyes at the sensation, then slowly rose and low
ered again.

Passion veiled her eyes when she opened them. She
moved again and sighed. "This is incredible, David."

He reached up and caressed her breasts so she coulc
see just how incredible it could be. He rubbed the taut nip
ples between his fingers. Her head fell back and she lollec
sensually into a wonderful rhythm as she repeatedly drew
him into her tight warmth and released him. Enhanced by
abstinence and love, the pleasure moved him in ways he
had never known.

He pulled her down toward him.

"Come up to me. Move forward a bit," he instructed

She slid up but halted. "I will lose—"

"You will not. Come up to me."

She lowered and he eased her forward until he coulc
take her breast in his mouth. She hovered above him
breathlessly, her body barely still joined to his. He felt her
grasping to absorb more of him, driving him mad with the
mutual caress they created.

"David," she gasped, her body shaking from the combination of tantalizing pleasures at her breast and betweer
her legs. He stroked her back down to its lowest curve
and continued to arouse her breasts. He felt the first deep
tremor and knew what it meant even if she did not.

"David," she cried again, frantically this time.

He released her and she slammed down on him with
a needful cry. Burying her face in his chest, she movec
hard again.

"Aye, it can happen thus, too," he reassured her, and

he held her hips firmly and took over and helped her find that different, more elusive fulfillment.

He had never seen a woman reach such a violent and complete release. Wonder, desire, and love echoed through her cries. She kissed him ferociously and gazed into his eyes as her passion peaked and her open acceptance of the magic made the intimacy fuse their souls as it always had. Her whole being seemed to fold in on itself, taking his own essence to its burning center, before flying out in all directions. At the end she rose up in a magnificent display of sensual ecstasy as she cried her abandon. Their mutual fulfillment momentarily obliterated time and space and consciousness.

She collapsed on him and he floated with her in their unity. Her love awed him and filled him with its innocent peace and grace. The hungry and needful response of his own soul astonished him.

Her face lay buried near his neck.

"Do you think anyone heard us?"

"Us?"

She giggled and playfully swatted his chest. "All right. Me?"

He thought about the open window and the silent city night. The whole household and half of Caen had probably heard her. So much for pretending that they were not content together.

It would not matter now. If the Comte thought to use her in that way, he would have already come for them both.

"I am sure that no one heard, darling."

She moved and settled down next to him. He had never known such peace and contentment, and he let himself savor it, knowing it would not last long and might never come again.

He probably should have told her everything.

Eventually he would have to. This love would not permi
long deceptions, even for her sake.

"Have you ever been there?" she asked. "To Senlis?"

"Twice. The first time some years ago, and then agair
recently."

"Did you go inside?"

"Aye. The Comte was not there, and I entered as a
traveling merchant with luxuries to sell. No one
will remember. The vanities absorbed the women, no
me."

"Do you want it? Senlis?"

"Who would not?"

She rose up and looked in his eyes. "*You* might not."

All the same, a choice awaited. "It is your fate that
decide as well as my own. I would know your will in this."

"I would have you with me forever, alive and whole
That is all that really matters to me, but I know that you
will not make your choice for your own safety, and I wil
not ask it of you. As to the rest, there is no clear right and
wrong here, is there? Both hold some pain and betrayal
England and France both have a claim on you. Both men
Edward and Theobald, deserve your loyalty." She paused
considering the dilemma. "I think that you should choose
the life that you were born to live, whichever you think i
was."

To the heart of things. Life with her would be fasci
nating.

"And what about you, Christiana? What about the life
that you were born to live?"

She smiled and rested her face against his chest. "I was
born to marry a nobleman, David. And you have alway
been one of the noblest men I have ever known."

CHAPTER 21

CHRISTIANA AWOKE TO an empty bed and the early morning light streaming in the chamber's window. The mellow memories of the night vanished at once. She rose and quickly dressed.

He was meeting with them now. It was being done. She could not pray for one outcome or another, even though she knew which she would prefer. He could give them the port, become the heir to Senlis, and live the life that few men had. Or he could refuse, be deprived of his old life but not given a new one, and maybe be killed. Not much of a choice to her mind, nor, she hoped, to his either. All the same, despite the status of Senlis and all that it entailed, she did not look forward with any enthusiasm to living in that strange place so far from home.

She paced the room but the confined space only increased her worry. She left the chamber and sought the stairs that led to the flat roof of this tall building with its many chambers for sleeping and storage.

Tubs of summer flowers and vines dotted the roof. As

she stepped out onto it she heard the sounds of activity floating up from the city below. The usual drone of commerce and movement had been replaced by a din of wagons and horses and men shouting orders.

David stood by the low wall surrounding the roof, looking down into the city streets to the west. Another man of middle years with a thick build and long brown hair watched beside him.

David turned and noticed her. He held out his hand.

"My lord, this is my wife, Christiana Fitzwaryn. This is the Constable d'Eu, darling."

Christiana met the inspecting gaze of the chief military leader of France.

"I am Theobald's cousin, my lady, and so a kin of your husband's." He glanced at David. "The daughter of Hugh Fitzwaryn, no less. You did well for Senlis. Theobald is pleased that your wife brings such blood to the family."

Christiana stepped to the wall beside David. In the streets beyond, she could see the feverish activities of an army preparing to move.

It was done, then. She glanced at David's impassive face.

"My lady, your husband will be staying here in Caen," the constable said.

She looked from one man to the other. Something was wrong. She could feel it.

"Are you saying that I am still a prisoner?" she asked.

"You are free to go. I will arrange an escort to take you to Senlis."

"Then my husband is now a prisoner?"

"A guest. Until the English land. He can join you then. He is not trained in warfare, and this battle is not his."

"I would prefer to stay with my husband."

The constable looked at David. David didn't react at all. The older man smiled. "As you wish," he said, and he turned away and walked across the roof to the stairs.

She waited until he had gone.

"Why must you stay here, David?"

"He does not trust me. He fears that I have lied to them. But your choice to stay with me has reassured him a little."

"But why keep you here if the army moves?"

"Theobald will take the army. He has already left the house. But the constable has decided to remain in Caen with a small force, to be available in case Edward comes a different way. The King's chamberlain is here, too. He agreed that this would be wise."

"And your uncle agreed to this?"

"Even the Comte de Senlis does not stand against the constable and chamberlain of France. Theobald wanted me with him, so that I could see the glorious French victory that I have helped bring about. The constable insisted that I stay with him here, however, so that he would have me at his disposal if I betrayed them in some way. He thinks that I might steal away from the army during its march, or that, if it came to it, Theobald would not take vengeance on his heir." He smiled. "The constable does not know his cousin very well."

He embraced her and placed his cheek against her hair. He still looked down into the city. She felt conflicting emotions in him and wished that she could say something to comfort him. This decision had not been an easy one, no matter what prize it brought.

"Why doesn't the constable trust you? Surely the logic of your choice should be clear to him. It is the decision any man would have made, and there will even be English knights and lords who recognize the fairness of it."

"He explained it to me just now. Almost apologized. It seems that if I were a knight, he would have no doubts about me. It is the fact that I am a merchant, and a London merchant at that, which gives him pause."

"That is outrageous. Does he think merchants less honorable?"

"Undoubtedly, as all do. Still, in a way, he credits me with more rather than less honor. He told me that he knows burghers, and has met many from London. He knows that we owe our first loyalty to the city itself. He does not claim to understand men who give their fealty to a place rather than a man, but he knows it is so with us and he has seen its power. He could accept that I would betray Edward, or even the realm, but not London. And so, while he and the chamberlain agreed with Theobald that the army should move with speed, the constable will stay here to organize a defense if I lied to them."

A steady stream of knights and mounted soldiers streamed across the gate bridge from the other side of the river. They moved through the city toward its southern edges. Foot soldiers, carts, and workers plodded with them. The streets looked like colorful, moving rivers.

David's gaze followed the lines. "I should have insisted that you go to Senlis, but I feared never getting you out later. Theobald can be ruthless when angered, I suspect. Still, it would have been safer for you. The constable assured your safety, but there are limits to his protection."

"What are you saying, David? Do you think that Edward has indeed changed his plans and that the constable will blame you in some way?"

He pushed away from the wall and walked across to the southern view with his arm around her shoulders. In the distance, past the lower rooftops, they could see the field on which the army gathered. At the front, with gold and blue banners, no more than dots to their eyes, sat three men on horseback.

"Theobald?" she asked.

He nodded. "There are five thousand here with him. Others will join the army as they pass south."

"They go to Bordeaux, then?" she asked, even though the answer was obvious. She needed to hear it said, however, so that she could begin reconciling herself to the future he had chosen for them.

She wished that she felt some joy, but her stomach churned in an odd way. She thought about his question last night before they slept, and of her response.

He had misunderstood. She had sought to assure him that she loved him no matter what his degree, and had found him noble even before she learned about his father.

He has done this in large part for me, she realized. *To give me back the life which this marriage took from me.*

The Comte and Duke began to ride. The thick, undisciplined mass of the army oozed after them.

"Aye, they go to Bordeaux," he confirmed.

He wore a peculiar expression on his face. His eyes narrowed on the disappearing blue banners. "Edward, however, does not."

She gaped at him. His gaze never left the southern field.

"I went to Edward before Catherine did. I told him everything, and offered to finish the game as I had started it. I would give them one port, and our army would arrive at another one. I pressed for him to consider Normandy, since half the French army was already in the south and if I failed he would still only face an inferior host. His experience trying to sail to Bordeaux had already inclined him to change plans, and a Norman knight has been at court these last months, also telling him about Normandy's unwalled towns and clear roads."

She glanced in the direction of his gaze. She could still see reflections off the Comte's armor.

"Edward will debark in Normandy? Here on the northern coast?" Tremendous relief swept her, but with it came a sickening fear for David and what he now faced.

"Assuming that he doesn't get clever at the last moment, which is entirely possible. Or that he doesn't grow to doubt me. Catherine probably told lurid tales of my duplicity, but I am counting on Edward knowing what he has in her. Godefrey, the Norman knight, and I were able to give him three possible ports, small and out of the way. He will use the one which the winds favor."

"Does the King know about Senlis and what you were offered? If he does, he may well doubt you. He will not understand your choice."

"I told him everything. I could not be sure that Lady Catherine was involved in your disappearance, or that she planned to betray me, but I suspected it. I could not be sure that she remained ignorant of my relationship with the Comte. It was well that I spoke frankly with Edward. When I finally got a hold of Frans, I had my suspicions confirmed."

"So you were never in danger in England? And you can return?" *Assuming that he could get out of Caen alive.*

"Aye."

"Still, having convinced Edward on Normandy, you might have betrayed him. When did you decide what to do?"

He still looked to the flow of the army. "Early this morning. Knight or merchant, you said. I took you at your word."

"And if I had spoken differently? If I had said that I wanted to be the wife of a comte?"

"I would have given it to you, and learned to live with my conscience." He looked down and smiled. "I suspect that I could have rationalized it. The power and luxury of Senlis can probably obscure any guilt. Such a life has its appeal. I will not pretend that I was not tempted."

She embraced him tightly. "You have sacrificed much for your city and your King, David. Edward owes you much."

"He owes me nothing, Christiana. He gave you to me. The debt is all mine."

His gaze had returned to the distant field. The Comte was barely visible now. She saw that peculiar expression on his face again, and a flicker of yearning pass through those eyes.

He had executed a brilliant victory, a daring strategy, a magnificent game, but no triumph showed in him. She doubted his subdued reaction had anything to do with the danger he now faced. She snuggled closer under his arm and tried to comfort him.

"In time he will understand, David. He knows about honor and the hard choices it gives a man. He may not forgive you, but he will understand."

He tensed at this mention of the Comte and the blood ties which he had betrayed.

She tried again. "David, I know there is pain here. He is your uncle . . ."

His fingers came to rest on her lips, silencing her. "I should have told you last night," he said. "I feared your reaction to the truth, and also did not know if he would try to learn what you knew. I have spent the last hour wondering if I would ever tell you."

She frowned in confusion. She searched his face for some explanation.

"Theobald is not my uncle, Christiana."

His words stunned her. It took a few moments for the full implication to penetrate her dazed mind.

"Are you that clever, David?" That audacious? You found a man whom you resembled in some way and plotted this elaborate scheme? You fed me this story so that I could convincingly support you if I was questioned?"

That peculiar, yearning expression passed over him again.

He shook his head. "It is much worse than that, my girl." He glanced to the speck of a man being swallowed by sunlight and haze. "Theobald is not my uncle. He is my father."

Christiana did not know how long they stood there with his words hanging in the air, but when he spoke again the straggling ends of the army were passing out of the city.

"He did not even remember her name."

They still stood near the roof wall. He rested his arms against it and he looked south, but at nothing in particular now.

"He seduced her, took her love, left her with child, and destroyed her life. I use her name, but it meant nothing to him. Both he and Honoré had been to London several times as young men, and he assumed that I was the product of one of his brother's sins. It was the final mockery of Joanna's timeless trust."

She spoke to comfort him more than defend Theobald. "It was thirty years ago. When you are fifty-five, do you think that you will remember the name of every woman you bedded?"

"Aye. Every one."

"Perhaps only because he did not."

He appeared not to hear. "There had been two rings, one gray and one pink. He assumed that I had Honoré's, the gray one, and never asked to see it. At Hampstead, he looked at me and saw only his brother."

"He knew his brother's face better than his own. How often do we see clear reflections of ourselves in glass and metal?"

"She meant nothing to him. She was merely a beautiful girl with whom he amused himself for a short while. A merchant's daughter who counted for nothing in the life of a son of Senlis."

She didn't know what else to say. He had watched Joanna's misery and patience. He had lived in the shadow of her disillusionment. He had watched the master whom he admired love her in vain. She doubted that his anger at Theobald could be assuaged by words.

"Why didn't you tell him the truth? Why let him think you are his nephew?"

"At Hampstead, when I realized his mistake, it stunned me. Otherwise, my plan had unfolded perfectly. I told myself at the time that correcting him might complicate things. For all I knew, he might resent the sudden appearance of a bastard son, or even suspect that I sought revenge against him. But in truth, it was my own resolve that I questioned. Meeting him was much harder than I thought it would be. I had fully intended to despise him. And then, there he was, and suddenly a hundred unspoken questions that I had carried in my soul all of my life were answered. The answers were mainly unpleasant, but at least I had them." He smiled ruefully. "The connection, the familiarity, was immediate. Unexpected and astounding. If he had known me for his own, and appealed to me father to son, I do not know what I would have done. So, I let him think otherwise."

He did not have to tell her this. She would have never known or suspected.

"So, Christiana. You are married to a man who lured his own father into disrepute and betrayed him. It is a serious crime in any family, especially noble ones."

He searched her eyes for disapproval or disappointment. She knew that he found only understanding and love.

She thought about the yearning she had seen in him, and her heart swelled with sympathy. "Do you regret it? As you watch him ride off, would you change things?"

"Only for you would I have done it differently and changed course. Never for him. I wish that I could say that I regret having started this, but I do not. I am what I am, my girl, and a part of me, the Senlis part, is glad that I have revenged Joanna a little."

"Do you hate your father, David?"

He smiled and shook his head. "It would be like hating myself. But I hold no love for him either. Theobald may have given me life, but the only father I ever knew and loved was David Constantyn."

He took her hand and eased away from the wall.

"What now, David?"

He glanced around the roof, as if inspecting it. "Now I see to your safety." He grinned down at her. "The danger that I face from the Comte de Senlis and the Constable d'Eu is nothing compared to what Morvan Fitzwaryn will do if I let anything happen to you. I think that you should ask the lovely Heloise to show me her house. All of it. Tell her that I am curious to see how Caen's wealthiest burghers live."

David and Christiana had their tour. David peered around without subtlety and effused compliments, and Heloise beamed with pride at the appreciation of this handsome London merchant. Christiana thought that he overdid it somewhat, but his praise dragged the afternoon out and gave him the opportunity to examine every chamber and storage room, every window and stable. He seemed especially fascinated with an attic at the top of the main building. Loaded with cloth and mercery, it could only be reached by a narrow flight of steps angling along the inner wall.

They finally left Heloise at the hall and strolled into the garden.

"There does not appear to be any way out except the front gate, short of getting a ladder to the wall," David said.

"Is that what you looked for? I could have told you that. There is one way, but you will need rope." She began angling him in the direction of the tree. She smiled at this simple solution. David would escape, she would join him, and then . . . what? A run to safety, to Edward and his army. How long was the Comte's reach if he sought revenge? Perhaps they would leave both England and France behind and go to Genoa.

As they neared the garden's corner, her heart fell. Where the tall strong oak had stood, they found only its stump.

"I went out this way a week before you came," she explained. "Theobald caught me. He must have ordered it cut after that."

"It doesn't matter. I doubt that we would have made it through the bridge gate."

She sought the comfort of his arms.

"How long?" she asked, bravely broaching the subject that she had avoided. "When does Edward land?"

"I calculate five days, maybe six."

"You must get away. You cannot be here when they

find out. Tonight, I will distract the guards at the front gate and you—"

"I do not leave without you."

"Then we must find a way," she cried desperately.

"If there is one, I will find it. But I think that it is out of our hands. Who knows? When the English army begins ravaging Normandy, the constable and chamberlain may be so busy organizing the defense that they will forget about me."

He said it so lightly that she had to smile. But she didn't believe that would happen, and she knew that he didn't either.

When she awoke to an empty bed the Wednesday morning after the army departed, she threw on a robe and went in search of him. She found him on the roof, gazing toward the west. Dawn's light had just broken, and the city still appeared as gray forms below them. Despite the stillness, the air seemed laden with a strange fullness, as if a storm brewed somewhere beyond the clear horizon.

She drifted up beside him. His blue eyes glanced at her, then returned to their examination of the field beyond the river.

"Look there," he said. "Approaching the bridge."

She strained to see. The light was growing and a large shadow on the field moved down the far bank of the river. She watched and the shadow broke into pieces and then the pieces became people. Hundreds of them.

They moved quickly, carrying sacks and leading animals. The sun began to rise and she saw that the crowd included women and children. They poured through the buildings across the river, past the abbeys built by William the Conqueror and his wife Matilda, and then began massing at the far end of the bridge, shouting for entry to the city.

"Who are they?"

"Peasants. Burghers. Priests. They are refugees, fleeing Edward's army."

Additional guards ran to reinforce the watch at the bridge gate. The mob of refugees coalesced and their shouts rose. On the near side of the river, two men mounted horses and began riding through the deserted streets toward the mayor's house.

"Is the army nearby?" she asked.

"I would guess only hours away."

"It comes here? To Caen? You might have told me, David. I would not have worried so much."

"I could not be sure. In April, by accident, I found a port on the Cotentin peninsula just to the west. Sieg and I waited there for the English ships to pass before I met with Theobald here in Caen. During the storm, a merchant ship was pushed inland toward the coastal town where we waited. It came within one hundred yards of the coast and did not run aground. The sea must have shifted the coast over the years and the port gotten deeper. Perfect for the army's debarking. Still, the winds may have taken Edward further east to one of the other ports I had found earlier."

"You did not want to give me false hopes," she said.

"I did not want to give you more worry, darling."

"Worry? This is good news! Edward will obtain your release. The flower of English chivalry comes to save you," she said, smiling.

"If the city surrenders, it may happen that way."

"Of course the city will surrender. There is no choice."

"London would not surrender."

"*London has walls.*"

"I hope that you are right."

"What is it, David? What worries you?"

But before he could reply, the answer appeared on the roof in the persons of two knights from the constable's retinue.

CHAPTER 22

DAVID PACED AROUND the small storage chamber. The space reeked of herring from the barrels stacked against one wall. A small candle lit the windowless cell, and he tried to judge the time passing by its slowly diminishing length.

He was fortunate to still be alive. Upon confronting him in the hall about his betrayal, the constable had barely resisted cutting him down with his sword. The panic and confusion brought on by the English army's approach had saved his life. The hall had been in an uproar as the constable and chamberlain tried to organize a defense of the city while their squires strapped on their armor. Word had been sent east and south, calling back Theobald's army and rousing the general population to gather and fight this invasion. David had been imprisoned in this chamber to await hanging after the more pressing threat had been defeated.

Before being led away, he had tried to reason with the constable and chamberlain and convince them not to resist Edward. He had told them that the English army numbered at least twenty thousand, while the constable had at best three hundred men still in Caen. He had reminded them that surrender would spare the people of the city and only mean the loss of property. Only the mayor had listened, but the decision had not been his. The French king had told the Constable d'Eu to stop Edward, and the constable intended to fight for the honor of France despite the odds. Caen would not surrender or ask for terms.

He strained to hear the sounds leaking through the thick cellar wall. The house had quieted and the more distant activity only came to him as a dull rumble. The real battle would be fought at the gate bridge. If the city could retain control of that single access, the river would prove more formidable than any wall.

For Christiana's sake, he hoped that the gate bridge held. If the city fell, she would not be safe from those English soldiers as they pillaged this rich town. He doubted that they would listen to her claims of being English, just as they would not listen to him when they broke into this storage room to loot the goods that it contained. He grimaced at the irony. He would undoubtedly die today, but if he lived long enough to hang, if Edward failed to take this city, at least Christiana would be safe.

He pounded his fist into the wall in furious frustration that he could not help her. She had been sent to Heloise and the other women immediately upon his arrest. She had fought the knights who pulled her away. Those knights had not returned, and he prayed that they guarded the chamber in which the women waited. It would be some protection, at least.

He lifted the candle and reexamined his tiny prison. He wished it contained other than dried herring, and not just because of the smell. Whoever went to the trouble to break down this door would probably kill him out of resentment at finding nothing of value for their time and labor.

As if echoing his thoughts, a sound at the door claimed his attention. Not the crash of an ax or battering ram, though. The more subtle tone of metal on metal.

Perhaps Edward had decided to move on. Maybe it would be hanging after all. He moved to the far wall and watched the door ease open.

At the threshold, her face pale like a ghost's, appeared a haggard Heloise. Christiana stood behind her holding his long steel dagger at the blond woman's throat.

"She knew it was the only sensible thing to do, David, but she is one of those women who only obeys her husband, so I had to encourage her," Christiana said. She replaced the dagger into the sheath hanging from her waist.

Heloise looked ready to faint. She leaned against the wall for support.

"What has happened?" he asked.

"The bridge has been taken," Christiana explained. Her own face was drawn with fear that she tried bravely to hide. "The knights protecting us left long ago, and I have been watching from the roof. Our army is all over the town, like a mob. It is as you said. In victory they are taking all that they can move. The people are throwing benches and rocks down on them from the roofs, and that is slowing their progress, but not by much."

"No one is here," Heloise cried. "The gate is guarded only by some grooms and servants. When the bridge fell, the soldiers all left, some to fight in the streets, others to run."

Christiana moved up close to him and spoke lowly. "She wanted to take her daughters and run, too, but I convinced her that she was better behind these walls than in

the city. They are not castle walls, and will not stop the
army long, but the soldiers are killing all they meet. Even
from the roof I could see many bodies fall."

He looked in her eyes and read her deep realization of
the danger which she faced. He turned to Heloise.

"It is well that you released me, madame," he said
soothingly. "Fortune has always smiled on me. Perhaps
she will be kind today as well." He eased the woman away
from the wall. "Let us go and assess our situation."

Bad news awaited in the courtyard. The servants
guarding the gate had fled, and the entry stood open to
the street. In the distance they could hear the screams of a
city being sacked.

He ran over to close and bar the gate. A group of six
women surged in just as he arrived. They looked to be
burghers's wives and they threw themselves at Heloise.

"That devil of an English king has ordered everyone
put to the sword," one of them cried. "They are stripping
the bodies of their garments and cutting off fingers to get
the rings. They are raping the women before slitting their
throats."

The other women joined in with hysterical descriptions of the horrors they had seen. David barred the gate
and looked around the courtyard. Christiana was right.
These were not castle walls and they marked the house as
that of a wealthy merchant. Eventually some soldiers
would decide to batter down the gate or scale their
heights. But they were better off here than outside in the
city.

Christiana stood to the side, listening to the tales of
mutilation and destruction with an ashen face. The sounds
of the pillaging army gradually moved closer.

He walked over and embraced her. "Do you remember the attic storage above the bedchambers? The one
reached by the narrow stairs? Take them there."

"And you?"

"I will join you shortly. It appears that I will need that armor after all. I never thought to wear it against Englishmen. It appears that my father will have his way in the end. It is an ironic justice that my betrayal of him has put you in such danger."

"Do not blame yourself for this. You did not bring me here," she said, instinctively knowing the guilt that wanted to overwhelm him.

"All the same, you are here." He hesitated, not wanting to speak of the horror that threatened. "If they come, let them know who you are. Speak only English. Claim the protection of your brother and the King."

"It will not matter," she said, turning to the knot of women nearby. "I have seen it before. At Harclow. It had begun before we left. My brother accepted defeat and possible death to save my mother from what we face today."

She approached the women and spoke to them. Grateful to have some instruction that at least offered hope, they fell in around her as she led the way to the tall building and the attic chamber.

David followed, but detoured to the room he and Christiana had shared. He slipped the breastplate of his armor over his shoulders and then lifted the pieces for his arms. He considered whether, with weapons and armor, he would be able to get Christiana alone out through the city streets. He shook his head. He had no jerkin that identified him as part of an English baron's retinue, and his shield bore no arms that these soldiers would recognize. They would think him French. In any case, he did not have it in him to abandon those other women and girls, nor would Christiana want him to. In death at least he could be the husband she deserved. Hoisting his sword with the other hand, he made his way to the stairway and the hiding women.

Christiana had already set the women to work. Lengths of cloth stretched on the floor, and they used his dagger to slice off sections of it.

"What are you doing?" he asked, setting down the armor.

"Banners," she said. "The white and green of Harclow. Thomas Holland's colors, and those of Chandros and Beauchamp. We will hang them from the windows. Who knows, it may attract someone who can help us."

She looked at the armor and stepped close. "I will do it." Her fingers began working the straps and buckles.

It took a long while to fit all of the armor, and he didn't even have the leg pieces. When they were done, she unstrapped the sheath from her waist and handed it to him, then retrieved the dagger from the women.

He looked a moment at the long length of sharp steel. Their eyes met.

"It will do me no good against armed men," she said, slipping it into its sheath on his hip. "And I am not brave enough to use it on the others and myself."

The women opened the windows and slid out the banners. The summer breeze carried the sounds of screaming death. As they closed the windows to secure the cloth, a crash against the gate thundered into the attic space. The noise jolted everyone into utter silence.

The air in the chamber smelled sour from the fear pouring out of its occupants. David glanced at the eight women and three girls. Their faces were barely visible in the room darkened now by the cloth at the windows. He drew Christiana aside and turned his back on the others.

He held her face with his hands and closed his eyes to savor the delicate softness of her lips. An aching tenderness flooded him, and her palpable fear tore his heart. "When I go to Genoa this fall, you will come with me," he said. "After this, crossing the Alps will seem a minor thing.